Whispers of Home

Drifters, Book Five

SUSAN RODGERS

Cover design by Alanna Munro. All rights reserved.
Edited by Kathy Gillis and Stephen Reaman.
Book design & formatting by Valerie Bellamy, Dog-ear Book Design.

ISBN: 978-1-987966-00-8

for my readers

Contents

"*G*uinness, please."

Jacob hesitated, and then called out to the Cuban bartender's back, "No, wait. Stop. I changed my mind. Uhhh…" He shifted his butt on the leather stool and ran a thumb absently over the rough three-day whiskers on his chin as the clean-cut forty-ish gentleman behind the bar paused mid-step. "Make that an IPA. Something popular around here. Local. Whatever you recommend, I guess."

His voice faded at the end of his request. Jacob was losing steam. By local he meant the 'city of magic,' Miami, Florida, where he'd quite surprisingly found himself working after Deirdre Keating decided he should branch out into acting. He'd caught a last minute gig as a singer on an American drama when the guy who was supposed to play the part bailed in favor of a high profile romantic comedy. Initially hesitant, Jacob agreed to audition after Dee convinced him he had the right look. After all, wasn't the 'look' half the battle when it came to taking on a new character?

He'd been in Florida now for two days, which wasn't so bad for this time of year since Vancouver was starting to cool down. A born and bred American anyway, Jacob had a certain comfort level with the practicalities, like currency, banking, and hip clothing shops, but he was missing the extras—friends, family…Jessie. It was a lot of change—from the States to Scotland to Vancouver, and now Florida, and *acting,* for God's sake. Add the fact that when all was said and done Jessie had gone and married Josh, so, despite this sweet career break, Jacob was downright depressed.

His beer slid under his nose accompanied by an offside Spanish-accented

1

remark about some kind of honey 'aftertazzzte,' but he hardly heard the guy. "Another arrogant bartender," Jacob caught himself rather unfairly muttering, "who can barely speak English." *This whole craft beer movement is getting out of hand*, he thought. Coffee was bad enough…who gives a shit about chocolate nuances and mouth feels? He just wanted a good cuppa joe most times and, tonight, a damn good beer.

He lifted the heavy frosted glass to his lips and took a sip, somewhat surprised to find the beverage pleasingly cool and crisp, indeed way more so than your average beer.

The slick, handsome bartender awaited his approval but stepped away after a moment when the scruffy unshaven guy at the bar rudely didn't respond. Jacob had paused, the glass halfway back down to the bar, when he spotted an image playing on the backlit neon green monitor above. His heart raced as it always did when he spotted Tom Ryan on the tube—this time, his famous singer-songwriter dad was being escorted down some back alley to meet an awaiting throng of press and admirers. The show was one of those entertainment blitzes, *gossip in a cup*, thought Jacob. It was designed to provoke, and was often dramatized and sensationalized. Jacob hated that whole shtick about this new chosen biz of his. Worst part? It wasn't the first time an uncomfortable gnawing in his stomach reminded him the biz was, as Jessie sometimes cautioned, a circus—one he seemed to be buying into. Did he want it? *Hell, yeah.* But that didn't mean he was immune to the media's manipulative power.

He watched his dad schmooze amongst fans with the grace and practice of an experienced dancer almost, as he wove this way and that so as not to leave anybody without the benefit of his charming smile. Signing autographs hurriedly and with a flourish each time, Tom Ryan was an experienced and popular celebrity on the world stage.

Grimacing, Jacob finally turned his head away from the man who dumped him as a youngster, when another powerful figure stole his attention. A ubiquitous cranberry silk tie over an elegant white dress shirt, the tie tucked beneath a staid perfectly tailored Italian suit jacket, was Charles Keating's announcement to the dimly lit extravagantly decorated lavish lounge that he was important, and he meant business. A tiny thrill traversed its way up

2

from Jacob's toes any time he got to experience Jessie's pseudo-dad producer in work mode, especially when Jacob reminded himself that he, too, was now under Charles' tutelage and care. Remembering this helped ease the burden of abandonment, both from his father and from Jessie. Charles was a power-house producer, here in Miami with Jacob to see, on Dee's behalf, that their new star was settling in and being treated well by the production company Jacob was now working for, and also to formalize plans for travel back and forth between Miami and Vancouver so Jacob could finish recording the last few tunes on his album.

He trained his gaze back to the fancy beer and frowned when he thought about the album. It would mean working with Jessie again. They'd agreed to continue to co-write. On the one hand, the plan to work with her was welcome. He ached for any time in her presence, begrudgingly accepting the crappy fact that Josh was a good guy whom Jessie obviously deeply loved. On the other hand it sucked that he, Jacob Ryan, would only have one part of Jessie from now on—the music part. Still—if that was all he could have, then so be it. He would just have to deal with it. But he would never stop loving her. His belly clenched with sensory remembrances of the old Jessie—Annie—whose body was his to touch and pleasure in Scotland and then, for a short time, in Vancouver. He shrugged his shoulders as he tried to talk his inner self into letting go. But the tingle in his groin betrayed his will to respect Jessie's choices. He groaned and slumped further into the bar.

Then, with a slap of a hand on Jacob's shoulder, Charles woke him from his melancholy reverie. Jacob jumped.

"Ryan! Thought I might find you here. How's Guinness taste in this part of the world? Somehow it just seems wrong in Miami." Charles slipped into the sturdy leather stool beside his artist and studied Jacob.

Jacob held up his glass. The clear IPA was a light golden color. It foamed just a little, serenely and rather otherworldly, in the cast of the prevalent neon light in the swanky lounge. "I've sworn off Guinness," he said in that lazy, quiet way of his. "But apparently the local IPA has some kind of exquisite honey aftertaste. Or should I say aftertazzzte." His eyes darted to the bartender.

Nearby, eavesdropping, the object of Jacob's derision turned his back

3

SUSAN RODGERS

and rolled his eyes. "Redneck," he muttered to himself before wandering off down the bar.

Charles chuckled and patted Jacob affectionately on the shoulder. He knew the boy was still down and out about Jessie's recent wedding, and that by cutting Guinness loose, Jacob was making a point of trying to cut Jessie loose. But Charles also recognized those kinds of attachments as far too deep and painful to let go of by virtue of refusing one's favorite beer. He called out to the retreating bartender, "Some of that honey aftertaste for me, too, please." Might as well show some solidarity. He turned back to Jacob.

"Cheer up, son. You're in a warm city where women dress in mini-skirts daily. Back in Vancouver they've already broken out the jeans and boots."

A low breathy grumble and a narrowing of his eyes telegraphed Jacob's thoughts on the subject. He clenched his teeth and shot Charles a sideways glare. *Jeans and boots. Hell, what I'd do to be with my gal and her jeans and boots* slid mutely across the tip of his tongue.

But Charles wasn't the man to cry to. The esteemed producer was thrilled about the album he and Jacob were recording back in Van, and he was over the moon about the adventurous foray into acting. He was whistling a happy tune even now, tapping his fingers on the glistening bar as he patiently awaited his beer. He was practically bouncing in his fancy seat in this artificial neon lounge attached to a restaurant where a simple Caesar salad cost seventeen bucks in *American* currency.

It occurred to Jacob then, that despite Charles' apparent easygoing good mood, the older man kept glancing towards the expansive mahogany framed entrance to the lounge. At the moment, he was twisting slightly around to look back over his shoulder. Beyond the entrance was a pristine hotel lobby, the floor itself a glistening geometrically patterned earthy rust-clay and sunshine yellow tile. It was moderately busy for this time of the evening as the hotel's guests wandered around seeking dinner after their busy days exploring Miami's hopping streets or traversing around from air-conditioned meeting to air-conditioned meeting, sipping sparkling waters and munching on seasonal fruits.

The singer turned singer / actor wondered who his keeper was expecting. He didn't have to wait long.

4

Into the vibrant dimness flew a willowy redhead on four-inch heels, which cracked upon the reflective tile like bullets. She landed next to Charles with a pronounced flourish of scarlet manicured nails as shiny as the floor. Promptly knife-slicing the nails through perfectly bobbed hair, the woman snorted in exasperation.

Jacob sat up a little taller and eavesdropped on the nearby conversation.

"I swear, that girl!" One swift fluid motion deposited a beaded evening bag on the counter, then both slim hands dropped to the woman's waist to adjust the wayward drift of her slinky silk jacket that, in all fairness, was a size too tight. An avocado green, it was a perfect warm weather Miami statement piece, and its low cut across her bust made it sizzle on top of an above-knee skirt. Even Charles, a happily married man, couldn't help but feel weak in the knees in the presence of this formidable woman.

The rant continued from between perfectly lined lips as the newcomer brushed a loose strand of bright red hair away from one eye and leaned a hip against the counter to face Charles. Her voice was musical, the words lilting. "She parties, she sleeps around, she's always late for call, and her tongue's as deadly as a viper. I'd throw her out except for the irresistible fact she makes my house and car payments, and I happen to enjoy cruising Miami in cherry red with the top down." She slipped onto a stool.

Jacob caught himself wondering if Charles had the discipline not to watch the woman's skirt slip further up her thighs as she sat. He—Jacob—didn't. Despite the fact the woman was likely in her sixties, as evidenced by tiny lines exuding from those pristine lips and heavily mascara'd eyes, Jacob surreptitiously leaned forward to peek around Charles for a closer look.

Martinique, as he soon learned the moneyed siren was called, half twisted towards the bar and rudely called down to the bartender, who was in the midst of serving another customer, "Tonio! Martini! Dry! Now!"

Antonio was obviously accustomed to Martinique's brusque and unprofessional behavior. He waved to acknowledge her and continued serving his customer. She turned back around to Charles and pouted openly. "What am I supposed to do with a girl like that, Charles?"

Charles was silent for a moment, and then he glanced back around at Jacob before responding. His eyes were suddenly pensive and, Jacob thought, a little sad. It wasn't all that long ago that the producer and his wife were asking themselves some very similar questions. When Charles faced the daunting woman again, Jacob strained to hear.

"Step back and let Ernesto handle her. That's what. He's used to hauling her out of bars, isn't he?"

A deep frown marred Martinique's pretty face. "I would, except he up and quit on me this morning. Well," she inhaled and revised her statement as Tonio deftly slid her drink towards her atop a tiny square cocktail napkin the same color as her fashionable outfit, "make that last night. Three a.m. was when I got the call, to be exact. Woke me in the middle of a dream. A *good* dream, may I add." Her dark eyes flicked up and down Charles' stately physique and Jacob thought she would have winked and teased him, had she not been so frustrated with...exactly *who* was she raging about?

"Uh-huh," Charles replied knowingly. "Her third in a year?"

"My usual go-to firm is swamped." She sulked, "Even if they had the manpower, no one will touch Kelly. Wouldn't matter if I promised them their own cherry red Porsche, or a Lamborghini, for that matter. She's poison."

Kelly? Jacob's heart sank and, beside him, Charles closed his eyes, hoping the dance music pumping through the bar drowned out Martinique's comment. But Jacob heard loud and clear. Kelly Reilly was his new co-star. He had yet to meet the girl but she, like him, was a singer, destined to star in the sexy new drama, *Mystic Nights*, a series about the artists signed to a fictional independent record label. Sure, Jacob knew his co-star had a reputation, but who didn't, in this crazy world of entertainment? He could handle her. Or could he?

Next to him, while Jacob pondered what he had gotten himself into, Charles was working his producer's calming magic on Martinique who, by now Jacob ascertained, was likely an old friend in the biz, and perhaps one of the connections that got him cast in the highly anticipated American drama.

"Look, I may know someone who can help you. A friend of a friend, you could say. Not Matt," Charles held up a hand quickly as Martinique's eyes lit up momentarily. "Not Matt, or any of his team," he repeated. "He's got his hands full with Jessie's security, and now with Jacob here. And I've got eyes on Dee, too, these days. She's on the road a lot with these shelters, including time in L.A. helping cast this show."

"She's a busy lady. You must not see her that often. You must…miss her?" Martinique's eyes narrowed.

His friend's expression was lost on Charles. He fingered his beer glass and stared at the tiny bubbles rising in a steady stream from the bottom. "Busier than I'd like, at her age. Retirement doesn't seem to be part of her vocabulary. 'Course I miss her."

"If it's the cuddling you miss, I can help with that," Martinique suggested, the corners of her lips slinking upwards as she sipped exaggeratedly on her martini, teasing the edge of the glass with her tongue.

That elicited a warm chuckle from Charles. "Martinique, I plan to be faithful to my wife until the day I die, and then likely after that, wherever I end up. You know that."

"Yes, as well as you know that I will never stop trying, Charles. I'm a woman who doesn't stop until she gets what she wants." She winked mischievously at him.

But it was obvious the two had played that game many times previously, because Charles responded by letting out a hearty roar that even managed to bring a smile to Jacob's pouty downcast lips.

Charles then deftly turned the tide of the conversation. "As I was saying, I think I know someone who might be up for the challenge."

"And?" Curious, Martinique raised an eyebrow.

"Well, not Matt exactly."

"Your Chief-of-all-things-Keating-Wheeler Security. No, we've established that."

"Yes, well…"

"Or is it Keating-Sawyer now?"

Jacob groaned as his frown expanded. Charles glanced over at him with newly sympathetic eyes.

"Yes, well Matt—"

"Has connections in the mafia, is that right? Because it will take the mafia to control Her Highness."

"Let me finish!"

Martinique smiled diminutively and gracefully waved a hand. "By all means. Master!"

7

Charles laughed again, then took her hand and gently brushed his lips across the back. "M'lady," he said gallantly while Jacob raised his own eyebrows.

"Matt has a brother who you may well know. In fact, Michael was instrumental in bringing Matt to the Keating camp in the first place. He's...in the industry. Or, well, he was. He kind of dropped out for a while." Charles shrugged his shoulders slightly, while Martinique stopped sipping her drink and pondered what he left unsaid. Charles continued. "My point is, he knows the ropes, all the backstage politics and innuendos. He's likely well versed in, well, Jessie's recent troubles and so he would have some sense of how to handle, well, a difficult personality, would you say?"

It was Martinique's turn to roar. She guffawed so loudly the whole bar heard, including the powerful Asian bankers meeting for an evening beverage in the back corner. "Difficult?! Difficult, you say? Kelly's not difficult! She's positively evil!"

"Martinique," Charles chided gently. It did the trick. His warm eyes flecked softly in the dim atmosphere of the bar. Martinique lightened up.

"Well, Charles," she swooned effusively, "Kelly's not Jessie Wheeler. Sawyer. She's not your sweet waif. She's...spoiled. You know, the whole Princess syndrome. Incorrigible."

"Nobody's incorrigible," Charles smiled quietly. Jacob rolled his eyes a second time, but they lit up, just a little. He twisted his empty glass in its wet puddle on the bar, and silently agreed with Charles' gentle inference that Jessie was, despite all, still a good influence in all of their lives. He wondered what she was doing right now...

"Okay, you win," Martinique was saying when Jacob tuned back in. "Get this Michael gentleman to call me, and we'll see if we can convince him to engage in security detail with the wicked witch of the—"

"Martinique!"

"I mean, with my lovely easygoing Kelly. That's what I meant to say." She nudged Charles, who laughed happily. He always enjoyed bantering with Martinique. Her American-Miami dramatics were an enticing breath of fresh air.

Martinique tilted her glass up, drained her martini and licked the edge of the glass with the tip of her small pink tongue. Delicately she swept down the hem of her skirt and slipped off the smooth stool with another wink at Charles. Jacob saw her glance up to see if the older man was looking downwards—he wasn't. The vivacious woman frowned noticeably.

She rallied quickly. "So," she said, proudly throwing her trim shoulders back, "who is this Michael? You say I might know him?"

Charles was suddenly subdued. He took a moment before responding. "Yes," he replied. "Well, maybe not know him well exactly, but know of him, at least. It's Michael Kelly."

Both Jacob and Martinique paused then. In fact it seemed the sound in the entire neon-mahogany trimmed lounge was sucked out for an extended moment.

Michael Kelly—huh, thought Jacob. He knew the man was a very successful singer in his own right, but that was years ago, perhaps even around the time Jacob's dad himself was starting out. That would put him at about… forty something? Mid-forties? All he remembered about the man was he sang a sort of light rock, maybe Van Morrison style, and he had suffered some kind of serious tragedy that resulted in his rapid departure from the business. Jacob—and apparently Martinique, too—had no inkling what the man was up to lately in terms of work. Jacob was also surprised to hear the guy had some kind of family connection with Matt.

"Kelly, is it?" Martinique threw in, effectively putting an end to the awkward silence. "Well at least they'll have something in common. They can chat about their low-blood heritage, starving on rotten potatoes or something like that." She paused. "I hope it's serendipitous, the two of them with the same name."

With that, Martinique regained her composure, inelegantly grabbed her evening bag, and graciously swept out of the cushy lounge.

Charles watched her go before wheeling his knees slowly around so he faced Jacob straight on. He seemed sobered. "Want to go somewhere quiet where we can think?" he asked his young prodigy.

Jacob's eyes were silent, watching, wondering. He ignored the question. "Michael Kelly still playing at all?"

Charles tipped up his cool glass and took a final swig of the delicious refreshing honey IPA. "Ahhh," he sighed with satisfaction. Then, "Nope," he added without looking at Jacob. "I don't think he has any intention of ever playing again, actually." He turned and peered closely at Jacob. "You know, Matt says he doesn't even play for fun anymore."

"Huh," was Jacob's rather thoughtful response. Despite the twenty or so years between them, he knew the man was still a highly regarded cultural icon, and his music still made the rounds on the radio as well as on a number of satellite stations. The thought of never playing music again, to Jacob, was simply unthinkable. But—to each his own. The guy must have his reasons.

He glanced up at Charles. "Something about his family, wasn't it?"

"Yep," Charles said matter-of-factly as he slid off his seat. "Lost a wife and daughter, if I do recall. Car accident. Nasty business." Both he and Jacob shivered at the thought. Neither wanted to even contemplate the possibility of such a heavy loss. Thoughts of Jessie and Dee flashed across both of their minds. Immediately Jacob chastised himself for his earlier ennui. At least Jessie was still in his life, on some level. He perked up at the thought of travelling back to Vancouver to write music with her again soon.

Just as he was exiting his chair in order to accompany Charles somewhere quieter where they could focus on some serious scheduling and planning, a ruckus at the grand Art Deco curved entrance to the lounge caught their attention. A blonde in her late twenties was being escorted in by two young male hotel employees who were, in fact, apparently trying to steer her away from the bar and back to the hotel elevator in the sumptuous lobby.

"Just one more drink," she was whining, swaying on tall glitzy Christian Louboutin heels as she did so. Her dress, an empire style gauzy silk shift, caused Jacob's throat to close. It was short, and she was around his age, so he felt a little less guilty for watching where it landed on her thighs than he did when he peeked at the well-preserved Martinique. Also, this girl's dress was much shorter than the older woman's. In fact, it barely covered her *there*, at all. His eyes couldn't help but dance over her thighs. He gulped.

Roughly, he fell back into his seat before glancing upwards and meeting the girl's piercing green gaze. One hand on her hip, she had paused, wavering, in front of Jacob, who felt suddenly very uncomfortable and conspicuous in his so-not-Miami plaid flannel shirt and threadbare jeans.

10

She spoke, her voice low and demanding. "I see. The redneck express has arrived. Or was it the turnip truck?"

Jacob couldn't bring himself to respond, which immediately gave Charles a terrifying moment in which to contemplate whether bringing the lonely inexperienced boy onto this shoot was, in the end, such a great idea.

The girl wheeled around then, lost her balance, and was caught by one of her pseudo-bodyguards at the exact same moment Jacob realized who she was.

Kelly Reilly. His co-star.

"Fuckkkk…" he stammered under his breath, but Charles got the gist of the word Jacob's round lips formed.

The older man turned back around to the bar, and a stunned Jacob soon followed suit.

"Tonio!" Charles waved at the bartender.

Jacob finished his sentence. " 'Nuther one of those honey bee chocolate flavored fancy after taste things, please."

Hell, he thought. *If she's gonna be calling me a redneck, I might as well be one.*

Charles patted Jacob's arm in consolation as, on the monitor on the wall before them, Tom Ryan lit up the screen once again.

Jacob hung his head and wished like hell he was back in a dark old pub in Scotland, a Guinness in one hand and an acoustic guitar in the other. Jessie's old warning flashed across his mind. *Be careful what you wish for, Jacob.*

Well, one thing was certain. Fer sure he was on one helluva ride.

Chapter One

"Okay. So Josh, if we're gonna live together, there's one thing we gotta get straight right off the bat."

Josh stood back from the glass stovetop he was polishing to a super shine, and couldn't help but smile at Jessie. She wanted normal? Well, she had it today. Hair up in a high messy ponytail and Lululemon pants over which she'd pulled one of his old T-shirts—excess length scrunched up and tied at the side of her waist—she was poised in front of the refrigerator with a small green compost bin at her side. Hands on her hips, she wheeled around to face her husband of just a few short weeks. She was trying to look menacing but Josh wasn't buying it, so Jessie reached over and swatted him lightly on the elbow.

"Stop! I'm calling 911!" he bellowed.

"Listen! I'm serious!" she replied, swallowing the laugh threatening to lessen the gravity of her housecleaning woes.

He threw his hands up in defense. "Okay, okay! I'm listening. Sir!"

"It's just that you need to cut down on the take-out." Jessie flipped back around and grabbed a paper box from amongst the mystery containers in their fridge, which she immediately tossed into the compost. "We can cook at home from now on. Well most times, anyway. Not including weekend brunch."

When he didn't respond, Jessie twisted back around and looked over at Josh. He had that silly grin on his face again, the one she wouldn't erase for all of the normalcy in the world. She softened and her diaphanous eyes blinked up at him. She had the same look too these days—happiness.

"*Home*, huh?" Josh was outright grinning at her now. He stepped forward and gave the fridge door a shove. It closed with a gentle *thwunk*. Wrapping his left arm around his wife's waist, he leaned in and brushed his lips against her forehead. "Why Mrs. Sawyer, I cannot tell you how much the sound of that word pleases me."

Jessie sighed and looped the fingers of both hands over his worn leather belt. "You sexy man," she said dreamily. "How am I supposed to get any work done with you distracting me with your puppy dog eyes and—and," she clenched his belt tighter with her right hand and hauled him closer, then wrapped both arms around his shoulders, "…this?"

"What, this?" Josh gestured happily towards his own body.

"Duhhhh!" She was laughing openly now.

"Break time?" he asked, wriggling closer.

She swatted him a second time. "With you it's always break time!"

They stood and shared some sweet kisses for a few moments before getting back to work. But both would never take for granted any of the time they had together, not anymore, not after the hell of the last few years and the heavy price they paid to be together.

Josh and Jessie were putting the finishing touches on officially making his beach house, in the UBC neighborhood of Vancouver, hers as well. They would keep her downtown condo, but mainly for the times when Jessie would need to work out a new song. Her baby grand piano was there, nestled in her cozy living room next to the floor-to-ceiling wall on the north side of the building. The place held all kinds of memories, good and bad, and she was ready to let it go in terms of living arrangements but, despite the bad times—the loneliness and the Deuce McCall assault, mainly—it was still, and always would be, her own space, a sanctuary of sorts.

Despite that, she was tickled to finally be moved into Josh's home, as his wife, nonetheless. Michelle's mark was still here, in the odd knick-knack here and there, or in smaller bits of furniture she left behind upon her hasty departure late last spring. Although Jessie couldn't help but bristle when she saw them, she had the grace to quietly ask Josh to remove such items. She didn't see any need for confrontation. For his part, he never paid much attention to household furnishings and décor, so he didn't concern himself with removing those things after Michelle left. But now he, too, was starting to see the home through Jessie's eyes and so he delicately tucked away a trinket here and there, or donated such things as Michelle's antique bookcase to the Deacon Foundation or to one of Jessie and Deirdre's shelters. He didn't bother getting in touch with Michelle. The two hadn't spoken since July, when she called him one last time to see how he was doing after his splenectomy. She was distant, sad, and so was he—but what they'd shared was a surface level love. Real, yes, but it didn't compare to the depth of emotion Josh felt when he looked at Jessie. Yes, the T-shirt his wife now wore was a bit scraggly, torn and frayed at the neck, but hell, it was still sexy. And as far as Josh was concerned, she could wear Lululemon pants any old time she got the urge to houseclean.

Later, after a shared shower and then a lunch of mixed greens and apple-cheddar grilled sandwiches, Jessie grabbed her bag. She pushed a pair of aviator Ray Bans atop her messy curls, which after her shower she coiled up into a messy bun as a tool to fight the Vancouver breeze off the Pacific. The couple climbed into Josh's King Ranch and Josh pointed it towards North Vancouver. Charles was landing home from Florida today, where he'd travelled to ensure Jacob's security in his new American drama, *Mystic Nights*, and Dee was home from a whirlwind trip to L.A. where she auditioned more actors as a favor to the *Mystic* producers, and where she'd checked up on the L.A. shelter at the same time. The family had lots of news to share and Jessie and Josh were both curious to inquire about their friends—Jacob, of course, in Miami, and Steve and Sophie in California. The entire extended *Drifters* family was so close now, after the tumultuous last few years, that a trip to L.A. for anyone would not be complete without a check-in with Steve and his fiancée, whose own wedding was imminent, and who were well situated in Cali while Steve worked on his new sitcom.

As they pulled into the curved driveway of La Casa and Josh drew the big truck to a halt, Jessie sighed. "I will never ever get over the peace I feel when I come here," she said, reaching out a hand and wrapping Josh's fingers around hers. She turned to look at him, an easy smile lighting her eyes. "It's home too, you know." Drifting back around to gaze at the Keating house through the passenger side window, she was wholly captivated by the home's arched welcome and the way the sunlight cascaded gladly down the front southern exposure, dotting the yellow with speckles here and there so the house seemed to glow with some otherworldly ethereal power. Wistfully she added, "All of a sudden I have lots of homes. Not so long ago I didn't have any…" She let the sentence fade off into oblivion.

She hadn't mentioned any references to home or her new-old Ontario family for a while, at least since coming back to B.C. and alerting Charles and Dee to the 'possibility' she might want to reconnect with the Martha Kilfoil branch of the Emily Wheeler family. Now, Josh reacted the way he always did when he felt Jessie might be threatened—he tensed, the little nerve on his cheek playing its own game of fear, twitching slightly.

He lifted a hand to his mouth, pinched his bottom lip, and studied her. Yes, Jessie did seem to be at peace these days, at least on some level. She was eating better, and a slight pink roundness in her cheeks had replaced the sallow tincture of fear that consumed her over the last few years. Sleep was welcome now, consecutive hours finally giving both Jessie as well as himself a measure of comfort and rest, and she startled less. Her eyes were attentive and focused, instead of desperate, sad and empty. Josh felt hope now as he watched her; it lit him from within, a rainbow of promise that inked its multi-colored faith from the bottoms of his toes to the tops of his ears. The last thing he wanted to do was rain on his new wife's parade, but Josh would do anything to spare Jessie any more unhappiness or disappointment. He did not want to see her hurt, ever again, but somehow he felt an uneasy twinge whenever this 'new' branch of her family tree was mentioned.

Jessie's smile turned upside down as he unwittingly telegraphed his thoughts across to her.

"Geez, Josh. Can't you just be happy for me?"

He sighed and a little whistle escaped from between his pursed lips. Josh turned away from Jessie and watched the cool light breeze buffet some fallen maple leaves over a tuft of earth before he answered. Jessie waited patiently, arms crossed. She held his gaze when he looked back at her.

He grinned slightly as he prepared to speak, disarming her entirely. She leaned her head back on the seat and placed a finger over his lips.

"Don't bother," she demanded. "I know what you're thinking, but if there's one thing I've learned over the years it's the art of self-preservation. Besides, you ought to know by now that you can't completely protect me. And," she tweaked him on the elbow, "I need this, Josh. I need to connect with my family. I need to know what in God's name drove my mother to break that connection with her first daughter—her *child*. And why my father let her. Also," she added, "I want to meet her. My *sister*."

"Look, Jessie, I'm not averse to you connecting with these people—"

"My family."

"Your family. Yes. But not one that knows you. Not one with your best interests at heart."

"Meaning watch my bank account."

"Meaning watch your heart, little one." Josh let a finger trail down Jessie's cheek and, despite her frustration, she felt a bubble of joy float in and around her, as seemed to happen a lot in Josh's company these days.

She resolved to spare *him* any more worry than necessary. Jessie would be at Charles' downtown studio tomorrow to work with Jacob, who was at this moment just back from Miami with Charles. The plan was to do more songwriting between Jacob's scheduled shoot days on the new show, but Jessie wanted to go early and spend some time on her downtown office computer looking for Aunt Evelyn, her mother's sister.

All George said via telephone when Jessie called him the other night about the aunt who was often Jessie's cushion after David Wheeler's death, was that she left after an altercation with Emily. Reading between the lines, Jessie figured it had to do with *her*, after she ran away. Did Evelyn know about the sexual abuse by Emily's wealthy third partner? (Husband? Not legally, Jessie now knew, since her mother was never divorced from her first husband in Peterborough).

Josh was pensive. He spoke quietly while watching a fat robin try to peck some nourishment out from underneath the stiff frigid grass. The bird darted a few steps, stopped and looked jerkily around, then rapidly switched direction and repeated the process many times over, quickly pecking at a frayed clump of grass each time it stopped. The bird seemed to be on the lookout for danger. Josh exhaled slowly and prayed he and Jessie could someday just *be*, without a constant threat around every turn.

"Jessie, have you stopped to consider Charles and Dee?" he asked. "What they think about you hunting down another family?"

"Not another family. *My* family. Of course I have." But she glanced down and twisted the hem of her knit sweater around and around an index finger. She shrugged. "I suppose they feel the same as you."

Jessie peeked up at him through long eyelashes, biting her lip at the same time. Her heart leapt when her eyes met Josh's solemn gaze.

"Damn it," she demanded curtly. "Stop looking at me like that!"

Laughing, Josh grabbed Jessie's fingers and gently eased the sweater hem out of her grasp. He, too, was a sucker when lost in Jessie's eyes. Their bond was strong, infinite, powerful. He swore sometimes she could climb right inside him and sit there, soaking up his essence and reading his mind until he broke the connection. He knew she felt he had the same dominion over her.

Jessie broke into his thoughts. "Josh, I know Dee has her reservations. But Ma and Pop Keating are grown-ups. They can handle this."

"You know what you mean to them, Jess." A tender pressure on her fingers accompanied the remark.

As if on cue, in his peripheral vision Josh saw Dee, in her gardening garb, pad around the corner of the grand home towards them. A pale pink cloth bucket hat kept the soft breeze from whipping her bobbed hair in front of her eyes when she knelt down to twist and encourage dead stalks from a garden grouping as she wandered by it. A three-pronged tool was clutched in one hand. As she made her way over to the King Ranch, Jessie pressed the button to let the window down so Dee could lean both elbows on the door, being careful not to let the tool drop and scratch the pick-up's shiny metallic grey finish.

Jessie forced herself to break her gaze with Josh in order to converse with Dee, but she wrapped the fingers of her left hand tightly around his knuckles. Chuckling at Dee in the silly hat, she felt a comforting wave of affection for the woman she often thought of as her mother.

"Deirdre Keating," she started, a bemused smile on her lips, "does your husband know you're out in public like that?" She let her eyes drop to the dirt encrusting her manager's perfectly manicured fingertips.

"After the craziness of L.A., I need some time in nature. And I'm letting

17

Carlotta have some time with her gardener man," Dee answered succinctly. "If it means I'm not acceptable to the general public, then so be it. Pride is one of the seven deadly sins, my dear." She drove the point home by gently tapping Jessie's arm with the gardening tool.

"And you're behind the fence," Jessie added, nodding southward towards the fence that bordered the home from the road. She yanked the brim of the floppy hat down over Dee's eyes.

Frowning, Dee adjusted the hat by wrenching it off her head, pulling strands of hair behind each ear, and replacing the hat. "And I'm behind the fence," she echoed definitively.

"Vancouver is saved."

"Vancouver is saved," Dee repeated. "From my fashion faux pas. As am I. From the fashion police. Coming in? Or are you two newlyweds planning to spend your visit cuddling in my driveway?"

"Well…" Josh threw in, winking at Jessie, who giggled and leaned over backwards for a quick kiss.

Swinging the passenger door open, Deirdre grasped Jessie's elbow. "Come," she demanded. "I need your opinion on where to plant my tulip bulbs for the spring."

Jessie groaned but went along with her. She slid down and out of the truck as Charles pulled in, in the passenger seat next to Matt who was behind the Audi's wheel. They'd dropped Jacob at his new place on Southwest Marine Drive on their way from the airport. Matt drew to a stop alongside the truck. Josh pulled the keys out of the King Ranch's ignition and stepped out to nod hello. Jessie waved happily, and then slipped a hand into Dee's as they sidled off to choose which color bulbs to plant where.

"You realize you have thousands of flowers, Dee."

"You need to learn to garden, Jessie. I'd think you'd be good at it!"

"If you mean I'd be good at planting, no problem, but plants and flowers don't do well in my care. The petunia I tried to keep on the back deck in P.E.I. was just spindly brown stalks by the time I finally let Josh toss it in the compost."

Dee eyed her girl mysteriously as they wandered away from the men. Her last words lingered in the cool November breeze.

"Patience, dear child. Let me teach you. We'll start with simple bulbs. Then we'll work our way up to grandbabies."

Jessie's genuine laughter warmed the hearts of the men as Deirdre and Jessie wandered out of sight around the corner. Charles leaned against the Audi and crossed both arms before fixing his eyes on Josh. Matt swept around behind the car and reached out to shake Josh's hand. He couldn't look at Josh without being consumed by guilt and the thought he'd failed both he and Jessie. He carried the weight of his failure with him always, a heavy manacle that gripped his intestines in a nasty clench every time he saw the couple together or when he awoke in the dark of night. Thankfully it was always quickly replaced with the realization Josh and Jessie were together now, married, and judging by the slow grin spreading across Josh's face now as Jessie's laughter receded, happy and safe.

"She's a handful, that one," Josh was saying to Charles.

"You talking about my wife?" Charles asked pointedly. A sly grin accentuated his next statement. "Or yours?"

"Uh…" Josh colored, glanced downwards, and dug a booted toe into the dirt.

Matt saved him. "Double trouble, if you ask me."

Their conversation took a serious turn fairly quickly. Charles was a man of action. He spoke like Shakespeare—most of his words carried weight. "Josh, you know Jessie's coming back into the studio tomorrow."

Josh glanced up at Charles and nodded. "Yeah, I know. She told me. It's good—I'm glad."

"She needs to work, son. I think starting with music is a good way to go."

"Yeah, for sure. I'm glad she's up for it."

Charles jumped in a little deeper. "Matt just picked me up from the airport, Josh. You know I was in Miami."

Josh shrugged. Why were his defenses crawling up his legs like a troupe of spiders? Barely there but still felt, just slightly tingly. "Yeah…getting Jacob settled in, I hear." A sense of satisfaction wrapped Josh up in a big smug bear hug. Jacob was now going to be mostly living very far away for the next six months, where he couldn't hope to be any kind of threat to Josh and Jessie's relationship. Josh knew about the songwriting pact between Jacob and Jessie,

19

and he could live with the brief meetings here and there to make that happen. If that was the price he had to pay to keep Jessie happy, then he could deal with it. But Miami…

Charles saw the tiny grin Josh tried to stifle. He and Matt exchanged glances. Matt ducked his head and watched an ant shuffle across the ground, carrying some particle five times its own weight. He knew how Josh would be feeling after Charles dropped this next bomb. He waited for the light in Josh's brown eyes to fade.

The older man was judicious, careful. He, too, was well aware his next bit of news might not be entirely welcome in the Sawyer camp.

"Josh, Dee and I had a long chat over Skype last night. We think Jessie needs to get back into some acting as well."

Josh bit his lip and stared hard at Charles. The man, in his ubiquitous fine cut white dress shirt and perfectly tailored fall tweed hunting jacket, had a way of demanding one's full attention and respect. It had something to do with the way his eyes lit upon the person whose attention he demanded, Josh supposed. Sometimes the man could be unsettling, usually when he was in business mode. But Josh also saw Charles through hard times when a girl he loved deeply as a daughter was hurting, missing. Back in those terrible days Jessie's producer was stooped, tired, his eyes fatigued and encircled with charcoal waves of pain. He was vulnerable. Real.

Josh adjusted his stance again and squared his body towards the man. Feeling suddenly inadequate in faded jeans and his scuffed tan leather jacket, he swallowed a rapidly rising lump in his throat. "Acting? On what, Charles?" he asked outright, his mind rushing to keep up. But suddenly he knew. *Mystic Nights.* In fucking Miami. He wasn't unaware of Matt's outright uncomfortable posture. He felt a little ganged up on and wondered if this 'news' was something Jessie was in on but had yet to share with him…maybe that was why she wanted to come here today…so much for their pact to never keep secrets from one another.

Charles read his thoughts. "We have yet to discuss this with Jessie, Josh. But we intend to. Today. During dinner. Or after. Whenever it feels right."

"She's already got a part lined up."

"I'm not talking about next spring. She can start now. If she wants to,"

Charles added cautiously, as if he would be surprised if Jessie said no to his and Dee's proposal.

"She needs time," Josh maintained, his thoughts swirling as he fought to remain in control against this powerful man.

Matt watched from the sidelines, rooting secretly for Josh.

"We just got back," Josh added in a subdued voice.

"This is small. Jessie can handle it. She can ease her way back in—the part was practically written for her."

"Jesus," Josh said, finally losing control. He turned half around, away from Charles, and swung an arm over the side mirror of his big truck. Looking back over his shoulder, he glared openly at Charles. "If you want her to get back into acting, then find her a fucking part in Vancouver. Away from…" He let the thought trail off, but inwards he thought it. *Away from Jacob.*

Sidestepping, Charles caved—a little. He glanced over at Matt who, he thought, was watching Josh rather apologetically. "Look Josh," he said quietly. "Jessie's a professional. She and Jacob have established some kind of safe rapport. She chose you, for God's sake! You know that, you know it's always been you she wanted. The thing about working with Jacob is this— it's safe territory. He can watch out for her, keep an eye on her. He knows the boundaries."

"You've got to be fucking kidding me. Charles, Jessie is just finding her feet again. Let her do her thing with Jacob in the studio, and find her a part here in Vancouver. Give—us—some time. Jesus, give *me* some time!"

"Give *you* some time? This from the guy who went off to shoot a film in Virginia last summer and left my girl suffering alone on the east coast? Give your head a shake, Josh!"

As their voices rose, Matt straightened. He touched Charles' elbow. "Easy," he urged, a voice of calm in the wilderness.

Charles shook him off as Josh stood glaring back at his pseudo father-in-law.

"She needed a wake-up call, Charles. She needed to get her ass into counseling."

"She needed someone with her, Josh. You bailed. Granted, I wasn't there and, in your defense, I trust you did what you thought you needed to do at the time which, in some way, was kick her lily white ass into action. Fine.

But don't tell me you didn't also go because you wanted the opportunity on that biker film." He let that one sink in and, judging by Josh's rapid blinks, he knew he hit his target.

Josh curled his fists into balls and the nerve on his cheek went into overdrive. He forced himself not to react because he knew Charles, at least on some level, was right.

Charles continued. "This is a good opportunity for Jessie. It's a few days here and there, at least at first."

"At least at first?" Josh's voice was low now, even and barely controlled. He curled and uncurled his fists.

Charles shifted his gaze back to Matt, who nodded slightly.

Might as well get this over with, the security chief was thinking. *Crush the guy with one fell swoop.* He worshipped Charles but, this time, although he could see the man's reasoning, he questioned the wisdom of putting a newlywed couple as vulnerable as Josh and Jessie on the hot seat so early in their marriage. But Matt also knew his boss was anxious to get Jessie back to work—back in the saddle, technically. The Keating king was afraid too much time off would make it too easy for Jessie to retire from acting altogether. If that was her choice, so be it, but…in the meantime…

Charles and Matt had just hashed over all these points on the way up the 99 from the airport, over the Lions' Gate Bridge and into North Vancouver. Matt knew Charles would accept whatever it was Jessie wanted—or didn't want—to do. But he wouldn't accept it without question and without putting some choices in front of her. *Some good choices,* Charles said in that strongwilled way of his as Matt steered them past the staid lions with the frozen eyes standing sentinel on either side of the bridge. *With Jacob by her side, Jessie will have a shoulder to lean on.*

But Matt also knew Charles wasn't seeing the whole picture, the one where the young man the Keating patriarch was so keen on nurturing these days because of some sort of flawless faith in his ability, mixed with an undying gratitude for urging Jessie back into music—who he was starting to think of as a son—was also Josh's nemesis. No, to Charles Jacob was the hero who destroyed Deuce McCall and ended Jessie's lonely terror. In Charles' eyes, Jacob was bathed in an all-forgiving ethereal golden-white light.

22

The boy could do no wrong.

And he was talented, to boot.

Josh was waiting for an answer Matt knew he wouldn't like. Charles jumped in headfirst.

"I admit, the part is open-ended. It could grow into something full time. The writers have some options available, put it that way."

"Full time." Josh's voice was dangerously low. Matt tensed, waiting to see which way this was going to go. They all knew of Josh's past propensity for violence, but this was Charles he was talking to. Still, Matt kept his hand on his phone should a quick need to call Ulysses or Dan arrive. The newest gal on the security team, Susanne, was away on a short trip with the NHL hockey player she was dating. The Vancouver Canucks were playing in Calgary. Silently Matt wished he could be there as well, with his wife Julie and young daughter Katy at his side. *Anywhere but here*, he thought.

Six months in Miami with Jacob, was what Josh was thinking. Another thought crossed his mind. He raised his chin and nodded at Charles. "What's the part?" he growled.

Charles didn't answer, but he didn't bow to Josh, either. He just held his gaze, which alone had the power to pierce Josh's heart. Charles was confident, but cautious. The last thing either he or Jessie needed was any kind of rift or grudge involving Josh.

Regarding the man, Josh cringed. Charles' reticence to respond could only mean one thing. He wondered if Jacob knew. The sultry, raspy musician would be over the moon.

Josh slammed a fist into the door of the King Ranch. Matt winced at the resulting dent, but it was small and could likely be hammered out.

"Seriously, Charles?" Josh was asking in a higher-pitched tone now, struggling to regain control of his emotions, which were getting the better of him. "Give me a fucking chance here, will you?" But he knew. He *knew* that not only would Charlie always rate higher than him on the Charles Keating scale, but so now would Jacob, as the singer had since the day he killed Deuce McCall.

Charles was watching him with a detached sort of interest. He, too, was tense, but he knew he had the upper hand. He was well aware Josh was the main key to Jessie's happiness, and in his heart he didn't want to mess with that. But this part was good, and Jacob could watch out for his and Deirdre's girl.

He acquiesced a little, and reached out to Josh, his hand waving a little in the suddenly stilled air between them. "Josh, c'mon, like I said, we haven't even asked Jessie yet. She may have no interest at all in going down to Miami."

Josh's stomach lurched and he caught himself thinking *score one for me*. He knew where Jessie wanted to go—Peterborough. A wave of guilt passed over him as he pictured the look on Charles' face each time Jessie laid that one bare and took off to Ontario.

In frustration he placed his hands on his hips and shook Charles' arm off when the older man tried to reassure him with a touch. Avoiding Matt's eyes as he stomped off around the front of the King Ranch, Josh felt his heart sink. Just when it seemed like things were getting better for him—Jonathon in his life in a way he never dreamed, Wes suddenly making sense, Jessie at his side *happy* for a change—life was taking more twists. He rallied when he paused around the corner of La Casa away from prying eyes, and leaned back on the sun-warmed brick in the cooling November air. But then another reality hit him right between the eyes and he almost felt sorry for the insurmountable Charles Keating. *Jessie's background on the Downtown Eastside. Were there photos and films? If so, how many, and where were they?*

His head spinning, Josh turned around to face the brick and leaned his forehead against the rough surface. He toed a hole in the dirt while he tried to catch his breath. *Jessie Wheeler. Yeah. Shit.* Earlier he'd been joking when he greeted Charles with the line about Jessie being a handful—yeah, he'd meant Jessie, all right. She was, indeed, a handful. A busy, recovering, sad, loving, kind, sweet, glorious handful. And she was *his*. Not Charles'. Or Jacob's. Manny, the skinny driver from the Virginia shoot, popped into his head. *She's worth it,* Josh thought, echoing Manny's sentiments the night Josh was out of his mind seriously considering an affair with the on-set hair gal. *I have Jessie, she is mine to love and care for, for better or for worse. I am her husband, goddamn it!* And then, the thought that calmed him beyond all others...*I trust her.*

He trusted her. In love, in marriage, and in the choices they would make together as a couple. If those choices brought his superstar wife to Miami to work with Jacob, or to Peterborough with an open heart to meet a long-lost family, then he would be there to support and cherish her, and to pick up the pieces if need be.

Joyous laughter echoed through the backyard and reveled on the breeze towards him. Raising his chin, Josh stilled the raucous thoughts careening for dominance in his head. He cocked his ears to listen, and couldn't help but smile when he heard Jessie's childlike voice teasing Deirdre—Jessie's *happy, playful* voice, in fact.

"Dee, give me that thing. You call yourself a gardener? Stick your hands in the dirt and dig! Like this!"

Suddenly that simple sound carried the utmost pleasure. Josh knew without looking that the woman he loved was just around the corner of the sunniest, most pleasing house he ever had the grace and good luck to enter, and he guessed that she was, at this moment, on her hands and knees with loose strands of curly auburn-tinted hair cascading over rosy cheeks as she dug, carefree, in the dirt. Josh tilted his head sideways and strained to hear when he heard her greet Charles and Matt, who had walked through the house and gone out the back door to the garden.

What would the years bring? Josh didn't know. Hell, he didn't know what the next month, or even day, would bring. But he stilled himself to be prepared for whatever might come their way, and he was glad because finally, for once, he felt he and Jessie would handle life together.

Inhaling deeply the invigorating North Vancouver dampness, Josh steeled himself for battle, shoved his hands in his pockets, and wandered around the corner into the fray.

Chapter Two

"Jacob, you scared the shit out of me!"

Jessie's heart was pounding as she sat, shoulders tensed and straight, just inside the roomy cozy studio high above Vancouver in the Keating Building. She'd been peering intently at a computer screen on a perch inside the door of the studio, at a post Charles installed for his musicians' use during lengthy recording sessions. Jessie meant to use her office that day, but a lingering love-making session that still tickled her senses put that thought to bed right off the bat. No, she didn't get to the studio as early as planned, and she didn't want to do this research at home and take a chance on worrying Josh further, so she was cramming a quick internet research session in just before the others arrived.

Maybe because of her new husband's forced ease during last night's dinner conversation, she cared even more about not upsetting him. Sure, Josh handled the difficult conversation with tact and a certain careful restraint, but Jessie knew him well enough to know Charles and Dee's suggestion— Jessie taking a part in Jacob's new series, *Mystic Nights*—upset him greatly. She could see by Josh's squared shoulders and the somber glint in his sorrowful eyes that he was, simply put, afraid.

A loud scraping sound startled her out of her reverie.

"Are you taking the part?" Jacob plopped himself down on the high wooden stool he'd dragged over from the middle of the studio. He tucked his brown leather desert boots—a new almost Hipster-y look for Jacob, Jessie caught herself thinking absently—onto the first rung of the stool and studied his ex-girlfriend carefully. The stool gave him an odd sensation of power over Jessie. He hovered over her and waited for a response.

26

"Hell, I don't know, Jacob," Jessie answered honestly, wheeling back around and staring at the Facebook profile on her screen. "Part of me wants to, but somehow it doesn't feel right."

"For Josh, you mean." Hard as he tried, Jacob couldn't disguise the jealousy edging his voice like a glistening sixteenth century rapier.

"No, for me, damn it." Jessie struggled to slow her heart rate. *Jacob really should know better than to sneak up on me like that*, she was thinking as she clicked the mouse. The profile of a woman who the page announced went by the name Evelyn Kilfoil lit up the screen. Jessie leaned forward and studied the woman's features. Her heart started to pick up its pace again.

From behind her came Jacob's plea. "Look, you. I need you there with me. The female lead's a freaking lunatic."

Jessie let her eyes drift away from the screen and she locked them into Jacob's deep blue cobalt gaze. She smiled, despite herself, and cocked her head at him. "Kelly Reilly, isn't it? Playing opposite you? I hear she's a bit of a firecracker."

"Firecracker? She's a fucking lunatic!"

"You said freaking, before," she chastised him, chuckling.

"I changed my mind!" Jacob decreed, narrowing his eyebrows in frustration.

"Matt said at dinner last night his brother Michael is taking over her security."

"Yeah, by the way, speaking of freaking…that completely freaked me out. The guy's a musical legend."

Jessie sobered. "Not just for his music, I think." Her own sordid story passed over her mind, an unwarranted slide show of a terror-stricken past with which she knew she would forevermore always be associated in peoples' minds.

"Yeah, damn straight for his music!" Jacob was adamant. "People get these things twisted up."

His crooked grin warmed Jessie's soul and she shot him a look of sincere gratitude. *Good 'ole Jacob. Good 'ole trustworthy Jacob. Leave it to him to read my mind and try to make me feel better.* She shivered when she remembered the large Celtic cross tattoo that ran across her ex's shoulder blades and down the center of his back. Ducking her head, she hoped he wouldn't see the pink flush she felt spreading across the tops of her cheeks. Josh flashed across her mind and she shrank a little in her seat. But Jessie's experiences with Jacob were surreal, the sex…hmmm…magical.

He took another tack, oblivious to Jessie's sudden discomfort. "I could use some support. This is all new to me, Jess."

"You need a guard, you mean!" Eyes alight, she finally looked up at him for an extended period. It was Jacob's turn to pause and recall good times in a small Scots pub, and then afterwards in his bedroom…he shook the thought away. He had to.

"Are you at least thinking about it?"

Jessie sighed. "Jacob, I don't deny it's a great part. And it would rock to sing on screen with you, it really would. But I think it would be dangerous to work with you that way. I mean," she reached deeply to find the words that would be fair to both him and to Josh. "What you and I had was amazing. What we *have* is amazing, musically, I mean." At his hurt puppy dog eyes she added, "And as friends. You're one of my best friends, damn it! And I don't want to mess with our dynamic." She watched him digest that for a moment before she added softly, "Do you?"

Shifting his butt on the hard stool, Jacob answered thoughtfully. "I can handle it, Jessie. There are lots of women on the show." He shrugged, as if by doing so he could dismiss his feelings for Jessie.

"Jacob…" Jessie laid her hand on his knee. *Old habits are hard to break,* she caught herself thinking later when she realized how easy it was to still be intimate with him. "The part is opposite you. You know there will be love scenes."

"It's American TV," Jacob said, chuckling, effectively burying the serious nature of what she'd just implied. "The writers will have me with every woman on the show."

She paused, and he immediately felt sorry for brushing her fears away like that. "Nah, Jessie, look, I know that's possible but we're professionals. We've gone our separate ways and we'll be fine. I promise you." Deep down, he hoped it was a promise he could keep. His stomach gurgled in fear. Hesitantly he asked her a question that had been on his mind from the moment Charles told him Jessie might become a part of the whole *Mystic Nights* scenario.

"Is Josh…" he hesitated. Then Jacob fortified his nerves and faced Jessie head on. "Does Josh know this part has been offered to you?"

"Yep. And he's about as thrilled as you can imagine. Although I know in the end he'll leave it up to me."

"He'll just have to trust you."

"Me, huh?" That Celtic cross…she shivered again, and averted her eyes. "Seriously, Jacob. I do trust me. My brain, at least. Not so sure about my body."

He smiled. "Well trust me then, Jessie. And you can tell Josh I said that." He paused. "Seriously. I want you there. And I won't mess around. My heart can't handle it."

"Pinkie swear?"

Jacob thrust out a baby finger, which he hooked around Jessie's baby finger. "Pinkie swear."

Crisp footsteps echoed down the hallway. Charles chose that moment to walk in. He tried not to appear pleased when he noticed Jacob and Jessie's fingers hooked around each other, accompanied by spicy grins.

"What?" he asked, his own finger itching to solidify the deal.

Jessie let go of Jacob's finger and shrugged. "Go ahead, Jacob. Make his day."

"You sure, Jessie?" Jacob asked, suddenly nervous. She was right—there were temptations in every situation when one partner worked away from the other. Throw in a hot ex, and…

"Yeah," she answered, instead of waiting for Jacob to confirm what Charles wanted to hear. She held out a pinkie to Charles. "I like the story. And the prospect of Miami versus Canada at least for part of this winter ain't so bad, either."

"And Josh?" Charles asked, letting Jessie's finger float alone in the air for a moment.

"He'll be cool. We'll work it out." She wished she were as confident as she sounded, but one thing Jessie knew without a doubt—Josh loved her deeply, and she loved him. They would find a way to make this work, even if it meant lengthy talks with the show's producers to ease up on any love scenes between Jacob's character and Jessie's character.

Besides, thought Jessie. *Jacob has the firecracker to deal with. For sure they'll hook him up with her—Kelly Reilly.* She grinned and shook pinkies with Charles, but not before a wave of jealousy seized the pit of her stomach. Flinching, Jessie swung her chair around again and hit the 'add friend' button on Evelyn Kilfoil's Facebook page before she closed the browser. Already Charles was barking orders to her and Jacob, and technicians were starting to arrive for the afternoon's session. *Miami...well, at least we'll be warm. And don't they have a pro basketball team? Josh'll adjust. We'll invite Steve and Sophie, and Charlie and Jane, and maybe Carter, Maggie and Sue-Lyn can pop down.*

The afternoon was broken up into chunks of songwriting versus chunks of laying tracks. Jessie and Jacob were tired when the day finally drew to a close. And Jacob still had to fly back to Miami that night. Big Dan lingered in the doorway, waiting to drive him home to grab his bag and then to YVR where the Keating jet was being pressed into service for the second time that weekend on a Miami run.

At the last second Jacob turned to Jessie, his eyes intent, curious. "What were you looking up, anyway?" he asked. "Earlier. On Facebook." He waved an arm listlessly towards the computer. "You're never on that thing."

"Oh!" Caught off guard, Jessie hesitated before answering. Then she decided honesty was a good place to start rebuilding a relationship with her new co-star. "An old family member I kinda lost touch with when I left Prince Edward Island as a kid. I'm on a mending fences kick, apparently." She winked.

"Ah. The whole life-is-short-why-spend-it-sulking thing, huh?"

She blushed. "Something like that."

Jacob's eyes danced, just a little. He was feeling playful after their afternoon of making music together. "So, about this mending fences thing."

"Jacob! You pinkie swore."

"No, that's not—Jessie, that's not what I was going to say. In fact, sometimes the whole world does not actually revolve around you. Capiche?"

"Hell, that's the best news I've heard in a long time! Finally!"

"Jessie!"

At the door, Dan grinned. Everybody was thrilled at the change in Jessie.

30

Her new married Vancouver self was like a fleshed out version of the old hollow Jessie. Happiness had settled into all of her features although, Dan understood, she still had a ways to go in therapy. But at least this Jessie had a spark or two in her. He was overjoyed.

Jacob was continuing. He spoke while holding Jessie's guitar case open for her so she could drop the Gibson in.

"It's just this family thing—I've been thinking I might drop in to see my grandparents some day when I get a few days off in a row, or get them to drop down to Miami. I haven't seen them in a few years."

"Oh," Jessie said, straightening as Jacob bent down and fastened the clips on the guitar case. "That's cool. I'm sure they'll be happy to see you." She was seriously overjoyed for Jacob. Seemed the hole in his bucket was filling in, too. Jessie was starting to understand a lot about her behaviors as well as the behaviors of others. Jacob, like her, was accustomed to being a loner, wanting to spend time away from the company of others. Reaching out to the grandparents who raised him was an awesome sign. "That's really great, Jacob," she added seriously, reaching into a pocket for her iPhone so she could text Josh that she was on the way home.

He held up a hand. "There's more, Jess. Listen for a sec."

"Uh—okay?" She phrased it like a question. Curious now, Jessie slipped the phone back into her pocket. "What?"

Sometimes Jacob had the capacity to look like a little boy. Now was one of those times. He shuffled his feet while he searched for the right words, hands buried deeply now in both front pockets of his jeans. He spoke haltingly, unsure. "It's just, I think I'm going to ask them to help me get in touch with my dad. That's all."

"Oh." Now the tables seemed turned. Jessie felt a real ache settle into her belly as she watched Jacob's eyes fleck from light to dark blue, as if a glow was now missing. Suddenly the serious side of him was back, the side that lost its innocence the day his father denied him. *Ohhhh boyyyy* she thought, as a silent understanding of Josh's reticence for her to meet her old family took hold. What she would give to never see Jacob hurt. Yet it seemed he might be setting himself up for failure in this endeavor.

"Babe, are you sure that's a good idea?"

31

His eyes softened and shone damply in the studio's dim lighting. He shrugged towards the computer. "Are you?"

"Ah."

"Yeah."

"Worth a try, I suppose."

"Yep. Can't hurt."

Jessie smiled and reached for Jacob. Wrapping her arms around him, she held on tight, basking in the comfort of his green apple scent. He squeezed her back. Just outside the door to the studio, Big Dan silently stole down the hall to wait.

"Pinkie swear you'll call me if things get weird." Jessie held out her baby finger for the third time that day.

Jacob raised his. "I swear."

"No, you have to say pinkie swear. It doesn't work if you don't."

"Sometimes I swear…"

"Jacob!"

"Okay," he laughed, the light returning to the cerulean blue eyes. "Pinkie swear! But you have to promise to call me too, Jess. Josh or no Josh. Okay?"

"Okay. I will. But I'm not keeping you a secret from Josh, Jacob. He's gotta know when we're around each other, or in touch with each other. That's the only way I think we can survive, you know? Honesty."

Shoulders slumping just a little, because Jacob was getting used to having Josh in his life by virtue of Jessie's marriage to him, Jacob nodded. "Deal, kid. Fair enough."

"Alright then. Let's shake."

They shook pinkies, and then wrapped their arms around each other for the walk down the hallway towards Dan, who would accompany Jessie to her SUV before driving Jacob to the airport.

"See you in Miami?" asked Jessie as they parted a few moments later in the underground parking garage.

"See you in Miami. 'Nite, Jessie."

" 'Nite, Jacob." Then, to Dan, "Drive safe, Big Dan. Precious cargo."

Dan shot her a thumbs up and then slid behind the wheel. He started the engine but waited for Jessie to pull away before following her out of the garage and onto Robson and then Burrard. He followed her until she had to turn off, and they beeped their goodbyes as Jessie slipped onto Fourth and headed towards the home she now shared with Josh.

Wistfully, Jacob watched until her taillights could no longer be seen, and then he settled back into the front passenger seat. He hummed along with a tune by The Zolas on The Peak and thought to himself, *Well, at least we'll have Miami.* There was a lot of comfort to be had in that, and he would have been even further assured had he known Jessie was thinking the exact same thing.

Chapter Three

"Damn it!"

Michael Kelly juggled as best he could but still his iPhone went tumbling to the floor on the passenger side of his pick-up, and try as he might to retrieve it, the phone remained just out of reach. The Rolling Stones' tune *Satisfaction* reverberated throughout the truck, reminding Michael of his brother Matt's gentle suggestion that it was time to download a new ring tone. "Aw, hell," he said out loud, slamming a fist on the steering wheel. "I'll change it when I want to change it."

He glanced once more at the phone and then, when he looked up to discover he was inching over the center lane in the snail's pace rush hour traffic, he over-corrected the vehicle, almost side-swiping a BMW in the lane on his right.

"Sorry, sorry!" he called fruitlessly to the driver, a sun-dyed blonde currently shaking a diamond-encrusted fist at him. Her bracelet caught the late afternoon sun and temporarily blinded Michael, but he shook his head and ran a hand through his hair, surprised at the way it felt to encounter short unruly spikes. He swung his right hand upwards and adjusted the rear-view mirror. Studying his reflection, he tossed another half-hearted curse at his brother.

"Matt, you're lucky you're married to Julie, because there's no way I would have listened to you, you candy-assed little rooster." He shook his head to get used to the feeling of having short hair. He'd just cut it last week, caving to sweet Julie's advice, although he knew Matt was the one who told Julie in the first place to state that he likely would make a better impression without the usual doe-eyed lost generation hippie locks to hide behind.

34

"Martinique'll demand you cut it if we don't," Matt had chided Michael over Shawarmas on West Hastings Street last week after Michael hesitantly agreed to test-run the new job. "Better it comes from us."

Sitting back then and studying Matt, the master of the Vancouver social elite vibe with his perfectly gelled hair and slick leather boots, and jeans rolled up just so, Michael had to nip his next thought in the bud, which was essentially *f-you*. He knew Matt was more concerned with what his Godlike boss Charles Keating would think than what some fake broad in Miami would think. But Michael's old red Ford was slow on the uptake and creaky on the turns, so in the interest of having money to finance his wheels for the next six months or so, he bit his tongue and eyed Matt with a little suspicion and a lot of hostility. But in the end he ducked into that old-fashioned barber shop near Revolver on Cambie in downtown Vancouver and, relieved at least to be handed a cold beer to sip on while he got his haircut, he watched the locks drop off, wilting in their downward flight to nestle against each other on the black and white tiled floor, already lonely for him and he for them.

What would he hide behind now? *Shit* he thought as now, in the hot southern city of Miami, he inched the truck forward in the sizzling heat, *nothing. There's nothing left to hide behind now.* He had to face facts. He, Michael Kelly, was famous in North America. But not just for his music. There were other, more sinister reasons for his fame. And, he thought of Matt and Julie again with a little warm spot lighting him up inside, *I'm here because I'm not alone. Someone out there genuinely cares about me, although for the love of God I can't imagine why.* He glanced at his reflection in the mirror again and tilted his chin up and down to see the top of the haircut. *Not so bad,* he thought, although the sight of his green eyes peeking out from the mirror shocked him. They were tired, bloodshot, intense…sad. He looked away.

Satisfaction erupted again in the blistering truck.

"Damn it!" Grunting, he unfastened his seatbelt, did a sweep of the congested city street for cops, and then ducked down behind the dash. Leaning over to his right, Michael nudged the phone towards him with his fingertips. He flicked it on and got it to his ear just in time to hear the caller curse.

"What's the point of having a fucking cell phone if it's never on?!"

He cleared his throat. "Hello?"

For a moment the caller was silent. But Martinique LaVois was never one to wallow in her own embarrassment. She recovered quickly.

"I assume this is Michael Kelly to whom I am speaking."

Michael winced. He could picture the grand lady in this very moment, shoulders thrown back, fancy drink in one hand, eyes glinting with ferocity, expansive view of multi-million dollar yachts many stories below in the harbor beneath her. His belly clenched.

"Yeah, uh, yes, this is Michael."

She cut to the chase. He could hear her take a sip before she spoke, though. Martini? *Who knows*, he thought, before responding to himself with *who cares*.

"Michael, I was hoping we would have a chance to bond over drinks and sort through this thing but as it turns out some things need sorting immediately." The indomitable Martinique paused dramatically before continuing, leaving Michael to think *who the hell says bond like bo-nd the way she did, and does anyone in the colonies really say i-MEdyatly the way she did?* He figured his new boss for a nouveau riche snob and not the old school aristocrat he thought she was pretending to be. But her musical speech at least got his attention. He hit the gas to get through a light before it turned red on him, and then almost stepped on the brake in the middle of the intersection when he heard Ms. LaVois' next words.

"Well you see, Michael…" he actually perked up at the way she said his name, her high-pitched lilt almost a song in itself, making his name somehow seem more worthy than the attention he gave it these days, these last many years, "the first of the crises I hired you to deal with has quite deftly arisen. And let's be honest, a few years ago I would have considered this a test but at this juncture in my tem-*pes*-tuous relationship with the lovely Kelly Reilly I would consider it only a smidgen of a bump in the road to welcoming you properly into our ex-*clu*-sive little fold."

Michael sat up straighter and swallowed past the fear rising in his belly. He waited.

Martinique continued gracefully, her even tone suggesting she was either damn tired of managing Kelly Reilly, or damn complacent with the role she was playing in her entertainment-biz life to the point of not giving a sweet damn at all. "Plug this into your GPS, will you dear? Palomino Sound Club on the corner of South and Friedmont. I do assume you're in the city, are you not?" The last query seemed to be an afterthought and Michael thought rightly if there was any panic at all in his new boss' voice it was in those few words.

"Yeah, yes, I'm in Miami, I'm just stuck, that's all. Barely moving."

"In this heat? Thank GOD for air conditioning. And GPS'es. Are you close to the club, dear?"

Groaning inwardly, Michael swept a palm over his forehead. It came away wet. Air conditioning? His 1994 Ford barely had wheels. GPS? At least he could enter the name of the club into his phone. When he got OFF the phone.

Martinique seemed to be singing directions to him. "I've texted Ricky your photograph—he'll be expecting you IMminently. He says Kelly hasn't moved from the bar so just GRAB her by the elbow and GALlantly bring her home, will you? Same hotel, Pacific Crest on Darnley. Text me when you're five away and I'll meet you in the lobby."

His brain lit up with questions and Michael jumped into what he hoped would pass as work mode. "And Ricky is…?"

"Ricardo, actually. Bouncer turned day manager of the club. He'll be watching out for you. Wouldn't want just anyone walking out with our super-star now, would we Michael?" She added drily, "Ricky's become a, how shall we say it, business associate of sorts. Keeps watch on our girl in exchange for concert tickets when we're in town."

"So just bring her to the hotel? What if she's not interested in leaving with me?"

"Oh, she loves attention, Michael. Especially from fellow musicians. One look at you and your long hair and those captivating green eyes and she'll fall right into your arms."

Literally, I'll bet, thought Michael, but he wisely kept that comment to himself. He swallowed back his next thought, which was *damn it, Matt* followed by a swift wistful glance in the mirror and a *geez I hope she likes short hair, too.* He'd have to make do if that Ricky guy protested and said Michael wasn't the fellow Martinique told him was coming for her singer, based on a description that included long hippie locks.

"What?" he said, catching the end of Martinique's next question.

"I said do you have any tattoos? Visible? Kelly loves tattoos on a man. Engage her in some conversation about where they are—on your BODY—and what they mean, and you'll be able to sweep her out the door like a piece of dirt."

Easing past another light, Michael glanced up at the street sign. *Montego…* is that anywhere near the club? He'd better get off the phone and punch something in Maps. But…what was that Martinique just said? Did she just inadvertently suggest Kelly was dirt? Kelly Reilly, one of the biggest names on the planet, who likely paid for Ms. LaVois' martinis and four inch heels?

Just can't wait to meet my new boss, he drooled, picturing her from any one of a number of high society event images he'd Googled. He leaned forward to glance up at another passing street sign. The heat rose up his neck in waves, accompanied by the stench of rotting garbage somewhere close by. He wrinkled his nose in disgust. *Air conditioning. Okay, I've been driving for days, I'm damn bone-tired and I need a shower. But for the thought of maybe being able to afford air conditioning someday I'll suck it up.*

"All right Ms. LaVois. I'll get your star to you."

"Martinique, please. Don't make me sound like an old spinster, even though I am, technically. Until Charles Keating gets divorced, that is. Oh, I shouldn't perhaps have said that since your brother, is it -"

"Matt."

"Works for him. At any rate, until he wants me I shall remain patient and single. In the meantime I will bow down to the likes of Kelly Reilly and console myself with a trip to Paris in the spring. But for now, just bring her home, will you DAHling?"

Harumph, thought Michael. *Likely she said that about Charles because she wants me to tell Matt. Whatever.* People were always trying to get something out of him once they found out he was one degree separated from the likes of Jessie Wheeler and her camp.

He signed off and immediately punched the name of the club into his iPhone's GPS. As luck would have it he was about a dozen blocks away, although in this heat and congestion it would take a while to get there. He eyed the interior of his old pick-up. He wasn't as meticulous as Matt, but he

38

did have a thing about not keeping garbage in his car so at least on that front it was clean, with the exception of a half-empty bag of nacho chips flopping over the passenger seat. One flick of his arm sent it flying into the glove compartment that he nudged open with his right hand. Kelly Reilly would be used to driving in luxurious entertainment-biz bought comfort. *Doesn't she have a usual car and driver,* Michael wondered absently? *Or maybe this IS some kind of weird test.*

He soon eased his old vehicle up in front of the club and shook his head at the valet. "Just be a minute," he insisted, flashing open his wallet so he could show the waiting club manager at the door that he was indeed supposed to be here collecting a probably inebriated superstar at five thirty in the afternoon.

His earlier inclination was correct. Ricardo eyed him warily until Michael practically shoved his ID in the man's face.

"What do you need, a blood test?" he growled under his breath so the guy couldn't hear him. He'd had too many altercations with bouncers over the years to test this guy's patience, and he needed those new stabilizer bars for the old Ford. *Besides,* Michael mused to himself, *I'm pretty used to having conversations with myself. Why break with tradition?*

He deduced correctly that Ricardo was probably just playing Ms. LaVois for concert tickets. The guy likely didn't really care who took the superstar away from his club—he just wanted her gone. In the end he let Michael in, gladly.

Michael found Kelly just where Martinique said he would—at the bar. The pretty blonde was out of it, all right, and Michael was somewhat relieved that what aided and abetted the young woman seemed to indeed just be alcohol and not something more sinister. *I can deal with alcohol,* he thought, pondering the girl and sorting out a plan of action.

She caught on to the fact someone was staring, and lifted her head off folded forearms, where she'd laid it while trying to focus on the Miami Heat basketball game playing on a monitor above an array of colorful glass bottles.

"And you arrre?" she asked point blank, slurring drunkenly. She raised her small pointed chin in defiance, and crossed one delicate calf over her knee. She was wearing a slinky yellow cotton summer dress that barely covered the tops of her thighs. Its green and white embroidery and simple lace collar depicted figurals—animals—that surprised Michael because he felt they made Kelly appear younger than her years. One crocheted figure—on the left lace collar—was a rabbit. The other was some kind of dancing horse. He was surprised to see a girl of Kelly's superstar status in such a childlike virginal outfit, apart from its short length, that is. On her feet were simple flip-flops, decorated only with tiny beads where the strap ran down between her toes.

Carelessly Kelly tossed her hair and stared at her rescuer, shoulders slouched now and arms wrapped around her waist as if she were trying to hold herself together.

He tested her. "Michael," he eased into the introduction slowly.

"Kelly?" She drawled, squinting and tilting her head sideways so as to focus on his features.

"Yes, ma'am," he said quietly, waiting for the inevitable *that singer?*

But it didn't come. Instead, his client started to chuckle but it came out mournful, half-hearted, as if she knew she should laugh but didn't really feel up to the challenge. "Kelly, huh? That explains everything."

He bristled.

She stared him down, the laugh gone now, her eyes bereft of light in the dimness of the Palomino Sound Club. "The name. Kelly. That explains why you're cursed."

It took Michael a moment to remember that this childlike girl was called Kelly too. He pondered that before responding. Then he tilted his head and joined in, with something like *if you can't beat 'em, join 'em* rustling through his musty brain. "The luck of the Irish," he mumbled, reaching out an arm. He nodded towards the club entrance, where a few curious folks were gathered to watch the great Kelly Reilly fall flat on her face in public…again. "Come," he insisted quietly, his words echoing in the half-empty lounge.

She raised her eyebrows and sat up a little straighter. "Why should I?"

"Well for one thing, I'm your new—"

"Handler, yeah I know, like I could give a shit. Got another reason?" She winked.

He smiled. "Martinique said I'm supposed to show you tattoos."

She grinned then, tossing her head towards the grimy faux-wood floor beneath the stool so that the blonde hair cascaded down and hid her face.

A pang of regret slipped sideways through Michael's gut at her movement, not for him or his messed-up life, but for some reason for this child-woman who was scrunched up in a ball on a stool in a mediocre bar with everyone staring at her. When she looked back up at him, Kelly's eyes were glistening.

"Tattoos, is it? You do realize that's Marty's way of inviting you into *her* bedroom. I could care less about tattoos. They're the devil's ink." She added, "Marty was playing you. She just wanted to know what ink you have on your body, and…where." Now her eyes flecked from somber to a slightly lighter countenance, and she raised her chin.

He rose to the test. "I guess I failed that challenge, then. I don't have tattoos." It was a lie, but his body and his ink were Michael's own business. Screw these crazy broads and their male fantasies.

She was laughing at him. "Bummer. Now how are you going to coerce me out of this club?"

"Thought you didn't care about—"

"Tattoos? Heck no. But I suppose a girl can still be curious." She smiled, then sobered. "I know what tattoos you have, Michael. Everybody does." At his chagrined panicked look she added, "The same way they all know what ink I've got on my body, and where. Google." She hopped delicately off the stool, one ankle turning over slightly in the light flip-flop. Michael caught her elbow before she slipped entirely. She didn't seem as drunk as he first thought. He sobered.

Kelly turned slowly to face him. "All right then," she said. "Let's go home, shall we?" She said *home* loudly, musically, as if Martinique's speech had rubbed off on her, because the word didn't sound natural coming out between Kelly's lips.

At the door, she paused by Ricardo and the waiting crowd, waved an arm, raised her chin and said gaily, "Isn't it fun, weekday afternoons in Miami? All sunshine and cock-a-tails!" Then Kelly allowed Michael to lead her towards his ragged pick-up, and his heart churned as he waited for her reaction, which he was certain would be a combination of sour-faced pouting lips and verbal outrage. But instead she simply leaned on his arm as he helped hoist her up into the sweltering heat, and she stared straight ahead when he climbed in the other side.

All she said were four simple words, and she didn't look at him as she spoke them, but somehow he knew that by saying them she was sending him a message—*I know who you are and what you feel.*

The words?

"Like the new cut."

Michael watched her straighten out the hem of the simple cotton dress with long tapered nails and a delicate touch. Then his superstar charge deftly flipped a lock of hair up over an ear, folded her hands on her lap, and settled in for the ride.

He turned the key in the ignition and trustworthy Jenny roared to life. She was a woman who never let him down.

As they started to trundle out into the mass of expensive cars on the street, Michael heard a few more small words slide between the girl's lips. "I can never marry you, you know."

Inwardly, he grimaced. *Why would anyone want to marry me?*

"I know," he said. "I'm way older than you. Like maybe," he studied her, "fifteen years?"

"Nah, that's not why," she said honestly, her face all innocence and open canvas. "It's because if I did my name would be Kelly Kelly."

This time Michael didn't hold back. He laughed out loud and, beside him, Kelly the superstar singer relaxed and hooted heartily as well.

"Why Michael Kelly, don't you think one Kelly is cursed enough? Imagine if I added another! Kelly Kelly? Think about it."

"Girl, it's not the name that's cursed. I'm proud of my Irish heritage, and you ought to be as well. We just have to look at it differently." Matt's voice echoed in his head. "Think of what our ancestors went through, what they managed to survive. Getting thrown out of their homes, starvation, loss…" He hesitated before finding his voice again. "Six weeks in steerage on a wooden ship with rats in the grain."

"Irish music."

"Hey! I like Celtic tunes."

"Only with Guinness."

"Fair enough."

And with that, Michael found the exit towards their hotel, and he pointed the old Ford south. *Maybe this babysitting gig won't be so bad.*

At the next light he pulled out his iPhone and texted Martinique. *On our way.*

Above them, many stories above the scorched city streets of Miami, Martinique LaVois finished her second martini before exiting her rented penthouse suite and sauntering casually towards the elevator. She would meet the famous Michael Kelly tonight, but she would not read him the riot act. Kelly Reilly would be riot enough for the man. And from what Martinique knew about Michael, the ex-singer, he'd had enough riot—and tragedy—in his life. This gig he could feel out on his own. Heck, Kelly needed a man in her life she could look up to. In the photos that popped up all over the web when one searched Michael, his eyes were a soft liquid green, etched in sadness and defeat, hiding behind all that hair. The wrinkles at the corners were road maps telegraphing his history, one filled with despair and defeat. *Was* he a man Kelly could look up to? *Maybe not,* Martinique mused, *unless you count his songwriting from before the pain hit.*

Musicians, she guffawed as she carefully clipped into the elevator on her high heels before turning gracefully to face the closing door. *They're all on their own planet anyway. Maybe he and Kelly can connect that way, through music.*

But in all honesty Martinique didn't think Kelly and her new security would connect at all. Because Kelly never seemed to connect with anyone. Instead, she generally just rolled over them with a bulldozer.

Martinique glanced down at the phone she held daintily in one soft palm. Five-fifty-two. *Well, I may just have time before they arrive to give Charles a call.*

A hint of an aristocratic smile touched her cheeks then, and Martinique settled in for the downward descent. She already had Charles' number punched into the phone before the door opened far below, so all she had to do when she reached the lobby was hit the round green phone icon to activate the call.

She did, then settled down in one of the lobby's comfortable wicker chairs, elegantly crossed her long legs at the ankles, and waited for the familiar voice to telegraph comfort, and take away the craziness of a stressful day.

Chapter Four

"Damn it Jessie, you promised me! We promised each other!" Josh kicked over the garbage bin and the top flipped open. Little bits of compost escaped; paper towel and potato peelings slid onto the floor. He winced at the mess, ran long fingers through his hair, and glanced up at his wife. From her perch on a stool by the kitchen island, Jessie eyed him warily but didn't speak.

"I'm sorry, look, I'll clean it up! But damn it Jessie, Charles Keating is not a God."

"Duh," Jessie responded haughtily, frowning as she crossed one knee over the other. "Referencing the cleaning up part, that is. And in future, you can take your hissy fits outdoors, Josh. Please and thank you."

"In future you need to consult your husband before committing to something this big."

A tiny twinkle flickered in Jessie's sea-pearl eyes. Josh knew what it meant, and a silent note of gratitude and relief passed between them. *Husband.* They'd get through this latest conflagration. He settled onto the stool next to Jessie and faced her.

"Look, I know it's a great opportunity."

"Yeah well, it's you who's been saying all along that I need to get back to work!" She cut him off and crossed her arms over her chest, refusing to acquiesce to Josh's temper tantrum by touching him. But it was hard to resist. She narrowed her eyes at the little piece of hair she loved to tuck behind his ear. He was so wound up now that it didn't seem to be bugging him the way it usually did. She uncrossed her arms and sat on her hands.

44

"Florida, Jessie, come on! We said we'd do this together, sort out our schedules and where we'd work, when."

"And…?" The twinkle in Jessie's eyes flickered out and was replaced with a determined, focused hard stare.

Shoulders sinking, Josh leaned his left elbow on the counter and sighed. "Jacob. Seriously Jessie. I mean…Jacob?"

"Let's not do this again, okay? You're just going to have to trust me. Period." She couldn't resist. Jessie leaned forward slightly so she could reach the rogue strand of hair. When she tucked it away behind his ear, Josh covered her wrist with his right hand and gave it a genuine squeeze. She took his fingers in hers and set both hands on her lap. The twinkle snuck back to the surface, accompanied by a sweet flicker of sincere yet gentle urgency. "Babe, I can handle Jacob. And as far as Miami goes, it'll be intermittent trips, and for some of them you can come with me. And anyways, we're just testing the waters now, to see whether this thing's even gonna go."

"Jesus Jessie, you, Kelly Reilly and Jacob on the same show? Duh yourself! Of course it's going to go. And you along with it."

"I can't say it doesn't intrigue me. Although I'm hearing Kelly's a real firecracker. Jacob's already feeling backed into a corner."

"Okay then, on some level I'm glad you're interested in working again." Josh sat up straighter and eyed Jessie carefully. "And I'm glad you're helping out that filmmaker you talked to when we were in P.E.I. But you and I have to start coordinating our shoots together, Jess. None of this going rogue and splitting off in two directions. We know how well that can go."

"Charlie and I were stupid," she chided him gently. "We didn't try hard enough." Inwardly Jessie was relieved and secretly thrilled. Just touching Josh seemed to be enough to bring him back to her, to calm him when he was upset. She stroked his forearm, reveling in the way his warm skin soothed her, as well. Silently she sent a little prayer up to Heaven. *Please God let me keep this man forever. Please God don't ever take him away from me.*

She opened her eyes to find him watching her closely, and Jessie let a small smile light up her man's eyes. Still, she could see the pain there, and the barely disguised worry, which shimmered across his face in fleeting gasps. Jessie sighed.

"Josh, stop this. Stop the worrying. Let's just soak up the good things and not let the bad get in. At all." Trudy's magic was working. Jessie felt a resolve of strength fritter its way to her brain that, a few months earlier, wouldn't have made it past her ankles. Grasping his other wrist, the one on the kitchen island, she yanked it close and faced him. She braced herself for another battle, although she hoped this one would worry her man less. She was wrong. He lost it as soon as the words were out of her mouth.

This time Josh jumped off the stool and threw her hands down, away from him. "How much grief can you take, Jessie? Is there going to be a breaking point? Tell me, at what point do we just live our own lives and stay the hell out of others'?"

She'd told him about finding her Aunt Evelyn on Facebook. Plans were in place to meet the woman Jessie hadn't seen since childhood, the woman who was often Jessie's sanctuary when the years between age twelve and fourteen became untenable and unimaginable.

"Think of it as a little getaway, Josh. Maybe we can turn it into a hunt for that ranch we've dreamed about."

That settled him a little. The lure of an Alberta ranch was a bright orange carrot dangling at the end of a shiny stick.

Josh turned back to his wife. "I'll go with you, Jessie, but promise me you'll take this one day at a time, that you won't go jumping on the next plane to Toronto. You'll think it through." But even as he said it, Josh knew exactly what Jessie would do with any information the long lost aunt would provide. She'd go hunting for family. She needed the blood connection, craved it, in fact. And, despite the ever-present fear of defeat and certain pain in dredging up a long buried past, he knew he would stand by her and pick up the pieces. As usual.

"One of these days you'll thank me for being cautious, little wifey," he said staunchly, his own stubborn chin thrust forward in determination.

Eyebrows rising, Jessie grinned. "Wifey? Seriously, Josh?"

He hesitated, then allowed a tiny smile to rest on his face, but he was still worried and slightly overcome by all these new developments in their shared life, so the grin came out lopsided and didn't quite go all the way to Josh's chocolate eyes. "I just worry about you, little one," he murmured quietly, stepping further back so he could memorize her, there in the kitchen where once he'd held her tightly in fear of losing her forever.

"I know, Josh, but I need this. I need to know whether these people are *my* people, you know?" She eyed him quizzically, still trying to reconcile the jagged fuzzy pieces in her brain with the ache of long ago loss in her heart.

"I know, Jess. Just..." he hesitated, and thought better of saying what danced across his brain just then, which was *I just don't want you to get hurt. Again.* There were only so many times he could stand to see the woman he loved in pain. So he cancelled that last thought and pulled Jessie to him. He held on tight, and tried to focus on the good times to come while she, enveloped in the strong arms of the man she loved, buried her face in the hollow she adored between his shoulder and neck, and breathed him in.

⁓ ⁓

Josh and Jessie were due to arrive in Canmore, Alberta three days later. It seemed like a good time to make the trip since Jessie was soon expected in Miami to shoot her first episode of *Mystic Nights*. The day before they left for Alberta, Jessie hired a real estate agent to take them through a few ranches within a day's drive of her aunt's home. It seemed like the least she could do to somehow convince Josh she was on his side, that she was committed and not out for only her own devices.

When Josh saw the Internet photos of the spreads they'd be visiting in the vast province, he was instantly subdued, because while Jessie was over in North Van with Dee lining up their trip and ranches to visit, he was secretly trolling the computer looking for a Downtown Eastside business owned by the mysterious couple from that weird day at Revolver when they first got back from Prince Edward Island. He found a Caryn and an Eric after less than five minutes of looking, which was great on one hand, but not so great on the other. Truth be told, Josh was sorry his intuition was right, because it meant finding out the tall couple were the owners of a black box film studio on the Downtown Eastside. What did they produce? His mouth suddenly dry, Josh poised a finger over the computer trackpad.

For a moment he paused with one hand on the laptop cover, ready to shut the whole thing down—the computer, his morbid curiosity about his new wife's past, his need to know. But then, almost in reflex—as if the universe

47

was prodding him along—his forefinger tapped the trackpad and the display changed.

Artistic Photographs
Tastefully Produced Videos
For the discerning client who seeks upscale erotica

Sickened, his mind swimming, Josh sat back and stared at the screen. His stomach churned as he rubbed the tips of three fingers over the throbbing nerve on his cheek. Upstairs, the compressor on the fridge clanked and he paused, tilting his head to listen. Purposefully he chose to sit in his downstairs media room to do this research. Josh figured he could close the pages quickly if Jessie should happen to arrive home. But now, as his somber eyes flitted around the darkened room, he realized his man cave, as Jessie jokingly called it, was an apropos locale for such underhanded investigating.

"Well, Mizz Jessie," he muttered to himself. "Here goes nothing. I hope."

Inhaling deeply, Josh clicked on the *photographs* tab before letting his gaze drift downwards. He studied the girl in the picture that appeared on the screen. She was young, maybe twenty, her straight blonde hair fanned out on some invisible light summer breeze. An indigo sky accented a cream linen top she wore unbuttoned so that just the tips of her nipples showed. Denim shorts completed the outfit; she sat on one butt cheek, leaning slightly forward, one leg pigeoned below, the other supported by hands that grasped it around the knee. Deep blue eyes peeked out at Josh from the safety of the screen, and he found himself instantly captivated, but it wasn't a physical attraction to the girl that struck a chord with him. It was more about the expression she wore. It was something he was familiar with. Those haunted eyes were Jessie's not all that long ago, and his belly clenched at the thought there were more of her out there, hurting and struggling to find a way to survive.

He rallied, and scrolled over the contact button at the top right of the screen. One click and he had what he needed.

"Jessie," he intoned quietly, as if she could by some miracle hear him from her tete-a-tete with Dee miles away. "This picture isn't much worse than some of those Gap or Calvin Klein ads I've seen hanging over the New York sky-line. But I'm not sure I'm ready to find you here."

He picked up his iPhone and tapped on the Notes icon. After typing in the street number from the contact screen on the laptop, he glanced again at the thumbnail images on the monitor. A quick scan revealed some of the models were in more compromising positions than others. The ages of the women featured surprised him. Not all were young. And not all embodied the perfect Hollywood size and shape.

"How many of you are there because you want to be," he queried them equally, voice low, eyes landing on each for a few extended moments as if they might sense his presence and actually respond. "And how many because you're lost?"

He exited the pages, erased his browsing history, shoved the screen closed, and then eased himself up from the depths of the comfy couch before bending down to pick up the laptop. "That's what I thought," he answered himself grimly. Kayla crossed his mind, as did Wes Sawyer, who once filmed Josh in his first sexual encounter years ago.

"You disgust me," he whispered to the inky darkness that enveloped him once the screen's glare disappeared. He hoped whatever association Jessie had long ago with Caryn and Eric was also now buried in some old black abyss.

Trudging slowly upstairs, though, Josh knew he had to know. When it came to Jessie, he would stop at nothing to protect her, although by the time he reached the fourth step it struck him as odd that, in her decade or more of film and songwriting stardom, that someone—no, not someone, this Caryn and Eric couple—hadn't released anything Jessie may have shot in those dark days when she lived on East Hastings. After all, he reasoned, Jessie Wheeler had quickly become worth a lot of money, and the rag bags were always looking for celebrity fodder to sell their supermarket stock. Jessie in the—?

He halted suddenly at the top step and grabbed the handrail for support. *No. It can't be. She wouldn't have.*

On the next level of the house, Josh turned a corner, trudged up a few more steps, and deposited the laptop in the back bedroom he and Jessie now shared as an office. His eyes caught the display on the digital clock in the corner of his desk. Jessie would be home soon, and he had promised to make her fajitas for dinner. Visiting the downtown studio would have to wait until later, until he was alone again and had enough uninterrupted—and alone—time to make that trek. At any rate, he still needed to get used to the idea, to ponder what he might find, to...prepare himself.

Should I tell Jessie? Nuh-uh. Not yet, anyway. Not until I know what I'm... what we...are dealing with. Not til I have a plan.

"Yeah, I'm breaking our code," he mumbled to the air as he yanked open the refrigerator door and poked around for chicken breasts which, in his haste to get to the less than desirable research, he'd forgotten to remove from the freezer earlier. He would have to microwave them now in order to get them thawed out. "But I'm taking certain creative licenses. And so, by the way, are you, little one."

As the timer on the thawing chicken worked its way towards zero, Josh rinsed and then cut strips of red and yellow peppers, and he hardly noticed when the knife slipped and gashed his finger. It wasn't until drops of blood colored the wooden cutting board that he finally growled and whipped on the faucet to clean the cut.

"Damn it!" he cried to no one in particular as he watched his diluted blood trail off into the sink and down the drain. "Damn it. Owww."

He leaned against the sink, the cut finger dangling loosely under the tiny waterfall. Hanging his head, Josh tried to think about horses. A ranch half-lost in the rough Alberta openness was starting to sound better and better. Miami, and all the press Jessie was going to garner from this new stint with... Jacob, of all people...intuitively felt like just another downward spiral.

Chapter Five

*K*elly slammed her script down on the table and petulantly thrust both hands on her hips. Glaring at the director of this week's *Mystic Nights* episode, she fumed.

"If you think I'm going to sing this cheesy kindergarten song on television in front of millions, you're out of your fucking mind." Her blonde locks teetered back and forth in cadence to the angry words she spit out of her mouth.

Behind her, Michael, who accompanied his new client to the table read, was slightly amused. The Kelly he met yesterday was demure and sad. This public Kelly was the one he'd been expecting to meet, the one his boss, Martinique, so royally primed him for, both on the phone and then after his arrival. Casually, he leaned back against the wall and, with an air of nonchalant detachment, watched the angry confrontation.

As the temperature heated up and already frayed nerves were tested, across the room from him he caught the eye of the young singer quickly becoming famous from the release of his first single, but already a household name thanks to liberating Jessie Wheeler from a lovesick stalker.

Jacob, eyes wide, echoed Michael's stance. He hooked a thumb in one jeans pocket while shifting his weight and gazing heavily from underneath long lashes at Kelly's new security. "Jesus," he was grumbling under his breath. "What the hell did I get myself into?" Mutely, he wished Jessie would make her appearance on this show sooner rather than later. Raising his head and narrowing his eyes he wondered why the older man across from him seemed on the verge of laughter. Everyone else in the stuffy room seemed ready to explode.

51

Suddenly Jacob realized the staccato beat of Kelly's high-pitched fury had ground to a halt. His eyes darted back to her and he jumped, surprised to find himself locked in a hard, angry stare. He gulped and straightened, but found a reserve of strength and held her gaze.

The scathing words she directed at him were bitter agents of defeat, designed to break Jacob before he even went before the camera.

"And you give me this…tadpole…Jesus. You take any acting classes, you weasely little frog? Or do you get a pass 'cuz you're Charles Keating's new pet project?"

Martinique interjected before Jacob could even open his mouth to communicate his own nasty riposte on the subject.

"Jacob read for the part, Kelly. He earned it. Now why don't you have a seat so all of you can get to work?"

"I'll work when I'm ready," the actor spat between clenched teeth. She wheeled around to face Michael but had to stifle a grin of her own when she spied traces of amusement flickering across his face. She cocked her head slightly in quizzical response, and then soaked up his relaxed scrutiny while half-heartedly tossing more angry words over her shoulder. "I'm going ten-one. By the time I'm back I'll expect a rewrite to be well underway for that effing kindergarten tune." She steadied herself briefly in the light of her new security's barely subdued grin before turning to the side, tossing her head, and stomping out the door.

The room breathed a collective sigh of relief at her departure and, while the top execs gathered for a tete-a-tete at the far end, Michael heaved himself away from the wall and calmly made his way around the end of the long table in the center of the room to have a chat with one of the objects of Kelly's scorn. He thrust out a hand.

Jacob paused and studied the man before hesitantly accepting Michael's friendship. After all, the two were connected, Michael and Kelly…

"She's a live wire, that one," Michael started, eyes glinting with amusement underneath the harsh overhead fluorescents.

"You can say that again," mumbled Jacob, eyeing the door through which Kelly disappeared and wishing to hell Jessie's character was in the current episode so she would land tonight instead of next week as planned.

"Tom Ryan's son? That right?" Michael was still hanging onto Jacob's hand. He gave it some pressure before letting go, as Jacob eyed him cautiously.

"So they tell me. Not that I give a sweet shit."

"Uh-huh." Studying the guy, Michael pursed his lips and nodded. "You have his eyes."

"You knew him?" The old curiosity flared up, annoying Jacob. He kept telling himself it didn't matter, but somehow when the opportunity to understand anything about his dad presented itself, some thin layer of pretense was destroyed and his vulnerable side poked its way through, unbidden and unwanted.

Shrugging, Michael backed off. "In the old days." He didn't seem to want to elaborate. Instead, he turned his head and hummed quietly while insouciantly examining the execs at the far end of the room, which pissed Jacob off further.

"Yeah, I hear you used to own the stage. In the old days." He didn't even attempt to disguise the sarcasm edging his voice.

At that, Michael whipped his head back around and scrutinized Jacob further. He shoved his hands in his trouser pockets, then pulled them out and straightened the black suit jacket he wore over a white shirt unbuttoned at the top. Silently cursing Matt's unwanted clothing advice and the months-old GQ magazine his brother had handed him that day when they met a while ago, he was glad he'd at least whipped off the tie. He'd left it lying on his bed this morning, like a snake ready to strangle him in his sleep in this new world. His shoulders relaxed a little as he realized the young singer opposite him was likely feeling very much the same way. And he liked the gentle flecks of light dotting the guy's eyes, despite that angry done-me-wrong hurt puppy dog look that made him such easy prey to the likes of her highness Kelly Reilly. Underneath the long lashes Jacob's eyes lent him an easygoing aura, although today it was plainly evident he, like everyone else in the room, simply wanted to be anywhere but here.

Michael ignored Jacob's dig at his age and dead career and started out on a new tack.

"So, Charles Keating, huh?"

"Yup. Matt?"

"Yep. Brother. Although you'd never know it. Haven't really spent much time together in years. But I suppose blood is thicker than water, so they say." He leaned to the side and plucked a grape off a bunch on the craft table which, even this early in the day, was already littered with used coffee stirrers and empty fake-sugar packets. Deftly sliding the grape between his lips, Michael added, "He means well. Getting me this job, I mean."

"Working with her highness? Hope you're getting paid well. Although I'm not sure any salary is going to be high enough for anyone on this show with her as the star." Once again, thoughts of Jessie's sweet nature passed over Jacob's mind. The two women were on completely different wavelengths, it seemed. One was fiery and insistent, the other quiet, a watcher.

As if on cue, Kelly breezed back in from the restroom. She eyed the writers, who glanced at her nervously as she waltzed over to the craft table and perched on one tilted high-heeled ankle, leaning in towards Michael. "I need a Starbucks. Can you be a doll and go get me a venti half-sweet caramel macchiato?" She leaned over enough for Jacob to be gifted a glance of her small bosom, and he felt something stir that caused him to shift his stance and look away. Michael noticed the young guy's color subtly change, and he tried not to smile when he looked back at his new charge.

"I'll get you your caffeinated sugar, darlin', but let it be known this will not be a regular occurrence. I'm happy to oblige, this once, but that's only because I, too, am in desperate need of a decent coffee. You TV people keep the most unholy hours."

Despite herself, Kelly laughed. Surprised, Jacob glanced back around and watched her face light up as the entire room exhaled slowly, hopeful the rough start to their day was over, and that the rest of it could be salvaged.

"Fair enough," the star was saying coquettishly to her new handler. "I'll just time my caffeine intake to yours." She parroted his voice. "But *let it be known* that the rest of the world moves with us TV types. It's you cheap destitute bar singers who live like vampires that are all messed up." She leaned into Michael again and brushed a breast against his arm. "Get used to it."

At that, she winked at Jacob, straightened her shoulders, and marched down the room to Martinique. Wiggling under the woman's arm, she asked easily, "Are they about ready to get going? I'd like to be done by noon so Jacob and I can go over some of these tunes." She purred, and looked back over her shoulder at Jacob. "Maybe the tadpole and I can play doctor; I mean, doctor up some of those appalling lyrics."

By the craft table, Jacob squirmed. Throwing another grape between his lips, Michael laughed outright and clapped a hand on Jacob's shoulder. "Nice to meet you, kid. Hope you've got your parachute on." He swung around and saluted to Kelly before waltzing out the door. Martinique, in her singsong voice, hollered after him as the AD called the room to order and beckoned everyone to their seats for the table read.

Outside the room, Martinique's high heels did nothing to slow her down and keep her from catching up to her new hired gun. Layers of dark mascara exacerbated an apparent lack of sleep; little bits and clumps rested below her eyes. Michael's intestines twisted as a sudden image of his wife and young daughter flashed before him, the child mimicking her mother in the washroom, each with a pointy finger under a facecloth, wiping excess mascara away from underneath gentle eyes.

Martinique caught the flicker of pain. "What," she demanded. She was nothing if not direct.

"Nothing," he stammered, his earlier good nature finally dissipating in a cloud of muck and fuzz. He rallied, a mask washing over his face, but the tired lines remained, leaking out from the corners of his eyes like dried, cracked mud. "What is it you need?"

"There's paperwork for you to sign back in my office. In my penthouse. Then I'm off to L.A. to police the sane actors on my roster." Martinique paused and touched a finger to her chin. "Wait," she exclaimed dramatically, musically, with a flourish. "I take that back. What I mean to say is I'm taking a well-deserved hiatus in an airplane where I refuse on principle to watch any type of filmed entertainment, be that movies, television, music videos, or homemade YouTube crap. Especially homemade YouTube crap. Although granted, sometimes that's far more engaging than what Hollywood pours forth on a daily basis." She started away before adding, "Let me know if you have any questions, and in the meantime good luck with that mucky little hoity-toity princess I'm thrilled to be leaving in your capable hands."

"I'm getting her a Starbucks and then I'll come up to do the paperwork. Ten minutes. Assuming this is like every other American city with a Starbucks on every corner." He yawned, as if to cement his desire for caffeine.

"She's already got you wrapped around her little finger, does she? Coffee boy?" Martinique flipped around on one toe and flashed him a Wicked Witch grin.

He frowned before dancing around the issue. "Coffee's for me. I just thought I'd be nice and get her one too."

"Coffee boy!" She poked a button by the elevator and crossed her arms, her manicured fingers shining and restless in the over-bright hallway. "I mean, I could call you whipped already but Charles assured me you've got balls." She eyed his crotch. "Do you? Have balls?" Her eyes narrowed and she regarded him closely.

Michael swallowed, his throat constricting his need to breathe evenly. "Yes, I get it, Martinique, you didn't hire me to fetch Mizz Reilly's coffee. Received. Loud and clear." He saluted his boss, flicking two fingers out and away from his forehead, a tiny nerve pulsating in his forehead. *Geez, Kelly I can handle,* he thought. *This one's the real bitch.*

The indomitable Ms. LaVois paused before entering the elevator, despite the fact that a businessman inside had to hold his finger on the 'open' button and wait for her. She fixed a solid stare on Michael. "On the contrary," Martinique commanded, her voice throaty and insistent. "I hired you to *handle* the little princess. Do whatever the hell it takes."

The elevator doors slid behind her with a *swoosh* that reverberated inside Michael's body, infusing him with a confused mixture of wonder and irritation. *No wonder Kelly's so messed up,* he thought. *Everyone caters to her.* Idly, as he took the steps downstairs to the lobby, easily leaping two at a time, he thought about what Matt recently told him about Jessie Wheeler. That the hardest part of dealing with her from both the Keatings' standpoint as well as Matt's bird's eye security detail was her irreverence towards protocols established to protect her. Apparently she was doing better these days, after the terror of the last few years, but still, sometimes she chucked all fear aside and went off on her own. Was she cruel about it? Mean to her staff? He didn't recall Matt ever saying she was. Instead, Michael thought his brother had referred to her as more childlike than anything, often feigning an innocence that helped her get away with behavior the others didn't approve of.

Michael, like Jacob before him, wondered exactly how well the famous Jessie Wheeler was going to get along with the blonde princess in the upstairs meeting room. He laughed outright as he hit the bright tiles in the lobby below. *One thing for sure,* he thought. *I sure as hell wouldn't want to be Jacob Ryan about now.*

Whistling, he strode purposefully towards the welcoming sunlight and embarked on a search for the nearest Starbucks.

～ ～

"Jess, you're gonna hate this gig. I'm sorry as hell for convincing you."

Jacob was reclining thoughtfully on a brushed suede sofa in his hotel room, staring out of the patio doors at the expansive ocean before and below him. He hoisted his booted feet up onto a large matching ottoman, and squeezed his bottom lip between his thumb and third finger. "I mean, it's not like I've been to an actual table read before, but Kelly was a bitch about the whole thing. She kept stopping and questioning her lines, and changing lines, not with a pencil, but with a pen, and everyone in the room just sucked in their breaths and let her do whatever the hell she wanted. I was wishin' I had a machete so I could cut the tension in there. But then while I was picturing all the air blowin' in through the crack I made with the knife, she started hollerin' at me to pay attention. What a bitch."

Through the phone, he could hear Jessie giggling on the other end. "Poor Jacob," she was saying as she pictured him all lonely and alone, prey to a well-known diva. "Don't worry, once Josh and I get our ranch picked out we'll come down there and rescue you from Kelly Reilly's evil clutches."

"Ranch, huh? Didn't know horses were part of the dream, Wheeler."

"Wheeler-Sawyer," she chided him gently, her reminder cutting through Jacob's heart like the machete he'd referred to earlier. "Though still just Wheeler professionally, I guess." Then she added, "Josh would love to have horses of his own again."

Uh-huh, and we all know what you're willing to do for loverboy, Jacob thought irritably. He grimaced and fixed his sight on a brightly colored spinnaker unfurling in the distance. The sailboat it was attached to wobbled unevenly as the crew tried to get control of the foresail in the gusty wind. He grunted.

Jessie swung around and tried another approach to lighten Jacob's funk.

Obviously he'd had a very rough start to his day, and she could clearly sense the ennui beneath the gruff cadence of his speech.

"What's Matt's brother like? Michael?"

"Thought you've met him."

"Briefly. I mean, we've been in the same room together, sat at the same dinner table, but usually with others in tow. He's a quiet guy, isn't he?"

"He's okay. Friendly, at least. In fact, he's the one person Kelly seems to be taking a shine to, for some inane reason."

"Well, if he looks anything like Matt, then I expect he's pretty cute. Although I would also think Miss Reilly would be all over you."

Jacob's ears perked up. Did he sense a little jealousy in Jessie's voice? Even the slightest teensy little bit?

"Princess Reilly doesn't give a shit about me. I stand between her and any possible chance at awards, apparently. She'd rather be working with Brad Pitt."

"He's a goof. Too cute, y'know?"

"She insisted I take acting lessons. Sucks. There goes any free time for y'know, mojitos and like, salsa dancing."

"Chill, Jacob, that's not a bad idea. Charles got you in the door, now if this is really something you want, then you have to commit. Jacob…is this even something you want?"

He paused before answering. Beneath him, the spinnaker was losing the battle. The boat tossed mercilessly in the wind, a child's toy in a giant's grasp, being flung to and fro.

"I thought I did," Jacob answered honestly, his voice tinged with defeat. He knew the reason he took the job was because it was another way to please Charles. And maybe…to stay close to Jessie. A pleasing tickle trickled up his body as remembrances of her tender touch came to mind. Maybe they would share some love scenes…he shifted in his seat, slouching down further and adjusting a cushion behind his head.

"Jessie?" he asked sleepily. "Just ignore me. I can handle Kelly. It'll all be fine once you get here."

"Okay," she said easily. "In the meantime, guess what? I got another note from my Aunt Evelyn. She's apparently already told my grandmother and my sister about me. That fer sure the girl they knew existed in P.E.I. all those years ago is me. You know. Jessie the singer, kinda thing. When we go to Alberta Josh and I are gonna plan a trip to Ontario to meet them."

Jacob's groan was profound. He figured on at least this one count he and Josh were on the same page. But then he also had similar plans—roots to reclaim and perhaps cling to. He hesitated and skipped the lecture on the tip of his tongue, choosing instead a simple, "Be careful, kiddo."

"Give me a break, Jacob. I'm not a child. Anyways none of *you* tried to take advantage of me."

Jacob was silent, although Jessie heard a slow exhale sneak through the connection.

"Okay," she admitted. "So maybe you might have, but in the end you won Charles' respect based on your own talent. And no one's ever asked me for money."

"That's because we don't give a shit about money. You met us at the Fringe in Edinburgh, remember? Artists? Starving artists, in fact?"

"You weren't starving. Far from it. Look, I'll keep my head up and Josh will be there keeping watch over things with his little hawk-like suspicious eyes, so there's no need to worry. I just want to connect with some blood relatives, that's all. I might find out some stuff I need to know, like who died of what when, that kinda thing. It's not like my mom's a regular chatterbox."

"Gruesome. Yeah, well, just don't let them suck you under. You don't know what you're going to find there. That's all I'm saying, Jess."

"Same goes to you, babe." She hesitated, and sucked in a breath. "Whoops."

Finally some light infused his voice when Jacob responded drily, "Whoops, my ass. You still want this, Wheeler."

She laughed. "Well, I don't know why you'd want *this*, Jacob Ryan."

"Awww, Jess," he murmured softly.

"I know, I know. Don't go there. Look, it's all good these days. I happen to like being married despite the fact that he constantly leaves the seat up on the toilet, which pisses me off to no end in the dark of night when I'm too tired to turn on the light and I end up sitting my ass down on cold porcelain. And the man can cook, when he puts his mind to it."

"Yeah, but in bed...?"

"None of your beeswax." But Jessie's stomach turned cold at the memory of her infamous orgasm comment to Josh that cold angry night in P.E.I. "I have no complaints." She managed a grin as a pink blush crested her cheeks.

Jacob's cell buzzed from its position on the end table next to the base of the room phone he was using. He grabbed it and held it up to study the incoming text message. "Damn," he groaned. "Her highness' new servant is requesting an audience in the ballroom. Fuck. Not up for this right now."

"Go forth and make beautiful music, Jacob Ryan. I'll see you next week, okay? Send me some texts if she gets completely out of hand."

"You'll be too busy riding the range with your cowboy, lovergirl." Jacob's spirits were sinking fast now that he had some idea of what the next few hours would likely bring.

"Never too busy for you, sweet Jacob," Jessie replied in a subdued tone. "I'm here for you if you need me. You know that."

"Fine," he retorted, sharper than he intended.

"Jacob," she chided him again. "I mean it."

His sigh was pronounced, deep, effective at pulling at her heartstrings. She could picture him making it; it was a genuine Jacob special. His cheeks would be puffed out and his eyes sad and downcast.

"Go make friends with Michael," she persisted. "He's been through hell. He likely needs a friend."

"He knew my dad once upon a time." This time, Jacob's voice was quiet, reflective. Losing energy.

"Oh," Jessie mumbled, unsure of what to say. She knew Tom Ryan as well, which was weird in its own supercharged kind of way. "Well, you said you wanted to meet the great Maestro Ryan. Maybe Michael's your bridge."

"Maybe."

"All right, kiddo. See you soon. Have fun with her highness tonight. But not…too much fun. Okay?"

"Hmmm? And why the hell not, should I ever wish to go there? Probably burn my pecker off if I did. Ha!"

"Uhhh, dork, because I don't trust her with your heart, that's why. We need to find you a nice little gal to settle down with."

In the distance, Jacob heard a door slam somewhere behind Jessie.

"My heart, huh?" Jacob sighed again, from the depths of his toes up to his already broken heart.

"I'll see you, Jacob." Jessie's voice was tiny now. Reminiscent. Worried. "You'll be okay, right?"

"Yeah. I suppose you have to rush now. Your cowboy's home. Wouldn't want you to get caught on the phone with me."

"Nah, it's not about that. But I promised to get dinner started and that ain't happening. So I guess I should run. Go make yourself some music."

"Married life. Pshaw! It's all yours, Jessie. See ya."

"Bye, Jacob."

After they disconnected, both sat for a moment and pondered this strange life both were now living. Their separateness seemed so final and profound, yet there was the upcoming gig that would draw them back together on *Mystic Nights*…

Beneath Jacob, in the harbor, the tipsy boat was now finally sailing smoothly along, spinnaker held high, its majestic arc gracefully leading its crew into a pristine sunset.

In Vancouver, Josh stole up behind his wife and wrapped his arms around her shoulders. He brushed his lips against her neck and smiled when he felt her body sigh into him.

"I'm sorry I haven't started dinner yet," she whispered as he continued to tenderly nuzzle her.

"Dinner-shminner," he murmured. Jessie pulled her husband on top of her on the couch. Dinner could wait.

In Miami, Jacob frowned and sulked all the way down the elevator to the ballroom. As he slowly approached he wasn't surprised to spot Michael leaning against the back wall of the elegant room, a beer cradled in one hand. But he was surprised—astonished, even -at the music emanating from the high-polished piano, a baby grand in the center of the capacious space.

The music had caught Jacob's ear before the elevator door even *swooshed* open. Now, inside the well appointed room, he saw Kelly seated on the piano bench, her back to the entrance and thus to him and Michael, a silky yellow sundress caressing her delicate frame and falling like a waterfall over her thighs. Backlit by the golden light from a low-lit chandelier, she was leaning into a classical piece that had everyone within hearing distance captivated in what was now a mystical space. If she noticed Jacob's entrance, it wasn't apparent. She didn't miss a note.

"Schubert," Michael breathed in a hushed tone to Jacob, spellbound eyes never leaving his charge's back as she bent over the ivory keys.

Huh, Jacob inhaled slowly, hands in his pockets. He stood near Michael, framed in the double doorway, ears inclined towards the complicated, haunting melody. *No wonder she hates the show's lyrics.*

Out of the corner of his eye he caught a glimpse of Michael as the man watched Kelly play. It was as if the new security guy had been pulled into some sort of trance—he barely seemed to breathe, and the only movement he made was to blink occasionally, or sometimes close his eyes for a few moments as the music took hold. The beer was left untouched, the elbow of the hand that held it, frozen. When the troubled man did look at Kelly, Jacob saw a sort of amity pass over Michael's features, as if a rainbow of perfect sound was making him a promise of everlasting peace, should he choose to listen.

Gently, confused at this unexpected glimpse into the soulful private worlds of two people he'd just met, Jacob backed away, slipping into the harsh reality of the too-bright lobby. He wandered deliberately into the nearby bar. Moments later he was back and, like Michael, was soon leaning up against the wall, silently sucking back a honey IPA, drawn into this strange, powerful new world.

Lost in the wonder of music, Jacob's melancholic mood was absorbed into some lost Neverland. Conjoined with the other lost souls in the elegant room, suddenly his suffering was no longer a solitary pursuit. Here, now, he was being given permission to feel, nurtured and encouraged by an angry golden girl in a soft yellow dress.

What he felt was pain, with soothing aloe vera layered overtop to ease the sting.

What he wanted was Jessie, to stand at his side and bear witness to this powerful music with him.

What he got—was bone-crushing drunk.

Chapter Six

Jessie knew Evelyn the moment she saw her but, since her aunt was still searching the crowds by Calgary's baggage carousel, she had the advantage. She wasn't prepared for the rush of emotion that surfaced at the recognition of her mother's features—the sharp nose, the angular chin, the pretty eyelashes, or the nervous way the woman studied the passersby.

When their eyes met, Jessie's softened but Evelyn's remained guarded. Inhaling deeply, Jessie touched Josh's elbow so he would know she was on the move, and then she made her way to the opposite side of the baggage area to greet her aunt properly.

The older woman accepted Jessie's hand when she extended it, but their hug was forced, loose.

"You made it okay," Evelyn stated unnecessarily, raising her chin almost defiantly.

Instantly, Jessie straightened, frowning. Truth be told, she didn't know what kind of a welcome she would receive from this woman, but she was hoping for at least a modicum of kindness resulting from the old familial ties. This arms-length lady with the subtle fireworks in the 'Emily Wheeler' eyes surprised her.

Josh wandered up behind them after scanning the carousel's baggage alert notice to make sure they were at the right pick-up locale.

"Uh, Josh, this is my aunt Evelyn. My mom's sister."

"It's a pleasure to meet you, ma'am," Josh said affably, extending a hand for a shake. Evelyn accepted the offering, a slight downturn to her lips and hesitation in her movement, but it was enough for Jessie to relax her shoulders and make the decision to go with the flow. She knew what Josh was thinking, which was fear of opening old wounds, but apparently Evelyn's actual thoughts about this reunion were being carefully guarded.

After gathering the couple's bags, the trio sidled out to the Parkade, where Evelyn led them to a late-model Range Rover. Shrinking uncomfortably from the stares and whispers following her famous guests like downwind smoke from a campfire, Evelyn loosened up somewhat when they finally hit the highway for the one and a half hour drive to Canmore, her small town at the base of the Rocky Mountains. Still, her discomfort with the visit was telegraphed clearly during the drive. And that, in a weird way, served to ease Josh's fears a little.

Evelyn ran a hand through the loose grey ponytail she wore high on her head like a fifties teenybopper, and pursed her lips.

Watching her hand grip the steering wheel, Jessie was impressed. The woman's forearms were tanned and muscular. She was quite obviously trim and fit. The pants she wore were Columbia brand, khaki green with deep pockets. *Designed for hiking,* Jessie thought. *My aunt's partial to the outdoors.*

Evelyn's forthright thoughts jarred Jessie out of her character study.

"I admire you for taking the time out of your busy schedule to look me up and visit, Jessie. But you should know your search for family should end here. You've done well for yourself." She let her gaze settle for a moment on the rearview mirror so she could see Josh in the backseat. His chocolate eyes narrowed immediately, and he straightened. She continued. "But all you'll end up doing by turning over timeworn rocks is find grubs."

Jessie angled her head to the right so she could study the perfect neighborhoods with their matching beige bric-a-brac houses. The fenced in subdivisions were perfectly aligned and similar, filled with doctors, lawyers, and oil company execs, she figured. She waited a while before responding to her aunt's declaration.

In the back, behind Jessie, Josh cleared his throat and leaned one elbow on the armrest.

"When was the last time I saw you, Evelyn?" Jessie casually tossed the question to the window as the distance between subdivisions lengthened. But Josh caught the underlying tension in her lowered voice.

64

"The night you left." The woman didn't hesitate. Nor did she glance over at her niece. Instead, her knuckles whitened on the wheel and her jaw clenched.

Josh's radar went on high alert. The day Jessie ran away from home was a subject he'd never raised in any depth. His theory was she would talk about it if and when she felt ready. Would she talk now? In front of this virtual stranger? While still in therapy for post-traumatic stress? He sucked in his breath and waited.

"Yeeaaahhhh," Jessie said, her voice now slightly higher-pitched and thoughtful. She drummed the fingers of her right hand on her thigh and avoided Josh's eyes in the rearview mirror. "The step-monster's birthday party. He had all his business cronies over for dinner. You and my mom made lasagna and Caesar salad. There was a lot of wine…" Her voice faded and she stared harder at the now vacant terrain. Her throat was suddenly as parched as the dry fields they slid by, which were crackling and stark in the late fall. Albertans had already been subjected to more than one snowfall, which was great for the ski resorts in the mountains, where the snow stuck, but only served to piss off the non-skiers. Yet the fields today were barren and wanting.

Jessie's insides lurched at the memory of the party. To this day certain wines turned her stomach. With them came the sickening smell of her step-father's sour breath when he leaned over her on those dank, dark nights. That particular night was a bad one. A painful one. The garlic from the salad and bread leached from the man's pores. Jessie shuddered in remembrance.

Josh leaned forward and touched her elbow where he could see it between the seat and the passenger side window. She jumped. But his movement served its purpose, both to gently remind her he was there, close by, and to keep her from sliding into a bad place. Trudy taught them that little move. He hadn't had to use it lately, but now…well, Josh was prepared and ready. But he still cursed his brand new wife under his breath for wanting to go back down a dark road that still haunted her with its black twists and turns.

Evelyn caught the subtle movement and glanced behind her. Josh didn't see her steal a look at him. When he sat back she was quick to look away.

He exhaled slowly and watched Jessie's aunt tighten and loosen her grip on the wheel again and again. In front of them, a breathtaking vista of the

SUSAN RODGERS

mountains drew closer, their imposing peaks jagged and snow-covered. The summits were all shadows and crags and mystery.

It was Evelyn who broke the silence. "I know why you left, Jessie."

"Ah, it's true what they say," Jessie responded coolly. "Old friends *can* pick up where they left off after long absences."

Evelyn chose to ignore the biting comment. "I knew something sinister was going on but I didn't know what, exactly. I thought maybe it was just the way your mother was treating you. Well that and the fact you'd just lost your dad. But I didn't know," her voice cracked, "I didn't know... exactly what that man did to you until a few months after you were gone. And when I found out, I hightailed it the hell outta there too. I never spoke to your mother again."

"Good old Emily was gone anyway, Evelyn. She started disappearing the day my dad died." Jessie finally looked over at her aunt. She wasn't surprised to see a moist sheen in the woman's eyes, but she saw Evelyn swallow away any pretense of tears and focus on the road. "You know that."

The older woman nodded and reached behind her head to pull nervously at the high ponytail. Her hands were shaking. She wiped them one at a time on the thighs of the khaki pants. "I do, Jessie, of course I know that. But still...she was your *mother*. She should have known."

Jesus, thought Josh incredulously. *Could the heavy shit not have waited til after dinner? How long have we been in the car? Less than thirty minutes? Damn!*

A small voice filled the void. It was Evelyn. "*I* should have known."

"How could you? After she married him, you weren't around as much." Jessie shook her head to keep the old cobwebs from filling her up and making her mind musty. "And anyways, it's ancient history now. It's over. Let's start fresh, okay Evelyn? I'm glad you were there. You were a bright light in those days after my dad died. A beacon of hope. You saved me many times. Remember?"

"Not as many as I should have, Jessie. And maybe..." She hesitated, trying out the words inside her heart before sharing them with her celebrity guests.

"Maybe what?" Jessie probed awkwardly, holding her breath to somehow help her accept the pointless answer.

"Maybe the rest of your life wouldn't have gotten so messed up if I could

66

have helped you back then. I could have had you removed from the home. You could have come to live with me."

A hearty laugh filled the car. "What, take me away from that swimming pool? And the big television in my room?" Jessie elbowed her aunt, who looked over at her passenger, surprise creasing the lines on her face. "Come on, Evelyn," Jessie added, winking. "How many kids in Summerside in those days could watch MuchMusic anytime they wanted? Like at three a.m. on a school night in their bedroom? Why would I give that up to go live with you and your man-of-the-week?"

"You were a child, Jessie. You should have been protected."

The dark nights—the slow creak of the bedroom door, the agonizing quiet footsteps making their way across her floor, the stark warning in her stepfather's low voice not to tell—came again unbidden, a shadowy nause-ating wave assailing the newfound peace Trudy was helping Jessie find. She cringed, fisting both hands tightly together and sucking so hard on her bot-tom lip she tasted blood.

Her almost soundless voice could barely be heard over the dull roar of the vehicle's steady motion. "It's done, Evelyn. It's over. If that's what I had to go through to appreciate my husband's touch on my skin today, then it was worth it. Because, Evelyn, I will never take him for granted."

Without looking behind her to see Josh, Jessie reached back between the seats. He grasped his wife's loving hand and brushed his thumb softly across her fingers.

Jessie continued, her words authentic and fueled by an endless capacity to forgive, to move on, imbued with Trudy's wisdom and patient counseling. She spoke quietly. "My husband's touch is luminous. His fingers on my skin leave trails of shiny glitter. I will soak him in and up and through me until the day I die. Evelyn…everything I have with Josh is more now than it ever could have been *before*, you know? I know that. And I will not ever forget that what I have with Josh is made that much sweeter because of *all the bad*."

At the wheel, Evelyn's lips parted. But there were no words to say that could possibly equal such a profound declaration of comprehension, of pure clemency, or of pure love for a man.

Jessie's aunt paused before glancing in the rearview mirror—her niece's sanguine peaceful words seemed too intimate and personal for her to let her eyes drift across Josh's features, but she couldn't help herself. A serene ripple traversed her hidden heart at the precious and silent joy tinting Jessie's husband's face and lighting his eyes.

Evelyn's grip on the wheel steadied. She swallowed the old sorrows and regrets, and changed tack by referencing the big TV Jessie mentioned earlier. "I thought I could hear Madonna's influences in your music. Could you not have listened to CMT instead?"

Groaning, Jessie countered. She spoke more volubly now. "Oh please don't tell me you're a country music fan." She sat up suddenly, knitting her brows together as a thought hit her. "Geez, Ev, is everyone in Alberta into country music? We're in rodeo country now, are we not?" She glanced in the rearview mirror and caught the twinkle in her husband's eye. "No," she said firmly. "I refuse."

It was Josh's chance to get a word in, finally, as the tension in the vehicle eased. "We're buying a ranch, Jessie. No pop music allowed. Only country."

"Listen, Sawyer, if you haven't figured it out already, my music's not pop, per se. It goes deeper than that. A whole other layer." She settled back into her seat. "You know the drill."

"You don't have to waste your breath trying to explain your music to me, Wheeler."

"Wheeler-Sawyer."

"It's just—if I wasn't married to you I'd be listening to Brad Paisley, that's all, Just sayin'. Or Alan Jackson. Garth Brooks, even. I really like that song about the thunder rolling, and isn't there one about a river? I seem to recall something about a river."

"*The* River," Evelyn tossed in helpfully, winking at him with a grin. She was enjoying the couples' banter. Slowly her grip on the wheel settled into casual cruise mode.

Josh continued, thoughtfully scratching his chin while Jessie twisted around in the front seat and rolled her eyes at him. "And what was that you were listening to on the flight? I saw what you were playing over and over on your iPhone!"

Jessie closed her eyes and covered her ears. Reaching forward, Josh pulled her hands away. He leaned in closely and whispered loudly in one ear. "Some song on the *Nashville* soundtrack methinks. One of the slow ones." He took advantage of having his lips so close to Jessie, and kissed her earlobe. She shivered with delight and then, eyes wide, she pronounced, "I was doing research for *Mystic Nights*! Some of the same songwriters from *Nashville* are going to be on the show. I was just being prepared!"

"Prepared, my ass! You're a closet country singer. I know it." He tweaked her earlobe with a finger.

"I hate to break up this lovely argument kids, but—"

"Discussion," Jessie corrected her. "We don't argue." She grinned back at Josh and squeezed his thigh above the knee, hard enough to make him yelp. He grasped her wrist and twisted it just slightly. "Owww!"

"Children!" Evelyn was now laughing outright. "One of the ranches you'll be visiting with the realtor tomorrow. Down that road on the left. Want a sneak peek?"

"Hell, yeah!" Josh responded heartily, letting go of Jessie's wrist with a warning light couched somewhere in his smile.

"Hell, yeah," Jessie echoed him happily, her eager pale eyes aglow as they settled somewhere deep in Josh's soul. If she could have purred, she would have. She tapped him on the knee and he tensed, ready, but Jessie just smiled sincerely, her gaze locked into his. "I guess I could listen to country if I had to. Living on a ranch and all."

He chuckled, took her hand, and ran his thumb over the fingers and the wedding ring he had only recently placed there—one day last month on a beach in beautiful Prince Edward Island. He cocked his head to the side and let his eyes land adoringly on his wife's hopeful lips, which he was already fantasizing about tasting. Silently he sent a prayer to the universe for Evelyn to have a large home and a guest room in the far corner so he and Jessie could play before fading into sleep that night.

He was so fixated on the lovely tantalizing thought that he almost missed Jessie's next words.

"I could *listen* to it, Josh, but I could never *play* it. Just so you know. Capiche? Country-smuntry."

The sound of their laughter followed the Range Rover off the main highway and onto a side road as Evelyn took them on a sightseeing tour of Alberta farmland. That night, they settled into a beautiful log home nestled into the side of a mountain in the outdoorsy town of Canmore. Jessie sipped on Bailey's and milk while Josh relied on his old stand-by, fizzy ginger ale, as they reclined in the hot tub with Evelyn and her hippie pony-tailed beau of the last ten years, Gary, and swapped the *good* stories of their lives. The bad stories were rustled under Evelyn's burnt-amber Navajo rug in the front hallway for the night.

Evelyn and Gary had a large home. Jessie and Josh thought it quite acceptable to play before sleep.

Evelyn fell asleep with a heart much lighter than the sad, heavy one she'd carried for years. As she slept, her cozy home was filled with light.

~ ~

"We bought a ranch," Jessie was telling Deirdre as Josh piloted the King Ranch from the airport towards their home at UBC. "Well," Jessie corrected herself, eyeing Josh sideways, "it's not exactly bought yet. But we're working on some of the finer details so hopefully within a few days we can solidify the deal."

On the other end of the line, Dee felt her nerves squelch up. "Already?" she asked. She leaned forward and took a sip of the green tea Charles placed on the coffee table before her. "That was quick."

"It's in the Kananaskis," Jessie bubbled brightly. "About an hour from Evelyn and Gary."

"An hour, huh?" Dee's voice was gravelly, despite the tea. "Only an hour? And how much time—realistically speaking—do you think you and Josh will actually have to spend there? Meaning free time, of course."

Jessie frowned at Josh and he grimaced. Both were expecting some resistance from Dee. To her the ranch meant downtime, meaning 'not working time,' and also, of course, distance.

"Look, we know it's not a full-time thing right now so we'll hire a caretaker. Gary knows a few fellas either looking for work—"

"In Alberta?" Dee cut in. "The land of golden honey? Is *anybody* in Alberta looking for work?"

"Dee! Listen."

"I'm listening." But her voice was edged with tension.

Jessie sighed. "We have the house in P.E.I. during the film shoot next May, if we can make it happen that fast. And maybe we'll stay a week or two after, but then I think the plan is to come out to the ranch for the summer and on into the fall. We'll spend the winters in Vancouver." She softened. "I promise."

The tea was soothing to Dee, who was nursing a sore throat. It calmed her spirit as well, but her next words were still cutting. "Don't forget about Miami."

"Miami. Yeah."

Curiously, Jessie watched in barely disguised amusement as the nerve in Josh's cheek twitched. He frowned when he glanced over and spied a note of glee flicker across her pink cheeks.

"So, about Miami," Jessie grasped Josh's right hand, lifted it to her lips and kissed it, "when do we leave? I can tell you about the ranch on the jet."

They ended their call with promises of a more in-depth chat during their flight the next day. As the couple pulled their bags out of the truck and headed indoors, Jessie reflected on the call. "You know," she said to Josh's back as he led the way down the flagstone steps towards the back entrance, "I think Dee's jealous."

"Of course she's jealous," came the response tossed over Josh's shoulder. "Suddenly she's no longer your only family." He turned and held open the gate so Jessie could squeeze through sideways. Her suitcase caught on the walk and he reached over to ease its passage. He looked up at Jessie when she didn't yank the handle and move. "What?" he asked impatiently. His belly was growling and they'd nipped into the Noodle Box to grab takeout before coming home. He was picturing his dinner cooling quickly in the crisp wintry air.

She was grinning widely, her eyes alight. "Yeah. Suddenly I have all kinds of family."

At that sweet remark, which Josh knew was meant mainly for him, he wrapped an arm around his girl and pulled her forward for a kiss. "This is only the beginning, little one," he murmured into her ear. He scooped her up and headed down the steps.

"Dinner!" Jessie squealed. "Hungry!" She made a half-hearted attempt at reaching behind her for their food. The suitcases could wait.

71

"That's what microwaves are for," Josh stated matter-of-factly. "Settle down! I don't want to drop you. 'Singer gets dropped by actor and gets bonked on the head.' I can see the headlines now."

"Never," Jessie whispered, her soft lips tickling his neck. "Never drop me, Sawyer. Ever."

"No worries, little one," Josh smiled and set her down in front of him so he could fish for his keys. "But I'm coming with you to Miami. Just to lay down the law with Jacob, at least."

A cloud passed over Jessie's face then. She was worried about Jacob. Their last call had revealed a deep loneliness Jessie understood, and which she feared. And she knew her ex's co-star was going to be no picnic to work with. Instantly, her mood crashed.

Josh scowled, and he paused before unlocking the door. "Jesus, Jessie," he said into the darkness. "Couldn't you at least *pretend* he's not two steps behind me at all times?"

She hooked a finger over his belt, and shivered. "You brought him up, goofball. Anyways he's not, Josh, you know that. It's just that…well, frankly, I'm worried about him."

Josh fit the key into the door and twisted it. He shoved her hand away from his belt and stepped past her into the light that he flicked on with a hasty fisted punch of the light switch. "Let's not do that thing where we tell each other everything, okay Jess?"

"Geez, I hate when you do that," she countered angrily, blood suddenly pounding in her ears. "Come on, Josh, enough with the twelve-year-old schoolyard jealousy! Jacob's old news. We've been over this."

He turned to face her, the nerve on his cheek going into overdrive. "You're right, Jessie, we've been over this. In fact, I'm so over it I've changed my mind about Miami. You and Dee go. Alone. Although I suppose Matt will attach himself to the two of you. I've got scripts to go over." He pushed past her and strode alongside the pool, which looked rather ghostlike and lonely in its winter garb, and he hopped up the steps to gather their bags and the takeout. Jessie followed after a shocked moment to collect herself, and they ate in silence in front of a Wes Anderson film on Netflix.

Josh kept his word. He mellowed before Jessie left to fly south, but he knew from the sadness in her diaphanous gaze that she was already missing him, and cursing his stubborn streak. But no way could he explain to her that he did trust her with Jacob (mostly, at least), and that he had an ulterior motive for staying home.

They had barely kissed goodbye when he hopped into the King Ranch and pointed it towards the Downtown Eastside. It was in his rearview mirror that Josh saw the Keating jet careen up into the clouds. His heart lurched when it disappeared but he told himself it was fine, that she'd be back in his arms soon. Still, it physically hurt any time they were separated, and silently Josh prayed Jessie would be okay without him for a bit. He squashed memories of other painful leavings, and pushed the image of her sad eyes out of his brain.

I'm doing this for you, little one, he muttered to himself as he skirted around a slow moving Dodge Caravan.

Twenty minutes later he was cruising East Hastings while, somewhere in the forever blue above the clouds, Jessie shoved earbuds into her ears and hit 'play' on her iPhone. While the soundtrack to the TV show *Nashville* filled her ears, she closed her eyes and willed away the lonely ache left by Josh's abrupt departure from their trip.

Chapter Seven

"*H*e's here? Josh Sawyer?"

The first thing Caryn did when her receptionist breezed into the studio where Caryn was directing a new film was glance at herself in the antique gilt mirror used for set dressing.

The receptionist, bronzed long legs scurrying with excitement on high-heeled black leather lace-up boots, had tossed her long raven hair when she delivered the news.

"I escorted him to the private waiting room. I offered him green tea but he declined. He looked nervous." She grabbed the lower hem of her tailored jacket, which she was wearing as a dress, and tugged it down but it still barely covered her butt.

A pale-skinned gal with Marilyn Monroe curls and deep set hazel eyes that danced in the artificial lighting as she reclined on the set bed, fluffed up a pink satin pillow and leaned back against it. "They're all nervous when they come here for the first time. What's he after? Male or female company? Or both?" She smiled coquettishly.

"Enough, Melissa." Caryn bit off her words. Besides having to shoot scenes for the new film today, she wasn't prepared for the emotional onslaught she knew would accompany a visit from Jessie Wheeler's new husband. "Roxie, back to your desk, please." She whipped around to the tall man at the camera, who regarded her cautiously. "Eric, rehearse that last bit for camera until you get it squeaky clean. I won't be long."

He stepped towards her. "I'm coming with you. He's got a rep for fighting."

"It's an old rep. He'll be fine." *Old because Jessie straightened him out,* she thought, feeling her husband's hard stare boring through the back strap of her skin tight off-white halter top as she strode towards the studio door.

The shift from the dark walls of the studio—where only the set lighting was employed at the far end—into the pristine white walls and warm architectural lighting of the reception and office space of the business, was like exiting a womb. Blinking hastily to adjust her vision, Caryn pondered the fact she was never quite prepared for either transition. Either the black was too dark or the light too bright. *Like my life,* she told herself. *No grey.*

She inhaled deeply and wiped both palms on the halter's tight matching pants before grasping the handle on the frosted glass door of the private waiting room.

Her first view of Jessie's man was of his back. He was standing in the center of the small room, square-toed boots a shoulder's width apart, frayed black denims skirting the floor, both hands thrust nervously into the pockets of his favorite vintage green leather jacket. His head was angled in one direction, which led Caryn to believe rightly that his sight was fixed on a large framed photograph on the west wall featuring a young African-skinned woman gazing seductively at the camera, one hand cupping a breast as she lay half on her back.

Josh heard Caryn come in, and he moved his body around to face her, pulling his hands out of the pockets at the same time as if he were about to suddenly yank a silver pearl-handled Colt from a holster at his hip.

Once his somber eyes fixed themselves on Caryn, she was immediately disarmed. Any pretense at confidence was gone. It took her a moment to regroup, to find her own guns and ammunition for this unexpected encounter at her downtown business.

Josh started them off. His voice was even and controlled, but low and not necessarily friendly. "You weren't hard to find. Your name—it's an unusual spelling."

Caryn ignored the comment and nodded at the photograph Josh was studying when she entered. "That one mimics a Rubens. You know—the famous European Painter from the Middle Ages?" She swallowed, her throat suddenly stuffed with cotton. Josh was undoubtedly a classically good-looking guy, and the blonde highlights from the Harley production lent him an

75

air of innocence. But he had also not bothered to shave this morning, and the fresh stubble completely beguiled Caryn. That and the way he always dressed so timelessly, plus his fame as an actor and as Jessie Wheeler's true love had Caryn grasping for something intelligible to say. She decided on an introduction.

She gathered her wits, leaned forward and stretched out a hand. "Mr. Sawyer. It's nice to more officially meet you. After Revolver a few weeks ago, I mean."

"Josh," he offered, taking her hand. "And I'm not sure I can echo that sentiment, Caryn." His eyes dropped to a tattoo on the bicep of the arm she'd extended towards him.

"It's also based on Rubens," she said, following his glance. "One of my favorite artists, although I would put Monet at a close second."

The tattoo was a naked woman in recline adorned by pink flowers. The way her body was inked on the arm gave it a graceful allure, and her breasts and pubic area were delicately and tastefully covered with loose flowers.

"You see," Caryn began, attempting to explain—or perhaps justify— what she did for a living, "my husband Eric and I started this business to offer tasteful erotica to the public. "What we do—"

"Porn, you mean. And I'm not sure that's ever tasteful."

"Uh-huh," Caryn said, folding her arms and opposing him, eyes flickering in time with her thoughts, which were rushing like a breached dam through her mind. *Never let him see you sweat,* she told herself. "Of course. You've watched porn. Who hasn't?"

"Lots of people," he shot back.

"If you'd let me finish."

"Please. Be my guest." He swept an arm loosely around the room.

"What Eric and I do is not porn." She raised a palm in the air to stop him from speaking. "And you may notice from the photographs in this room that we are an inclusive company. Body type, gender, race—we cater to many different audiences by providing tasteful erotica to help stimulate relationships and promote the body—and intimacy—as a beautiful, healthy, natural thing."

"I gather you're used to defending your shady business."

"We are a legal, legitimate company."

"That uses vulnerable young girls to make a buck."

"Our youngest model is 20. Our oldest, you may be interested to know, is 65. Her and her husband both, in fact. Although I think he may be a year younger, actually, come to think of it."

His voice lowering a notch further, Josh's eyes flashed. "Jessie wasn't talking when she knew you. When she apparently *worked*…for you. Age is one thing, mental state quite another."

Caryn stayed locked in his gaze but didn't speak until she saw the nerve in his cheek settle and the sudden fists at his sides unclench. She blinked. "Jessie was not our typical model, Mr. Sawyer."

He didn't bother reminding her to use his given name.

"Please," she stepped towards the door and pulled on the handle. It opened with a small *shuff*, letting in the cacophony of a busy office. Strangely, one of Jessie's tunes was playing over the lobby speakers. Caryn hesitated before continuing, listening to the song for a moment before lifting her chin and gently urging him forward with a nod of the head. "Let's go to my office. It's more comfortable there. I can explain a few things that might help you make sense of Jessie's life back then. And the choices she made."

"The choices she…?" Josh was incredulous. How does a traumatized young woman come upon any choices? He expected the *choices* of which Caryn spoke were in fact made for her.

Caryn waited, again choosing not to take the bait. Eventually Josh wiped a hand through his hair, bit his bottom lip, took one last lingering look at the compromising photos in the room, and followed Caryn's lead.

Her office was at the far end of the hall. A large tidy room, it felt out of place to Josh. He had to remind himself, as he dropped carefully into a seat on a white butter-soft leather chesterfield against the east wall, that he was visiting a shady business on Vancouver's Downtown Eastside. This place was luxurious, elegant. Caryn's space was, like her, dressed in shades of white and off-white. A large antique mahogany sideboard with a silver tray resting on a linen runner sat in front of a tall window. On the tray were crystal goblets from which Caryn poured Josh a sparkling water infused with cucumber and lemon. She handed it to him, then leaned against her desk, a heavy glass contraption on which sat a large-screened iMac computer.

"I don't have a lot of time," she said, clipping her words as if she had rehearsed them on their walk down the hallway. "I know your motives in coming here, Josh, and frankly I'm not surprised. But I'll cut to the chase."

He laid an ankle over one knee and settled against the chesterfield. "I'm listening," he spat back. The brown eyes were less somber now, and more firm. He wanted something, and he intended to get it.

"When Jessie first showed up here, on the Downtown Eastside, she did like most homeless do, and found a corner."

At the word homeless, Josh cringed. It was hard to reconcile the woman he now knew with the image he knew he was going to hear about here, today.

Caryn continued. "I passed her those first few days. I recognized right away that she was new here, because," she swallowed, "well, because I live here, for one, and also because yes I do look for new talent on the streets. But it's not what you think. I give the girls choices. And sometimes this job is a means to an end. They get a few paychecks, a little self-esteem…"

He scoffed at that but she wisely ignored him.

"A few friends…and off they go. There are some stipulations, things I look for. One," she tapped these out on her fingers, "no addictions issues."

This time Josh swallowed uncomfortably. He blinked, and she went on.

"Two, they go through a rigorous interview. Most times." She hesitated, thinking about Jessie's voiceless entry into her life, and not looking at Josh where she knew she would see a certain *harumph* in his eyes at that particular protocol. "I need to know they are not running from the law and that they sincerely want to put their lives back together."

Her voice softened, and she gripped both edges of the thick glass desk with her fingers as she leaned back against it. She was a beautiful woman, her longish pink-blonde hair glistening from the corner light and, as she moved, the daylight from the expansive window caught both high cheekbones and the space between Caryn's breasts that the halter top didn't cover. Her office, too, was decorated with attractive scantily clad—or nude—women in positions of recline. Josh was starting to become uncomfortable for more reasons than one. He adjusted his seat again and took a sip of the cool water. He glanced around the room, his troubled eyes landing on each photo for a moment until he was sure…

"You won't find her in any of these pictures, Mr. Sawyer. She's long been deleted, I assure you. We delete the girls' files as soon as they leave our employ."

He stared at her, unsure.

Caryn continued. "It became apparent rather quickly that Jessie was in trouble. She was sick. Not just traumatized, Josh. Sick." She sighed and turned her head towards the window. The memories were, indeed, tough to recall. "After a few days Eric and I went and got her. She was wearing one of those grey blankets around her shoulders, the kind your friends Charlie and Jane deliver around here. But it was loose, like she no longer cared to try to keep warm. Although she was in a small alcove under an awning, it was freezing rain, the sideways Canadian kind of freezing rain the wind whips around, you know, and she was blue from the cold. She didn't resist when Eric picked her up and, by the look on his face when he touched her, I knew she was in pretty dire straits."

She gazed at Josh to see if he understood. He did. Tears pricked his eyelids and he moved his thumb and forefinger to his face and squeezed his bottom lip.

"Jessie was desperately feverish and yes, you're right, she didn't speak, but then at that time she was so sick it was all she could do to blink. We brought her here and gave her a bed."

No shortage of those around here, Josh thought wildly.

"Then we called in a doctor who does rounds on the Downtown Eastside. He diagnosed her with pneumonia and called an ambulance. She spent two weeks in the hospital but she still wouldn't speak, any more than her name that is, which, by the way, in the beginning she told us was Emily. I now know that's her mother's name, but at the time, well…" she shrugged.

Huh, thought Josh. *That's interesting.*

"In the end they wouldn't release her from the hospital unless she had a place to go. So Eric and I," her voice softened so Josh had to lean forward to hear her, "took her home. To our place."

"She lived with you?" Shocked, Josh's mind started to race. Why wouldn't Jessie have told him that?

Caryn nodded, and at her admission a wave of sadness washed over her.

She slumped against the desk and gathered her wits by studying a spot of dust on the exquisite Persian rug at her feet.

Josh set his glass on the end table next to the couch and eased himself into a standing position. "How long?"

Again, Caryn shrugged absently. "About a year."

His voice was a whisper. "A...a year."

This time when Caryn looked up, the old mask was back. It was a look Josh recognized, which startled him. "I told you, she wasn't a typical client, Josh. She did a few films, yes, and by that time she was communicating a little here and there. She started with photos and, in the end, those were her first choice. She chose what to do and, in some cases, she turned work down. Eventually she started to play her guitar again, so she gradually stopped working for Eric and me. Then, finally, we let her go."

"You let her go. From here?"

A rock-hard lump of coal formed in Caryn's throat. Unbidden, the moistness in her eyes leaked out. She turned her back to Josh and grabbed a tissue, but not before adding a few last words. "Not just from here. From home, too. And then...from our lives."

When she finally turned back to Josh, he was staring at her, shaken.

Caryn murmured in wonder. "She didn't tell you."

He shook his head slowly. "No."

"Well. I don't know what hurts more. That we weren't worth mentioning or that she's never invited us to a concert."

Josh fought a rising nausea. Why wouldn't Jessie speak about this time in her life? She lived with these people. After they'd met at Revolver, and memories seemed to be coming back, she must have remembered living with this couple.

Something else occurred to him. He fought the urge to just walk away, to leave this oppressive white cave and its sketchy business and just go, and pretend he'd never met this captivating woman with the perfect breasts and runner's butt crammed into tight-fitting white pants. But he had to know. So he felt compelled to ask. The words came out gruff, the tone business-like. "You got attached to her. You kept her in your home—in your life—for a year. She was like a daughter to you." He waited for the answer he knew was coming, despite the fact he also knew he didn't want to hear it.

Caryn moved her head side to side slowly before choosing her words carefully. "No. Not like a daughter, Mr. Sawyer."

He swallowed a rising bile from deep in his belly. "What, then?"

Unmoving, she regarded Josh and waited for him to fully grasp the answer himself.

He croaked out an answer. "Your husband. Was he in love with her?"

"No, Josh." Again, Caryn waited until Josh's eyes telegraphed his comprehension. Then she dove in for the kill. "Not my husband, Josh. She needed *me*. For a time."

The shock factor of that admission turned Josh's knees to jelly. He knuckled his hands into fists and struggled to remain standing. "But—you were married."

"Yes." Caryn shifted her stance and crossed her arms. She raised her chin. "Eric was very understanding. He still is. Look, Josh. What you need to understand is that Jessie was a very different young woman then. She was alone, and hurting, and she needed to feel love. She needed me."

"You took advantage of her." The old demons were hard to fight off now. The words were forced through gritted teeth. Josh's fists clenched and unclenched.

Caryn took notice, and she straightened. "Easy, Josh. Jessie never did anything she didn't want to do. And like I told you, in the end *we* had to let *her* go. It wasn't like she wanted to leave."

This was also a new and surprising revelation. The words caught in Josh's throat. "She didn't leave on her own?"

Another tear left a salty trail down Caryn's pretty cheek. A graceful finger rose delicately and gently swiped it away. "No. It was Eric in the end. He gave me an...ultimatum." Her last word was almost sung, high-pitched and musical. She stared hard at Josh. "It was either her or him. One had to go. And since I was married, well...you get the drift." She shrugged. "Truth is, I got in way too deep with her. She was a very troubled woman. Still is, from what I hear, so I'm guessing you know what I'm talking about."

He didn't speak, but didn't detach himself from Caryn's steady gaze, either. The fists tightened until Josh's knuckles were white.

"The thing is, Mr. Sawyer. I learned early on that Jessie Wheeler is a hard woman to love. And despite the fact she was starting to come around, which is what love can do, as you know, it can melt and thaw people…well, despite everything we did for her—clothes, warmth, food in her belly—she was still hurting and deeply troubled at that time. You could hear it in her music; you could see it in her eyes when she played. She was in pain. And after a while that became my pain too, you know? And then by association, Eric's, and then everyone around me was feeling it. Eric was right. I had to let her go. I had no choice."

"Where?" He rasped. "Back out on the fucking streets. In the goddamned freezing rain." Now it was Josh's turn to wipe a hand across a stubbly cheek.

"We took her to Arnie. He was always, like, the angel of these streets. He watched out for folks then, and he still does now. We took her there and she slept at his place on the cold nights and out in the streets on the warm nights." Quickly, she held a hand up in the air again, an air palm against what she detected rightly was Josh's blood pressure rising further with what he likely thought transpired at Arnie's. "No, it wasn't like that with Arnie, it was never like that. She slept on his couch and sometimes he fed her and some- times she brought pizza home to him. They were good friends, and still are."

"I can't stand the man."

"Because he spirited her away that time. Which, by the way, likely saved your goddamned ass."

"I don't trust him."

"Well, Jessie apparently does, so you might want to get used to the guy." She sighed, heaved her slim yoga body away from the big desk, and started towards the door. "Look, Josh, I need to get back to work. And I don't thank you for coming here today and raising a lot of old sad memories. Jessie has a special aura, she does, but she has always been, and always will be, a deeply troubled woman. You should have kept that Michelle chick if you knew what was good for you. I'm sorry," she added, with a wave of a lily white hand. "But it's true."

"Not that it's any of your business, but she's working on things. On her life. She's working with a therapist."

At this point Caryn was standing between Josh and the door. He started to walk towards her, ready to make his exit. But Josh felt something stir in his body and in his soul in the presence of this formidable woman, who was both a savvy businesswoman as well as a victim of his own sad Jessie. Their eyes met as he passed and, despite his anger at what he supposed must have happened years ago with the hurt young woman he loved, he felt the strange need to hug Caryn. But he held back, although at her sudden blink he thought she might have felt it too.

"Take care of her," she whispered, taking a chance and reaching out to graze his hand with the back of hers.

"I'm doing the best I can," was Josh's honest reply. Startled at her touch, his eyes flicked down at Caryn's elegant fingers as they floated between them. Then he remembered the main purpose for his visit. He paused, and then appealed to what he hoped was her continuing concern for his wife. "Caryn…I need those files."

"I told you. I deleted them." Again, the jade eyes flickered.

"I'm not buying that. You cared about her. You didn't delete them."

She chewed on a lip while she regarded him. Then, the bare shoulders sank so the tattooed nude on Caryn's arm settled below Josh's line of vision. He forced himself not to blink downwards and gape at it, but he wanted to. He wanted a closer look.

"Look, I may have…I may have a few photos. That's all. Give me your phone." She could see its outline in his coat pocket. He retrieved it, handed it to her, and Caryn opened the Notes Ap and added a street address. "Here. That's where we live. Come by tomorrow, anytime after six, and I'll show you what I have. But I swear, they're not going anywhere, Josh. They're…well, they're sacred to me. You know?"

He hesitated, then took the phone from her outstretched hand and stowed it away again.

"Yeah. I know," he muttered ungraciously. "I'll see you tomorrow, then."

As he strode out of Caryn's white tomb, Josh was surprised at how deflated he felt. He was drained, like he'd shown up at the gym without enough protein for fuel to get through a workout. His limbs were heavy, weighted.

Jessie was just what he told Charlie she was that day outside La Casa when they'd arrived back in Vancouver after time on P.E.I. He'd said she was just simply…Jessie. Caryn was right. She would not change. Ever. Regardless of how much help she received from a professional like Trudy, Jessie would always just be that troubled girl with dark surprises around every corner.

He slammed a fist into the brick when he exited the building. The rough exterior was hard enough to scrape his knuckles raw, as well as wake him up to the realization there was one thing Caryn did say that was unequivocally true. Jessie responded to love. And he had lots of that for her. As did Dee, and Charles, and Steve and Sophie and Maggie and Carter, Sue-Lyn, Charlie and Jane. And…Jacob.

"Damn it!"

Josh yanked open the door of the King Ranch, climbed in, slammed the door as hard as he could behind him, and then leaned his forehead on the steering wheel. "Damn it."

He wrenched the truck into gear and abruptly squealed the tires before speeding down East Hastings towards home.

From the building, Caryn watched him go, and then she strode purposefully down the hallway, her head held high. *Jessie Wheeler* was a long time ago. Who knew she would become a big star? How could she, as vulnerable as she was back then?

Caryn opened the door to the black box studio, and entered the darkness once again.

Chapter Eight

At took Josh a while to get up the nerve to call Jessie in Miami that night. For one, he was sneaking around behind her back, investigating a past he was damn sure she would rather have left alone. Two, he had no intention of ever telling her. He just wanted some certainty that any evidence of her association with Caryn's sketchy business would never appear.

He was a good actor, but lying to his wife was going to be Josh's toughest role of all.

After an easy dinner of oven-melted skillet chicken pizza (an invention from his bachelor days), which he ate on a baguette right out of the skillet, he finally speed-dialed her. He caught Jessie as she was about to knock on Dee's hotel room door.

"Hey, little one."

"Hey, cowboy." She retraced her steps and plunked her butt down in a comfy wing chair by the elevators. She'd chat with Dee in a bit.

"Cowboy?"

"Jacob's new nickname for you. On account of the ranch. It seems to be sticking."

"And how is the new female fodder for the masses? Was he happy to see you? How long did it take him before he tried shoving a hand up your dress?"

"Easy, boy. Down. I wasn't wearing a dress. Vancouver's freezing right now."

"Miami's not."

"Well, Vancouver's where I got dressed this morning."

"Okay, okay, whatever. Let's not do this right now, okay?"

"You started it."

"Jesus, Jessie." Caryn wasn't kidding. Jessie was a handful at times, no doubt about that.

"Okay, fine. What the hell's eating you? Still pissed about me working with Jacob? Because let me just remind you that you were supposed to come on this trip."

The ennui in her voice concerned Josh. But he fought the urge to console her. He needed to keep up his charade in order to keep Jessie on another track. He decided to take the bait, even though he was trying to trust her around Jacob, for the most part. He had no choice or he would go stir crazy.

"Tell me what the latest is on this part you've signed up for. How often will you be working closely with him?"

Jessie sighed. "Enough. Like us on *Drifters*."

"Lovely."

"This is more soap opera-ey, though. So our characters are likely going to be moving around a bit."

"Sleeping around, you mean."

"With tact."

"Of course."

"But yeah, there are moments with Jacob." She didn't add they would also be singing together—starry-eyed love songs on intimate stages.

"This day just gets better and better," Josh mumbled.

"Why? What happened in the rest of your day?"

"Nothing. I'm just missing you, that's all. You're right, I should have come on the trip."

"It's fine, Josh, I won't be gone long. But we have to make a point of trying to travel together when we can, okay? We promised each other that. No long breaks."

"I know, kiddo. I promise."

"Okay, so have you found any scripts that'll be shot in Miami?"

He laughed, a sound she found heartwarming and which eased her mind about both his moody temperament as well as her plans for the evening, which she wisely chose not to share with her new hubby.

"Nada. Toronto's looking promising."

"Toronto?"

"Yeah, Jonathon wants to shoot a pilot for a new series. Steve's in on it as well, if he can make it work with his other jobs."

"Steve! Awesome. When?"

"It's too early to say, Jessie. But for now I'm just gonna go through a few more scripts, then there's this press junket coming up in the new year for *Freedom Ride*—"

"*Freedom Ride*? I take it the producers finally settled on a name for the Harley film."

"You got it. It's okay. It'll work."

"Little cheesy there, husband."

"It's an American film, what do you expect? It's got to have that Hollywood flair, kiddo."

This time it was Jessie's turn to laugh. "Hollywood shmultz, you mean."

"Tell that to the voting members of the Academy, little girl. They might revoke those two shiny handsome statues I happen to be staring at right now."

"Yeah, I know. I don't mean to be ungrateful, but sometimes I want to go to Denmark and shoot movies, you know?"

"Ouch."

"Oops, sorry, Josh. I forgot about the Susanne Bier film I so unmercifully got you kicked off of."

"Hey, ancient history, remember? Her team has already called me about doing another film. Someday I'll get to work with her. Maybe the two of us. Actually, Jessie, there is a script in this pile I think you should take a look at. It's one of the new Marvel films."

"Ah, no. I'm not interested in blue skin or green skin or…pointy ears."

"It's the best script in the pile, kid. Sweet story and lots of humor. And we could work together. Bring our kids, maybe."

"Our kids?" Down the hall from Jessie a door opened and closed. Dee poked her head out and waved to Jessie, whose smile was now lighting up the entire wing of the fancy hotel. Jessie returned the wave.

"When we're ready," Josh was saying.

"Of course."

"Can't wait, Jess."

"Neither me."

"Luv you."

"Luv you back. Dee says hi." To Dee she mouthed *Josh*.

Deirdre rolled her eyes. She mouthed back *Of course it's Josh. You're a mushy mess.* Out loud she called, "Hello, Josh. Jessie's fed, clothed and housed."

When they signed off, both Josh and Jessie sat and reflected on their brief conversation. Neither was being completely honest with the other, for reasons they told themselves protected their partner. But in both situations it left a sense of unease and discomfort.

Jessie glanced over at Dee, who was now waiting patiently in the opposite wing chair.

"I know that look," Dee said, her eyes narrowing suspiciously.

"Favor?" Jessie asked tentatively. She held up her thumb and forefinger and pinched them together. "Just a wee one?"

"Will anyone be maimed or killed?"

Jessie frowned.

"Oh, poop. Sorry, honey. That was careless. I'm sure I can help you. What's up?"

After explaining her plan for the evening, Jessie sat back and studied Dee. Her pseudo-mom made no attempt to disguise her surprise—and displeasure—at Jessie's audacity. She raised her eyebrows and crossed her arms.

"Dee, I've been thinking about this since long before I saw a poster advertising tonight's show. This won't be a complete shock to Jacob—he and I have talked about this."

"Talking's one thing, Jessie, showing up on the man's doorstep with his estranged son in tow is entirely another."

Still, she acquiesced, like she usually did where Jessie's wants and needs were concerned. She was all melty butter in Jessie's effusive warm embrace.

Half an hour later Jessie and Jacob were on their way to the airport, escorted by Matt and a hired limo driver familiar with the city. Matt, yawning, was scratching his head. Beside him sat Michael, and opposite him in the large Lincoln was glamour girl Kelly.

Jessie was frowning, her pouty downturned lips aimed straight for Matt, who appeared, besides tired, rather displeased and very irate.

Jacob, who at this point only knew they were heading out of town for some concert, sat at the far window of the back bench seat next to Kelly, who was in the middle, and watched the blonde singer apply layers of makeup. At this moment she was working on mascara. The car hit a bump, and she yelped and cursed the driver. Jacob took a breath and glanced sideways past Kelly at Jessie by the other window, who silently met his eye and bit her bottom lip.

She turned to Michael then and smiled genuinely. "Well, it's a surprise, and was such short notice, but I'm really glad you and Kelly could join us on this adventure."

He allowed a small grin before responding. "I would say the same, except I haven't got a clue where we're going. Big brother isn't talking."

Matt trained his sight on Jessie, his annoyance barely concealed, and then poked a number into his cell phone. Soon he was listing off instructions to the security chief at a concert. He stuffed a finger in one ear to block out any conversation in the big car so he could better hear the guy, but it was a use-less move. All occupants of the limo were quiet. They could hear the security chief loud and clear. He was screaming obscenities. Matt eyed Jessie stonily, removed his finger from his ear, and held the phone out aways, but she just winced and shrugged her shoulders.

"Okay, it's a concert. I know there will be some...finagling...to make this happen in your universe, Matt. You know if it was just me and Jacob here, we'd throw on hats and line up in the first row."

"At a Tom Ryan concert? Are you nuts?" Kelly cursed when her lip-gloss zigzagged after another bump. "Damn it driver, is this how it's done down here? Y'all use potholes for target practice in Miami?"

From her right side came a swift intake of breath.

"Jesus, Kelly," Jessie groaned softly.

"What? He's a shitty driver!" She read the guarded expression on Jessie's face, then swung her head around and stared at Jacob. "Oh. Sorry. But it's no secret he's playing in Atlanta, right? Is that not where we're going? I just fig-ured with Jacob here and all..." She glanced at Jessie and then back again at Jacob who, suddenly white as a ghost, was silently cursing Jessie. "I mean, it's a weekday. His concert would be the only reason I figured we'd leave Miami. In a jet."

89

"I think it was supposed to be a surprise, Kelly." Michael's gentle voice was quiet and understanding.

"Oh." She dropped the lip-gloss into her makeup bag and zipped it shut. "Sorry, Jake old buddy." She didn't offer an apology to Jessie, but Michael did, by silently mouthing *sorry*.

Jessie leaned forward in her seat and spoke across Kelly's lap to Jacob. "Dee's arranging backstage passes for all of us but we don't need to go meet him if you're not up for it. I just thought you'd like to see his show, at least. We can compare your fingering styles."

"Fingering styles? Is that what they call it these days?" Kelly hoo-hawed at her own joke, which clearly, in bad taste, referenced Jessie and Jacob's past as a couple.

Thankfully, the vehicle swung into the private area of the airport and disembarked its passengers before anything else could be said. Soon the little group was on its way to Atlanta.

Jacob was pensive on the flight, although he didn't hesitate when Jessie patted the seat next to her.

"Jacob, I'm sorry for the short notice. I only just saw a poster today, at the hotel. It was past its date, he'd already played in Miami, but Atlanta seemed doable. I jumped at the chance. Your dad's a legend. And like I said, we don't have to meet the guy, especially with…" She glared across the aisle at Kelly, who was openly flirting with her new handler *and* his brother.

"I get it, Jessie. I'm just not so sure this is the way I want to meet the old man. Plus I'm equally sure it's not the way he will want to meet me. In fact, to be honest, let's call a spade a spade here. He doesn't want to meet me at all. If he did, ever, he would have years ago. I'm feeling a little gun shy."

"You don't know what drove him to the decisions he made. Look at Josh and Jonathon. All those years Jonathon could have said something to his kid, but he didn't. He kept it quiet for Josh's sake."

Jacob was annoyed enough to face palm Jessie. "Can you maybe *not* bring up loverboy in front of me? Especially his tragic story? Cuz I really don't give a shit."

"Sorry." Jessie sank lower into her seat, a frown creasing her brow.

From across the aisle, Matt stepped over Kelly's long legs and laid a hand on the top of Jacob's headrest. He was wearing his serious 'don't mess with me' expression. But before he could speak, Jessie jumped in.

She winked at Jacob and used her favorite singsong speaking voice. "Matt, did you get those spiky little tips in your hair highlighted? You're just so trendy." She dropped both hands on Jacob's thigh, leaned over him and fixed her vision on Matt's boots. "New leather desert boots! I knew it. Just like Jacob's. You two go shopping together?" She elbowed Jacob, who jumped and cursed her. "These ones have kind of an auburn tint to them. I like it! And I see you're now only rolling your jeans up once at the cuffs instead of twice." She looked up at Matt and sat back, tossing her hair for good measure. "Thank GOD we have Matt, Jacob, to be our barometer for Vancouver fashion. Though I'm not really sure what the deal here in Miami is. More like…flowered shirts, big flowers, you know, red ones—"

"Damn it, Jessie."

"Geez, Matt, your eyes are on fire. I'd rather you don't look at me that way. In fact, I insist." She gave him a serious look of her own that suggested Matt take a moment to remember just who his boss is. Generally Jessie didn't play that card with him, ever, especially given the extensive guilt she knew he carried over not reading signs that could have prevented a lot of pain for all of them in the past few years. But Jessie was drumming her fingers on her lap now. She was nervous enough. She didn't need Matt's judgment right now. She needed his help.

He got the message, but there was still a serious edge to his voice, and the fire in his eyes didn't fade. He would never forget how things went down a few years ago, and the responsibility he played in that. But Jessie's rogue behavior pissed him off and made them all vulnerable. He took a breath.

"This is how this is going to work, Jessie, Jacob. Security is arranging a limo from the airport. They'll deliver us directly backstage. We'll be escorted to a private box above the arena. The opener has already started but we'll be there in time for Tom Ryan's set. He's playing two hours straight with no intermission. When the concert is over, we'll be escorted directly to his dressing room. He's been informed that his special guests will include Kelly Reilly, Jessie Wheeler-Sawyer, and," he looked at Jacob, "Jacob Ryan."

Kelly tossed in, "Don't forget about the after party, hotshot."

SUSAN RODGERS

Matt twisted his head and glared at Kelly and then Michael. "There will be no after party. All of you have an early start in the morning, and we don't need any unplanned PR hitting social media overnight."

"Party pooper." She winked at Michael, who shook his head and stifled barely contained laughter. "Your brother's an old fogie."

Matt turned back to Jacob and Jessie. "Look. I'll see that the two of you have a few private moments with Tom Ryan. But Jacob, this man's an old school entertainer. You should prepare yourself. It's no secret he likes his weed and his booze."

"Just not his kid."

"Jacob, easy." Inadvertently, Jessie laid a hand on Jacob's thigh again. Matt's eyebrows raised and he caught her eye and slowly shook his head.

"Oops."

Frustrated at the turn of events and the still difficult emotional situation he found himself in where Jessie was concerned, Jacob grasped Jessie's hand and set it on her own leg, and then rose, pushed past Matt and stormed off down the short hallway to the small washroom.

Jessie exhaled slowly and turned her head to stare out at the inky night sky.

Tired and wound up tight as a ball with the unexpected concert security Dee asked him to arrange at the last minute, Matt dropped into Jacob's vacated seat.

"I'm real sorry about this, Matt," Jessie told him. "We've been talking about Jacob meeting his dad. I thought it would be simple—you, me and Jacob. I didn't expect her highness to overhear and want to tag along."

"It's done now, Jessie. We'll manage. But no more stunts like this, okay? I'm getting too old. It's hard on this old guy's nerves." He thumped his heart with a closed fist.

"At the very least, it must be nice to have your brother around. He's a musical legend too, I hear."

Matt glanced over at Michael, and allowed a small smile to form on his lips. His brother was engaged in serious conversation with Kelly, and both seemed happier than Matt had seen either of them all day. He looked sideways at Jessie. "Yes, it is. But to be honest, I'm nervous about how that's all going to go down, too. Kelly has a less than stellar reputation, and Michael's been out of the music industry for years."

"Why did he leave?" Jessie spoke quietly so Michael wouldn't hear.

Matt's eyes darkened. "A bad tour. He walked away."

"I heard his wife and daughter were killed. Is that true, Matt?"

"Like I said, a bad tour. One that ended before it started, Jessie. An accident. That's all." He tapped a few knuckles on the armrest between them. "Now. None of this leading Jacob on, okay? I know you're just being nice, but us guys can only have our hearts broken a little at a time."

"Matt, I'm not so sure that me taking this job was such a good idea."

"You still have feelings for him."

"It's not that. I mean, I do, of course I do, but not in the way you think. I love Jacob lots, and I always will, but Josh is…well…Josh is everything to me. You know that, Matt."

He smiled. There was no greater pleasure than seeing Jessie's eyes light up from within when she spoke about Josh. "I know."

"It's just that…well, maybe I should have given Jacob a little more space to get used to the idea that I married Josh. And to be fair, Josh isn't thrilled about this either."

"For now, let's just get this concert over with." Matt moved to go, as Jacob had closed the bathroom door and was heading back towards them. "See how the next few days go, and figure it out from there. I'm sure once you get into a routine, the shoot will fly by pretty quick." He got up and Jacob slid back into his seat, a sulk on his pretty boy face.

Matt had a final order to add. "I mean it, Jessie. No funny business tonight. You and Jacob do exactly as I've outlined. If you have to pee, I'm going with you."

"Okay," she said quietly. She could almost read Matt's mind and, in truth, she appreciated his attention to detail tonight. The last thing she needed was for some rogue video of her and Jacob together to make its way onto YouTube. She hadn't told Josh about accosting Dee for the jet and securing passes to see Tom Ryan. The way she saw it, he didn't need to know she was helping Jacob bridge the gap to see his dad. But there was something else in Matt's expressive eyes, something hurt and wary. It hit Jessie like a lightning bolt.

It was the fact they were going to Atlanta. The southern city was not quite five hours' drive northwest of Charleston, South Carolina—the home of Deuce McCall. Was there still any danger from McCall? No. Jacob himself had pulled the trigger on that ordeal. But his family was surely still around, and they didn't need to know Jessie and Jacob were anywhere in the vicinity. She nodded at him, and swallowed past the gritty lump forming in her throat.

Then Jessie reached down and took Jacob's fingers in her own. They felt familiar, and instantly she sensed the movement comforted Jacob. She didn't look back up at Matt. He wouldn't approve. But sometimes there were things that just needed doing, and this was one. Tonight, Josh was fine, but Jacob needed her. And having a ring on Jessie's finger would never—could never—entirely displace her feelings for Jacob Ryan.

Chapter Nine

"Nuh. You stand the same way. That thing you do with your shoulders."

Chins resting on their hands, elbows pointed sideways on the ledge in front of them, Jessie and Jacob pondered the man on stage a hundred feet away. Bathed in blue light for this song, a folk ballad, the man they'd come to see was mesmerizing to watch, regardless of his personal connection with Jacob. His voice as he sang was dusky and sincere, and he moved one knee in time to the music. The backup band consisted of the same guys he'd played with for years, testament to enduring connections he'd been able to keep, unlike the one with his son.

Tilting his head and squinting so he could see better, Jacob disagreed with Jessie's proclamation. "Nah. I don't think so. I don't look like that."

Secretly, Jacob was proud. *That's my dad up there...a legend.* He was determined to succeed in the same way, if only to spite his father's blatant ignorance of him over the years.

Jessie smiled. She fixed her eyes on Jacob, to her right, and watched him as the mellow music overtook the two of them. In the dim lighting his cheeks were sculpted, all shadows and crags. His eyes, apprehensive when Tom Ryan took the stage, were aglow now, wide and hopeful, as if he were once again the little boy who waited day after day by a picture window dreaming his dad would, by some miracle, drive up and take him to hockey practice.

A few rows behind them sat Matt, unforgiving and tense. Michael, who was leaning against a stand-up bar with Kelly, left her side with a gentle touch of a finger on her wrist, and eased into the seat beside his brother.

"Chill out, Matt. The only people getting in are the servers. She's safe."

He gestured to the only door to their private space, ten feet away above and behind them.

Matt swiveled around a little and nodded at the man assigned to secure the door. His eyes picked up Kelly as well. She was flirting openly with a twenty-something waiter who likely won some kind of draw in order to get to bring snacks and drinks to this exclusive crowd.

To Michael he said simply, "Local security. The guy's got less training than a puppy at doggy school."

"Appears that's enough for some people."

Shooting him a look of disdain, Matt said, "Martinique was desperate. And Kelly needs a babysitter more than anything."

"And Jessie?"

"Don't go there, Michael."

"What, you don't want to get into a pissing match over which princess deserves trained ex-RCMP for security?" He was only half joking.

"You know what I mean."

"Yeah, I sure as hell do. Jessie's the real deal, while Kelly's just a hack who pops out meaningless shit." The image of Kelly at the grand piano playing the delicate haunting Schubert piece slid in full glorious technicolor across his mind. "You think she's fly-by-night. A cookie cutter star."

"No, Michael, I would never lay judgment on Kelly. And I'm not saying my gig with the Keatings isn't a babysitting job half the time either. But at this juncture, Kelly Reilly has proven herself to be a party princess who spends most of her time getting carried out of bars. Your biggest challenge with her is keeping eyeballs on her and knowing when to pull the plug." He glanced at his brother and pointed two fingers towards his own eyes to illustrate the eyeball point.

Michael's response was dry. "And your biggest challenge with Jessie is apparently going to be keeping her from fucking her ex. Didn't know you were her moral police as well, bro." He plunked his feet up on the chair in front of him and watched Jessie lean in to Jacob and whisper something that had both her and Jacob laughing heartily.

"I'm not even remotely worried about that," Matt answered stoically, although he chewed the side of his lip thoughtfully as he watched the two ex-lovers in front of them. "Jessie gave up a lot for Josh. There's no way she'll mess that up. She and Jacob have established boundaries."

"Yeah, I can tell," Michael responded sarcastically as a second server came by with a plate of nachos. "Sneaking around to concerts behind your new husband's back with your ex somehow got left off that list. Have Jessie and Josh even been married a month yet?"

Matt didn't even bother to disguise his frown. "It's not my business. But I trust her. She'll be fine."

"Didn't think it was your job to trust her." Michael stood, balancing the nachos in one hand and stepping past Matt. "Just to babysit her."

"Great to have you around, Michael." After that caustic comment Matt reached up and grabbed a cheesy tortilla chip. A pile of nachos came off the plate with it, so he put his second hand underneath the first to catch any stragglers that might otherwise drop to the floor. He bit down on one and crunched thoughtfully, watching Jessie and Jacob laughing openly and sharing apparently secret jokes.

"I was thinking the same thing," Michael replied, his lips curving up just slightly as he placed his free hand on his brother's shoulder. Matt looked up and let his eyes linger on his brother for a moment. A slight quiver of energy passed between them, and he finally relaxed enough to allow a small grin to broaden his lips. He nodded, just enough to let Michael know he truly was glad his brother was around. On the planet. Period.

Michael stepped to the stand-up bar and set his plate of nachos down in front of Kelly, who was still flirting with the staff. At her bodyguard's approach, the server hightailed it outta there.

"Party pooper," she teased Michael. "You made him go away. Didya see that pirate tat on his bicep? Sexy! Go get him back for me!"

"Pick up your own men, Kelly," Michael chuckled. "I'll sit here and cheer you on."

She giggled, and their cheerful banter surprised Matt, who knew firsthand the horror stories that followed Kelly Reilly around the superstar circuit. He turned to watch them—their foreheads were almost touching, and they seemed so engrossed in each other that he would be surprised if they would later be able to recite any of the tunes on Tom Ryan's playlist. Yet…Matt was somewhat relieved the two were hitting it off. Michael had been living in his own self-imposed dungeon for so long, and apparently had shut music out entirely. So this was good. Very good. At least…it was a good place to start.

In front of Matt was a similar vision. Jessie, who for so long lived in her own isolated, lonely world, was also happy, finally, and giving off a beautiful light Matt knew was a result of her renewed relationship with Josh. Yet here she was with Jacob…

Matt shook the thought away and settled lower into his seat. On the stage, Tom Ryan was just launching into a fan favorite. It was a love song that left Matt feeling crushed and lonely—for his pretty wife, his busy daughter Katy, and for the pain so many people seemed to suffer from in this crazy thing called life.

Halfway through the song he saw a flash of light above him—the door to their space was opened and closed. Out of professional habit he glanced around, heart racing. But it was just the first server, back to flirt some more with Kelly. Matt raised a hand and the youngster strode over.

"What can I get for you, sir?"

"Budweiser, please." This would be his second, but Matt knew it was a two-hour show. Coupla beer couldn't hurt. He added, "Thanks," as the guy nodded and went off to fill the order.

He sank back in his seat and leaned on his chin, one elbow on the armrest. A huge yawn brought moisture to his eyes, and he swiped at it. He closed his eyes, and let the music carry him away.

～⌣〜

Matt awoke with a start as a thunderous ovation rocked the arena.

"What?!" He sat up in time to see Jessie leap to her feet, then clap and even jump up and down a few times. Jacob was slower to rise, but his cheeks were glowing, Matt noticed, as Jacob leaned in and turned his head sideways to holler something in Jessie's ear. Matt let his shoulders down. *Phew. Thank God that doesn't happen often, dropping off to sleep like that.* He'd been up early to deal with a family issue—he and Julie were selling their home, and there were legalities to deal with that he didn't have time to settle during the day. Anyways, he sure as hell hadn't expected to have a late night tonight. Besides, they were fine. Jessie was fine.

When Matt stood to go, he started to stretch catlike but stopped halfway. Kelly and Michael were nowhere in sight. *What the hell?* He looked questioningly at the local security dude at the door, and then at the number of beer bottles and glasses on the stand-up bar.

Jessie moved up behind him. "Michael said they were just going to get a head start on the after party."

"What? I told them, *no* after party! I thought I made that pretty damn clear, actually!" Matt wiped an anxious hand through his spiked hair, which made Jessie smile.

"I always thought you were cute when you were angry, Matt." She reached out and teased a few spikes back the way they were supposed to be, but he swatted her hand away.

"Jesus, do any of you people care what I think?"

A wistful blush bloomed across Jessie's cheeks. She hooked an arm in Matt's. "Trust your brother, Matt. If he's anything like you, then her highness is in good hands."

"Humph."

Jessie's eyes followed Matt's to encompass the litter of beer bottles lined up on the stand-up bar. "Huh. Okay," she said. "I take that back. Well, let's get Jacob and I down to see Tom and then you can go on a search for Party Girl."

Matt was already texting Michael. If the nerve in his forehead hadn't been twitching so hard, Jessie would have leaned forward to see what he was typing, which she figured was likely a few not so thinly disguised threats, but as it was, she just sucked in a breath and twisted around to holler at Jacob to hurry.

But she paused when she saw her musical partner silhouetted against the emptying arena. The lights were on in the arena now, but not in their little private box, so a thin line of yellow light outlined Jacob as he stood, hands in his pockets, sleeves of his ubiquitous checked shirt falling over his hands, curly hair more managed than when they'd first met, but curls still tickling his neck.

There was something different about him now—he was holding his head high, as if by being at his father's concert he somehow found roots that connected his soul to his own music and songwriting. His stance was proud, sure, and he seemed to be lost in something Jessie couldn't see but that she could guess at. She knew it had to do with the music and how it wound from his father's soul on stage to somehow encompass Jacob himself. And she felt a wrenching pain grab her gut when she realized that no matter what happened when they went downstairs to meet Tom Ryan, Jacob had a dad who played music, and that man was still here, on this planet.

Matt was about to raise his voice to Jessie to demand they leave, but he stopped himself when he turned and saw the happy light in her eyes flicker and sway. He breathed slowly and watched as she fixed her gaze first on the stage, and then to Jacob, who was as frozen as a cat who spotted its prey and knew that in order to grab it he would have to remain still so as not to startle it. Matt had been in the Keatings' employ for a number of years now—he knew Jessie as well as anyone, he often prided himself. Regarding her now, he saw a woman who had pushed her own pain away to help a friend, as misguided as that may have seemed to both he and Deirdre, and even Jacob at the time. Now, he understood exactly what Jessie was seeing, and he guessed rightly at what she was feeling. Her father was absent. His music was gone. Yet Jacob had a chance to make age-old reparations with a father who was still here.

Cursing at Kelly and Michael under his breath, Matt sucked in his gut and took a deep breath. "C'mon kiddo," he said to Jessie, not unkindly. "Let's give Jacob a minute and go see whether this dude is on the ball enough to be able to lead us to Tom Ryan's dressing room."

He wrapped an arm loosely around her shoulders, and she sniffed and followed suit, placing an arm around his waist. "I did the right thing, Matt, bringing him here. I know I did."

"Yeah, kid, you did," said Matt quietly. "Let's just hope the old man doesn't burst the bubble Jacob's in right now."

"I'm not sure he can, at this point," Jessie replied. "Actually," she corrected herself, "even if he tries, I won't let him. I'll talk Jacob through this."

"Will you?" Matt searched her pale eyes, resolving to get them all on the jet as soon as possible. Jessie was fighting a yawn now, too, and her face was pinched and drawn, despite the success of the evening and the musical high she was riding.

"Why is everyone so worried? Yes, I'll watch out for Jacob. And maybe even find him a nice young gal to play with while I'm at it so everyone can stop pointing fingers at me. Yeesh!"

Soon they woke Jacob from his reverie and headed down to the dressing rooms. A few curious stares almost resulted in stops, but Matt swept his charges along efficiently, and wouldn't allow for any autograph signing or photos.

"Keep your heads down," he growled more than once. Silently he was impressed with the local security. He had asked the men and women assigned to their little group to be sure to 'pleasantly encourage folks to put their phones down' if anyone they passed seemed to be attempting to take pictures of the celebrities in their midst. So far the locals were doing a great job and, as Matt's eyes continuously scanned those around them, he saw no reason to panic over the potential release of videos on YouTube.

Outside the musical legend's dressing room, Matt stopped short. Tom Ryan himself was leaning against the wall by the door, a brew of some type or other in his hand, with Matt's own brother Michael engaged in conversation with him. Kelly was there, too, tottering on gold heels, one arm hooked in Michael's.

He glanced at Jessie, and she shrugged and grinned. Then she followed Kelly's lead and gingerly hooked an arm through Jacob's. He was trembling, and Jessie gave him a sideways look and frowned.

"You can do this, Jacob."

But Jacob was rendered mute at the sight of his dad sedately lounging against a wall less then twenty feet away; the dad at whose concert he, Jacob, had just been completely blown away. He felt like he was standing on the edge of something mysterious and unknown, but instinctively he knew it was powerful and deep.

They approached quietly, the entourage of yellow-jacketed security physically falling away, but their curious stares remaining.

Tom straightened when he saw his son. A brief recollection flashed across his face, but was immediately replaced with fear. He swallowed, forcing the fear to wash away. He could do that at will, aided by years of avoiding reality where his son was concerned. Neglect and inattention? *Pshaw*. He did what he always did when the boy invaded his brain. He hid him; he callously pushed the kid aside, along with any crumbling need for a child left behind years ago. Yet—there were things to consider. The hair, the curls, the shoulders, the stance...the woman so long ago who was this boy's mother, once upon a time.

He took the high road, but he chose a distant one; this road was a thousand miles away with a great stone wall in between. His careful stance took in Jessie Wheeler, with whom he'd once shared the stage, and then the soulful eyes flitted down to her hold on his son. His forehead knitted together in curiosity.

Then the legend that, at the moment was embroiled in a sentimental discussion with an old friend, a man also considered a musical legend, thrust out a hand and took Jessie's.

"Yes, Mizz Wheeler, always a pleasure." His throaty voice cracked as he spoke; it was a rare old dreamy recognizable soft burr. It was the man's recordings, coming to life in front of them.

Jessie smiled broadly, hopefully, eyes shining, and accepted his handshake. "Tom. Great to see you." Silently she prayed he would invite them into his dressing room.

Behind her, Matt was eyeing Kelly, who was teetering on her heels and signaling to Michael who, Matt noticed, seemed quite sober despite the upstairs evidence of his evening's copious libation. Kelly was clear in her intentions, mouthing the words *after party*. Finally, Michael heeded her, and he flicked Matt's arm as he walked past him, and pointed down the hall. Matt rolled his eyes and stepped back. At least the party was close by. He could watch both rooms—both musical princesses—at once.

Jessie was introducing Jacob to his father, but Tom's eyes were roving, distracted. He couldn't seem to focus on Jacob. Jessie tried harder.

"Tom, hey, Jacob and I write a lot of music together. He's got your touch on the guitar." She peered closely at Tom. *Is he high?*

A harried, excited journalist rushed over, her high boots clicking an uptempo tune on the floor. "Jessie, do you think I could have a word in a minute? When you're done here?"

Matt was on the woman instantly—long enough to give Kelly time to accept a ride to a club in town with a member of the back-up band. Michael nodded, glanced back at his brother, and ducked away with her. As he strode away with his pretty blonde charge, he pulled out his phone to text Matt.

Jessie knew the journalist. She smiled warmly and said, "Yes, in fact I'd love to. Just give me a moment, please." Inside, she was seething. *Damn, guess I will be telling Josh about my night after all.* And *Damn this man. Does he not see his kid in front of him?*

By now, Tom was calling the journalist back over and ignoring Jacob entirely. The awkward moment had Jacob staring at his feet, confused. All those years of wishing and wondering...hoping...

Studying him, Jessie's heart was sinking downwards alongside Jacob's solemn gaze. She tried again. "Tom, you ought to come check out a show. We'll be doing one in the spring, with the cast of our new show, *Mystic Nights.* Did you know Jacob got a lead on it? It's kind of a big deal."

Her words faded into the ether as Tom nodded absently and muttered, "Great, that's great," without acknowledging Jacob at all.

The great Tom Ryan then sauntered into his dressing room, turned and nodded once at Jacob, and remarked, "Too bad about your mother's death, kid. Can't imagine the grandparents were a picnic. Damn sorry about that."

And with a wave and a final, "Thanks for dropping by, hope you enjoyed the show," he closed the door.

Chapter Ten

Astounded, Jacob stood motionless until Jessie grabbed his arm and led him away. She waved a hand at the journalist and called, " Another time Amy, okay? Sorry."

But she didn't have time to deal with Jacob's myriad of confused emotions then, for it only took Matt a moment to realize his brother and Kelly were gone.

He flagged the security sentry that guarded their private door for the last two hours. "What's your name again? Cecil? Get these two into a private room and lock them in. Now please. And thank you."

"Sweet Matt," Jessie murmured calmly to Jacob. "Always remembers his manners." Inside, her belly was roiling. Looked like not much about this night would be a success, after all, and tomorrow they would feel the fall-out—fatigue and disappointment, not to mention the raking over the coals she would likely be getting from Josh. She was even feeling guilty over the carbon footprint from this extra use of the jet.

A deer caught in the headlights, Cecil, wordless, only took a moment before figuring out where to take Jessie and Jacob, while Matt disappeared around the corner, yanking his phone out of his pocket and reading as he moved.

Once they were alone in a small, dim dressing room rank with the refuse of hockey players' malodorous sweaty gear, Jessie collapsed on a low wooden bench next to her friend. "Geez, if I'm going to have to work in rooms this smelly, I might have to back off that hockey film I signed on to in P.E.I."

Jacob didn't bite. He sat silent, stoic, staring at the rubber mat on the floor designed to cushion sharp skate blades but not so effective at mitigating the bitter stink of rejection.

"Come on, Jacob," Jessie tried, her voice weaker than she wanted it to sound, "he was okay. Just scared, I think. Really. We caught him off guard."

"Hmmm, if by okay you mean he was an asshole, you're right, Jessie." Jacob stood and paced across the small room, then leaned on one outstretched arm against the pockmarked yellow cement wall. "Doesn't matter anyway. I got the best part of him. The music part."

Tenderly, Jessie steered him around a different corner. "What was your mom like, Jacob? Was she musical?"

"Nah. I think she was just a fan, that's all. A groupie."

A thought crossed Jessie's mind. She wrinkled her brow as she pondered how to ask it. "But...your name is Ryan. They were married, or did you just take his name?"

"They were married. My grandparents refused to talk about them so I have no idea how they hooked up. Just that they did, for a bit. Must have sucked cause I don't think he married again after they split up. Then of course...well, she died when I was small so unless I go to a séance, it looks like I'll never get any solid answers."

Jessie eased herself up from the low bench and crossed the room. She touched Jacob's arm lightly, then gained confidence and grasped his elbow firmly, turning him around to face her. "Babe, I realized something when I was watching you tonight."

"About time you came to your senses." His tiny attempt at a smile lightened Jessie's own sorrow at the failure to launch any kind of relationship between Jacob and his dad.

"Dork," she grinned. "No. I'm never leaving him. Stop asking." She swatted his arm. "No, Jacob, it's just that...I know this isn't what you want to hear right now, but the thing is...you've got so much of your dad, you know? His music? You can go to iTunes and download his songs...and you can listen to the melodies he wrote, and study the lyrics and...and...try to figure out what made him tick, y'know? And..." she tried to swallow but somehow a mist covered her eyes and sticks got all crackly in her throat.

Jacob softened and finished her sentence for her. "And you can't."

Slowly, Jessie shook her head from side to side. "Nope." The word was cottony soft. It was finite. She tilted her head to the side and peeked up at Jacob from underneath dewey eyelashes. "I can't. All I have is the memories. That's all. Sometimes…sometimes I can't even dredge up his voice anymore, y'know?"

"I know." Pulling her close, Jacob closed his eyes. "I'm sorry, Jessie. I know I'm being a dick. I'm a selfish bastard."

"Nah. You're not. I am, bringing you here, unannounced like this. Catching both of you unprepared." She leaned back out of his embrace, just far enough so she could peer into the never-ending deep cobalt of Jacob's eyes. "I wanted to be your savior, you know? To do something good for you after…well, after I…"

He groaned loudly. "Bringing up your cowboy again, are you? Why don't you just drive the stake in all the way so we can just get this over with."

Opening her mouth to protest, Jessie caught sight of a slight twinkle in Jacob's eyes and she broke out into a fit of laughter. "Enough! I feel bad enough."

"So, speaking of voices," Jacob said, referencing their earlier meeting with his dad, "I did think he had a pretty cool tone going on there. Kinda low and husky."

"Yeah, but classic, eh? Like you knew when you were talking to him that you've heard his voice a gazillion times on the radio. It was kind of surreal." She poked Jacob in the ribs as they sat down on the wooden bench again to wait for Matt. "Hey. D'you think people think that when they meet us in person?"

"That our voices are weird?" Jacob chuckled.

"Ha! No. You know, the whole 'surreal' thing."

Jacob stared at Jessie in awe and wonder. Sometimes it seemed she didn't 'get' her fame at all. He sighed, and wrapped an arm around her shoulders. "You continuously amaze and frighten me," he murmured quietly.

The door flew open then, and Matt rushed in, his stylin' leather blazer flinging from side to side at the hips. "Let's go," he growled. "I found them. They're supposedly being driven to the jet as we speak." He wheeled around and held the door open for Jacob and Jessie. "I'll believe it when I see it,"

106

he added, in a voice Jessie knew meant business as she sidestepped around him.

But she couldn't resist one last poke to try to lighten the darkened mood of their earlier joyous adventure.

She reached out and patted down a few of the tufty small spikes in his hair. "Sweet Matt," she whispered adoringly, gazing into his frustrated eyes. "Even your hair's on edge. It's standin' straight up."

Her childlike giggles had always been hard to resist. Matt let the door *shuffftt* behind them and, as he followed his famous charges down the tunnel towards the exit, where the waiting Lincoln would swift them to the airport, he was surprised to find himself outright laughing.

Behind the three of them, a ways down the hallway, Tom Ryan was outside his dressing room again, this time engaged in a serious interview with Amy, the persistent journalist. He got stuck though, in the middle of a sentence, when he spotted the son he did not know heading towards the exit. His shoulders sagged, and Tom took a deep pull on his beer.

"What was that again?" he asked the woman, his gaze still locked on Jacob's back.

She said, "Can you tell us what you think of your son's songwriting?"

"Uhhh…" Down the hall, Jacob disappeared from sight. Tom paused and, around him, time froze. He stared down at his toes, the way his son had done earlier. He shifted his feet. The floor looked weird, unnatural, and for a moment he didn't know where he was, or when. The woman's southern twang jarred him back to the present.

"Your son's songwriting? How do you think it compares to your own? Do you think Jacob Ryan has a shot at a success as enduring as yours?"

Once he was focused on the question, it only took Tom Ryan a moment to answer. "Hell, yeah," he said. "And don't bother asking me why. The answer should be obvious. He's my son."

The real telling was, of course, in the music.

He nodded a thank-you and saluted the journalist, effectively ending the interview, and trundled around to plod back into his dressing room. In the room down the hall, the after party was roaring fun for those inside the hallowed walls, but Tom wanted some privacy.

He closed the door and shut the world out, and then he flipped open the cover on his iPad. He slid his hand over the screen until he found iTunes, and he selected *Favorites* and chose *Jacob Ryan*.

Then he got up, flipped off the lights, made his way back to his chair, positioned his feet up on the counter, and sat back and listened.

He hummed along, and sometimes the humming erupted into a word here and there. It was easy. Tom Ryan knew the lyrics, and he knew the melody of this, Jacob's first big hit single.

He was, after all, Jacob Ryan's dad.

~ ~

"Hey. It was Kelly that got carried to the jet on Michael's shoulder. Jacob and I only had a coupla beer each."

"Great." In Vancouver, Josh sighed. He rubbed his temple with his thumb and forefinger. He had pulled over to the side of the road when the phone rang. The truck was parked a little crooked, but he didn't want to miss the call. The YouTube video featuring Kelly Reilly being carried to the jet from the limo—taken by a fan who followed the limo to the airport, hoping for a glimpse of the stars within—also managed to capture Jessie and Jacob hurrying up the stairs into the jet as well. Considering he and Jessie had talked likely less than an hour before she would have had to fly out to Atlanta, well… Josh was less than impressed.

Frustrated, Jessie tried to make up for what she now knew was poor decision-making. "Look Josh, I know it was wrong not to tell you, and I pinkie swear I won't do it again, but let's face it. You were in a shitty mood yesterday and I just didn't see the need to piss you off further."

"At the time, you mean."

"Yeah, well, delaying your reaction sometimes does have its benefits."

"Listen, Jess, I don't want to argue with you. Remember who you're talking to here—a guy who gets the whole complicated dad thing. On some level I think it's sweet that you took Jacob to see his dad's show. Kinda sounds like a Jessie thing to do, actually. And you and I both know there's not a damn thing we can do about how the media or social media for that matter wants to interpret you and Jacob together for a night on the town. So let's just let it go, okay?"

Surprised and somewhat taken aback at his terse but apparently tolerant tone, Jessie responded with a hesitant, "Okay?" She recognized the fatigue in Josh's voice but figured it had nothing to do with a lack of sleep and instead was more because he sometimes found her exhausting. At that thought, she couldn't keep a tiny ping of sadness from bouncing around in her heart.

Josh cut into her thoughts. "What's golden boy up to now? How's he adjusting to acting?"

"He's getting there. He's with his new acting coach now. We had some publicity stills to do this morning but our set call isn't for another hour— we're night shooting tonight, groan, lovely way to start acting again, huh?" She continued, " I think Jacob would be fine if he could get past his fear of Kelly Reilly. Strangely enough, the only person she doesn't intimidate seems to be Michael. He just tells it like it is and she responds to that."

"Or he's a white knight, carrying her over his shoulder up the steps of an airplane."

"I guess any guy who has to resort to that deserves a little respect."

"Matt's a pretty cool and collected guy too. Maybe it runs in the family."

Jessie snuffed at that comment. "Ha. Matt was rather incensed last night. It wasn't one of his better nights overall."

"Do you blame him?"

"'Course not. But regardless of how cool and collected he and Michael are, I still can't put my finger on why Michael and Kelly are clicking so well. It's not like they knew each other before he got hired."

"Maybe it's just you singers. You connect on some deeper level." Josh eyed the time on the dashboard of the King Ranch. He would have to end this conversation soon in order to meet Caryn.

"I dunno. Something like that, maybe." She avoided the sarcasm edging Josh's voice. She knew he was trying here, as far as Jacob was concerned, and he sure as hell deserved to get angry with her for her little escapade last night.

"Hey Jessie, I've got to run. I've got some errands to do downtown and I want to get back home at a reasonable hour so I can give Hilary a call. We need to figure out what direction I should be going in, where to go from *Freedom Ride*."

"You know, Toronto's pretty close to Peterborough, I hear."

"What am I gonna do with you?"

"I can think of lots of things, big boy. Evelyn's trying to set up a trip for January so I can meet my long lost relatives. Time Toronto with us, if you can. I'm sure they'll want to meet you too."

Josh's heavy sigh managed to deflate Jessie's spirits a little further. These long distance phone calls plainly and simply sucked. She needed to see his eyes to know how he was truly feeling about, well, everything. She sucked in a breath and let it out in a slow whistle. Then she threw a curve she thought he'd like.

"While you're at it, sort out Christmas plans with Hil and Zach, okay? See if they'll come up Vancouver way so we can do the Keating Boxing Day extravaganza. The more the merrier!"

From Vancouver came a lengthy pause and then a slow, "Yeah. You bet, Jessie."

It seemed like that last desperately lonely Christmas was eons ago. Sitting at the Keatings' gorgeous Rosewood dining table, Michelle by his side, and then Jessie's voice coming out of the blue singing a song that was, essentially, a message to him…well, this Christmas would be special. Midnight Mass, friends and family…Steve and Sophie's wedding over the holidays…and in January, Charlie and Jane's baby would be making its arrival…there was a lot to look forward to. As long as…if…

He had to get those files from Caryn.

"I gotta run, little one."

In Miami, Jessie went all tingly. Over the phone, Josh could hear her smile.

"I'll see you soon, Josh. Five more days. Then a break for Christmas."

"Okay, Jessie. And take it easy on golden boy tonight. None of those little tricks you like to use on inexperienced male actors, okay?"

"Well, someone has to take the lead sometimes."

"Ah, if the general public knew what you really got those Oscars for."

Her laughter was a balm for the soul, and Josh soaked it in, because he would need it when he landed at Caryn's condo in half an hour.

"Bye, Jess."

"Bye, Josh. Luv you."

"Luv you back, little one."

He sat on the side of the highway, the phone in his hand, and summoned up the courage to put the big truck in *drive*. In the end, Jessie's reminder of the upcoming Christmas holiday was enough to spark some action on Josh's part. He wanted happiness and goodness here on in for them as a couple, Christmases included. No more pain, no more lonely nights, and no more sadness.

Despite an earlier call from Deirdre warning him about Jessie's little Atlanta adventure, and the fact he'd see and hear about it on social media, Josh had mostly avoided the Internet, with the exception of his morbid curiosity leading him to check out the YouTube video. He had long since figured out his and Jessie's lives were their own, and that in order to keep some semblance of privacy and normalcy, they'd have to ignore the sensationalistic interpretation outsiders would be taking of their comings and goings. In his heart his relationship with Jessie was secure. And—Jessie being Jessie—it made perfect sense that she would be flying Jacob to Atlanta to see his dad. Miami was a quick flight away. Jessie wanted everyone's world to be better, and Josh knew she was also well aware of just how badly Jacob was hurting because of her marriage.

Leave it to Jessie, he muttered, and finally started the engine and looked over his shoulder to merge back into traffic. He flicked on the radio. A Kelly Reilly tune filled the cab, and he cranked it up. Soon Josh was singing his way down Fourth in Kitsilano, and he caught himself chuckling as he thought he'd better not tell Jessie he was singing to one of her obstinate co-star's tunes. Ten minutes later, as he nosed up to the curb on East Hastings, he reminded himself that suddenly it seemed there were a few things he'd better not tell Jessie…ever.

Chapter Eleven

While Josh was screwing up the courage to exit his truck and make his way up to Caryn's condo, Jessie was diligently studying lines and character development for the night's shooting. Jacob was studiously working with his new acting coach. Matt and Deirdre were having a drink in the bar with Charles, who flew in that evening to spend some time with his wife and peek over the shoulders of his two stars.

On set, however, all hell was breaking loose.

"I will NOT play her like a petulant two year old! These lines are NOT working for me, and I refuse to be seen on national television wearing zebra striped pants!" Kelly threw her sides—the day's script excerpts—onto the floor, where they crumpled up in a heap.

"Somebody's having a PMS day," mumbled the production's wardrobe assistant.

"Somebody's got chronic PMS," muttered the wardrobe key in response.

They watched as Kelly stormed off set, yanking a green plastic Perrier bottle off the craft table as she passed. Her antics didn't faze the crew. Most were seasoned veterans in the TV and film biz, and they were accustomed to nervous actors dealing with their insecurities by throwing hissy fits. Slowly the crew gathered in small groups here and there and waited for a producer to come to set and sweet talk their star into working again.

Michael, as usual, was close by. He let Kelly stomp off and then he grabbed an Aero bar from craft and followed her at a distance, tearing off the wrapper as he walked. He set up camp outside her dressing room, stuffed bits of the chocolate in his mouth, and waited.

It didn't take long. The frazzled producer knocked but made no headway. When Kelly was sure he was gone, she opened the door just a bit and made eye contact with her handler. "Can you come in?"

Michael used his foot to give his body a shove away from the wall. He teetered slowly over to Kelly's door and wandered in. She held the door behind him, peeked once into the hallway at the execs huddled at the far end, and then she closed the door and turned to face Michael. He was watching her somberly as he popped the last bit of chocolate in his mouth.

"I got the bar for you but you were taking too long. So I ate it," he hedged, then added, amusement edging his voice, "the wardrobe girls think you have chronic PMS."

Dropping onto the large comfy couch on the north wall, Kelly groaned. "I don't have PMS. That was last week. Wardrobe on this show sucks." She plucked a handful of zebra skin spandex and stretched it away from her thigh. "They wouldn't go on television in these. Why should I?"

"I think you look kind of cute. The way those pants wrap around your butt wouldn't offend anybody watching you on TV," Michael winked, and Kelly threw a cushion at him, but she did allow a tiny smile for his benefit.

"I just get tired of this sometimes, you know?" She tucked her legs underneath her and leaned on the arm of the couch, grabbing the second cushion to hug as she spoke honestly to the one person she figured wouldn't judge her. "Everyone thinks acting is so damned glamorous, but then you're asked to do things out of your control. Like wear these stupid pants, or send your character in a direction you don't personally believe that person would go."

"You're a hired gun, Kelly." Michael spoke quietly, his attempt at unveiling the truth carefully unleashed so she wouldn't fly off the handle again.

"I know, I know that Michael, but that only adds to this sense of, I dunno, lack of control it seems has taken over my life these days. Like I'm on some damn roller coaster and I can't get off."

"That's show biz, kid," he said, tossing the cushion back over at her. "Why'd you get into it in the first place if it wasn't what you wanted?"

"Why'd you?" she fired back at him.

Wordlessly, he pondered her. Then, "That was a long time ago, Mizz Reilly. You may recall I left the performance side of the biz."

113

"Why?" She was persistent, but in a softly encouraging way. She knew why. Everyone knew why, at least the basic outline of *why*.

He shrugged, and melted a little in his seat, but held her gaze. "Nothing mattered anymore. That's why."

"Your wife and daughter." Her voice was a whisper, but the air in the small dressing room was sizzling. An unseen electric blue light crackled between them.

He blinked, cleared his throat, shifted in his seat, and nodded. "Yeah."

"They were killed."

He paused again, and studied her. "Yup."

"Do you want to talk about them?"

He always answered *no* when someone, usually a drunk in a bar, asked that question. But Michael's gruff response was uttered before he had time to process it. "Maybe. Someday. Not now. Okay?"

"Okay," Kelly smiled softly.

"How is it that everyone out there is afraid of you?" Michael asked in a low murmur, his eyes taking in the pretty girl with the gentle smile sitting with her legs in the striped pants tucked up underneath her.

"It's not me they're afraid of," Kelly replied, her expression expanding into a convivial smirk. "It's their own inadequacies. They don't know how to fix the problems."

"The on-set problems. Like the zebra pants." He grinned and pointed towards her black and white legs.

"Yeah. Those." Kelly smiled wholeheartedly now. "I'm here if you need me, Michael."

He took a second before responding. "Why?" he asked carefully, aching for a connection—a real connection—to another human being.

"My new bodyguard picks me up in an old rusty truck, I figure he needs me more than I need him."

"She ain't rusty." The words came out gravelly, like an old abandoned road.

"Michael...your songs are still on the radio. Why are you driving a truck that leaves a trail of broken parts on the road behind it?"

Michael ducked his head. He spoke while staring at a used Q-tip on the floor that missed the garbage bin next to it when it was tossed. "I don't want the money from my music, Kelly. I give it away."

"Oh." She twisted her fingers in her lap and then brightened after a moment, as if the truths behind his statement were too much to face at the present time. "Speakin' of rusty," her eyes were dancing now, the on-set drama already behind Kelly since suddenly she had more perspective about the important things in life, "I wonder what Jessie Wheeler will be like to work with. It's been ages since she's done any acting."

He shrugged. "She's a pro. She'll be great."

"I hope she can knock some sense into Jacob."

"He's terrified of you! Lay off him and he will be fine too."

"I don't get why everyone's always walking on eggshells around me."

A knock startled the two, and Michael winked at Kelly. "Let's see how you handle this, and then we'll revisit the eggshell discussion, okay Kelly?"

"Loser," she decreed, and flung the cushion at him again. Michael laughed, and got up to open the door.

Later that night, after having taped the scene wearing the zebra striped pants, and after doing her first scene with Jessie which, by all accounts, was spectacular, Kelly breezed out the door of the hotel with a few of the *Mystic Nights* crew. She'd smiled kindly at Jacob when he arrived on set to do his first scene with Jessie. They'd passed each other at the studio door after Kelly wrapped.

Watching him trudge his way up the hallway and into his dressing room, she had shaken her head and said to the grip next to her, "Like a sad puppy dog. Scared of its own tail."

Many hours later Jessie and Jacob were wrapped, too, after a magical night of shooting, and had just been driven back to the hotel for breakfast, when Kelly arrived after a night of heavy drinking. Michael had gone off shift and passed the torch to a local hired bodyguard who had, not surprisingly, long ago been ditched by the experienced singer. Matt, too, was off shift but it was apparent to Jacob and Jessie that Kelly was in need of some assistance. She was, as usual, in a short mini with four-inch heels, and she kept dropping her tiny gold purse as she slipped her way across the lobby.

Jessie was the first to reach her. She called back to Jacob, " Give Matt a call, will you? He'll know how to reach Michael."

"It's 6 a.m.," Jacob yawned.

"He'll be up. He gets up at 5:30. In fact, he's likely already at the gym." She bent and grabbed Kelly's small handbag from the floor.

"Oops," Kelly slurred, reaching out for it. "Dropped my bag." She stood tottering and stared at Jessie. "You must think I'm a real old bitch, eh Jessie? Jessie-the-perfect-Wheeler? Everybody's saint?" Tears pricked the corners of Kelly's eyes. Nothing like a night of hard drinking and disconnection to fuel one's perceived failures.

"Oh, here we go," murmured Jacob as he punched Matt's name on the phone.

Jessie frowned and crossed her arms, facing Kelly. "Nobody's perfect, Kelly. Least of all me."

"Sure as hell ain't me, is it?" Kelly laughed sardonically.

Then, without warning, she lunged forward and shoved her co-star, hard. Jessie landed on her backside on the hard floor.

"Jesus," Jessie cried, rubbing her butt. "What the hell'd you do that for?"

"Just seein' if you would break," Kelly answered hotly. "I hear you have a lot of breaking points."

His mouth gaping open, Jacob spoke quickly into the phone. "Catfight, Matt. In the lobby. You might want to hurry."

Easing herself off the cold floor, Jessie winced. Kelly stood opposite her, poised and ready for a fight, but Jessie didn't budge. Instead she simply gazed at Kelly defiantly, sizing her up.

"So I know you want me to hate you, Kel, but you're shit out of luck. I don't know what your game is, although I am guessing it's the ensemble cast thing. You need more attention than you're getting, so you piss everyone off trying to get it. But you know something? You're not gonna get what you want from me. I don't play that princess game."

"Bullshit. You play all kinds of games." Kelly snickered at Jacob, who stood just behind Jessie, alternately eyeing the very drunk teetering blonde and the elevator.

"I came here to work, Kelly. Period."

"With him."

116

"Oh! Is that what this is about?" Jessie almost laughed. "You want Jacob?"

Kelly pressed a fingertip to the corner of her left eye. She managed to wipe away a tear without Jessie noticing, she hoped. "I'm not into your castaways," she snarled. "I don't like sloppy seconds."

"You bitch," Jessie growled, just on time for Matt to come hurling out of the elevator, shirtfront open and top button of his jeans undone.

"Ha! That was way too easy!" Kelly laughed fiercely and narrowed her eyes at Jacob. "Poor puppy," she said, putting her hands up in front of her to resemble paws. "Still Jessie's little toy, though, eh? Just far enough away from freezing Canada so her movie star husband won't know her dirty little secret."

Jessie lunged at Kelly then. "You leave him alone! You little bitch!"

Matt slid the last few feet across the floor to grab Jessie, and Jacob had no choice but to quickly pocket his phone and wrap his arms around Kelly's biceps and chest. Both girls were swinging and kicking, and Kelly's bag went skittering across the floor once again.

"What's the problem, Jessie, your boy toy not give you enough on set last night? You can't tell me you can just leave a guy after fucking him for months and somehow just be friends! I don't buy that. But I will say one thing. I'd take Josh Sawyer first, too. In fact, if you decide to take Jacob back full time, you just send Josh to me. Let me at him in the bedroom and he'll be crawling out on his hands and knees. *Puurrrr!*"

"You're not a nice person, Kelly." Jessie stopped struggling against Matt, who relaxed his grip a little. "Let me rephrase that. The alcohol's not nice. I'm going to give you the benefit of the doubt and acknowledge it's the drink talking. Because even you couldn't hurt someone intentionally as bad as you just hurt my friend."

She watched as Kelly's eyes fluttered open wider as she took this in. Her lips pursed together, Kelly gave up the fight too. Her arms were being held tight against her, so she couldn't wipe away the tears sliding down her cheeks. Glancing down, she saw by the plaid sleeves that the person she had just viciously attacked was the one hanging tightly on to her. She could feel his warm body against her, and it brought back memories of another man, one in a similar flannel shirt, one who smelled like brandy and aftershave. The sodden memory curled her belly into a vicious ball of fury and ache.

Everyone jumped when she screamed. "Let me go! Let me go, you hea-then! Let me the fuck go!" Her sudden movement, after Jacob had eased up on her, startled him and so he did let go. Kelly went slipping and slid-ing onto the floor, her heels and the alcohol conspiring against her. In the end she was on her hands and knees, groping for the fallen handbag, sob-bing uncontrollably.

Shaken, Jessie's feet were frozen to the floor. She forced her eyes up to Jacob's, which she knew from experience would be wounded and hurt-ing, the blue eyes she loved downcast underneath his long lashes. He let her sorrow envelop him just for a moment, because then the elevator door slid open and a sleepy Michael, beckoned earlier by Matt, rushed towards Kelly. He and Matt hoisted her off the floor and towards the open eleva-tor, and soon they were gone, a backward glance from Matt warning Jessie that she needed to hop in the next elevator and go upstairs to bed after her long night of shooting.

When Jacob's eyes flicked back from the closing elevator door to Jessie, they were unsettled, nervous and darting. He took a deep breath and stepped towards the bar.

"Jacob?" Jessie asked after him, an anxious warble coloring her usually even tone.

"I need a drink," he declared sullenly. "And none of this local watered down chocolate-honey shit. A frikkin' Irish Stout, that's what I need."

"For breakfast?" she hollered after him. "At bloody six a.m.?"

"Damn straight," she heard him answer, barely. "We just got off work, didn't we?"

Jessie rotated her head a bit to stare solemnly at the closed elevator doors. Then she followed Jacob into the bar.

"Well, as long as they serve Eggs Benny with their Stout. Count me in."

Once seated, she pulled Jacob's hand into her lap, but he yanked it away.

"She's got problems, Jacob. It's nothing to do with you. People don't drink the way she does for no reason."

He looked up at Jessie then, and shrugged. "Everybody's got problems, Jessie. Just seems like today everyone's problem is you."

The waiter, stifling a yawn and a bad bedhead, came to take their order then. But suddenly Jessie didn't feel like Eggs Benny anymore. She slid off the seat and, without a backwards glance at Jacob, left the bar.

~ ~

"Ouch! Easy, Michael!" The cry came out in a whine.

Kelly was sitting on the edge of her King-sized bed, gripping the side to keep herself from slipping off as the room spun. At her feet, Michael was nudging a heel off, but he couldn't get the thin strap to unfasten, and so he ripped it over her heel and down.

Whining women were not Michael's usual forte. He grimaced and tossed both shoes aside, then stood and faced his charge.

She peeked up at him, and touched her bun to see if it was still intact. Most of it wasn't, and her hair flew out in all directions as if she'd been the main volunteer at some science world's electromagnetic lecture.

"Now what?" she wailed. "Are you gonna quit too?"

"You want me to?" he asked as he signaled for her to stand so he could pull back the covers on the bed.

She obeyed, but Michael had to grab Kelly's elbow with one hand to steady her while he drew back the covers with the other.

"Noooo," she moaned, and flopped down on the bed. Michael pulled one delicate foot up and then under the sheets, and then did the same with the other. He gripped the top edge of the swanky duvet and hauled the whole kit 'n caboodle neatly up under Kelly's nose.

"I'm still dressed," she sniffled.

"Yeah, and you're staying that way as long as I'm in the room," he fired back.

"Come on, Michael. I need you."

"You need a good kick in the arse." But there was a glint in his eye when Michael spoke, so Kelly responded with a tiny smile.

He perched his butt on the edge of the bed and studied the young woman snuggled beside him. "That was pretty shitty. What you said to Jessie. Especially with Jacob there."

"I know. Sometimes I just…I just…" She palmed her forehead with one hand and held it there, avoiding his eyes.

"You give it so you don't have to take it." He finished the thought for her.

"You need to ease up on that Jacob kid, though. He looks heartsick enough without you rubbing his nose in it, Kelly."

"I know. I will. I'm sorry."

"It's not me you need to apologize to, Mizz Reilly."

"I think you should marry me. Keep me close by forever and we could develop some kind of hand signals that teach me when not to speak."

"You'd be Kelly Kelly. I don't think you'd like that much, Mizz Reilly."

"Ah, well I'll just keep my own name then."

He laughed and tucked her in the way his father used to tuck him in, with hard pokes of the fingers under her body so the covers adhered themselves tightly and created a sort of cocoon around her.

"Ohhh, that's nice," she smiled, eyes closing with pleasure and a deep need to sleep.

"I'm off then," Michael said. "To finish my own beauty sleep. Promise you'll stay put? Not provoke any more international singing stars into fist-fighting on the floor of Miami's best hotel?"

"I promise."

"Kelly?"

Her eyes drifted open just a little. "Yes, Michael?"

"I know what sets me off. But I don't know what it is that pisses you off so much."

"One day we'll swap our war stories, okay Michael?" She slipped a hand out from under the covers and grasped his fingers in hers. "But right now I just need to sleep."

"Promise?"

"Promise."

He grabbed the wastebasket from the corner of the room and nudged it next to the bed. "Kelly? I'm leaving a bucket for you just in case, okay? It's here by your head."

"Aaahhhh this sucks."

"Tell that to your future self, will you? I'm serious about losing my beauty sleep. Makes me a monster. Trust me."

From the bed she murmured something that sounded like *I'd like to,* but Michael couldn't be sure.

He exhaled slowly, then dropped into a wing chair and watched Kelly's chest move up and down until he was certain she was in a land of sweet slumber, and then Michael made his way to the door and eased it quietly open. He slipped outside into the hallway before closing the door gently behind him.

He started down the hall, and was surprised to run into Jessie at the other end of the hallway. She'd been crying, as evidenced by the dark mascara running down her cheeks. She was cursing, and fiddling with a card key that didn't seem to want to co-operate. Without asking, he took it from her and tried it on the door. They heard a small click, a green light flicked on, and when Jessie turned the handle, the door opened.

She looked up at Michael and whispered a soft, "Thank you."

Her pale, startling eyes caught him off guard, and he wondered how his brother had stayed sane over the last many tough years in the Keating employ, in charge of this sweet wild young superstar with the hurting soul. He knew that when he looked at Kelly, his own heart broke, and they were barely getting to know each other.

"We'll help her," he said to Jessie, surprising even himself with the admission. But Matt had told him enough about Jessie over the years for Michael to know she was a gentle soul who cared about others. Whoever the woman in the lobby screaming *bitch* was, he didn't know. But it sure as heck wasn't the Jessie he'd come to know through Matt.

A hint of a smile snuck through Jessie's tears, a rainbow in the storm. "I know," she said, referencing his comment about helping Kelly. "She reminds me of someone I once knew, anyway."

"Who was that, Jessie?" Michael started to walk away, but he turned to see if she would answer.

He got what he figured he would get. She cocked her head to the side and whispered "Me."

A slow grin bloomed across Michael's cheeks. He nodded and said, "Yeah. Me too." And then he walked away.

Inside, Jessie started hauling her clothes off before she had taken two steps. She left a trail of clothes from the door to the bed.

As she snuggled under the covers and sank into sleep, her last thought was *Ahhh. Now I know why those two get along so great—Michael and Kelly.*

121

It's the same as me and Josh. Hmmmm. I know why Michael is hurting, but I don't know shit about Kelly...

And, as she made it a point to find out, Jessie's last thought went to Jacob, and so it was his sad eyes filling her daytime dreams that morning after the night shoot, while in Vancouver, where it was three-thirty in the morning, Josh's dreams were haunted by Jessie's.

Chapter Twelve

The evening before, after the call with Jessie, Josh finally got up the nerve to leave his vehicle and walk the few short blocks up East Hastings to Caryn and Eric's place. To his surprise, their building was the nicest on the block, a tall well-kept tastefully restored high-rise surrounded mostly by darker, dirtier lower edifices. Characteristic of the twenties or thirties, its charm was a class above the more downtrodden surrounding it, as if it were Queen of the block while the other buildings and their dingy crumbling rooftops were its subjects.

The facade was pristine, like Caryn, seemingly untouched and virginal, whereas its Downtown Eastside surroundings remained—at least to the uninitiated—dull, lifeless and used. A well-tended tiny row of petunias and pansies prospered hopefully in a small flowerbed by the building's entrance; their buoyant upturned faces and leafy spines lifted Josh's spirits a little. He couldn't bear the thought of Jessie ever living any kind of derelict life, and he didn't want to picture her in the slums. Still, he didn't expect the kind of excess he found upstairs after Caryn buzzed him in.

Her condo was large, perhaps even two units modernized into one. On the top floor, the twentieth, the view from large windows was spectacular, and an expansive deck lined with repurposed iron filigree incongruously matched with modern tempered glass windscreens gave the occupants a stunning bird's eye view of Burrard Inlet and North Vancouver. A large open concept kitchen, dining room and living area were decorated with contemporary art sculptures and expensive designer furniture, mostly in white, like Caryn's office, with pops of girly pinks and purples here and there.

Near the windows, a few steps up led to more art in the form of sculptural railings surrounding a raised level on which sat the couples' King-sized bed. Low creamy leather cushioned benches and pristine glass shelves fit seamlessly in between low posts amongst the railings. On the shelves stood exquisite Inuit soapstone carvings—whales and polar bears and Northern folk in parkas. Some of the Eskimo people grasped spears held high at the ready, seemingly meant to either extinguish prey or perhaps to warn away uninvited guests. Sucking in his breath, Josh found it unnerving to see the couple's bed so visible, set up almost on a pedestal or a stage, so that it likely afforded its own solitary gorgeous view of the mountains across the Inlet during the day. Now, on this December evening, Josh was treated to a stunning vista of twinkling stars and dancing planets.

Caryn welcomed him with an air of false bravado, urging him with a nervous wave towards the living area in her and Eric's home. As he made his way to a modern Scandinavian white leather chair, Josh noticed Eric in the kitchen, fixing drinks with what appeared to be some expensive fancy blender. He nodded a silent greeting, and Eric did the same. Something about the man intimidated Josh, and he was starting to regret having accepted Caryn's invitation, when the coup de grace was delivered. As Josh's eyes drifted to the oversized contemporary art on the walls, his vision fixed itself on a five-foot high semi-nude image of a young woman who, he realized with a shock, was his wife.

The excessive photograph was simply framed in a light wood, perhaps birch, to match the corresponding modern furniture. It seemed the background had been removed with a program like Photoshop, as all that was apparent behind Jessie was a shadowy white expanse. She was sitting on a flat surface, left knee up and right knee angled out and crossed in front. She was wearing panties, for which Josh was relieved, but they were pale and faded into the background and against her light skin. Her left arm was loosely wrapped around her raised knee, and her right wrist rested on the left, almost enough to cover her bare breasts, but not quite. Jessie's hair was longer than Josh had ever seen it, the loose curls at the ends teasing her nipples, and the hair was uncombed, unkempt.

It wasn't so much the overall image itself that made Josh want to toss his sushi dinner; it was the childlike vulnerability in her eyes. What was most striking about this younger version of Jessie was the haunting depth of those sleepy sea-pearl eyes, the cherished eyes Josh longed to bury himself inside and stay lost in forever.

There was a slight downward twist to Jessie's sensual mouth, which was open just the tiniest bit. A hint of the pink tongue Josh loved to tease and kiss peeked out. But most disturbing of all was a single tear sliding down Jessie's right cheek—her soul was laid bare for any viewer to see. She didn't have a 'come hither' look, like some of the portraits Josh saw at the studio; instead she appeared exhausted, thin, and desperately lost.

Yet—the photograph was scintillating and decidedly erotic. Josh was speechless and, at the same time, breathless. This stripped-down young version of the woman he loved was perhaps the most beautiful image he had ever seen of her. And he had seen many, some in Haute couture gowns and thousands of dollars worth of gold and diamonds.

Quiet footsteps stole up behind him.

Josh found his voice while, at the same time, tilting his head so the bit of hair Jessie always flipped behind his ear fell loose and cascaded towards the floor. He pointed at the picture, and when he spoke his breath was ragged and husky. "I hope to hell you never have company over for tea."

He didn't look at Caryn. He couldn't. The image of his wife up there in all her semi-nude erotic glory stunned him. It spoke legions about who Jessie was back in those early Vancouver days less than two years after her first boyfriend was murdered in front of her, maybe even less than a year earlier. And it spoke legions about the depths of Caryn's feelings for the hopeless waif in the photo.

Josh added brusquely, "You have a helluva lot of nerve."

Caryn touched his elbow lightly. "Josh, please, sit. Eric's making us some drinks. I told you we'd talk about this...so let's just do that, okay?"

It was on the tip of Josh's tongue to say *I don't drink* but then he thought, *what the hell, I need a fucking drink.* The way he rationalized it, his problem was never with alcohol, anyway. But Caryn and Eric knew his story; in fact he soon learned they knew quite a lot about him. And so the highly perceptive Caryn delivered a strange cerulean drink with a kind admonishment when Josh accepted without asking.

125

"Non-alcoholic, Josh. A virgin cocktail. One of Eric's specialties—don't ask me what it's called or even what's in it. He just likes to experiment with color. Yesterday's were green."

Wrapping his trembling fingers around the stem of the glass, Josh couldn't care less if his beverage was purple with pink polka dots, but he sure as hell wished it contained a few ounces of vodka or gin.

"Talk," he demanded, as Eric disappeared wordlessly back behind the kitchen bar and Caryn sat delicately down on a white chaise, kitty corner to where Josh halfway perched himself on the edge of the modern chair. He fixed his eyes on Caryn and prayed he could get his breathing under control. This was the closest in some time that Josh felt an impending panic attack coming on. Blood started to pound in his ears and his face suddenly seemed very hot.

"Honey," Caryn started. "First of all, when we know someone is coming here we remove the picture. We tuck it away under the bed where no one can touch it. Second, the only person who truly remembers Jessie even living here is Arnie. And he's not the kind of man to give away confidences. In fact, he would give his life to protect your wife."

"Yes, I seem to recall how good Arnie is at keeping secrets." In some convoluted way Josh found relief in that, but his words were tinged with a bitter building anger now that the realization of Jessie's extraordinary photograph was settling deeper into his bones.

"The first thing you need to understand, Josh, is that we—Eric and I—did not force Jessie into anything she wasn't interested in. She was a willing participant."

His response was a forced whisper. Eyes narrowing, flickering dangerously, Josh breathed, "She was a child. A hurt, scared child."

"She was in pain, yes, we knew that, it was obvious. But she needed us, Josh. She needed someone to love her and to nurture her back into the world."

"Not to drag her to bed and take advantage of her! That's not nurturing! That's sleazy and wrong on every level, Caryn." Josh was trying not to lose his temper. He needed those damn files. He tried to keep his voice even and controlled but it seemed the tremors had made their way to his voice box.

Caryn shimmied up to the edge of the chaise and placed her fingers over his around the glass containing the weird sapphire drink. Her hands were soft, small and fragile. Picturing them touching Jessie intimately, Josh pulled away, but not before a new tremor started in his body. It disturbed him. Roughly, he deposited the drink on the coffee table, creating a rippling wave within the glass so that the contents almost spilled over, then he stood suddenly and circled around to the back of the chair.

Caryn rose too, quickly, and in a pitchy voice she called out to him. "You have to understand, our relationship wasn't based on sex. It was a part of it, yes, Eric and I have an open relationship and we do have sex with other people, but with Jessie it was more about helping her overcome the demons that brought her here. She was so delicate, you see, and after her being so sick I couldn't leave her alone. She needed me!"

"She didn't speak. How could you know anything about what she needed if she didn't fucking speak? She was a child, yes; I know she was likely pushing twenty but Jesus, Caryn, that's a child! How much older are you? And…and him?!" The thought of Eric also being involved with Jessie in such a vulnerable state was too noxious to even contemplate. Josh was sickened. A metallic taste formed in his mouth and his eyes got spotty. He groaned and sank down against the wall, and shoved the heels of both palms into his eyes. "Goddamn it." He ran all ten fingers and thumbs through his tousled hair and, through the incessant pounding of fear and distrust assaulting his ears, he stared up at Caryn through stunned misty eyes, albeit eyes not too upset to miss that she was in her own personal agony as hard memories came rushing back like tidal water on a quest to break over the shore.

"Look at that picture, Caryn. Look at it. That is a heartbroken child. She's crying in that photograph. She's fucking crying." Josh uttered the painful truth so low that even he could hardly hear himself. "How could you? How could you." He covered his eyes again, struggling inwardly to settle his breathing and cool the steady pounding in an attempt to ward off the rising panic.

The woman in white paused and then knelt slowly down before him. This time when she grasped his hands, Josh let her. She pulled them away from his eyes and exerted a gentle pressure upon both sets of trembling fingers.

"Sweet Josh," she murmured, her voice so soft and lilting and musical he had to look, despite the nausea and threatening tears, "Baby, the young woman you see in that picture is not the Jessie who arrived here, broken and battered. That girl was frozen. She was incapable of speech, or any communication, not even through music. This girl," she waved an arm in the air behind her, "is the one who was starting to play guitar again, and to sing, even."

She leaned closer to Josh and this time took his cheeks in her palms. Something about her pleading eyes softened his agony. Silently he begged her to help him understand this, any of this—the big man in the kitchen who scared him, the bed on the pedestal, the luxury and softness of this place. It was like living in a cloud. And then, with Josh's realization that this was some kind of insular padded safe place, came the most remarkable words.

Caryn's beguiling lips were pink and small, her teeth as white as the lacey cotton top she wore despite the freezing temperatures outside. Josh focused on those lips as she revealed what she believed to be the truth behind the erotic image.

"She was an iceberg, Josh. When she came here. And what you see in that image up there, what you see in Jessie is…the iceberg starting to melt."

She was still pleading with him, diving deep into his eyes, begging him to understand. And on some level, all of a sudden he did.

She carried on, her words tumbling slowly over each other. "You were right, in my office yesterday. What you said. I loved her. I did. How could I not? So scared she was, when she first came here! I didn't touch her right away…how could I? But then one day she came to me, and folded herself into my arms, and it just happened. It was like she was begging me to touch her and to love her. Not a word," she murmured softly. "Just those lovely, haunting, tortured, terrified eyes, begging me to show her what it was like to be loved again. And…when it was over, she lay on her side in the bed, curled up in a little ball, and the tears started to come. For the first time. Finally there was emotion coming from this haunted girl. I got out the camera and I started snapping. She didn't mind. She knew. She knew what was happening, that things were starting to change. And I think…I think for the first time she realized maybe, just maybe, it was possible everything might someday be okay. My iceberg, Josh. That's what she was when she came here. But she melted, you see? And then I had to send her away."

Both Caryn and Josh were desolately entranced now, locked in a snowy cocoon loving a woman who, hours later, far away, would be crying herself to sleep, lonely and wishing her man was spooning her and whispering soothing sweet nothings in her ear.

In the kitchen in the East Hastings condo, Eric stood silently transfixed and watched his wife with Josh. He had long ago learned not to speak of Jessie in Caryn's presence, yet he also instinctively knew his lady often thought of the singer, especially on nights when her shoulders sank and she was lost in some dark reverie in which he was not invited to partake. Now he was a complete outsider although, in the Jessie days, he sometimes cuddled the girl as well, depending on Caryn's mood. Then, he knew Jessie was just going along with it, but he also recognized that she derived pleasure from his experienced touch. That was how he knew she would not last with Caryn. That she would break his wife's heart. That she would want a man of her own one day.

Caryn was sitting on the floor by Josh now, her head resting loosely on his shoulder. Both seemed to have forgotten entirely that Eric was even in the space.

"You have more, " Josh was saying. "You said you were snapping pictures that day. Plural."

"Yes. I do have more." Caryn pushed herself up with one arm, and strode over to a cabinet against a side wall near the photograph. In a bottom drawer were a number of photo albums. She bent and retrieved one from underneath the rest, and she brought it over to Josh and handed it to him, at the same time sliding down again against the wall.

"Here," she said simply as he took the brown leather album from her and opened it, his heart in his throat.

His first word was husky and low. "Jesus."

As he turned the pages, Josh saw more of the same, although most of these had a clear background image—the bed. In some, Jessie was on her side, in some she was on her back. In most she wore the haunted image that terrified Josh, the one he hoped he himself would never have to see again. But in a few towards the end of the album he saw a tiny, minute little light in her eyes. And also in those—a hint of a lopsided smile.

When he finally closed the album, Josh pondered leaping up and running

129

out the door of the luxury condo with it stuffed securely under his arm. But something stopped him, and it wasn't Eric in the kitchen, staring confused daggers at him. Instead it was Caryn, her soft touch, the delicate fingers, and the lonesome longing for Josh's wife so many years ago. Suddenly, like sunshine after a rainstorm, Josh understood that her love for Jessie was very likely reciprocated.

And so when he drove home in the dark a half hour later, he was no closer to solving his dilemma, which was to somehow remove the incriminating photos—and videos, damn it, he forgot the videos!—from Caryn and Eric's possession. His mind was a fog, his head and heart reeling, and he was suddenly lonely as hell for Jessie.

He wanted to fold her into his arms and hang on forever. He wanted to hold tight the hurting part of her and run his fingers over the sad cheeks, and demand she listen to him. He wanted to hold her captive in his eyes and implore Jessie to understand one thing—that he, Josh Sawyer, would never let his girl feel that kind of debilitating pain again, ever. He wanted to love her and love her and love her until all he ever heard escape that pretty soul or those perfect lips was the laughter of the Gods; or the joy of a universe that giveth and never ever taketh. He wanted to lick the spot on her cheek where the tear seared and scarred it in that unforgiving photo, and he wanted to drive himself inside her so he could hold his wife in a tender cocoon where they would always be one.

He just wanted…her.

Chapter Thirteen

*S*he arrived home in a whirlwind, towing a fluttering pack of Christmas shopping bags, precisely five days later.

"So weird," she hollered at Josh as she picked her way down the metal steps of the jet, bags clutched wildly in each hand as she navigated against the biting wind, "Christmas shopping in Miami is just wrong. Not a smidgen of snow anywhere. Santa's elves were in bustiers!"

She leaned forward and brushed her lips against Josh's, and was starting to back away and speak again when he clutched her hard to him and teased her neck with the tip of his tongue.

"Come home," he murmured seductively into her ear. "Now. Please."

"Okay, cowboy," she giggled. "Or do you want to do it right here? Drop right down on the asphalt?"

"Too much information," breezed Matt as he sidled by and grabbed the shopping bags from Jessie's hands. He headed towards Josh's truck and deposited them in the back seat of the extended cab, and then he swung open the tailgate to make room for the forthcoming suitcase and carry-on bag.

"Uummmm," mouthed Jessie, wrapping both now-free arms around her husband's broad shoulders. She pinched his shoulder. "Hmmm. You've been working out."

True, he'd spent a lot of time at the gym while she was away. Something about doing a good hour on the elliptical helped Josh bear the agony the trips to East Hastings had unleashed. Well, that and a trip to the pharmacy for some gut relieving antacids.

Jessie grinned and peeked mischievously up at him while wrapping one hand around the buckle of his belt and dropping the other just below and behind it.

"Hmmmm. Nice abs, too, cowboy."

Exhaling slowly, Josh placed a hand behind his wife's head and pulled her close. "I was missing you," he breathed. They lingered there, together, until Jessie started to wriggle. She leaned away and studied him. Her brow wrinkled in confusion.

"What is it?" she asked.

"What's what?"

"Spill it. I can read you, you know."

"Hope not. You might not like what you see."

"Something's up." His eyes had a new sadness to them. From somewhere deep inside, Josh's soul was telegraphing its hurt to the woman he loved and trusted most in the world. Jessie lifted a finger and touched the corner of his eye and then, with a touch as soft as down, let her thumb brush his cheek. She cocked her head and regarded him, biting her bottom lip in concern. She waited.

"It's fine," he said, placing both hands on her cheeks and drawing her to him so their foreheads could touch. "I was just lonely for you, that's all."

He was speaking the truth. After leaving Caryn and Eric's virginal white palace-cloud, Josh found himself longing for his girl in a way that frightened him. It was as if now that he knew another of her truths, he needed her even closer, so he could offer shelter and protection. It didn't make sense because, for one, in her own weird maligned way Caryn had apparently given Jessie just that. And what could Josh do now, all these years later? But it was like looking at pictures of World War II flyers, or Vietnam soldiers, or Depression era starving children—you wanted to hold them and take their pain away, even though the days when you could help were long past.

"Well then, take me home, big boy." For some reason, Jessie's internal alarms were ringing. Something had changed. Was it because of her escapade with Jacob? Maybe. But whatever was bothering Josh, it ran deep, because the corners of his lips were turned down and he felt heavy in her arms, as if a great weight burdened him here, today. Turning away from him, she looked over at Matt who, now standing by the Audi, was waiting to say goodbye. He caught the quizzical glint in Jessie's eye and glanced behind her at Josh. He, too, detected a sadness he couldn't quite fathom, but he chalked it up to Jessie's absence and the Atlanta foray.

"Thanks for everything, Matt," Jessie said, letting her fingers slip out of Josh's hand and wandering over to Matt so she could wrap both arms around his neck. She hugged him tight and then backed away and smiled, curls softly tossing in the breeze. "I'm sorry I teased you about your hair. It's good on you, that spiky look." She reached up to touch his hair but he grabbed her wrist and stopped her.

His smile was genuine, the tension over the Miami trip eased somewhat now that they were back on Canadian soil. It was just the two of them— Deirdre and Charles were catching an evening United flight to L.A., and Jacob was staying in Florida to shoot a few more scenes before his schedule garnered him a break.

"You do realize you're crossing a line here, Jessie. Never mess with the security dude's hair."

"You might want to share that bit of news with your brother, Matt." Jessie winked and, behind her, Josh's ears perked up.

Matt frowned. He did catch a vibe between Michael and Kelly, but he was hoping his brother was wise enough to keep his relationship with his charge platonic. He was also hoping no one else had noticed.

Jessie continued, softening. "Look Matt, Kelly's not so bad. And from what I saw, Michael seems good for her. If nothing else, at least he's a buffer that keeps her off Jacob's back."

Matt, whose grip on Jessie's wrist had slipped casually down to her fingers, lightly rubbed his chin with his other hand, absently wishing he was one of those guys who could go a day or two without shaving, like Josh today. Right now he needed something to hang on to. Something rough to scratch. At Jessie's allusion to the possibility of Kelly and Michael as a couple, he could feel his blood pressure spike. Why the hell did he get his brother this job anyway? He should have stayed the hell out of his life. If what both he and Jessie detected were true, then all of a sudden Michael would be vulnerable again. And Kelly Reilly was unpredictable and, more often than Matt wanted to admit, even cruel. She was also younger than

Michael by about fifteen years. She wasn't exactly Matt's first choice for his brother.

Watching him, Jessie saw the complex emotions play across Matt's face. "Hey!" she said, with a little friendly pressure on Matt's fingers. "Guess I shouldn't have brought that up. But Michael's a grown-up. He seems to be handling Kelly just fine. This could be good for him, don't you think?"

"No. I don't think."

"Ah. I get it. You think she's too complicated for him. Being a singer and actor and all." Sobering, Jessie pensively studied Matt while, behind her, Josh stepped forward and tucked an arm loosely around her waist.

"That's not what Matt's saying, Jessie. He's just being a big brother. They get concerned about their little brothers when it comes to matters of the heart."

But Jessie knew otherwise. Matt, true to his nature, was quietly returning Jessie's gaze. He, more than anyone, was well aware of the cost of fame, and of relationships constantly scrutinized by fans and the media. And he was damn sorry about the price his brother had already paid to the music biz.

"It's okay, Matt. I get it," Jessie said quietly, letting go of his fingers. "You don't want Michael dating a screw-up."

"Jessie." Josh spoke her name in earnest. With the revelations of the last week, suddenly his wife's thoughts had deeper layers rising to the surface. "Jesus. Let it go."

Shifting his weight on polished boots, Matt sighed and looked away. He realized he was completely exhausted by this girl now gazing imploringly at him as if he was her sole judge and jury. Maybe it was time to find himself a less troubled celebrity to shadow.

He shoved that thought away as instantly as it crossed his mind. Regardless of her troubles, Jessie was family. Still…

"Kelly is technically Michael's boss," he said.

"Ouch," Jessie whispered, recalling her underhanded comment the other night to Matt on the jet. Obviously he was still a little pissed.

He ignored her. "He has a job to do, and he needs to do it."

She wiped a strand of hair out of her eye and tucked it behind her ear. "Touché, Matt. But okay. And I *am* sorry about our unscheduled plane ride.

And the stupid thing I shot between my stupid lips on said unscheduled plane ride." *And about the last few years,* she thought inwardly. She shivered as the bitter December wind flittled its way down her neck. "Go home. Get some sleep. Hi to Julie."

As she wheeled around and walked hand in hand with Josh towards the King Ranch, she could feel Matt's eyes on her back. But Jessie tossed her head and screwed up her courage. She knew he was mad about Atlanta, on some level, but usually he didn't let Jessie's impulsive rogue behavior dwell on him. Today it was obvious he was still pissed. Likely didn't help that Kelly was seemingly in a bad place, slipping and sliding drunkenly around a shiny hotel lobby. Maybe he was simply worried about his brother. After all, the man suffered his own personal tragedy at one time, and for sure Matt felt the agonizing repercussions from that.

Jessie was quiet on the way home. As Josh pointed the truck north on the 99 she sat back and watched the traffic fly by. She knew Matt would never intentionally hurt her, but she'd felt some judgment in his words, in his response towards her. Was she like Kelly? As hard to handle as Kelly? Hell, yeah. She'd pretty much fucked everyone over, Matt included. Given her behavior over the last many years, Jessie was surprised that anyone remained her friend. Her mood sank even deeper as she pondered Jacob back in Miami. He was pretty isolated there, and hadn't made any real friends on the set of *Mystic Nights,* although Michael and he seemed to share the odd coffee or beer now and again. Taking him to see his dad's concert had illuminated something reflective about himself, but Jessie wasn't sure it was necessarily a good thing. Meeting the music icon himself had, undoubtedly, only served to strengthen Jacob's self-loathing.

Another thing preyed on Jessie's mind as Josh steered around a small blue sedan. Being back in Vancouver took her life off hold. Christmas would, as always, put it back on for a bit, but it was still a few weeks away and Jessie had squeezed in some shopping in Miami. But she hadn't heard from her Aunt Evelyn in a while and she was anxious to see about these Ontario relatives. She wanted to set that January date and get things in place for a trip east.

Josh's own brooding mood was starting to get to her as well. She let her eyes flit down to their hands, which were joined together on her lap. His touch was intoxicating, as always, and she longed to crawl inside his soul and see what was troubling him. He was steering with one hand, for the most part, pulling away his right hand from Jessie when he required two hands to signal or change lanes. He did this now, and didn't return his grip to her. Instead, he leaned his right arm on the wheel and chewed his fingernails, which was something he never did. Jessie was mystified, confused and concerned. She narrowed her eyes at him.

"So what all did you do while I was away? Besides read scripts?"

Glancing over at her, Josh was surprised to see her glaring at him. *Damn it,* he thought. *Sometimes I swear this girl can read my mind.*

He shrugged. "Thought about you." It was an attempt to get her to chill, but Josh knew he would have to somehow let what he'd learned over the past while just breeze past him. Jessie and he were so in tune that unless he could change his frequency she was not likely to let up wondering what was bothering him.

"Ach," she groaned, settling further back into her seat. "Fucking men."

"What?" Now Josh laughed. "Don't let Matt get to you, Jess. He's been away from home. He needs a good lay with Julie. He'll be fine."

"Oh, so is that your problem too, Sawyer?"

She was frowning, and Josh felt his heart melt at the sight of her. He could almost see the silent tear from years ago, sliding down that pretty cheek. A wave of ennui washed over him. He reached out and touched the cheek where the tear lay frozen in the photo.

"Yeah," he said softly. "I need to feel your skin, little one. I need to take you to my bed."

He'd never worded it quite that way before. Jessie's ears pricked up at the word *my.* But she slid the weirdness around the word away, and leaned over to him. With her right hand she rubbed his belly and then she lowered her hand and pushed gently on the soft places in his crotch. She scratched a little through his jeans and relaxed a little when she felt his body give and sigh under her caress.

"Uuhhhh," he moaned quietly as the pleasurable reverberations her touch sent throughout his body ignited his senses.

"Drive faster," she whispered, leaning closer and taking his earlobe into her mouth. She sucked gently, and then ran the tip of her tongue around the inside of his ear.

Soon they were parked crookedly in the driveway of their home, and Josh scooped up his wife and carried her down the flagstone walk, by the winterized pool, and in through the back door.

"Ouch!" she yelped when he got her a little too close to the side of the door while passing through it.

"Oops, sorry," he responded. "Hope I didn't knock you out. I need you right now, Mrs. Sawyer. In a big way."

"Trust me, I'm fine. How big? Hmmm?" She squeezed her arms around his neck as he took the stairs two at a time. "Don't drop me. K?"

"I might," he answered, teasing. "Just how much Guinness did you drink down south, anyway?"

"It wasn't the Guinness, big boy," she murmured into her favorite cozy place between his neck and shoulder. "It was the peach pie."

"I'll give you peach pie," Josh winked, laying Jessie on the bed and sliding over her body. He grabbed both hands and pulled them up over her head, held them with one of his own big paws, then used the other to unbuckle her jeans and yank them down. He relaxed his grip on her hands when he lost himself in the delights her body offered, sinking his tongue into her and almost losing control at the way her body responded to him. He fought to dispel the thoughts and images conjured by Caryn and her history with Jessie, but somehow they had replayed so many times in his mind that Josh found having Jessie finally here, underneath him, was incredibly erotic. Thinking about her with Caryn—and Eric, he reminded himself distastefully—was definitively and decidedly stimulating. It charged the way he made love to Jessie now…he was anxious and hurried, and even rough. He had two desires, one, to somehow heal her through his touch, as he had been learning to do through counseling, and two, to make her his own again. Strangely, in this erotic moment it didn't feel dirty to him, the way it felt when he first gleaned that Jessie'd been involved in some shady business on East Hastings. Instead, he saw her as he did in the photos in Caryn's album—needy, hungry, erotic, sensual, sexy as hell, and…touched and loved intimately, the way he desired to touch and love her now.

He reached up and pulled her top over her head, then grasped clumsily at her bra and pulled it over her head, too. Her jeans had caught around her ankles, and he bent down quickly and pulled them off so she could spread her legs wider. When she did, and he got back to his favorite place on her body, Jessie's moans increased and she arched her back to meet him. She grabbed his head and directed him, and groaned when he stopped flicking his tongue against her to pull a nipple into his mouth, but then he shoved two fingers inside her, roughly, and Jessie almost lost it then and there.

"Jesus," she cried. "Jesus, Josh!"

He hadn't even pulled off his jacket, the green vintage leather one she loved best on him. She didn't bother either, instead Jessie just grabbed at his shirt and shoved it upwards so she could feel his hot skin on hers. She poked at his belt until he had to give in and help her, and then he got the fly down on his own. He went down on her again, sucking hard, and she couldn't hold on any longer. She started to come, and he gave her a few more pushes with his fingers until she clawed at his back, begging him, with her moans, to go inside.

When he did, Josh came quickly, too, and they rode the wave together until it subsided, leaving in its wake beautiful tingles of sweet sweet pleasure.

"Jesus," she whispered again, holding him close, enveloped in the vintage jacket she so desperately ached to touch back in April at his birthday party. "I'm going away more often."

Josh buried his face in her neck because suddenly, with Jessie in his arms, and himself still embroiled in her body and soul, he was overcome with a wave of emotion. She felt his body crumbling, and the tremors that overtook him, and it scared her.

"Josh. Josh! What the hell?"

She tried to lift his head, but he refused, so she held him and let him sob until he quieted.

After, he released her from his grip and rolled off the bed. He pulled off his jeans and then the jacket and shirt, and dropped them on the floor as he stumbled into the adjoining washroom and turned the knob for the shower.

Jessie waited a few moments, her thoughts going a mile a minute, then followed him. She let the spray wash over her, and then she touched him gently on one trembling shoulder blade. He was standing with his back to her, and didn't turn when she touched him.

"Babe," she murmured. "Tell me everything is okay. Please? I don't... I don't understand."

He paused, lathering soap into his hair and rinsing it out before summoning the courage to face his wife.

Then Josh touched her cheek gently with the backs of his knuckles and pulled her towards him so he could brush his lips against her forehead. "I'm sorry," he whispered, the ache in his voice enough to cause new worry lines to erupt on Jessie's face.

She took his grizzly cheeks in her palms. "Tell me," she begged, a sick feeling seizing her insides. She didn't add *tell me you didn't cheat on me,* which was one of the many crazy thoughts plummeting through her desperate mind.

He shook his head. "Not now, Jessie." He looked into her eyes and begged her to understand. "Can't. Okay?" He still didn't quite trust himself to speak.

"No," she demanded. "No. We tell each other stuff, remember? You and me?"

That almost unleashed a new wave of agony, but Josh drew upon some of his acting training and found the strength to fight the overwhelming emotion of the last few days, and of the way he felt he just used his wife. He'd gone behind her back to find out things about her past that both terrified and intrigued him, and he felt justly ashamed and afraid of what she would do if she found out.

"It's fine," he murmured to her, kissing her swollen pink lips tenderly. "Just some old shit I had to work out."

Her anxious eyes saddened him, and so he felt a need to offer some explanation. He evaded the truth more, and further sickened himself, by remarking, "Just...you and Jacob...you know."

"You can trust me, Josh. You know that. I told you that. Why isn't that enough for you? Or for anyone, for that matter?" She thought about Matt's warning eyes from earlier in the week. "Fuck, men!" she cried, exasperation adding to her anger. "You're all from another planet!"

She turned her back to her husband, who squeezed his eyes shut with shame, and then Jessie lathered her hair and rinsed it, cursing under her breath.

Finally, Josh wrapped both arms around her shoulders, and she gave in and layered her own arms over his. They stood together, the water cleansing their fears and worries, at least for a little time, until their fingers turned to wrinkled prunes and their bellies rumbled. Josh took a large fluffy bath towel and patted Jessie dry, and they kissed softly and held each other close before padding into the bedroom to dress.

As they snuggled up under a quilt and watched a movie later, they managed to push the world aside.

But soon, the world invaded again, unbidden, as it always managed to do, and the fears they pushed away that night came rushing in like a swollen river in spring.

Chapter Fourteen

*B*esides cherished time together, the highlight of the Christmas break was reuniting with the old *Drifters* gang for Steve and Sophie's wedding. It was a lavish affair, held in the gorgeous gauzy Emerald Ballroom of Vancouver's Fairmont Pacific Rim. With an exquisite view of the North Shore mountains and Vancouver harbor, the wedding had an added feature—in the background, seaplanes touched down or departed on feathery light pontoons, foamy wakes trailing behind their privileged passengers.

All of the old gang flew in for hugs and champagne. Jessie stood at Sophie's side as her teary Maid-of-Honor; Maggie, Sue-Lyn, a very pregnant Jane, and Ashley all also attended Sophie, who was the only daughter of a wealthy Vancouver surgeon. The women reveled in the opulent ceremony and dance, and thrilled at the opportunity to celebrate the union of two of their closest friends in marriage.

Sophie, a delicate blonde who once trained in classical ballet, now the writer of more than one popular blog—including one that educated readers about hot topics like Vegan foods and environmental issues—stopped all hearts beating when she convened with her girls at the far end of the aisle to journey towards her husband-to-be on her father's generous arm. Her Israeli bridal gown designer, Berta, would have humbly blushed had she witnessed firsthand the appreciative hushed response to the stunning plunged neckline on tiny Sophie's white lace and silk silhouette gown, a trademark feature for which Berta was famous.

Blonde hair swept back into a tight bun, the diminutive Sophie waltzed down the aisle with careful precision. A stylish, sensual vision, her husband-to-be's knees almost gave way when he first spotted her.

Besides the wedding gown, Berta also designed the attendants' mid-thigh length dresses; caramel lace highlighted the silk, and they were mostly backless, leaving the men in the ballroom completely beholden to Berta's daring designs.

During the reception after the ceremony, comfortably gathered in white ladder back chairs around a large round table sumptuously adorned with expensive wine and artful displays of off-white roses, the friends caught up on each others' lives.

For starters, Maggie invited the gang to New York to see her new play on Broadway.

"It's a depression era story about a family who tries to beat extreme poverty by going on the road as folk singers. The director is Anthony Turner, that prodigy from Princeton who did such an amazing job on the adaptation of 'A Streetcar Named Desire' in Houston last summer. It's surreal, working with him. He's just a kid, but what a talent! We're selling out."

"I'm going to New York!" gushed Jessie. "Who's meeting me there? I want to go to that ice cream place from John Cusack's film *Serendipity*. What's it called? Mmmm…"

"Duh, Jessie, how about 'Serendipity?'" Steve was grinning at her, one arm resting on the table and the other loosely tossed around his new wife's shoulders. He was glowing and, as the memory of his and Jessie's brief but difficult time together as intimate lovers washed over his face, he exchanged a look of genuine joy with his old gal-pal. In this moment, he was eternally grateful to be celebrating the sincere happiness he'd rediscovered with the lovely Sophie. On this surreal night, he had no regrets over his and Jessie's short-lived one time dalliance.

"Mmm, yes, I go to Serendipity once in a while for their frozen hot chocolate. De-lish!" confessed Maggie. She added, "Don't tell Anthony. I'm supposed to be poor and skinny in the play." Turning to Carter, who was quietly drumming on the table with his and Ashley's unused spoons, she asked, "How about you, Chad Smith?"

"I wish." Carter chuckled at the reference to the well-known Red Hot Chili Peppers' drummer. But he colored, and dropped the spoons. "I'm mostly hanging out in L.A. with Ashley these days. This girl," he took his girlfriend's hand, "did such a good job on Joss Whedon's last film that she went and hooked up with another one of his gigs, doing sets on one of the new Marvel films." Beside him, Ashley beamed. He continued. "As for me, I'm still auditioning. Lots of auditions…" Carter's voice faded and he shrugged. "Life in the biz. We're not all as gifted as Josh and Jessie, apparently." He let go of Ashley's hand and grabbed a spoon again, tipping it up so that it took on a new role as a medieval catapult. He made a small ee*rrroooom* sound as he faked the launch of some invisible boulder in the general direction of his old co-stars.

Sue-Lyn leaned forward and laid a hand over his. "Something will come up, Carter. If you don't get a part soon, come teach acting with me. I can always use a good-looking homegrown guy to bring in the female students. They'll die for those cheekbones!" She tweaked his cheek with a thumb and forefinger, but he shyly and self-consciously pushed her away. She twisted around and fixed Ashley in her gaze. "Is that okay with you, girlfriend? I promise to send him home at the end of class."

Ashley laughed, eyes sparkling. "By homegrown I take it you're referencing Carter's aboriginal background?"

"Native, Ethnic, Indian, take your pick," Sue-Lyn teased. "You've got yourself a good looking man, Ashley. Hang on to him."

"I will," Carter's on-again off-again girl declared happily. These days the couple was more on than off, and collectively the small group of friends were relieved Carter wasn't alone during a time in his life he was finding challenging.

All of them were thrilled to soak up the old friendships again, but Carter's reference to tough times in the biz humbled Jessie.

"Carter," she started carefully, anxious to sidestep around her friend's pride, "Let me talk to Dee for you, okay? Until something better comes along, at the very least maybe she can set you up with something on *Mystic Nights*."

Clearing his throat, Carter sat up straighter in his seat and gave Jessie a slight nod. He mumbled, "Thanks, Jessie, but it's okay. I need to earn a part on my own. Maybe something that's not, you know, the whole Custer's Last Stand kinda Native American bullshit."

"Just talk to Dee. Meet with her. See what's up." Jessie was cautiously insistent.

Ashley broke in. "What can it hurt, Carter?"

Throughout the discussion, Josh watched his old friends chat. Sure, acting was a tough business for everyone, but he knew from personal experience it was ten times harder for people who were already stereotyped for one reason or another—as a villain maybe, because the actor had piercing eyes or a certain build or, in his case, a particular reputation. Or they could fall into the cultural pit, like Carter, who was an indigenous actor with very distinguishable features. Josh knew Carter's pride as an actor was at stake, and in truth it felt awkward to suddenly be one of the film world's newest stars while his friend and past co-star was struggling.

He caught Carter's eye, though, at one point, and Josh wasn't surprised to find what he thought he'd find—sincere friendship and trust. There was no judgment in the dark eyes. If anything, what he spied in Carter's soul was a gentle kindness and a sense of gladness that at least some of the old *Drifters* gang—meaning Josh and Jessie, for the most part—were on track.

Jessie mellowed a little as the difficult conversation came to a close, and she leaned into the comfort of Josh's side, one hand on his thigh, her slight tension dissipating in the knowledge that all of them would be looking out for their friend in the months—years—to come. What a relief to be here amongst the company of such great soul mates again. What a blessing to be alive and joyous here in Vancouver with her *Drifters* friends at her side.

A loud guffaw from the direction of the dance floor caught the gang's attention. It was Charlie, who was well past feeling his bourbon. Jane had him by the hand.

Steve reached over to the next table and yanked on an empty chair, which he dragged to a stop by his own seat. Josh followed suit, and stood to help the very pregnant Jane collapse into her chair.

"He might as well enjoy it," Jane was saying about Charlie and his bourbon as she settled, using her toes to nudge off wide-strapped champagne-glitter Jimmy Choos as she spoke. She caught her breath with the sudden sweet relief of removing the glamorous shoes. "Ohhh that feels good." She added an addendum to her previous comment. "Soon Charlie'll be stuck at home changing diapers."

"Can't wait," Charlie roared, while the others playfully tried to shush him.

"This one's gonna be so freaking spoiled. I'm jus' tellin' y'all now so you're prepared." He nodded affirmatively and almost tipped the bourbon glass over when he tried to set it down, narrowly missing the edge of the table. Next to him, Sophie's quick reflexes saved the expensive drink from soiling Charlie's lap. He ignored her hasty save and continued. "So none of you hicks comes over and wonders why my kid is up watching the Vancouver Canucks with his proud papa on a school night."

"And if it's a girl?" Maggie teased.

"It's okayyy," Charlie slurred. "Girls play hockey these days too."

At that, Jane shook her head at the others. "She can play hockey if she wants, but I'm waiting for the day my little girl is old enough to wear her first tiny pink tutu. Hmm, Sophie?"

As the conversation turned to children, with reference to similar hope and pleasure coming Steve and Sophie's way someday too, Jessie leaned into Josh's ear and whispered, "How many children did we say we're having, Sawyer?"

He wrapped an arm tighter around her shoulder and leaned in. "As many as you feel like carrying for nine months at a time, little one."

"You'll have to change my nickname." Her pearl eyes shone as she rotated her body further around to lay her left hand against his tight abs and lean in for a soft kiss. "Big one."

"How about little-and-a-half one?" he offered, eyes alight.

"Or just baby mama? Change the vibe altogether?"

They shook their heads at that. "Nahhh," they agreed simultaneously. Little one was Josh's pet name for Jessie from the start. It was part of their magical growing collection of memories, the ones they were carefully guarding and setting into a special box for some enchanted day down the road.

As they snuggled and sighed into each other, from the dance floor Jacob spied them. He was at the party too, as Steve and Sophie's friend from his Jessie days, and he wandered over on a stumbling zigzag path with one of Sophie's gorgeous blonde cousins floating less than gracefully on his arm. He raised a glass to Steve and Sophie, and arrogantly leaned an elbow on Josh's shoulder. Josh looked down at his toes and swallowed the urge to tell Jessie's falling-over-drunk ex to take a hike.

Jacob bent forward and offered a garbled toast. "To lifelongish uhhh... life. Looovvee. May you two beautiful pee-pul both never lose the...uh... never forget..." He thought for a second. "The maaahhh-giccc." From behind Josh's back he tried to focus on Jessie. Her eyebrows knit together and she shot him a warning look, which Josh caught. But Josh understood the toxic curse of deep-rooted hurts soaked with alcohol, so he dropped his right hand over his wife's knee and exerted a gentle pressure. She met his eye and he shrugged lightly—*no worries.*

Jacob stood taller then, removed his elbow from Josh's shoulder, and swallowed uncomfortably. "How'zzz about a danzze, Jezzie?" he managed, as the beauty on his arm bristled.

Hesitating, Jessie glanced at Josh while the table went completely silent. Her husband shifted in his chair but in the end Josh acquiesced with a nod. "Go ahead, Jessie. He needs someone to hold him up."

Always amused at Jessie's adversarial men, Charlie howled and slapped his thigh. Jane shushed him but he roared anyway as Jessie stood and fixed a solemn gaze on him.

"Jake," Charlie slurred, pointing a finger, "take that pretty honey on your arm and grab the next flight back to Miami. Jessie's off the market." He leaned an elbow on the table and faced Jacob with a scrunch of his brow. His voice lowered an octave. "You and I, we got to love Jessie from a distance now. That's all we get, these days." He said the last few words with a flourish of one wrist in Jessie's general direction, as if the movement could erase the hard memories where Jessie was concerned.

"Charlie, geez," groaned Jessie, glancing at Jane's round belly and then letting her eyes drift up to the pixie blonde's patient face.

Jane smiled genuinely and touched Jessie's hand. "It's okay, honey," she offered. "If I couldn't handle his attachment to you I wouldn't be here all fat and craving sushi, which I hate. And about to pee for the fifth time in an hour." She swatted Charlie's knee. "Right now, he's not really on my good side anyway. But he'll be back in my good graces in about, oh, a month, I think." She placed a hand on her large belly.

Jacob was regarding Charlie closely. At that point, Josh realized Charlie hadn't looked away from the singer. It was as if he were now mutely sending the younger guy a telepathic message that said *I feel your pain*. Suddenly neither Charlie nor Jacob appeared drunk anymore. The others at the table remained silent.

Jessie gave Charlie a curious look which he did catch, and which, by virtue of her movement, finally motivated him to come back to earth, to the wife beside him he knew he'd just hurt, whether Jane cared to admit it or not. And in the old Charlie eyes was happiness, yes, but still a sweet sad longing for the days of old which he was well aware he'd royally fucked up. He moved back in his chair and reached for Jane's small hand, and then he finally shifted his glance from Jessie to the bourbon on the table, which he grabbed and sipped on loudly while avoiding Carter's inquisitive glance across the table.

Managing to pull Jacob away from Charlie's gaze was easy. Jessie just smiled at the woman clinging to Jacob's arm, and then she slipped her fingers in his. Sophie's exquisite cousin let Jacob's other hand go, but by her hard glare it was plainly obvious she wasn't happy about it.

Jessie led Jacob towards the dance floor. She didn't look back at the *Drifters* table to see if Josh's somber eyes were following her. They weren't. He didn't need the visual reminder of Jessie's romance with the man who apparently gave damn good orgasms.

On the dance floor, Jessie chided her drunk dance partner. "Jacob," she admonished, while trying to ease through a slow Sarah McLachlan ballad with an air of detached grace, "why'd you go off and get drunk? You oughtta know better."

He avoided the question. "Just one danze, Jezz…for old timez sake." Her old boyfriend stroked a thumb against Jessie's bare back and tried unsuccessfully to avoid eyeing the lovely half-round moons of her breasts in the plunging neckline of the dazzling short dress.

"Up here, Jake old buddy," Jessie snipped, placing a forefinger under his chin and rather harshly raising his head. She poked two fingers towards her eyes. "Here."

He chortled. "Oops. Sorry." But it was everything Jacob could do not to reach out his own finger and brush the backs of those beautiful breasts, ones to which he not so long ago had exclusive access.

Exhaling slowly, Jessie felt rather sorry for her one-time flame, so she pulled him close and breathed in the green apple scent of his hair. "Good ole Jacob," she sighed. "But Charlie's right. Move on, babe."

"I will when I'm ready," was Jacob's not-so-seemingly drunk response as they moved back and forth slowly, their arms delicately around each other.

Jessie could feel the heat of Jacob's body through his black dress shirt. Unable to stop herself, she pressed her hands a little harder into his back, envisioning the Celtic cross underneath her graceful fingertips. She let herself remember the way his hair tickled her face when she pressed her cheek against him. Betraying her will, her body tingled in secret places. She gulped. "And when will that be?" she asked him, somewhat distracted.

"When you really let me go," was Jacob's pouty, unexpected, murmured response.

There was a certain undeniable verity to that statement. Still, it also held a definite shock factor. Jessie leaned away from Jacob. She moved both of her hands up to his biceps, and lost herself for a brief moment in the blue puppy dog eyes. She sucked in a breath and shook her head slowly from side to side.

"I did that already, Jacob. I let you go."

"Did you." It wasn't a question.

Her next words were barely heard over the ballad. "You promised," she chastised him. "You promised we'd be okay. Together."

Jacob didn't answer. *Liquid courage*, he thought, thereby absolving himself of responsibility for his outright declaration. His lips parted and his eyes searched hers, transmitting a raw ache for Jessie's sizzling touch, which Jacob desired directly on his hot skin, and not just through his damn shirt.

They stood suspended, locked in each other's eyes, watched now by everyone at the *Drifters* table except Josh who, his back to them, hung both shoulders and fought with his brain to trust his wife, despite a rapidly increasing heartbeat.

And then Jessie spun on her heel and abruptly left Jacob in the middle of the waltz. He stood alone in the center of the grand Emerald Ballroom of the Fairmont Pacific Rim, unmoving, wanting; the object of Charlie's mute bemusement, and Jane's silent pity.

Chapter Fifteen

"*D*amn it." Jessie squinted at the words on the laptop in front of her, as if by doing so the typed letters would rearrange themselves and form words she wanted to hear.

Josh was on his way into the office from the kitchen, where he'd put together a platter of sliced fruit to munch on. He placed squares of chocolate on the side while he was walking, the tray held high in one hand and the chocolate in the other. He shoved a pile of unread scripts aside and set the tray down in a spot on Jessie's desk that both could reach while they worked.

"What?" he asked, glancing over as he dropped into the office chair across from Jessie. "Straighten up, Jess. You're all hunched over."

She sat back instantly, lips screwed up in annoyance. "It's an email from Aunt Evelyn." Waving a hand abruptly, she explained, "The Peterborough relatives don't want to see me. She says my so-called sister isn't interested in dredging up the past."

"Huh." *Well, on the one hand,* thought Josh, *unless this is a bluff, it at least makes me feel a little better about their interest in Jessie for her money.* To her he said, "It doesn't mean it's not going to happen, Jessie. It's likely a helluva shock to all of a sudden find out you're related to an international star."

"Star, shmarr," she frowned, plucking a square of chocolate off the tray.

"Fruit first, Jessie," Josh admonished, using his fingertips to push the tray a little closer to her.

"Oh, screw off," she mumbled under her breath, but she reached out, took a slice of pear, and popped it in her mouth.

"What'd you say to me?" Now Josh was frowning, but his brown eyes

149

were alight. He switched to a wide grin, and gave Jessie a look that had her squirming in her chair.

"I said oh, *few* of…the pears. We need more pears on this tray." She grabbed a nearby cup from Rebel On A Mountain Coffee and gulped back a healthy swig of her mocha, avoiding Josh's playful stare.

"Yeah. Okay," was his response, and he turned to his own monitor and scrolled through his emails. "No offense to the Christmas season," he declared, "but I'm glad it's over so we can get back to normal. I need to know what city I'll be living in for the next few months."

"Duhhh, Miami," Jessie threw in. "At least part of the time." Using her toes, she swung her chair around to face his. Leaning forward, she grabbed another slice of pear and held it high in front of her so he couldn't help but see it, then she narrowed her eyes into slits, dropped it into her mouth, and quickly followed suit with chocolate.

Laughing, Josh pointed a finger at her. "Just be glad I'm taking care of you, little girl. If I wasn't watching out for you, God only knows what you'd be eating or…"

A cloud washed over his face and he turned his chair back around to face his emails. He moved his right hand up to his chin and rubbed the three-day grizzle he hadn't felt like shaving over the recent holidays. Once Steve and Sophie's magical wedding was over, and the couple flew tearfully back to L.A., he and Jessie had totally cocooned.

"Or what?" Jessie asked quietly. "Josh?" It seemed her past would never leave her alone. Always there would be a dark cloud over Jessie's head, filled with the eyes of the people who loved her, watching, wondering… worrying.

"It's nothing," he said, chiding himself inwardly for almost spilling the beans, for alerting his pretty wife to him digging around in her past. He rounded up some courage and faced Jessie. "I just happen to like taking care of you, that's all. And I'm glad it's me doing it."

"Mmm," she answered. *The Jacob thing again.* She changed tack and pointed towards his iMac screen. "Anything?"

"Yeah," he said. "There's a note from Hilary." He scanned the email. "And?"

"Patience, little one." Then, "Humph."

"What?"

"Okay, well it looks like I'll be able to fly with you to Miami in a few days. But then I'll be meeting Steve in Toronto to shoot some test scenes for Jon's new series."

"Ya oughtta start calling him dad, y'know. Somehow I don't think he'd mind." Jessie's smile was sweet and chaste, all hope and longing for anything to make Josh happy, to see golden light in his eyes and peace in his soul.

He shrugged. "Can't see that happening, Jess. It's enough to know that he is, though, you know? My dad? Notwithstanding all the lost years...with Wes and his version of child rearing. Or should I say Josh-rearing. He did fine with the other two."

"Well now you've got me—and Jonathon—to make up for what you've lost." She pushed herself up out of her chair and flopped into his lap. Wrapping her arms around Josh's neck, she leaned in and let her lips drift over one fuzzy cheek. "Ouch."

"Hmmm?" Eyes closed, Josh was relishing the feel of her sweet body in his arms. "I'll shave," he said, his voice muzzy with pleasure.

"No, don't," she murmured. "I like your old west look. It reminds me of *Drifters*."

"Ahhh, *Drifters*. We had some good times, didn't we, Jessie?"

"Most of the time."

"Third season pretty much sucked. And come to think of it, number one wasn't a piece of cake, either."

"Okay, so some of the time. Let's not rehash the past. Let's just move on to the future, okay cowboy?"

She felt a chill pass through Josh's body then. Beneath her, he stiffened. Jessie chalked it up to the bad memories engendered by her stalker, Deuce McCall, and the terrible sadnesses the old days conjured up.

"Babe," she breathed into his neck, "it's all good from here on in. I promise you."

"Yeah," he said quietly, turning his face so he could run the tip of his tongue over her lips. "But while we're on the old shit..."

She stopped kissing him, and sat back a little so she could see his face.

"Plan on coming to Toronto with me, and maybe we'll take a little field trip out to Peterborough, okay?"

"You think that's a good idea, Josh?"

"I don't know," he answered honestly, plucking a strawberry from the tray and popping it into his wife's mouth. He smiled at the way she had to use a finger to push it all the way in, and at the way her cheeks pinked up a bit 'cuz she'd dribbled a little red juice down her chin. "But I suppose it wouldn't hurt to at least drive by and see where your grandmother lives. Look, Jessie." She sat back and listened. "You'll just have to prepare yourself. They may not want to see you even when you're in front of them. But—"

"But maybe they will. When they see me in person."

Her childlike expression, all expectant and hopeful, touched Josh deeply. He thought of her again in the large photograph at Caryn's, and wondered at how she hadn't come out of that experience all crisp and hardened like a burnt and blackened steak. He slipped a hand underneath her pink T-shirt in the back, at the waist, and moved his hand upwards.

She straightened, her face twisting. "Oh," she cried. "Scratch!"

He did, smiling happily as she contorted this way and that as she tried to eradicate an itch.

"Not there! There! To the right! No, up! Not that far up! Ach! Josh! Down!"

Amused, Josh scratched until he found the right spot. She melted into him then, both arms hugged tight to her body while she lay against his chest. He sighed and scratched gently.

"Oh God that feels good," Jessie murmured, her voice vibrating against his body. "Orgasmic, even."

"I know something else that feels good," he breathed into her ear, pulling her closer against him.

She wriggled in anticipation. "Yes, all that holiday prep and then dinners and church and the wedding and all that...I'm feeling a little deprived, Mr. Sawyer. We have some catching up to do. How much time do we have?"

"My appointment's at two, so if we just have a quick lunch we can make it."

"Doctors are never on time, and this is just a check-up, so—"

"We'll get there on time. If we hurry," he growled menacingly, the corner of one lip inching up playfully.

Jessie leaned back and lifted one leg up. She circled it around him, and then placed both feet on the floor so that she was facing her husband. She nipped her hands down to his jeans and slowly unfastened his belt. "Well, Mister Sawyer, we don't want you to be late for your check-up." A frown creased her brow as she unsnapped his shirt and eased it open, and then drew two fingers up and over his splenectomy scar. "We need that clean bill of health."

She bent forward and teased his nipples with her lips. They hardened immediately, and Josh moaned and arched his back to help her out. His hands were caught in his shirt and on Jessie's lower back, but he made no attempt to struggle free, and instead let his wife do as she wished to pleasure him.

But he felt it was quite all right to give her some direction. "Lower," he begged softly, as her pink tongue drew circles around his right nipple while her left hand tugged gently at the other.

"Oh?" Jessie murmured, then she sat back further and traced the middle of his chest and belly downwards with a lone finger until she could ply his belt fully open and pull the zipper on his jeans down. "Tell me what you like, Sawyer." She slipped off his lap and knelt on the mat on the floor in front of him. She helped him pull down his jeans and boxers, and then she slipped him into her mouth.

"Ahhh," Josh moaned loudly, moving himself towards the edge of the chair to facilitate his own pleasure. But, despite the electricity flowing through his veins, today there was still a niggling voice in the back of Josh's mind. It was saying there was an agony inherent in Jessie's lovemaking, that it was hard earned and maybe, just maybe, she was doing this for him today as some kind of remorse or payback because he would be seeing the doctor this afternoon to have a check-up on the spleen removal not yet a full year old.

Josh tried to push the thoughts away, replacing them with Trudy's gentle encouraging voice, teaching both he and Jessie that it was okay, they loved each other; this was natural and welcome in the intimate life of any couple. But he hadn't confided to Trudy anything at all about Caryn and Eric, and what Jessie had remembered and done in their employ and...in their household.

"Jessie," he moaned gruffly, moving rhythmically to her ministrations, which were quickly stripping his mind of any rational thought as she sent him over the edge, "do you like this? Do you like doing this?"

But if she heard him, she didn't answer and, although she paused, it was brief. Lost in the intoxicating build-up of pleasure, Josh didn't notice her pause, and soon, when he couldn't stand it any longer, he pulled her away from him and urged her onto her back on the floor. He only needed to flick his tongue against her a few times before she was begging him to go inside, and that was fine with him, and soon they were riding the sweet wave that was such a gift to couples in love.

When they were done, they stayed embroiled in each other for another few moments, and Jessie stroked Josh's hair lovingly, murmuring his name as if it were itself a beacon of hope for the future.

"Josh, you are everything to me." Then, murmuring softly, she answered his earlier question, in a way that pleased him but also saddened him, because underneath it were truths he wasn't sure how to interpret. "Of course I love pleasuring you. Of course I do. I'll do anything to make you happy. Anything."

For the second time that day, Josh shivered, and fear and sorrow encapsulated his soul. He damn well knew she would do anything for him; that she would forsake her own happiness *for him*. And what was he doing? Lying. Running around behind her back, trying to get some answers to misguided questions. Thinking he just needed to know the truth and get his hands on some files when, in fact, he was completely intrigued by the dark side of his own personality, the shadow side wanting to peer into a past that, somehow, made him ache for Jessie the same way…well, the same way Caryn ached for her. It made him sick to think of it, to recognize that seeing Jessie in all her vulnerability in those photos excited him. Because she was defenseless and scared then; she was exposed and hurting. Yet, somehow knowing that about her made the photos all that much more erotic.

Conflicted and ashamed of himself, partly for the untruths between them, and partly for the physical desires the images conjured up, Josh pulled himself away from Jessie and kissed her tenderly before he stood and left the room.

"I'm sorry, little one," he inhaled under his breath as he started to close the door behind him. Then he paused, turned, and let his gaze drift up and down his wife's body. In the afterglow, Jessie was laying on her back, watching him with pale sleepy eyes, one hand playing with a nipple and the other up and behind her head. Her hair was splayed out every which way, her jeans discarded in a pile nearby, tangled with her panties, and her T-shirt and bra were close by. She was still moving her hips a little, rhythmically, and her lips were half open.

"Babe," she begged quietly, "I still need you."

Aw hell, he thought tenderly, as he watched Jessie move one hand down her body and widen her legs just a little more. *Who needs lunch? We have chocolate.*

He lay back down beside her and cradled Jessie's head in one arm. With the other, Josh placed his hand on top of hers and, while he helped his wife find another sweet round of electrifying pleasure, he sucked on an earlobe and whispered *I love you* over and over. He slipped his fingers inside her and she clenched around him, and he held her while she cried out and convulsed into him, and as he did so he realized he and Jessie were not all that different. He would do anything to please her, too, and to give her a safe and caring home.

With Caryn's voice echoing in his brain, he thought about what else he could do to make Jessie happy, and Peterborough came to mind, and then Miami, and with that came tolerating Jacob, and then he thought *I hope I have a good check-up today, because I want a lot more of this.* He kissed his wife as she started to come down from her second orgasm to lie trembling, spent and moaning, in his arms, and he held her and rocked her until she was ready to let him go.

Chapter Sixteen

"Saw your film last week."

Jacob yanked a couple of sweet potato fries out of a paper lined red plastic basket and dipped them in chipotle mayo, and then he bit off the ends and double dipped. He looked up at Josh expectantly.

"Why?" Josh asked Jessie's ex point blank, staring at him straight on.

"I dunno. I guess because it's the hottest film in America right now. Thought I might learn something." Jacob leaned forward and whispered conspiratorially, "This acting thing is a helluva lot harder than it looks."

Josh chuckled and poked around at the haddock burger on his plate. He picked up his fork and ate a few bites of the haddock before putting down the fork and grabbing the top of the bun to place over the haddock. The tomato slid off and he frowned and picked it up with his fingers. Once he got the whole thing put together, he took a big bite and murmured appreciatively. Then he got around to answering Jacob.

They were sitting alone in a pub near the hotel in Miami. Kelly and Jessie were with them, as were Michael and Matt, but the four actors had signed autographs while waiting for the meals to be served, and the girls had stuck around to chat with fans. They were over by the cash register, their security keeping a close eye as they posed for pictures.

"Well, we're not saving the world but we're doing our bit to relieve some stress, I guess."

"I feel like a hired monkey sometimes," Jacob admitted candidly. "Do you ever feel that way?"

"I used to. But I see what a good film does for people who need some escapism and so I've learned to let the hired monkey bit go."

"What about the promotional shit? The press tour? Junkets and stuff?"

"It's tedious as hell and, believe me, sometimes there are reporters you want to dig a big hole for, so you can dump them in, because they just don't get it, but you just have to grin and bear it. They mean well, and you need the promotion, so you live with it." *Kinda like you,* Josh caught himself thinking. *I don't like it, but I have no choice but to accept it.*

Jacob grinned diffidently and looked down. He had a feeling he knew what Josh was thinking, and he felt the same way.

Josh continued. "The press tour for *Freedom Ride* was okay. I was glad *Mystic Nights* did some rearranging so Jessie could come along. You too. Thanks for changing your schedule," he mumbled.

"Yeah, it's all good," Jacob said, avoiding Josh's scrutiny and glancing to the right to see how the girls were getting along. "Gave me a chance to bond with Goldilocks over there." Jessie and Kelly were arm in arm, all smiles, as they posed for pictures.

Nodding towards Kelly, Josh tossed in, "She seems to have chilled a bit? Or is that just for our benefit?"

"She's settled down over the last few months, since Christmas. Michael has some kind of hold over her. Father figure or something, who knows?"

"Are they a couple?"

"Not that I'm aware of. I dunno. I think Matt would have his balls if he went there."

"What about you, then? And Kelly?"

Jacob pushed another sweet potato into the dip and chewed thoughtfully before answering Josh. "What, so you can get me off your radar? Tell me how you really feel, Sawyer."

"Just layin' it out, Ryan. Kelly's a singer, you're a singer…she's fucked up, you're fucked up…"

At that, Jacob threw his head back and laughed boisterously. Despite the ever-present tension when Josh was around, he couldn't help but like the guy. "Jesus, Sawyer," he said, "I'll let you know when I find someone, okay? I'll send you a carrier pigeon or something. So you're the first to know."

It was spring now, April 5th, and the gang were celebrating Josh's birthday. Over the last few months a steady rhythm had occupied the minds of the actors, with lots of travel to Miami to finish *Mystic Nights*, a few auditions here and there, some recording and music video shoots in Vancouver that Jessie and Jacob both cherished as their own special soul-time together and, of course, Josh's hectic promo tour for *Freedom Ride*, the Harley film.

He and Jessie had taken a side trip to Peterborough to scout out her relatives but, as Evelyn predicted, they got nowhere and, in fact, faced only closed doors and seemingly empty houses. Broken-hearted but resilient, Jessie chose to take a stiff upper lip about the whole thing, and so she continued to bug Evelyn for emails and contact info (not forthcoming, which made her wonder if this was all Evelyn's doing), and then Jessie simply pushed her relatives aside and continued her busy acting and singing lifestyle, filling any 'spare' time with awards shows, fundraising benefits for her and Dee's shelters, and visits with the old *Drifters* gang.

Now, in Miami, nearing the end of the season one *Mystic Nights* shoot, she felt healthy and happy. Jessie's husband was by her side as much as possible, and she also carried a sheer exuberant joy for those in her circle of friends. By doing this, Jessie could project the love she wanted to give her family onto those who were her constant protectors and sincere pals.

The latest to receive her unequalled love and sincere joy were Charlie and Jane, whose baby Stella came into the world in January. Every time they were home in Vancouver, Josh accompanied Jessie to their house so she could hold the baby and gush over her in the way women who wanted to be mothers often did. She and Josh had talked about having children of their own soon, despite Deirdre's nervous caution to wait a little while. *You haven't had a lot of time together as a couple yet, Jessie.* But Jessie's response was always *we've already lost a lot of time, Dee. The clock is ticking.* She didn't have a family, per se, not a biological one at least, and she wanted one. A big one. She stopped taking birth control the day Stella was born.

In the last few months, Josh relaxed a little over Caryn and Eric, and Jessie's involvement with them. But he was still inexplicably drawn to them, in his voyeuristic attempt to soak up everything about his wife, including a past most would consider sketchy. He went twice to see Caryn, and both times the stoic Eric stood watch twelve feet away in the kitchen. Josh had yet to walk away with any files, and when he left the East Hastings home he always asked himself what the hell he went there for. Inside, he knew. While he was there he sat quietly drinking colorful virgin drinks Eric made them, and he and Caryn shared stories and secrets about the person they loved the most—Jessie. There were more photos than the ones Josh saw upon his first visit and, as she grew to trust him—or draw him in—Caryn pressed a few of these into Josh's palm. Her eyes suggested he hide them from Jessie, but some uneasy part of him also thought perhaps she wanted them to be found.

He hid them in his underwear drawer, underneath a pair of never worn red Snoopy Valentine's Day boxers with *I luv u* emblazoned across the butt.

Now, the girls bounced over to the boys' table, Matt and Michael close behind.

"Geez," Jessie was saying, as if she had already forgotten she had just signed a bunch of autographs and posed for pictures, and that she was, in fact, an international star. "My quesadilla's gone all hard. It's not gooey anymore." She lifted the top tortilla and the bottom came with it. She grimaced.

"I'll order you another one." Kelly waved at a server and hollered, "Hey! Another quesadilla for Jessie Wheeler-Sawyer over here!" She teetered on her stool and smiled at Jessie.

"Yeesh Kelly, it's okay," Jessie said, lifting a hand to grab her co-star's arm and pull it down. "This one's fine. There are kids starving in the world. I'm not going to waste it."

Josh eyed her carefully as he chewed on the corner of his lip. He glanced over at Matt, who caught his eye. Lately it seemed the homeless Jessie was on Josh's mind a lot; he could see in the flicker of sadness lining Matt's face that he, too, was not likely ever to forget where Jessie came from, or the pain once encircling her that now, thankfully, seemed to have evaporated.

"Jacob," Jessie asked tactfully, oblivious to Josh's dark thoughts, and inhaling deeply for courage as Kelly sat fuming, embarrassed, next to her, "how did it go with your grandparents last week?"

Jacob had finally dropped up to New York for a visit. He was welcomed warmly, and he sat up straighter now, eyes bright, and regaled Jessie with tales of his trip—the over-protective grandmother, the silent thoughtful grandfather.

As she listened, Jessie's reaction was the opposite of his. Her shoulders sank, and she tried to smile but it was tough. Watching her, Josh resolved to try to break down Aunt Evelyn himself, despite concerns about Jessie meeting up with her long-lost family. They'd be going out to their new ranch next month, maybe then he could corner the aunt.

Due to some red tape with funding, the P.E.I. hockey film was delayed until further notice, so that opened up some time in their crazy schedules. However, Jessie's role on *Mystic Nights* had grown, as Charles predicted, so that didn't help. But he'd make time. *They* would make time.

It wasn't all roses in Jacob's world. Jessie asked him about his dad.

"No, I haven't heard anything from him, Jess. He's off my radar."

But a silent look passed between him and her, which Josh caught and that caused his belly to tighten. He was well aware the 'music-dad' thing was just one more point Jacob and Jessie had in common that excluded him entirely. He stared hard at Jacob's beer and cursed under his breath. *Damn it, sometimes a cold beer would be fucking welcome.* Josh sometimes wondered if he could handle alcohol. After all, a beer was a simple drink. It was not a complicated cocktail of street drugs. He shook the thought away and sucked on the colored straw in his ginger ale.

The discussion around the table turned to an upcoming *Mystic Nights* end of season live concert that would be followed by the wrap party. As she spooned salsa onto her quesadilla, Jessie tossed a question in Michael's direction. "I hear you've been asked to play a few tunes with us."

He tensed noticeably. "I won't be playing."

"Why not?" Kelly whined, as she started on her fourth strawberry daiquiri.

"I don't play anymore, Kelly. You know that." Michael glared at her drink. Seemed that over the season of *Mystic Nights*, he was less amused by her and more annoyed. At least, that's the way it felt this evening, in the small air-conditioned pub in downtown Miami.

"You're just being a baby," she pouted.

"Miss Reilly," the usual quiet Matt warned.

"What? A lot of people would come to see the great Michael Kelly play live again. And anyways he's always pushing me to do stuff I don't want to do."

"Like what," Jacob demanded, amused. "Let him carry you out of bars?"

Viper Kelly appeared out of nowhere, egged on by the drink and by being cornered. "You know, you're a schmaltzy little thing, aren't you, Jacob?"

"Cool it, Kelly." Michael was nonchalant, sitting back in his stool and sucking on a toothpick. But his eyes were wary. Over the season he'd seen a lot of Kelly Reilly's moods, and he was starting to feel he knew her well.

"Oh, fuck off," she spat at him. "You and your fucking secrets. I'm tired of people hiding things from me all the time. Or not telling it like it is." She waved a hand drunkenly at Jacob. "You *are* schmaltzy."

Jacob turned to Jessie and whispered, "What the hell does that even mean?" Then he turned back to Kelly and gestured lightly to her. "Go on, your Highness."

Non-plussed, she crossed her elegant knees and continued. "For one, all of your songs are life-sucking ballads."

"And yours are no-brain pop songs."

"And when you kiss me on camera, you smother my nose and I can't breathe."

Josh stifled a chuckle and angled his head away so Kelly wouldn't notice. Michael raised his eyebrows, and even Matt laughed. Jessie just groaned and hung her head in her hands.

Kelly continued. "In our last love scene, you didn't even get hard."

"Jesus, Kelly," came from Michael who, Jessie noticed, actually seemed to be getting a little hot under the collar.

"As if you would even notice, you little princess," Jacob muttered, taking a healthy swig of his Guinness. "You are always so tanked up I'm surprised you even know what set to report to. Amazes me that you know any of your lines." He leaned towards her. "In fact, I've long figured out that's why you always want to change lyrics, and lines. You don't fucking know them, so you figure if you change them, no one will have a sweet clue!"

Kelly slid off her stool and staggered towards Jacob, who tried to grab her to keep her upright on the ubiquitous tall heels. Josh and Jessie exchanged glances. This little altercation was quickly losing its amusement potential.

Kelly threw off Jacob's grip. "Let go of me, you schmaltzy little creep!" She turned to Michael. "You're playing at the concert." A dim light faded in her eyes, and she went to grab her drink but she missed it, and knocked Jacob's over instead. It went flying into his groin, soaking him.

"Oops, sorry," she mouthed to him, arrogant and unapologetic. She pulled a linen napkin off the table. "Let. Me. Just. See. If. I. Can. Clean. You. Up." Her eyes drifted downwards and she shoved the napkin towards Jacob but he grabbed the delicate wrist and stopped her. Taking the napkin out of her grip, he mopped at the mess himself, sliding off his own stool to do so, cursing under his breath all the while.

Matt caught Michael's eye and nodded sternly at him.

"Fine," Michael said. "Pay the bill, will you?" He stared irritably at his brother and rose, the chair screeching loudly backwards on the wooden floor.

"You know what?" Kelly interjected, raising her hands to stop him from coming towards her. "I think we should trade tonight. What do you say, Jessie? Trade men? You take Michael, for a change, and maybe you can convince him to sing. I'll take Matt. He's so sweet." She smiled cherubically at Matt, who straightened nervously. This was a Kelly Reilly special, about to happen.

Out of control and gaining momentum, Kelly continued. She pointed a wagging finger at Josh. "Actually," she preened, smoothing down her yellow mini-dress with her other hand, "I want Josh. You take Jacob." She whipped her head around to face Jessie. "What's it like when you're with Jacob on set? I mean, I know he's mostly my character's love interest now, but when he's with you, does he…you know?" She gestured to her crotch, and Matt turned slowly around to see if anyone in the pub had cellphones out. He relaxed when he saw no evidence of recording, or even of interest in the celebrities at this time. Miami was mostly immune to celebs on the prowl. It was often the tourists Matt and Michael had to watch for.

"Go, Michael," he demanded. "Take her home."

Jessie groaned and avoided both the bristling Josh's and fuming Jacob's eyes. "You're gonna miss the cake if you don't settle down, Mizz Reilly."

Tossing the soaked napkin on the table, Jacob gestured to Kelly. "How about I take you up on that offer instead, your highness?"

The table floated into shocked silence. Jacob's face was flushed and he was shaking.

Teetering on one toe, Kelly turned to him and smiled seductively. She tilted her head sideways and looked at Michael. "That okay with you, Michael?

If I go home with Jacob, I mean." She leaned forward and rested both elbows on the table, so that her low cleavage was clearly displayed for the men at the table to see. She whispered loudly. "I think he has something he wants to prove to me."

Standing next to Josh, across from Kelly, Michael's eyes were flashing. Everyone at the table tensed, waiting for his reaction. It was no secret something was at play between Kelly and her security, and no one really knew whether they'd consummated any kind of relationship or not, but, regardless, there were feelings openly at play between them. Now, for Kelly to blatantly throw Jacob in his face, it was obvious he was hurt, and at a loss.

"You're drunk," he said quietly, thrumming his fingers on the table. They echoed hollowly throughout the pub, which just happened to have its satellite playlist between songs momentarily. "I'll take you home."

"Nada," Kelly replied, her voice edged with sarcasm. "Coward." She spat the word at him, and it pierced him the way she hoped it would—through the heart.

"Jacob." Jessie's face was pale, her eyes wide. She shook her head.

"Oh, fuck you, Jessie. I hope you and your cowboy enjoy your goddamned cake."

He looked down and grasped Kelly's hand. He was sick of her attitude, and sick of Jessie and Josh making eyes at each other all through dinner and, in fact, any time they were together. He'd heard rumblings of them trying for a baby, and that sickened him further. Lately it seemed that apart from music, all he and Jessie had left was their loneliness for family connections. And, not counting his grandparents, most of the family shit didn't seem to be going so good. Jacob was tired, he wanted to get laid, and Kelly was apparently willing.

He turned to Michael. "Yeah, if it's okay with you, I think Matt will come with us tonight." He fired a direct stare in Matt's direction. "*Matt*." He didn't pose it as a question. It was a demand. Matt was his security as well as Jessie's these days, although Jacob had never—not once—abused this or usurped Jessie's needs. But tonight he was tired of being second.

Matt's gaze landed squarely on Jessie. He waited, swallowing his pride and realizing more was at play here than Jacob and some stupid playboy routine. He saw the hurt in the boy's eyes every time he looked at Jessie, and by God she didn't help matters any by constantly touching his thigh or leaning over to whisper to him on set. Now, he spied a deep hurt pride in Jessie's eyes and he could see by the way she sucked on her lip and then ran a finger over her top lip and then the bottom that she was less than impressed with Jacob at this point in time. She was looking at him now, and he was staring right back, challenging her. Between them, a current of electricity was flying back and forth. If he would have looked closer, Matt might have seen the shadow of a Celtic cross flit across Jessie's icy eyes. Jacob sure as hell saw it, and he drew back his shoulders as he fired bullets back at his co-star.

Jessie had heard the rumors about Kelly and a supposed love of tattoos. Whether it was true or not, she swallowed past the lump in her throat as she pictured Kelly's manicured nails digging into the cross on Jacob's back. An unbidden memory of the way he pushed himself down on her when they made love in the old days crossed Jessie's mind, and she didn't dare meet Josh's eyes as her nipples and thighs tingled in remembrance. It was easier to keep Jacob as a friend, as a pet, almost. It hurt like hell when she thought about him driving himself into someone else, especially…Kelly. Also, she knew he was drunk now, too, and pissed at Kelly's comments about him. But the Jacob she knew wouldn't hurt Michael this way.

She looked over at Kelly's handler, bypassing Josh's dark eyes, and she sucked back a breath. Michael was white, silent and stiff.

A rustle accompanied Jacob and Kelly, hand in hand, as they moved towards the door, and high-pitched giggling forced its way into Jessie's ears. Matt's stern voice jarred her to action.

"Jessie?"

She exhaled slowly, emitting a tiny whistle, then forced herself to look at Matt. She shrugged, trying to pretend she didn't give a shit. "Whatever," she said, managing to hide nothing. Finally, she found the courage to look at Josh. The sight of him almost crumpled her, because Jessie was powerless to hide how she felt about Jacob, but also because she loved Josh so deeply that it killed her to know she'd hurt him by virtue of her reactions here, tonight.

"Michael," she said, still lost in Josh's crushed eyes, "I hope you like cake."

Chapter Seventeen

"Wham, bam, thank-you Ma'am, is it?" Kelly was languishing on top of the duvet, eyeing the inked cross covering Jacob's back as he sat on the edge of the bed, his back to her, shoulders sagging. He reached towards the floor and grabbed his jeans, and started to pull them up when Kelly stopped him by grabbing his elbow.

"Seriously. Jacob, it's fine, you don't have to run away." She was speaking quickly, her voice almost a falsetto.

He sighed and inched around to face her. Lifting a hand, he ran it through his scraggly hair. "Look, Kelly, I just needed a lay, okay? That's all."

In silence, she watched him get back to the business of dressing.

Jacob was only the slightest bit remorseful at leaving her this way. All season she had been almost nothing but bitter and mean to him, with only the slightest ray of sunshine here and there if for some weird reason she happened to be in a decent mood, which was a rare and special treat. On set, she was almost always cruel, to other cast, to crew, even to the guest directors, some of whom were big stars in their own right. The producers who had the guts to call her on it were edgy and nervous when they spoke to her. She carried a lot of power on *Mystic Nights*. If she had a hissy fit and left—for a day, or a week—she would cost them a lot of money and cachet on their production.

"Why?"

Now it was a tiny voice, floating up to Jacob from Kelly's prone position on the bed. Without turning, he forced on his boots and thought before he spoke.

"Because you're not a nice person, Kelly. And because it kills me that,

165

despite myself, I can't help but like Josh Sawyer. And because it kills me to lie beside his wife on set and touch her, and have her touch me, and even be asked to go so far—in the name of the production, you hear—as to touch her between her legs, and then have to walk away. Or limp, I should say. It fucking kills me." He was surprised to suddenly find himself choked up. "Jesus," he cursed at himself. "Get it together, Ryan."

Kelly stroked his back. Her fingers felt like cotton as she traced his large cross.

"You still love her," she acknowledged in a whisper, her emerald eyes gossamer in the moonlight wafting into the darkening room.

"I do, yes," Jacob admitted, pausing in pulling on his second boot as he responded. "If you want the truth, then yes I will love her til the day I die. And then some." He finished yanking up the boot, and bent over to pull his jeans down over it.

Kelly's voice was soft, her words tinged with a barely concealed pain. "What is it about Jessie that has everyone all googly over her? I can't stand her. That shy way she has of looking at everybody around her…to me she's just some weak child everybody feels they have to cater to. You included. And her music is—"

"Surreal." He, too, was soft-spoken now. Lost in the mystique of Jessie Wheeler.

"No. I was going to say…saccharine."

Jacob twisted around again to regard Kelly. This time a small grin lightened the darkness playing around his cobalt eyes. "That's a big word for you, Kelly."

"Oh, fuck off." She tossed a pillow at him. "Alcohol fires my brain."

"Oh, so that's why you drink so much." He tossed the pillow lightly back at her. She grabbed it and hugged it, and then sat up on one elbow and studied him.

"I started drinking when my mom killed herself."

"Ah." The shock factor of that statement took a moment to sink in. Unnerving goose bumps prickled their way up Jacob's arms. "I'm sorry, Kelly. Really." He paused before pronouncing, "So you have more in common with Jessie than you think."

"Her mom's still alive."

"Her dad died when she was twelve."

"My mom killed herself when her boyfriend decided he wanted me instead." She didn't blink as she disclosed this to Jacob. She just lay there on her side, propped up on one elbow, staring at him, willing him to react in some way, in any way. She needed him to react. Wistfully, she touched the sleeve of his plaid shirt. "He always wore these kinds of shirts."

"So I take it you liked the guy too?"

"I was sixteen. He was thirty-two. But yeah. I liked him all right."

"Where'd he go?" Jacob asked carefully. "After your mom died?"

She played with the corner of the duvet while she considered what to tell him. "She killed herself. She didn't…*die*. Like of some disease." The corners of her lips turned down in disgust. "She chose to die. And the thing is…she killed him first."

The shock of that disclosure rippled through Jacob, and he felt a chill in the warm room that left him shivering. He expected to see a cold hardness in Kelly's eyes, but instead he just saw moisture forming there. She was looking at him in a plaintive inexpressive way, yet the brightness of her eyes gave away her pain.

"I'm sorry," he said honestly, reaching out to flick a strand of honey-blonde hair away from her cheek. "But as much as that sucks, Kelly, we've all got pain. It doesn't give you a reason to hate and devour everybody in your path. Look at Jessie—"

"Yes, look at fucking Jessie! Jesus, I'm so tired of everybody touting all her virtues, all of the fucking time! She's not a—a God!"

She leapt off the bed and, naked, marched over to the drapes. With a hard pull on each, she forced them closed. The room darkened further, but Jacob could still see the angst in his co-star's eyes as she whipped around and faced him.

"Kelly, the thing about Jessie is—"

"I don't care! I don't care about Jessie!"

"You tried to order her another quesadilla! Admit it, you've fallen under her spell too!"

Kelly threw up her hands in disbelief. "What spell? What fucking spell?

I can't stand the little bitch! And I can't stand you!" She shook suddenly as sobs overtook her—sobs of sorrow at the loss of her mother and a man she thought loved her at a tender, fragile age…sobs for Michael's eyes at the table that night, silent and guarded.

She sobbed for the confusion and hurt she seemed only able to voice through sarcasm and cruelty, there were sobs of anger at Jacob for finally calling her on her cruelty and ruthlessly using her to couch his own pain, and there were sobs of loneliness for a man with whom she somehow seemed to connect but who she, earlier tonight, heartlessly tossed away like last night's refried beans.

"Oh fuck!" she cried, dropping to the floor, her body heaving with a pain she could only express now through great waves of tears.

Watching her, Jacob considered what to do. He tried to touch Kelly, but she recoiled and screamed at him to get away. It was like he was lightning, and she was cold hard metal…his touch both electrified and terrorized her. It sent great jolts of memory and recall through her body, knocking Kelly senseless with an anxiety so overwhelming she was rendered helpless.

Ten minutes later a frazzled Jacob stood in front of a hotel room door and considered knocking. He realized he had two choices here. Kelly had a lot of power on *Mystic Nights*, and be damned if he was going to be responsible for her carrying out any kind of self-harm, like taking pills or jumping out a window. He figured rightly she needed help, but who best to ask? He knew both Jessie and Michael were likely pissed at him, and it was now twelve-thirty, so both were probably in bed. The thought of Jessie snuggled up to Josh repulsed him, and so he chose what he considered the lesser of two evils. He knocked on Michael's door.

Matt's brother took his time answering. When he did, it was apparent he should have been asleep—his eyes were red-rimmed and lined with fatigue—but he was still fully dressed. He was clutching a Budweiser, from which he took periodic pulls as he glared at Jacob.

Jacob shoved both hands deep in his pockets, hunched his shoulders nervously, and inhaled deeply. "She's kinda messed up right now, Michael."

A cold flush swept over Michael's face. He pondered Jacob while sucking the beer in between his teeth, which made a sort of hissing sound.

It disconcerted Jacob, so he shifted his weight uneasily and avoided the man's stare by eyeing the toes of his boots.

"What do you mean she's messed up? What the hell did the two of you get into?" Michael grabbed Jacob's shirtsleeve and yanked it up, then roughly lifted it so he could get a good look at the inside of his arm.

"Ow! Lay off, man!" Jacob stepped backwards, taking his now sore arm with him. "I don't do drugs and, from what I can tell, neither does Kelly. Just booze, man." He eyed Michael guardedly, from a position out of reach a few feet away. He changed his stance so he was square on to Michael, feet a hip distance apart. "Look, if you're not interested in helping her I'll go get Matt. Go back to bed or watching TV or whatever the hell else you were doing in there." He stole a quick look behind the man, and was rather astonished to spy an acoustic guitar leaning against the foot of the bed.

A questioning look replaced Jacob's nerves. If Michael realized why, he didn't give his thoughts away. And he wasn't budging. Raising his hands in defeat, Jacob grumbled, "All right," and backed away.

Michael hesitated, but only for a moment. After Jacob turned his back, he disappeared inside, cursed while he grabbed his card key and then the spare he kept for Kelly's larger suite, and then he accosted Jacob in the hallway seconds before the singer would have knocked on Matt's door.

"All right," he demanded gruffly. "What the hell happened?"

Flustered, Jacob stammered, "I don't know, she just…well, she got on this lame stupid kick about Jessie and then she told me about her mom, about what happened to her mom, and about some guy from years ago—"

Michael froze and stared death rays at Jacob. "What about her mom? What about some guy?"

"She didn't tell you?"

Once again, Michael's hard glare unsettled Jacob. The man didn't speak and, instead, just waited, solemnly, anxiously. The only clue Jacob had to the guy's rapidly increasing anxiety was a little pulse at Michael's neck, which started to flicker faster and faster. He swallowed.

"Her mom killed herself." He waited for the inevitable shock to pass like a wave over Michael's eyes. Then he continued with the grisly tale. "Supposedly she killed her lover first. Because he had turned to Kelly. When Kelly was sixteen."

It was late and Jacob was damn tired, sick of thinking about what Jessie was doing in bed with Josh, and fed up with the hurt and pain consuming so many good people and distorting so many lives. His voice was flat, his declaration of Kelly's troubles, flat, unemotional. He didn't wait for Michael to react. He started walking again, towards Kelly's door. He could still hear her wailing, although the eerie sound was now more like a baby bird crying for its mama.

He gulped past the nausea suddenly assaulting his senses, and waited for Michael to unlock the door.

Inside, it took a few moments for both men's pupils to adjust. Kelly hadn't moved, and for some reason Jacob was relieved to see that—perhaps because it also meant she hadn't consumed any more alcohol or perhaps something else of a more sinister nature. He stayed just inside the door while Michael approached the *Mystic Nights* star. He waited until Kelly accepted Michael's soothing tone and warm, welcoming arms, and then Jacob—numb, sick, and disgusted with life as well as himself—swung around, wrenched open the big door, and let himself back out into the light.

Chapter Eighteen

"For God's sake, can you please just stop doing that?"

Jessie clamped a hand onto Josh's to stop him from clanking his spoon around his coffee cup. The sound was driving her over the edge. She hadn't slept well, and had awoken with a massive headache and an upset belly, and so was not in the mood to tolerate harsh sounds this morning. It was five thirty, and she was trying to stomach some breakfast—some fruit and yogurt, maybe—before climbing into the production van to be driven to set.

Just as she was wondering where Jacob was, he waltzed into the banquet room the production used for occasional early morning breakfasts at the hotel, and he plonked his iPhone down at an empty place next to Jessie. His bloodshot, tired eyes drifted over to Josh, who appeared even more bleary-eyed than the two actors on this show. He wasn't at all surprised when Josh fired him a silent *fuck you*.

His own mood having not improved since the drama of the night before, Jacob fired back. "What's the matter, Sawyer, didn't get laid last night?"

"Jesus, you two," Jessie moaned between the fingers she was using to try to keep the light out of her eyes.

Josh stood and faced Jacob, but it wasn't a fight he wanted. He glared, but his response was fair. "As a matter of fact I didn't, Ryan, Jessie and I actually have a helluva lot more between us than just sex." He studied Jacob's own inflamed eyes. "What's the matter with you? Awww, let me guess, you *did* get laid last night."

A groan accompanied Jessie's head landing on her now folded arms on

171

the table. Josh reached down and pulled her sliced fresh fruit bowl away from her hair, some of which was now a little sticky.

"What's wrong with her?" Jacob asked testily, still standing by his place setting.

"Headache," Josh answered, lifting Jessie's hair to peek at her flushed face. He laid a hand against her cheek to see if she was running a fever and, concerned, his liquid chocolate eyes softened noticeably.

Thumping his chest lightly, Jacob screwed up his face. "The two of you together just make my heart break, you're so fucking cute." He swung around and strode over to the breakfast buffet, yawning as he opened the metal lid on the scrambled egg pan.

Heaving his chair around, Josh reclaimed his seat and bent down to his wife. "Jessie? Hey little one, maybe you need to sit this one out. Why don't I see if they can do some rearranging this morning, okay? You might feel better in a few hours."

"I'm fine," came the tough voice Josh knew and loved from their time on *Drifters,* from the strong woman who intended to do a massive concert hours after being viciously raped and beaten. "I can work. I'll be okay."

Just then, one of the show's producers breezed into the room. A man of Charles' age, he commanded the attention of the assembled cast and crew merely by scanning the room's occupants. Something in his expression was amiss this morning—usually confident and amiable, today the Armani clad producer was intent and serious. He clapped his hands unnecessarily, as everyone was already looking at him, with the exception of Jacob, who was fighting a losing battle with a sausage he was trying to clasp between a long set of tongs.

"People, listen up," the producer was saying, clasping and adjusting his tie anxiously while he spoke as dollar signs flashed before his eyes. "We will be starting late this morning. We will be rearranging our day. Miss Reilly is unwell and won't be working today." His large curious eyes swept the room again and landed on Jessie, who was twisting around in her seat, watching him, one set of white knuckles clasped on the back of her chair, the other fisted into a ball in her lap.

"Jessie, you can go back to bed for an hour. We'll wake you when we know what's up. We may need to keep you a few extra days."

At her gasp, which he ignored, the producer turned to Jacob who, finally with a sausage on his plate, was frozen. "Same for you, Jacob." He turned back to the general presence in the room. "The writers are helping us with this but I would also appreciate everyone's silence and discretion until Miss Reilly is feeling better and is up to working again. All of you signed non-disclosure agreements. This is one of those times when we'll be enforcing those agreements with gusto, should anything untoward regarding Kelly's illness be leaked to the press. Let me remind you—all of you are replaceable."

"Wuss," Jessie breathed softly, only half-kidding, as she sat back and looked at Josh, who was watching her with a mixture of worry and frustration.

"If they keep you longer, I'm going to have to go, Jessie. I've got to be in Toronto Friday to shoot that pick-up."

"I know," Jessie sighed wistfully. "But I'll be right behind you. Hopefully just a day or two. I'll meet you in Van."

Jacob made his way back to the table and set his plate next to Jessie. He dragged his chair back until there was room for him to sit, and then he dropped heavily into it.

"What'd you do to her?" Josh asked, sarcasm coloring his tone.

"Wouldn't you like to know?" Jacob grinned, despite an overpowering worry for Kelly, and for Jessie now too, apparently, according to her drawn and pale appearance at their early breakfast. He winked at Jessie, who shot an imaginary bullet between his eyes and shook her aching head at him.

"Mmppff," muttered Josh as he stood again and took his and Jessie's dishes to the rectangular gray collection bucket by the door.

"Jacob, must you really antagonize him?"

Smirking, Jacob forked up a big bite of sausage and chewed happily. He enjoyed these little mini-battles with Josh. They gave him some sort of one-upmanship that somehow massaged his delicate ego and broken heart.

"Kelly was in bad shape when I left her last night," he offered, instead of responding to Jessie's comment.

"I don't want to know," she snapped. "Jesus, Jacob." She shoved back her chair and rose, intending to follow Josh out of the room. She could see him now in discussion with an AD, and she wanted the information she felt he was likely receiving, in terms of scheduling issues.

"Not that," he cut in, just as quickly. "Relax, Jessie." He waved a hand in the air towards her chair, indicating she should sit back down.

With one more glance towards her husband, her heart lurching in the process as she silently appraised his choice of jeans, white V-necked T-shirt, square-toed brown leather boots and tan leather jacket, Jessie sat back down, aware as she did that many of the female eyes in the room were also on her husband. He was big news now, with his critically appraised lead in *Freedom Ride* the talk of every entertainment show and gossip rag in the world these days. She swallowed her worry and blinked anxiously at Jacob.

"She had some kind of meltdown," Jacob explained. He gave Jessie the abbreviated version, declining to mention Kelly's state of undress at the time, Michael's late night rescue while she was in that state, and that he, Jacob, felt helpless and afraid but also, sadly, only mildly so, given her treatment of him over their months of shooting.

"Shit, that's not good," pondered Jessie thoughtfully. "I didn't know anything about her past."

A new current passed between her and Jacob as they recalled their own now united and terrifying past, which ended with Jacob killing Jessie's stalker. She forced herself to quell her trembling, to not ask him whether Kelly liked the erotic Celtic cross emblazoned across his back, and whether it had enticed her more deeply into earth-shattering sex. She shook her head and blinked the thought away.

Soon, the cast and crew had the news they needed. With the rearranged schedule, Jessie had no choice but to stay in Miami longer than originally planned. She was also at the mercy of the producers in terms of rewritten scenes Jacob would shoot with her instead of with Kelly.

Kelly would be seeing some help, but at this point nobody was able to cajole her out of bed. Jessie was sorry to hear that. She had her own memories of such days and, despite Kelly's irascible temperament, she didn't wish that kind of deep pain on anybody.

Josh flew to Toronto on schedule, having negotiated some sort of middle peace with Jacob again that gave him a modicum of trust with Jessie and, as soon as he left, Jessie slipped into the bar to chat with a crew member she trusted, a woman AD, who knocked on her door later that evening and handed Jessie a home pregnancy test. The last thing Jessie needed was to be spotted purchasing it herself.

Michael sat in a chair at the head of Kelly's bed and held her hand. When she awoke intermittently, he tried to talk to her, but she buried her head in the pillows and drifted back off to the fantasyland offered by sleep.

The day before Jessie flew back home, Josh, back in Vancouver—seemingly unable to help himself—acted on a simple text sent by Caryn, and sent his and Jessie's lives spinning once again.

Chapter Nineteen

The text from Caryn read simply *good day to see set, drop by.*

She had long ago invited Josh to drop by her and Eric's black box studio, but Josh, despite his few visits to their home, had hesitated about going to the studio. Reasons? Well, for one, he was terrified of conjuring up the old memories of the stint he did for Wes Sawyer, the man whom he thought was his dad, for whom he likely made a ton of money by unwittingly acting in a child porn flick at age fourteen.

Second reason? He'd seen the photos Jessie posed in for Caryn. He knew there were 'a few films' but he didn't know how many or what they featured, exactly. He was sickened at the thought of his girl doing any kind of porn (although Caryn called it erotica, *bless her heart,* he thought sarcastically), but still—it frightened him.

But his shadow side was intrigued. The photos were old news now. It was time to assess the film studio.

Driving downtown, Josh told himself he was still just on a quest to get control of the photos and films. It was easier to do this today because he was a little pissed at his wife for her blatant heartsick stare at Jacob the night of Josh's birthday. He trusted her not to act, yes, but he knew she was still—and always would be, on some level at least—in love with Jacob.

Damn it, Jessie he cursed as he piloted the King Ranch towards East Hastings. He sighted a parking spot on the opposite side of the road to the studio and slid the big truck into it. Flicking off the ignition was like shutting off an essential heartbeat. Suddenly the silence of the ticking, quieting engine was a roar in his ears, echoing a pulse that threatened to erupt somewhere on his body; how, he didn't know, maybe through his ears or out of his chest like in that old Alien movie.

Josh slammed the driver's side door and, like a well-rehearsed child, looked both ways before crossing the street. His footsteps hammered on the pavement, keeping time with his nervous heart. He waved when he saw Caryn arriving at the same time as he, a tray of coffees in one hand and a wide smile on her exquisite, elegant face.

"Hey," she called enthusiastically. "I'm glad you decided to come." She held out the tray. "Caffeine?"

"Drip coffee?"

"Yes. Rwandan. It has a nice citrus and chocolate aftertaste."

The coffees were from Revolver. Josh's heart lurched, but he stilled it with a quick and silent *leave me be* as he took a coffee from the tray. Inside the building, he added milk in Caryn's office before she took his coat, hung it on a mahogany rack inside the door, and led him towards the studio.

"I should warn you, we have a guest today, Josh."

"Oh?" *What? Who…?*

She tugged open the door between the offices and the studio, and Josh followed her in. Once his eyes adjusted to the dim light, he recognized a man who approached from behind the camera. It was Arnie, Jessie's Downtown Eastside friend. Arnie—the man who helped her escape her life a few years ago.

Arnie nodded at Josh but didn't extend a hand. "How's my girl doing?" he asked simply, tilting his head back somewhat so he could better see Josh, who was almost lost in the semi-darkness and who was also slightly taller.

"She's fine," Josh said in a clipped response, his mind firing a mile a minute. He, too, didn't offer to shake. He took a pull on the hot coffee and yelped when he burned his lips and spilled a few drops on his hand. "Shit."

Arnie wandered over to a makeup table nearby and yanked a few tissues out of a box. He handed them to Josh. "Here."

"Hot." Josh said.

"Yeah, well, it is coffee."

No shit, Dick Tracy. Josh regarded Arnie carefully. The man was wearing a tight T-shirt, navy blue, and his biceps bulged beneath the short sleeves.

His broad chest was obviously well earned. Josh seemed to recall hearing something about the man spending time in a boxing ring. Arnie set himself up to Josh's right, and it was only then, as Josh watched Arnie, that he realized the man was watching something else—the actors were blocking their shot with Caryn, who was directing this particular 'episode.'

Arnie distracted him. "She's in Miami today? Shooting that new television series?"

"Yeah." Despite his tensed nerves, which threatened to snap like a guitar string, Josh resolved to be amiable. There was something beguiling about Caryn that helped him relax in the weird situations he found himself in around her. He figured it had something to do with her predisposition towards white. She always seemed to be surrounded by the virginal, innocent color—her clothing, her furniture, even her boots were often white. *Or maybe she's a wolf in sheep's clothing*, he muttered inwardly.

He extended his answer to Arnie's cordial query. "She's fine," he said for the second time, a little more confidently, as he sipped on the super hot beverage. "She's happy."

"I see that in her interviews," Arnie agreed. "I'm glad. I'm glad she came back and worked things out."

"Why are you here, Arnie?" Amicable was one thing, but it didn't mean Josh couldn't ask questions...

"Caryn asked me to drop by. To help explain some things."

Josh tensed further. *Explain what?* He eyed Arnie's muscular forearms. *And explain how?*

Shooting him a sideways look, Arnie chuckled. "Relax, Josh, I won't damage your pretty movie star face. I know what you want, coming around here. I just need you to understand that we have a code down here, on the streets. Not everyone adheres to it, mind you. But Caryn and Eric do, and I'm in on it as well."

"Meaning?"

"Meaning nothing Jessie did back in the past will ever see the light of day in any public forum. We give you our word."

"That's not good enough."

"It's going to have to be." Arnie turned and looked at Josh. "Think about

178

it. We're talking about digital files here, Josh. Even if we gave you some—
and I'm being brutally honest here—how would you ever believe we gave
you the only copies? That we didn't make copies that could still be leaked to
the media? And let me ask you this—why isn't Jessie worried?"

Josh had pondered that himself. "I don't know," he offered quietly. "Look,
I know she trusts you folks, but even if none of you release these files, what's
to stop someone else who gets their hands on them from releasing them?"

Just then, Eric caught his eye. The tall man was apparently acting in this
sequence, which almost stopped Josh's heart entirely. He averted his gaze.
Eric wasn't undressed yet, but he was in a robe and was barefoot. He was talking quietly to a young actress Josh recognized from a framed photo in the
hallway leading to the studio. She was not wearing a robe; in fact she wasn't
wearing much of anything. Swallowing nervously, Josh could not bring himself to avert his eyes from her pale body. Arnie noticed.

He used his own steaming coffee cup to gesture towards the bed. "She's
a sweet little thing," he said matter-of-factly.

"You—you know her?" Josh asked, some weird constriction in his throat
keeping the words from flowing smoothly.

"Yeah. She came from Saskatchewan. Regina, I think. Her parents were
killed, hit by a truck that did a 360 on icy roads. She has no other family. She made
her way to Vancouver, refused to get involved in any sorts of drugs—like Jessie—
and Caryn found her soliciting patrons, as it were, on the street one night."

"Like Jessie."

"Not like Jessie," Arnie corrected him. He slurped the hot coffee before
going further with his explanation. Josh waited. "Jessie was very sick when
Caryn rescued her."

"Rescued, my ass," Josh said, but his tone was low, even and controlled.

"That's right, Josh. These kids, you don't know where they're coming
from, but you know it's from a bad place. All of them, without exception.
If they do what this girl was doing, hooking on a street corner, they risk all
kinds of abuse without someone to protect them. Caryn and Eric give them
choices. If the girls aren't interested, they go on their merry way. The ones
who stay work for a few years and earn some money to sock away in a bank
account for the future."

"Yeah, yeah, I've heard all this before. Caryn's some kind of white angel or something. She helps the girls and then she molests the girls."

"Watch it, Sawyer." Arnie's adam's apple was moving. His biceps twitched. He didn't look at Josh, and instead took another drink of coffee as, on the bed, Eric moved over the girl, who was now lying on her back. "Why did you come here today, Josh?"

Josh sighed deeply. "I thought I came here to exorcise some demons. That if I saw this place I wouldn't feel so bad about how…about how I feel about this place. And places like this."

He was surprised at the tears now pricking at the corners of his eyes. His shoulders sagged and he suddenly felt extremely weary—of this strange erotic world that caused a physical response when he looked at the young girl on the bed with a man twice her size; at the look of longing in Jessie's eyes when she stared at Jacob with Kelly the other night; at what he thought was his own low moral character regarding misguided desires for his new wife.

"Arnie," he started quietly. "Do you ever get the feeling your world is spinning out of control? That you couldn't put the brakes on if you wanted to? That you think you've got it all figured out and then one day it all comes back to haunt you?"

In front of them, Caryn was swiftly directing the scene with confidence and ability. Before Arnie had a chance to answer him, Josh nodded towards her and said, "She could be in Hollywood."

"She's in her own version of Hollywood, Josh. What she's doing is legal and professional. She's helping women who need her, and she's good at it. And by the way, I used to feel that way—confused and out of control—but I don't anymore."

"Why not?" Josh spoke with fear he didn't bother disguising. Watching Eric rehearse with the young girl whose face Josh now couldn't see totally unnerved him.

"Because I've found some peace with my life, I suppose. I have a woman I love and a place where I feel at home. Enough work to keep me going—"

"Work, huh? I heard it was you who got Jessie that gun."

Shrugging, Arnie acquiesced. "I do what I have to. I was afraid for her,

Josh. She didn't tell me any more than she told the rest of you. I thought maybe it was you who was hurting her—"

"So did everybody else."

"—until I saw the look in her eyes when I mentioned it. So sad. So scared."

"Fuccckkkk. This is all too fucking much, Arnie."

Josh was nauseous and aroused at the same time. But in the end, when he dropped his half-drunk coffee into the garbage and went barreling out of the studio, it was the image of Eric that propelled him. That big man with his Jessie…it made him sick.

He leaned against the outside of the building and dropped his head. "Jesus," he moaned, angry with himself for spinning his wheels in terms of getting his hands on any files, and disgusted for becoming aroused at the sight of the girl on the bed.

"Damn it," he cursed, walking in circles in front of the building. He'd forgotten to grab his coat in Caryn's office, and the April cold was starting to sink into his bones. Just as he knifed a hand through his hair for the umpteenth time, the door opened and Caryn tiptoed out. She held out his jacket, which he took sheepishly but gratefully.

"S-sorry," he muttered.

She folded her arms in front of her chest and smiled genuinely at him. "It's not for everyone," she admitted. "That's why I wanted Arnie there. I wasn't sure how you'd handle it. I thought maybe he could talk you through it." She mimicked a show of strength with Arnie's biceps. "He's a big tough guy," she said in a put-on husky voice.

"Yeah, I gather that," Josh replied, leaning back against the brick.

"Look," Caryn said, reaching out and touching Josh's arm. "Meet me tomorrow at…" She looked around. "Well, how about Revolver? We can have a coffee and digest this shit."

Hesitating, Josh studied her. His eyes were still moist, and he knew it was time to extricate his body and soul from these dangerous people. Maybe Arnie was right. The files would be endless, anyway. Josh would just have to pray they never see any public light of day. But Caryn…there was something so captivating about her. To Josh, it wasn't all sexual, really. Maybe on some level, but he knew he had no sincere interest in going there with her or with anyone except the wife he'd suffered so long for. But Caryn's past history with Jessie…she was another tie or, if you wanted to put it this way, another weighty godforsaken anchor in Jessie's life. What would one more meeting with her hurt? At the very least, he could say his goodbyes properly, and not out here in the street bawling like a baby on the inside.

He nodded and agreed softly, "Yes. Okay."

They decided upon four p.m.

Caryn gave Josh a gentle hug good-bye, and he left with the scent of lilacs in his nostrils. All the way home he thought of her, of her lily-white skin, those enchanting jade eyes, and her successful questionable business. His mind flicked back and forth to the scene she was, by now, surely filming, and to the big bed and the photos of Jessie taken in Caryn's large dwelling.

At home, Josh stripped off his clothes and stood under the shower. Jessie would be home at some point tomorrow, and he didn't need Caryn's lilac scent to leach its way onto any furniture. Later, he tossed a load of laundry in, and then he made homemade pizza for dinner. He turned on Netflix and watched a subtitled French film, silently commended the French for their filmmaking skills (there was some nudity—where do you draw the line, he wondered?), took a call from Kayla and listened while she nattered on about her life as a dancer and with Paul, and then he went to bed.

He slept, pushing unwanted thoughts away deep into his brain where they could hide in the dark. After all, tomorrow would be a brand new day. He would say his goodbyes to Caryn, push any thoughts of Jessie's old exploits out of his mind forever (he hoped), and celebrate her arrival home.

In the dark of night he awoke, jarred awake by a bad dream where he was back in Wes Sawyer's black box studio, and Jessie was the woman he cried in front of. He awoke with the pillow wet underneath his cheek, his breath quick and uneven, and his body shaking.

No, he thought angrily, throwing Jessie's pillow across the room. *I can't forget about those files. Just like Jacob, they'll be haunting me forever, standing over my shoulder and taunting me. They're another fucking noose around my neck.*

What he didn't add was that Jessie, too, was a noose. For he was power-less to escape her grip—he didn't want to, regardless—but she came with a lot of heavy rope. It was big, it was scarred, and it was rough to the touch. And was it worth it, to be under her, to be caught up in her?

Hell yeah, he thought. *Every damn second.*

He rolled over and, after a time, while the blue moon carved ghostly patterns on the wall, his breathing returned to normal and he went back to sleep.

Chapter Twenty

*M*iami was starting to get hot again, blazing hot, the scorching kind of heat that melts wide-eyed children's popsicles at the snap of a finger, and that wickedly sucks salt from pores to leave folks gasping for water.

The tension on set was even hotter. *Mystic Nights* was close to wrapping its first season, yet the production was missing the final scenes featuring their top female star. Kelly had yet to return to work. She declined to act, and she refused to record the last few songs the show needed for its soundtrack. Also, the live concert was coming up, soon, a few days after Jessie flew back to Miami after a week's time off at home.

The production was floundering. Jessie was anxious, but unable to leave. She was held over in Miami until her role on the show officially wrapped, which couldn't happen without Kelly. Josh had sounded off on the phone the last few days so she wanted to get home, to put her mind—and his—at ease. Once again she chalked his unease up to Jacob, but despite her closeness to her musical partner and co-star, she knew in her heart Josh trusted her. She couldn't put her finger on the actual trouble. It was freaking her out.

And Kelly's plight had them all worried.

To calm her increasing anxiety, Jessie went for a choking hot morning run with Matt. As they slowed their heart rates down afterwards with a walk, she asked him what he thought about the whole situation. Had he been to see Kelly? Had he spoken with Michael? Was there any progress? What would happen to *Mystic Nights*?

Matt reported he had been in to see Kelly but so far she wasn't stirring.

"Ouch," Jessie said, her breathing starting to return to normal after the sweaty run in the intense heat, "that's gotta be bad. I got up after a few days. And I was miserable."

"Michael's with her. He knows what's up. After his...troubles...he was in bed for a month."

"Matt?" Jessie looked over at her security chief, friend and occasional running partner.

"Um hum?" He sucked back some water from the bottle he gripped with his right hand, and wiped perspiration from his forehead with his left before glancing over at Jessie. "What?" he asked, eyebrows knitting together in curiosity.

"Well...we've all heard Michael quit music because he lost his wife and child. But...what exactly happened? How did he lose them?"

Matt sighed deeply, and then sucked in a breath as the horrible memories came flooding back. He turned and leaned his back against the heated metal rail of the boardwalk where they were running. Directly behind him, a large white yacht was parked at a marina, its nose barely bobbing in the musky overheated stillness of the hazy day.

"Let's just say he was all hot and bothered for music in those days."

"He was good. The guy's a legend." Jessie's eyes lit up the way everyone's did when they talked about Michael Kelly's music.

"He was, indeed." Grinning at Jessie's childlike enthusiasm, Matt continued, sobering as he got deeper into the story. "But he was in too much of a hurry, and he didn't realize it until it was too late. One day he had a big fight with his wife before heading out to catch a bus for a tour. When he stormed out he forgot a little gift his daughter had picked up to remind him of her during the trip. It was...I don't know, some kind of stuffed animal, I think. A bunny, maybe."

He shifted his vision to his water bottle, which he thrummed casually against his thigh. The rest of the story emerged slowly, like ice-cold honey from a jar on a frigid day.

"It likely didn't cross his mind at all. But Cindy...his wife," Matt's cool eyes clouded over at the memory, "well, she didn't forget, and she likely had a little girl in tears at the thought of her daddy on his big tour without that stuffed animal. So Cindy packed herself and her daughter up and drove off to where the bus was leaving from, planning to catch Michael before he left."

185

He paused, and Jessie could see Matt's throat working as he dredged up the horrific memories of a very bad day.

He looked away before continuing, clever eyes sweeping over the boats in the harbor, the light in those same gentle eyes fading with remembrance in the daylight. "She caught him, all right. She drove into the parking lot just in time to see Michael with his arms around one of the dancers on the tour. Cindy got out of her car anyway, and handed him the toy, and then she got back into the car and pulled out in front of a truck. That's it," he said, his voice constricted with remembered grief. "That's what happened. He saw it happen. People who were there say she did it on purpose, but the theory I choose to believe is that grief does terrible things to people. In Cindy's case I expect she couldn't see for crying. So I doubt she saw that truck at all."

Jessie took Matt's hand in hers. She brushed her thumb over his fingers. "Poor Matt," she said softly. "My friend. I'm so sorry you and your brother had to go through that."

He returned the touch and smiled, just a little. His eyes were wet. "It was a long time ago, Jessie. Michael stayed in his shell for years, but he is doing better now."

"You must still be worried about him. With Kelly going through this… trauma, I mean. They seem to really care about each other."

Matt nodded. "Yeah. I suppose I am. But mostly I'm impressed as heck he's made it this far. Most of her security only lasts about a week." He draped an arm casually around Jessie's shoulders and they started on a slow trek back towards the hotel.

"Yeah, well, they're not all as easy to handle as I am, Matt." Jessie laughed genuinely, a happy laugh that Matt soaked up and put in his memory banks to cherish, to replace the bad memories of yore.

"Dear God, give me strength," was his quick response, though, and Jessie laughed even harder at that.

"Listen, Matt," Jessie started after the warm fuzzy passed, scratching her chin as she considered what she was about to say. "Do you think it would be okay for me to go up and see Kelly?" She stopped walking, and trained thoughtful eyes on him. "I mean, I've kinda been through all that crap. Feeling awful and hiding out in bed…" She drifted off.

Frowning, Matt leaned back against the walkway rail on one elbow. "I'm not sure why you would want to, Jessie. Kelly hasn't exactly been Miss Congeniality towards you."

"That's just her defense against the world, Matt."

He guffawed in his crisp and hip Matt way. "You blow my mind, Jessie. Kelly's not a nice person. Period. She's all about the me-me-me's."

Pursing her lips, Jessie shook her head slowly from side to side. "Nah. Nobody's really all about the me-me-me's, Matt. Most are hiding something, their own insecurities or whatever. Kelly's one of us."

He raised his eyebrows. "Meaning? I'm not following."

Speaking so low he could barely hear her, Jessie answered truthfully, taking his hand in hers as she implored him to listen, to understand. "Tragedy, Matt. Like us, she's been around that block. Frankly, I don't know how she kept it from the media, but apparently she's a master of publicity, because she did."

"Martinique LaVois, that's how. The woman's a mastermind."

"Her manager? I guess." Her eyes sparked as she remembered something. "Hey! Isn't she Charles' old flame?"

Matt's boisterous laugh caught Jessie off guard. Rarely did she see him anything but serious. She grinned.

He pointed a finger at her. "Don't be telling Charles that. He says they had a thing once but swears it didn't last. He doesn't seem to want to talk about it. It's in the past."

"Well, if there was anything between Charles and Martinique, apparently Dee holds no grudges. They've run into each other a few times out here on *Mystic Nights*. I even had dinner with them once. They were perfectly civil to each other."

A young mom jogging with a dog on a leash beside her and a red baby stroller in front paused and threw Jessie a second look after she passed. She slowed and stretched her neck back further. Sobering, Matt touched Jessie's shoulder to signal they should keep walking. "We don't need you to be recognized," he said. "Go."

He added, "Everyone has a past, Jessie. And some of us have learned the hard lesson that it's possible to love more than one person. Which is likely why Charles doesn't want to talk about it."

187

"Uh-huh. Charles? I can't see it. Not with Martinique, anyway. Not love. Not *true* love, anyway." She grimaced and looked over at a grouping of mysterious tropical pink flowers lining the pretty path. "Although I suppose that explains why he fell hard for Dee, after the stormy Ms. LaVois. And by the way, *hard* lesson my ass. More like *agonizing* lesson. Loving two people…"

Jacob's sad blue eyes came to mind but were quickly replaced with Josh's earnest smile and adorable dimple. She blushed, wiped a strand of hair out of her eyes, and looked down at her runners so Matt couldn't see her face. A thought struck Jessie, and she gazed back up at Matt. She hooked an arm in his and practically started skipping as they moved along the path. "I suppose there's one good thing about having more than one love in your life."

"Hmmm?" Distracted, Matt was scanning the grounds and the upcoming joggers. Just as they left the presence of the young mom, he'd noticed her pulling her cellphone out of a pocket in the stroller. He wanted to get his charge safely back to the hotel before word got out about Jessie Wheeler-Sawyer jogging on that particular trail.

She jumped in, oblivious to his growing nerves. "Michael," she said simply. "He's totally enamored with Kelly. And she with him. Second chances, Matt. They just need a boost, that's all."

That got Matt's attention. "Don't go there, Jessie. He's her bodyguard. And she's a—"

"Matt! I'm shocked. And bodyguard, shmodyguard. Heck, I'd date you, Matt!" She leaned closer and whispered in his ear. "That spiky hair is sexy as hell. Although it's looking a little limp and melty in this heat."

"Mmphmf!" He pulled his arm away and steered her by the elbow instead. "Leave my hair outta this. I was going to say she's a lot younger than he is. C'mon, pick up the pace, matchmaker, let's get you home. You singers are all the same," he winked back over his shoulder at her as he let go and started to jog a few paces ahead. "Your heads are always in the clouds." He waved to Jessie to catch up, which she did, laughing happily. "Race you back, youngster," he called. "Just try and keep up."

"I'm melty too, Matt! Wait up! I can't get any air in this scorcher." Jessie stopped and bent over, pretending to struggle with her breathing.

Feigning concern, Matt dropped back. He rested a hand on one shoulder.

"You okay there, kid?" Then he straightened and gave her a little shove. "Move it, Mrs. Sawyer. What, you think I just got off the turnip truck?"

But she was quick. One uproarious laugh and Jessie was off and running.

She beat her security pal back to the hotel fair and square. Matt didn't have a chance. He found it hard to run in the heat while his chest was bursting with unfettered joy.

A soft knock on Kelly's door startled Michael awake, but after he padded over and pulled it open he simply nodded at the visitor and then dropped back into the wingback chair he'd just vacated. He crossed his arms, hung one leg over the arm of the chair, closed his eyes without speaking, and faded back into oblivion.

His chair was now at the foot of Kelly's bed, on the side where she was facing which was, as far as Jessie, her visitor, could see, not its natural home in the room. According to the mussed up Navaho rug underneath the chair, Michael was moving it back and forth so as to likely keep an eye on Kelly as she shifted positions.

Eyeing him carefully, Jessie tiptoed past and pulled a smaller wooden ladder-backed chair over to Kelly's bedside. It screeched on the wooden floor and she squeezed her eyelids together and winced. "Oops! Sorry," she said to whomever was listening, which, she thought, might in fact be no one. Kelly seemed solidly in dreamland, and Michael was not interested in conversation, apparently.

Sighing, Jessie sat down and studied Kelly.

Her co-star, skin flushed yet pale underneath, had one semi-naked arm flung around a pillow. Her face was barely discernible under a tangle of blonde hair that carried with it a significant unwashed bedhead tang. Scrunching up her nose, Jessie considered getting up to tweak the air conditioning in the stifling room, but instead she decided to suck it up and just try to wake Kelly instead.

She reached forward and tentatively touched a few strands of the girl's hair so she could better see her face. Kelly huffed and snuffed at the touch before slowly opening her eyes. She squinted at Jessie.

"Running out of scenes?" The words grated over gravel.

"Nah," Jessie replied stoically, hands now folded in her lap. "I just want to go home. But I can't until you get your stupid princess ass out of bed and come work with me."

Yanking the duvet up higher so she could burrow more deeply underneath, Kelly groaned. "Go away. I need to sleep."

"Look, Kelly." Jessie wasn't in the mood to mince words. She really did want to go home, for a number of reasons. She wrapped her hands around her belly. Josh would be there, waiting for her, and lately Jacob was less than stellar company. In fact, most of their time together over the last few days was spent bickering and sniping nastily at each other. Thank God for Matt, at least. He was a big ole Charlie Brown security blanket.

Jessie continued. "The thing is...I know where your head is. And your heart. I've been there."

"Keep it to yourself, Wheeler. Or Sawyer. Whatever. I don't need your misguided saint shit, okay? Go. Go far away." Kelly ducked her nose under the covers before using a few fingers to tuck the sheets around her ears as well. One hand snuck out and gave Jessie the middle-fingered salute.

"Nice. Hear me out, Kelly. Choose not to listen if you don't want to, but I'm going to talk anyway. I know you're tired, okay? And I know you've been through some shit in your life, but hell, who hasn't? We've all been there. We've all got shit, some of us just have bigger piles in our looney bins."

She tilted her head to one side and watched Kelly for any further signs of encouragement or reaction, but she wasn't getting any. At the same time, there weren't any pillows being thrown at her, or curse words for that matter, so Jessie Yoga-inhaled through her nose and tried again.

"The thing is, if you're depressed, then listen to the doctor and get some help. I happen to know a very good therapist who is likely due for a holiday down south. If it's pills you need to get you through this, then so be it. She can help with that. But if you're just pissed off at yourself and at the world, then talk to me, for now. Like I said, I have some idea of what you're feeling. Please? I'm not kidding, Kel. I want to go home. I want to see my husband. Hell, I *need* to see my husband. I need his big arms around me and I want to run my hands over his back." Jessie leaned back, then stared at the ceiling and exhaled slowly, as images of Josh floated across her mind. Her cheeks colored at the thought of just how scrumptious he looked the day he brushed his lips across her forehead and left for the airport. *Oh, what I am going to do to that man when I see him again...*

She was startled to look back down at Kelly and see her staring up at her. The girl's eyes narrowed and she perked herself up on one elbow. "Give me a break," she whined.

Jessie colored even deeper but she couldn't avoid the tiny grin that lit up her eyes.

"Can't help it," she said matter-of-factly, leaning further back in the chair and placing her toes on the edge of the box spring of Kelly's bed. She crossed her arms. "He's adorable." Her smile upended itself. "And I miss him. I want to go home."

"Jessie?"

"Hmmm?" *At least I have her attention.* She steeled herself for whatever weapon Kelly planned to throw although, upon close inspection, the girl's eyes were pallid and moist instead of the usual expected edgy and narrow.

"I was just wondering...what made you decide to get out of bed and keep going? When all that shit was going down."

"Huh," Jessie said, barely realizing she'd spoken aloud. She was surprised to hear anything serious come from those pale lips. She shrugged and decided to go with it, for now. "That's easy," she answered, her own sea-pearl blues flecking with joy as she spoke of the one thing that fueled her every move, that floated on every breath. "Loving someone. The hope that I could be with him again. That's what kept me going. That's what *keeps* me going."

"Josh."

"Hell, yeah." Jessie's smile was wide now, her eyes big and luminous.

"I don't have a Josh."

Jessie paused. "You sure about that?" She nodded towards Michael, asleep or feigning sleep in the nearby chair at the foot of the bed. He didn't move a muscle, so whether he could hear the girls chatting or not wasn't evident. However, his presence in the room spoke volumes. "He's been here all week, Kelly."

Kelly adjusted her position on the bed so she could better see her security detail dozing nearby. "I know," she whispered conspiratorially.

"D'you see the scruff? On his face?" Lifting a hand, Jessie fingered her own chin as an example and screwed up her nose. She leaned towards Kelly and breathed decidedly, "He hasn't even bothered to shave. And it's sexy as hell."

That comment drew an actual low-pitched giggle from Kelly. She sat up finally and heaved her pillow against the headboard, then leaned back against it and regarded Jessie. She was feminine and pretty in a nightdress with lovely laced cap sleeves that Martinique had drawn over her head late one night. She pulled the sheets up over her body and hugged them tight.

"I know I've been a bitch to you."

"Whatever. You've actually been a bitch to everyone." Jessie's tone was casual, but a glint in her eyes suggested she was, at least in part, joking. She took Kelly's hand. "Honey, nobody goes to bed for days on end without a reason for it. And the way I see it, nobody treats everyone else like shit for no reason, either. I'm not saying it's an excuse and I'm not forgiving you for the way you treat people, but I am saying it helps me understand."

"I know I'm not nice." The voice coming from the bed was tiny, accompanied by slow tears that caught the light on their downward drift. The result further softened Jessie's disposition towards her co-star. Kelly was genuine in her acknowledgement of her own cruelty. She continued, her voice barely discernible, her pleading eyes making up for it. "I don't know why someone like Michael would have any interest in me, Jessie."

"Lots of reasons, honey," Jessie said, looking over at him all hunched over in the chair. "I'll give you the biggest."

Curious, Kelly raised her eyebrows. "What?"

Jessie spoke as if she was surprised Kelly didn't get this one on her own. She raised her hands in a great flourish. "Music!"

"Music?"

"Well, yeah! Music. He's a musician, you're a musician."

"He doesn't play anymore."

"Bullshit. Jacob said he saw a guitar in his room. Anyways, you know what music's like. You can say you're quitting it, but it's futile. It won't quit you."

"No?"

"No. I mean, sure, maybe he doesn't play for money anymore, but sometimes I think that's the best way. Anyways, I can't see the guy carrying a guitar case around for years that he never opens. Doesn't matter anyway, he wrote some beautiful songs in his time and I'll bet there are lots more up his sleeve we just haven't had the pleasure of hearing. And as for you, well, even if nothing ever happens between you and Michael, you've got music too. And it won't quit you, either. Even if you end up living alone with ten cats."

The first hint of a genuine smile flickered over Kelly's lips. "I guess," she said, as she loosened her grip on the duvet.

"Kelly, get out of bed, okay? Take a shower and get dressed, and then come downstairs for something to eat. Jacob and I are heading out to the studio to record those two tunes we need for the soundtrack, and we're really hoping you'll come along and do that other one the producers are begging for. In the morning maybe we can get a few scenes in the can so I can fly home later in the day, okay? So I can, you know," she wiggled in her chair and smiled, "be with my own sexy man tomorrow night."

"You shoulda kept Jacob." Grinning sardonically, Kelly caught Jessie off guard.

Jessie eyed her, and exhaled slowly. "I love Josh."

"Yes, but you said it yourself…the biggest reason people like us are interested in others…is music." She knitted her eyebrows together in curiosity. "Do you and Josh have that?"

"Depends how you look at it." Squirming uncomfortably, Jessie sighed. "He likes my music. He gets it."

"Ah. But he doesn't play it. Not like Jacob. Don't you feel like part of your soul is missing with Josh?"

A noise from behind them saved the shocked Jessie from responding. Michael was stirring, and he tossed a few words into the conversation. "Don't you, Kelly? Feel like part of your soul is missing without music?"

Taken aback, Kelly looked past Jessie to meet Michael's eyes while Jessie fidgeted in the hard wooden chair.

A broad smile widened on Kelly's flushed cheeks and she wiped a palm across her forehead to settle any damp misplaced strands of honey-blonde hair. "Yeah," she said. "I do."

Jumping up, Jessie squeezed Michael's arm as she passed. "That's my cue," she called out behind her. Turning to Kelly, walking backwards, she added, "I'll see you at the studio, okay Kelly?"

A wistful look followed her first few steps but then, as Jessie looked back one more time, she saw Michael taking Kelly's hand and gently drawing her out of the bed. His words followed Jessie to the door, and then were lost in their own private sphere. "Come on, girl. Jessie's right. You need to shower and get on with the business of living."

"She just needs to get laid." Jessie tossed the words casually over one shoulder.

As his laughter echoed behind her, she let the door crunch shut before pausing and chuckling quietly. *Sneaky bugger,* she thought. *He was listening all along.*

She whistled one of his old tunes as she skipped on down the hallway, hands in her pockets.

"Jacob Ryan, I hope you're in a good mood today. Cuz we got us some tunes to sing."

Chapter Twenty-one

"Aw geez, I was counting on going crocodile hunting today. Me and the electrics got it all planned out."

Trying to replicate a southern drawl wasn't working for Jacob, and neither was his ploy to piss Jessie off when she told him to get ready, that the studio was booked and ready for them, and that there was a good chance Kelly would show her pretty pale face.

He crooked one knee and shoved a foot backwards up against the hall wall, crossed his arms, and pouted. "Just can't wait to get home, eh Jessie? Not enough excitement to keep you busy here in good 'ole Miami? Oh no, pardon me. I got it all wrong. Not the right guy here in Miami." He grabbed his crotch before shooting her a look of pity and striding away.

"Oh for God's sake," Jessie muttered under her breath. She was getting damn tired of Jacob's sulking and, after her brief meeting in Kelly's dark suite, she needed some brightness and positive vibes. Caring for others' dark moods had too much sway over her own these days.

"It's work, Jacob. Recording. Us. Her highness up there in her palace. Singing. You know, music?" The sarcasm and frustration underlying her message were blatantly clear. "In fact," Jessie hollered after him as he headed towards the elevator where one punch of a button would summon him a ride downstairs to a waiting chauffeur, "I admit. You're actually right about one thing."

He stopped cold but remained standing with his back to her.

"That comment you made about the right guy. The right guy, as you call him, would move on with his life. He'd stop wandering around in a funk bringing everybody down. He'd stop sulking and find himself a good woman to warm his bed at night."

One foot pawed the ground before Jacob turned, and when he finally faced Jessie and drew his shoulders back to fire at her, she prepared herself for the worst. Rarely did she see Jacob so incensed that his eyes fired bullets directly into her heart. She'd seen him hurt, yes, and the remembrance of the puppy dog eyes fading with the pain of her rejection was enough to sink any fire Jessie had left in her to fight back.

"As I recall, Jessie, he did. Find a *good* woman, I mean. Fairly quickly, I recall, after you dumped him and climbed into my bed." The emphasis was on the word good. Jessie cringed and knuckled her fingers together. She inhaled through her nose and stared at her ex over a chin raised in defiance. "Okay. So that's the way you want to play it, is it Jacob? Dirty?"

"Hey," he waved an arm carelessly in the air as he took a few steps backwards before swinging around on one heel. "It's your cesspool. I'm just tired of swimming in it."

"Circling the edges, you mean. Like a goddamn shark."

"Hell, no. Why would I want to go there again? Kelly's right. You're used goods now, *Sawyer.*"

Well, can't dispute that, thought Jessie, as Caryn and Eric slid into her mind. Her sessions with Trudy floated in a hazy mist somewhere on the edges of her consciousness. She blinked and swallowed but couldn't keep a sharp sword from piercing her belly. She wrapped her right arm around the ache and gripped her left just above the elbow. Her nails were sharp, and they dug deep. *Caryn and Eric. Thank God Josh seems to have let that shit go.*

She followed Jacob down in the next elevator, not even bothering to hide the fact that he'd hurt her when she finally slid into the SUV waiting for them outside the hotel. They each clung to their own side of the big car, slunk down into their seats, and gazed mournfully out of the windows.

Jacob looked over at Jessie once, and instantly noticed the red crescents newly formed on her arm. He ached to touch her, but the wall of pain was too great. It blinded him. He was immobile, helpless. She came with baggage, tons of it. He'd always known that, and for a while it seemed they were able to let the past go and just hang out together, but lately…well, Kelly exacerbated the issue by calling it like it is, Josh's occasional presence in Miami was disconcerting, Jacob's father added to the shit-pile by making Jacob feel unwanted, and then, add to that…

With Kelly's meltdown had come new scenes by the writers, scenes containing actions with the power to push people maybe into directions where they didn't really truly want to go. The *Mystic Nights* producers didn't want to lose their shirts, their homes, their fancy shiny cars while Kelly recuperated. They had Jessie and Jacob on set, so…well, suffice it to say the revised scenes pushed the comfort zone Jessie and Jacob had cautiously retreated to in an effort to rebuild some kind of relationship. It wasn't a huge stretch for the show—early in the season their characters flirted, but Charles Keating had graciously (and unknowingly, to Jessie and Josh) waved his magic wand. He and Deirdre swayed the producers enough to keep Jessie out of Jacob's bed when the cameras were rolling.

But now…well, the last few days of shooting had come as a shock to both cast. The worst part was that their only chances to discuss the new scenes were in front of Hair and Make-up, or at lunch, when they couldn't seem to find time alone. So they were deer caught in the headlights, literally, and they had to cope with little notice and even littler prep. Now, Jacob recoiled, thinking about it, making a *snuffing* noise in his throat that caused Jessie to glance over, briefly, while the streets of a blistering Miami glided by.

He figured it wasn't so bad for Jessie for two reasons. A, she was a pro, an experienced actor, in fact a storied actor with two golden statues on a shelf at home. B, she got what she wanted, yeah she had to go through hell to get it, but still…she got Josh. So she also got sex, for one thing, on a regular basis he presumed (rightly), and she got a warm body and soul she loved deeply to hold at night, should her nightmares return, as Jacob knew they did on an occasional basis.

As for him? *Well shit,* he thought, hanging his head and staring at the scruffy toes of his brown leather boots. *I get to live with the truth that I killed a man, that I wanted to kill another (and sometimes even now I still…*he shook that thought away quickly, in case Jessie could read his mind, 'cause he figured she'd either strangle him or jump out of the moving vehicle if she could), *I am lonely as hell, and I am a very green actor.* The coaching helped, and was still helping, and in fact was what got him through those scenes with Jessie, period. But then…most nights he went to sleep alone, usually after a few sodden hours at the hotel bar.

Although last night…at least he got to take a detour first, up the elevator with the only woman working as a grip on this show. She was twenty-six, slim (*too slim*, he thought, *nothing to hang on to*), strong-willed, cavalier, and working her way through the male crew on the show. She told Jacob she'd just given up trying to seduce one of the electrics, who was married and faithful and had laughed in her face, saluted her, and vacated the bar moments before Jacob's solemn entrance. The girl wasn't a Department Key on the show, and only Keys were permitted to be present when love scenes were being filmed, so Jacob knew she hadn't seen him with Jessie, but still…at any rate, the girl was a determined, quick lay (*I have to get some sleep, she'd said, peering at him intently right before driving her hand down his pants and grinning seductively at his immediate arousal*).

The sex was good, pretty awesome actually, but that wasn't what Jacob was missing. He was missing the *soul* part. And, as far as he figured, the only person who could give that to him was the gal sitting a few feet away scowling out of the window, arms wrapped around her belly, and ugly new gashes in the shape of fingernails on her arm.

He closed his eyes and let his mind take him back there, to yesterday, when the toughest of the love scenes was filmed. The writers hadn't been that creative—he and Jessie were in bed in Jessie's character's home, and thankfully it was a night scene, so it was dark. There were set lights, of course, but these were minimal. The largest was a 2 K with blue gel fastened over the light with clothespins, designed to imitate moonlight swathing the bed. Jessie seemed right at home when they had to reconnect in this weird, fake, intimate way. But him? His heart was racing long before the scene was scheduled. By the time he was on his back, in bed, with his ex-girlfriend's knees on either side of his hips, playing out a scene they'd played out for real many times in the past, his heart was palpitating so hard he thought he might explode.

There were clauses in their contracts designed for their comfort. Jacob had the most protection. Bare breasts were common practice, though. There was a sheet to play under, at least. The only way Jacob got through take after

take was by connecting with real emotion, as his acting coach had decreed…
so he caved and let his mind take him back to the old days…to loving Jessie…
to caressing her breasts as she arched her back and laid her soft palms over
his…to brushing his lips alongside her nipples…to pulling her down on top
of him, to rolling her over and inhaling the lavender scent he so desperately
missed as he gently allowed his hips to grind on top of her…to letting himself soak up those small hands as they ran over and over the cross on his back.
She delicately traced it first, as sighs of pleasure escaped her lips and his, and
then Jessie'd pushed down hard on his back as she pressed her breasts into
him, and then her own hips, too, which Jacob was told by the director he was
permitted to bare 'if the moment is working and it feels right.'

Well hell, Jacob thought, squirming a little now as somewhere in his body
a new fire was starting with this remembrance, and then squeezing a fist on
the armrest as he stared at an arrogant white poodle on the sidewalk outside that, in all honesty, he really didn't see…*of course the moment was going
to feel right. Of course I went there.*

The weird thing was, when he pulled off Jessie's (well, her character's)
jeans, he thought she was going right along on the ride with him. Her sighs
of pleasure were the same he remembered from before, that haunted him at
night when the hot desire got so strong he couldn't sleep. Yeah, she was there,
in that room with the artificial moon, with barely perceptible shadows on the
perimeter all curious, all watching how Jessie Wheeler makes love, how she
once made love with him, Jacob Ryan…and her eyes were doe-ey and her
lips soft and delicious when he teethed her bottom one, sliding it between
his teeth and groaning to show her how much he wanted her, when all of a
sudden, as his hands groped for her jeans and pulled them down, his tongue
only inches from that electric spot he longed to taste…she stopped him.

She grabbed her panties to keep them from going down with the jeans,
like they usually did *back then,* came down with the jeans, that is, before she'd
spread her legs wider and beg him to *go there,* and he would, Lord Tunderin',
he would. He'd drive himself into her just at the last second while she writhed
underneath him, already coming sometimes, losing her mind with the pleasure
of it all. The searing scorched feel of her fingers raking over his back would make
Jacob cry out in his own laid-bare ecstasy, and then their hot bodies would

release together, as one, her legs wrapped tightly around him, with him deep inside her as they rocked and she twitched and clenched around him, her little sighs and moans ebbing and flowing somewhere off in the distance as his heart raced and then eventually slowed exactly in time with hers.

He wondered now if her fingernails back then left little crescent shaped moons in his back. Not that it mattered. The scars she left him were well intact in his soul. They had ravaged his heart, where they still remained, twisting and turning and wrenching so hard when he breathed that he felt a rising anxiety even now, thinking about how deeply she was embedded in him. And she was just sitting there, nearby, on the other side of the car, scowling at the flying-by trees planted in the sidewalks. *If looks could kill,* he thought…*every damn tree we pass would shrivel and die.*

The moment when she'd grabbed onto her panties was the clincher. That was when Jacob realized this make-believe world they were living in was, in fact, just that—make-believe. None of this bullshit made-up Miami television world was real. He could pretend it was, when Josh wasn't around, at least until the damnable insatiable desire took over. The moment Jessie stopped him when he tried to bare her beneath his hungry body…he cringed now, remembering.

And that's when he knew for certain…that as much as he actually found himself liking Josh, he still wouldn't hesitate to bed the man's wife if the opportunity arose.

He'd thought he wouldn't. Jacob thought he was better than that. That if he looked into Josh's eyes more than once and saw kindness there, and a deep abiding love for Jessie—who lost herself in Josh's eyes so many times in Jacob's presence that it drove him nuts—he would not *go there.* Jacob told himself he would not mess with that kind of love with people he really did consider his friends. Damn it, he promised Jessie he could handle it, way back in the fall. But Jesus, yesterday on set he was an inch away from tasting her, in fact he did taste her, that beautiful mouth, at least. He'd sucked her lip and kissed her and tongued her, deeply, feeling an old exquisite pleasure rock him inside and out, so how could his body not want to finish the job? Later, the female grip had eased some of the ache. But sweet Jesus, not nearly enough.

Part of the ache came from the panic in Jessie's eyes when she so quickly put a stop to how far Jacob could take the scene. He'd raised his head, shocked almost, and met her eyes, which were narrowed in an angry sort of warning, he thought. She'd whispered sharply to him *fuck off, Jacob,* and he heard the boom guy, who was wearing headphones, snicker. Her sharp reprimand cooled things off to a point, but the rest of the long shoot day was never as magical as that first master take. Not to him, not to the director, not to the producer standing by with his arms crossed, and not to...Jessie.

That was part of the reason Jacob was so pissed off now. He knew, he *knew,* she was into it yesterday. He could tell by the lust in her eyes, the deep-seated desire he sensed smoldering beneath her skin every time he touched her or ran his tongue over an arm, a shoulder, a breast. Her hips were trembling, pressing into him...he wanted to look over at her now and demand she admit it, that she only stopped things between them because she got suddenly scared that somehow it would get back to Josh, how hot things were during that take. That she wanted it as badly as he did, despite her feelings for Josh. *We were under a fucking sheet,* he considered. *Nobody would have known the difference.*

The driver turned the final corner, and drew to a rather abrupt halt in front of the studio where they'd be recording today—recording love songs, of all things. They got there just in time, because Jacob was feeling uncomfortable in his tight jeans, and he moved his hand slightly, to adjust himself, when Jessie made a move to open her door. He felt like his face was beet red but, even worse, it was gonna be painful to walk.

Grimacing, he pushed open his door, and stepped out onto the heat-hazed pavement.

Penny for your thoughts, he wished miserably, hopelessly, as he looked up in time to see Jessie's slooped shoulders disappear behind a palm tree beyond the walkway. But he knew that wish was futile. He already knew Jessie's thoughts, hell, he felt like he knew her soul. And, sadly, that took some of the fuel out of his fire because, the truth of the thing was—in fact the whole stink of the thing was—he knew she still cared about him. She would never stop caring about him. They loved each other—they did then, they did now. But their love would have to be expressed in music, and not in any other way.

Because, and the truth fucking hurts, Jacob admitted, as painful as it was, tears springing to his eyes, *she loves someone else more.*

Chapter Twenty-Two

They were supposed to try to get the guitar and vocals of their first song laid before Kelly's expected arrival which, they were told, would be in about four hours, if she chose to show up at all. A week earlier this would have been lots of time for Jessie and Jacob, but today, with tensions running as high as the summit of Mount Everest, it was taking forever.

"Jesus, Jacob, will you get it together?" Jessie was perched on a high wooden stool, microphone placed strategically in front of her, and Jacob was a few feet away, on a similar stool. Visions of yet another lonely night in Miami were stretching before Jessie's mind. She missed Josh so badly she ached. Guiltily, she softened her glance towards Jacob who, Jessie was sorry to see, was shuffling his feet on the stool rung and throwing her his sad puppy dog look, lips curled down and long eyelashes moist. Sometime during the session he had folded a red bandana and wrapped it around his head, over his ears, to absorb some of the sweat from the overheated room. His curls beneath it were droopy, which only added to the overall aura of heartbreak surrounding him.

Jessie sighed deeply, then reached out to run a soft finger down the front of his grey T-shirt, which read 'Thar She Blows' around an image of an old ship's wheel. The shirt was tight enough to nicely display his broad chest and bicep muscles and, below that, his faded jeans had holes in all the right places. Add the scruffy boots to complete the picture, and...

"Okay," Jessie said quietly, shifting on the hard stool, "I'm sorry. Is that what you need from me right now? An apology?"

Jacob stared hard at her. He blinked, and then shook his head in

202

astonishment. "I don't need anything from you, Jessie. I just don't fucking want to be here with you right now."

Matt, who had driven in with them in the front seat of the limo next to a chatty Cuban driver whose 'Spanglish' he couldn't hope to understand, stiffened beyond the glass wall separating the artists from the sound engineer. He leaned on the edge of the soundboard and watched the two ex-lovers spar. The long-haired long-faced engineer raised his own eyebrows, one hand pausing over the button which would allow him to ask his singers to start at the beginning, when a look from Matt stopped him.

"Let them duke it out," he said simply. "They need a good old fashioned yelling match to clear the stink out of the air." He'd heard about yesterday's tough shoot from exhausted crew who worked a triple overtime day in order to get the love scene shot. He'd seen the layer of fury underscoring Jacob's eyes when he escorted him back to the hotel, and discerned the concerned stare in Jessie's as she watched Jacob from sideways glances all the way back in the car.

Today, he knew, something had to give. Matt considered telling the sound guy to take a smoke break, but instead he stilled his body and eavesdropped, ready to enter the room and play referee if need be.

Inside the studio, Jessie slid off the stool and stood facing Jacob, thinly disguised fury in her voice, which shook as she unleashed what had been on her mind these last few days. "You wanted this, Jacob. When we first came back to Vancouver I warned you there would be times when it would suck. But you didn't listen. You went for it anyway! Now you've got the career you wanted, and you're so bloody bitter I can't even talk to you!"

He bit his bottom lip so hard it almost bled, and glared at her. "I didn't expect you to be part of the package, Jessie. Not after…" he stopped, and shoved their bitter break-up out of his mind.

"Liar," she spat back at him. "You knew Charles would at least try to put us in the studio together right from day one. You've wanted that all along!"

"I didn't ask him to! Ask him yourself!" Jacob dropped off his own stool and squeezed past his mic. He paced a little before facing Jessie again. He pointed a finger at her nose, which she had to force herself not to reach out and grab. The ferocity in his eyes was rising. "You have no idea. You have no fucking idea, what…what it's like…"

His eyes darted to Matt in the booth, who stood stock still, watching, a deep frown creasing his brow. The man crossed his arms and shifted his balance, but didn't make a move to silence Jacob, or to enter the studio.

"What what's like, Jacob?" The words were even; they were leveled at Jacob's capacity to be reasonable which, by now, was insanely and irrevocably diminished.

Jacob forced himself to look back at Jessie. She almost disarmed him completely — she had her hands placed staunchly on her hips over faded denims. A red-print empire halter (mostly backless, he noted earlier with dismay) flared overtop her waist, and the ubiquitous brown cowboy boots peeked out from beneath frayed hems. She'd pulled her hair high up into a messy pony, but a few strands had escaped, and were obviously bugging her, as evidenced by the quick swipes she was making at one rogue curl in particular.

He glared angrily at her and resisted the urge to help her locate the misbehaving swath of hair. Instead, Jacob laced her up and down with everything that was pissing him off these days, regarding…well, her.

"To be so close to you and not…and not to have you, that's what! You want the truth? That's the fucking truth! I can't do this, with you! I can't be here, with you…I thought…I thought I could. But I can't." He was gasping now, and Matt glanced around the small sound booth in search of a paper bag, should the boy in the studio start to hyperventilate. There were none.

Matt held his breath, and finally signaled to the engineer to go out for a smoke. But he held his own footing, despite knowing he was eavesdropping. He was, after all, responsible for these two, and should their anger erupt into a shoving match, they may need an intervention. He heard footsteps behind him, and turned around to see Michael escorting a pale Kelly into the small sound booth. It didn't escape Matt's eyes that his brother's arm was gently around the girl's waist.

"What's all this?" Kelly was asking quietly as her heels clicked on the parquet floor.

"They just need a little airing out," Matt said drily. "They'll cool down in a bit."

Inside, things were anything but cooling down. Jacob had swung around and strode up to a mic stand, thankfully with no mic attached, and belted it across the room. It skidded angrily over the floor, bounced off the wall, and rattled to a halt. The room was eerily silent then, with the exception of Jessie's breath, which was now coming in anguished gasps.

"For Christ's sake, Jacob!"

When he turned around again, Jacob was sorry for the fear in Jessie's eyes, which he knew he'd quite succinctly placed there. Yet he hammered another mic stand, backhanding this one, and actually took some guilty pleasure from watching Jessie tense up further and back away. Daggers shot directly from his eyes to hers.

In the booth, Michael took two broad steps forward and reached for the door to the studio. Matt's hand shot out and grabbed him around the forearm. "No," he demanded. "Not yet."

"S'your funeral!" Michael backed away, throwing his arms up in resignation.

"Jessie, you were into it yesterday. I know you were!" Jacob was yelling now, not even trying to hide the anguish in his voice, or the white rage ravaging his body.

"It's called acting, Jacob! Fucking acting! That's what we were doing!"

"Liar!" he screamed, nose-to-nose with her now, so he could smell the pink-peppermint breath he longed to inhale. "Feel free to tell yourself that all you want, Jessie, but it's bullshit!" He stepped even closer, and she put out her hands to stop him, landing them on his chest, and grabbing a few fist-fuls of 'Thar.' He had her backed up against the wall now, and Jessie's short breaths telegraphed a rising panic. She knew Matt was close by but, in the heat of this battle, she didn't waste time wondering why the hell he wasn't in the room. There would be time for that later.

Incredibly, Jacob started to sob. "Jessie," he started, wavering, and then he finally lowered his voice so that only she could hear. "You responded to me. Yesterday. And I need that...from you...you know I do. And you...you were right there with me. It wasn't any different than it was before. Before..."

She shoved him away, hard, and he almost toppled over backwards, over one of the mic stands he'd so carelessly thrown around.

"Before what, Jacob?" she spat, incensed. "Before you weaseled your way into Charles' good graces and all your dreams came true?"

"No!" he cried, tears now running openly down his cheeks, and somehow, in the heat of it all, chastened to see Jessie swipe at one on her own pink cheek. "No! Before I…before I fucking shot McCall, that's when! When I could have shot your fucking cowboy!" He pointed a finger again at her shocked, frozen face. This time his voice was lower, even and controlled, too controlled. "When I *should* have shot him, Jessie."

Jacob watched Jessie struggle to comprehend the wicked declaration before he wheeled around and left her standing there. She was trying to regain control of her breathing, which was shallow and quick, but Jacob didn't care. He called back over his shoulder in a thick voice soaked wet with pain, "Not all my dreams came true, Jessie. Not all of them." And he stumbled out of the studio, into the hallway, and out into the blinding sunlight, where he leaned over the bushes and puked until he was dry.

"Oh for God's sake," came a high-pitched female voice from the sound room.

Matt gave Michael a look that said *go keep an eye on him*. He marched purposefully into the studio. Grasping Jessie's face between his right thumb and fingers, he grabbed her left shoulder with his other hand and urged her to focus on him.

"Look at me, Jessie," he demanded, starting to count slowly. "1…2…3…4…5…Breathe. Jessie, look at me." She was fighting him, sobbing, unable to breathe, and collapsing, all at the same time. He went to the floor with her, bending down in front and continuing to try to get her to focus. "1…2…3…4…5…Breathe. Easy now. Better? Okay?" At her nod, he wiped a tear away with his thumb, and then he spoke quietly. "He'll be fine, Jessie. He needed to get that out, but he'll adjust. A little time away from each other will help."

"What if…what if he is right, Matt?" Her voice was tiny, a whisper. From the depths of her eyes, Jessie pleaded with him to understand. She gripped his forearms tightly as he held on to her.

"About what, Jessie?" But he knew already, and he was sorry before she even spoke.

"About…me." Her eyes darted around the room as she took this in herself, maybe for the first time. Then she looked at him directly, sorrowfully. "About me wanting him."

He frowned, his cheeks going a little pale at that revelation. Josh flitted across his mind.

"Do you?" he asked her, begging for honesty.

"Just…it's hard to explain, Matt. I don't, not really, but sometimes… when I look at him…Matt, do you seriously think it's possible to love more than one person?" She was thinking of their earlier conversation, during the morning run.

"Sure, kiddo," Matt replied. "I said I do. I'll stick by that. But in the interest of this discussion I also know that, despite how much I know you love Jacob, I've never seen you look at him the way you look at Josh. That little— twinkle—you get in your eye, right there." He smiled, and mimed where the twinkle would be. "And I am quite certain you would not even come close to cheating on Josh if…" He looked down at a spot on the floor and wrinkled his eyebrows, pausing to think.

"If what?" But she answered before he could get the words out. "If I wasn't pushed? Matt, I didn't consider cheating on Josh. At all. But," she peered into the eyes of the man she trusted with her life. "But I can't lie. Jacob's…well, he's sexy as hell, Matt, and we do have a history. It sucked being put in that situation with him yesterday, despite the fact we're supposed to be professionals. It's too soon. It hurt like hell…the look on his face when I…Matt, I had to push him away at one point. It sucked so bad!"

He sighed and said, "You need to talk to Charles, Jessie. Or maybe Dee in this case. Either back off on this show, or get them to cut back on the storyline with you and Jacob. A little distance wouldn't be a bad thing, I think. Although I'd hate to see the kid skulking around alone all the time."

"Me too. He's still my friend."

"I think he's warming up to Michael. And it's actually good to see my brother warming up to him, too, for that matter."

"Good. Although," she smiled through her tears, "Michael may soon have his hands full, if my spidey-sense is working."

An uneasy grin animated one side of Matt's face. "Kelly."

"Yeahhhh." She brightened when she saw Matt's grin widen, although he shook his head at the same time.

"Ouch," he said. "He must be a glutton for punishment."

They stood, Matt first. He extended a hand to hoist Jessie up.

"I wouldn't get too worried yet, Matt. I don't think anything's transpired between them at this point." She grimaced slightly, remembering Jacob's tryst with Kelly just a short time ago.

Matt whipped an arm around Jessie's shoulder and led her to a big soft black leather couch against the far wall. "Sit," he demanded, depositing her. "I'll get someone to grab some coffees, and then we'd better get you prima donnas back to work."

"Matt!" she hollered at him as he left the room, throwing a cushion in his general direction. "Meanie. Prima donna. Humph."

In the sound room, Matt found Michael deep in conversation with the sound engineer, who smelled smoky enough in this anti-smoking age that Matt caught himself recoiling. "Uhhh…" He looked around the room and raised his arms questioningly at Michael, who broke off from his chat about the sweet pure sound of a vintage Gibson to answer the unasked question.

"She wanted to go with Jacob instead," Michael thumbed towards the door. "Outside."

"All right then," Matt mumbled. With a last peek at Jessie, who was sitting disconsolately on the couch with her knees drawn up and both arms wrapped tightly around them, he wandered off to see what kind of damage control the blonde princess was managing with Jessie's ex.

He found them sitting side-by-side on a large concrete block, their toes barely touching the asphalt below. Tufts of smoke rose steadily from cigarettes clutched between Kelly's painted blue nails, and Jacob's thicker fingers.

Matt made his way over to them, plunging his hands casually in his pants pockets as he did so.

"Hey," Kelly said seriously as he approached.

Jacob mumbled something incoherent and didn't look up. Instead, he shifted his glance towards a clump of brown grass trying to survive through a crack in the asphalt.

"Hey," Matt responded, looking disapprovingly at the disappearing smoke. "Ready to go back to work? Jacob?"

It took a great reserve of strength for Jacob to respond. He eyed Matt wearily. "Not so much. No. Actually, Matt," he said, "I'd like to call it a day."

"So would I," Kelly echoed between puffs. She sent Matt a challenging look that said clearly *I dare you to mess with me. See how much power I have?* She added, "We want to go to the Sound Club. Nachos." She blew smoke rings at Matt. "Go get Michael."

Matt stood his ground, assessing the two of them. *Exactly when did they become friends* was running through his mind. *Oh, likely after they slept together,* he decided, despite Kelly's meltdown. He could feel his temper rising, despite the sympathy he felt for Jacob. He had a hard time mustering any sympathy for Kelly.

The thing is, if these two stars wanted to end their day, they had the power to do so. One of the exec producers was expected to drop in to see how things were going. Matt shrugged. The guy wouldn't be impressed. But there wasn't much Matt could do to change the minds of these two. He was just a hired gun. A babysitter. A tired exhausted babysitter who missed his wife and daughter. He turned and trudged back into the studio.

When Matt opened the door to enter, guitar chords wafted out into the parking lot. He sighed. *At least Jessie's in the mood to play. Maybe the sound guy can coerce something usable out of her until these two nimrods get their shit together.*

Behind him, Jacob straightened.

"What?" Kelly asked, eyes narrowing as she took one last puff before butting her smoke against her rough concrete seat.

Gesturing towards the door, Jacob offered quietly, "I recognize that tune." He cocked an ear and tried to listen, but the door had closed shut. "Huh." He jumped down and turned to assist Kelly in her heels. Butting out his own smoke and dropping it into a can filled with sand and other old butts, he turned around and strode towards the door.

"Wait up!" Kelly tripped across the pavement behind him.

She caught up to him in the sound booth and stopped in astonishment.

"Thought so," Jacob murmured. "That's one of his more famous tunes."

"Oh Lordy," Kelly breathed. "He hasn't played in…well, years. Right, Matt?"

It was Matt's turn to struggle with his breathing. "Yeah," he managed, his eyes locked on his brother who, in the studio, was singing into Jacob's vacated microphone as Jessie pushed her own stool away with her foot and adjusted the height of her mic. She had grabbed her Gibson from its case and hoisted it over her head, tuned quickly, and jumped in with some strong bar chords that added depth to Michael's old classic rock tune, one every singer on the circuit learned and played. The captivated souls in the sound booth watched, spellbound, when Michael angled his hips towards Jessie and they sang together, their song infused with the simple joy of playing music.

"This is too good to pass up," Kelly mused, breezing by Jacob. She whipped open the door to the studio and tiptoed over to Michael. She touched his hip, smiled, and he scooted over a bit to make room for her at his mic. She got there in time for the first chorus. She broke into harmonies just as a studio drummer who arrived for the same call time as Kelly dropped down behind a drum set. His rhythm was a perfect balance to the two guitars and three voices.

Matt didn't notice Jacob pull open the door and enter the studio until the boy grabbed his own guitar and settled in by Jessie. He, too, tuned quickly and added his gentle husky voice to the party. Without breaking stride in the music, Jessie managed to lean sideways and brush her lips against his temple. She stopped singing long enough to whisper *sorry*.

Strumming along, Jacob let his gaze drift over the light Jessie gave off when she sang. It surrounded her, just like it was enveloping Michael and Kelly now who, in their own bubble of perfect peace created by the magic of music, were lost in each other's eyes, their voices blending perfectly in harmony.

Jacob and Jessie glanced over at them, and then back towards each other. They shrugged at the same time and broke into laughter while they sang, because both knew each other was thinking the exact same thing.

Those two will have it all—the music and the sex and the warm body and the hugs and the sex and the sex.

But somehow, at that moment, it didn't seem to matter.

Joy was joy and, even in the darkest depths of loneliness and heartache, when it was brought forth by the union of souls in music, it was bliss. Sheer bliss.

They played on, going over the chorus a few times just because the moment Michael created, sacrificing his own deep pain and hurts to help heal others, was too sublime and surreal to let go. Then, when their hands were forced and they had to find an ending, a few well-placed chords did the trick. Afterwards, Michael tossed the borrowed guitar he was using back over his hip, and he leaned in to give Kelly a hug. Their laughter was dear and the joy in their eyes was meant only for each other. Their fingers lingered, entwined, long after the music ended.

Jacob nodded apologetically at Jessie. She threw off her guitar and grabbed him fiercely around the neck. She shook him from side to side, and let the tears flow for the second time that afternoon. He reached a hand up to grab her arm, then let it float around to her almost bare back, and he felt her shiver when he pressed her as close as he could against him with his guitar still between them.

"You dork," she groaned, grinning widely as she grabbed his cheeks and held his face between her palms. She planted a kiss firmly on his lips. "I love you, I will always love you, but that's all you get. Okay?"

Flushed, he ran his hand lower down her back and winked. "You sure about that?"

"Yeah!" She laughed. "Yes. Jacob, you mean more to me than you will ever know. But don't let me ever hear you making threats against my husband again. Okay?"

"I didn't threaten him, Jessie." His eyes deflated. "What I said was in the past. Old thoughts."

"Uh huh." She eyed him warily.

He pulled her as tight against him as he could get, swearing silently. His guitar was still staunchly in between their bodies. For the first time ever, he cursed its presence.

"I like the old fart. I like you being happy with him. But—if you ever need me, Jessie—you know I'll be here for you."

She rubbed his stubble thoughtfully, then leaned in and kissed him again, this time more tender and loving.

"I know," she whispered, and couldn't help herself. She removed his guitar from around his shoulders, and he held it to one side. Jessie reached up under the back of Jacob's T-shirt and pressed her hands against his cross, over the shoulder blades. He trembled under her touch, and at the warmth of her gentle breath on his cheek. His lips drew downwards as he tenderly reached his free hand behind his back, grabbed one of her arms, and pulled it out of his shirt and away.

"This is what got us into this shit in the first place," he reminded Jessie, holding her wrist high in between them. He bent and kissed her knuckles. "No more," he said softly, and then added, to her still fisted hand, "go forth and make another man happy." His body sighed and the deep blue eyes looked sadly at his friend.

She tilted her head at him, a slow blush spreading across her cheeks. "Thank you, Jacob," she murmured fondly.

"Rrrrr," was his response, as he lifted his guitar higher out to his side like a trophy. "Thar she blows! Who wants to play some music?"

Chapter Twenty-Three

H̶ey! Jet's landing at 6 c u then, Matt's car there he will drive

Josh eyed his phone warily. "Six," he muttered. "Okay. Lots of time to say my goodbyes to Caryn." Inwardly he echoed the thought with *and try to walk away trusting her not to share my wife's sexy body with the world.*

He texted back *can't wait I need u c u soon luv u*

His meeting with Caryn was at four. He spent the morning doing odds and ends to settle his nerves. He and Jessie had talked about hiring a house-keeper to help with the cleaning—Carlotta had a second cousin in need of work—but they hadn't gotten around to it. Josh did the rounds himself, eyeing this and that with a critical eye. He wanted the place to look nice for Jessie, who he knew would be tired when she landed. He cranked the tunes on the PEAK and went for it, scrubbing the toilet on his hands and knees, and shining the faucets with enough elbow grease to keep his Harley run-ning smooth.

He ran a hand over the bed to ease out any unwanted wrinkles, and glanced around for clothes he'd lazily tossed on the boxy black corner chair. "Oh, that's where that was," he grumbled, finding a script he'd been read-ing buried under a grey hoodie. Josh tugged on the script and threw it over his shoulder to the bed. Grabbing the hoodie, he studied it for a moment before putting it on over his black T-shirt. He folded a pair of jeans and laid them on a shelf in the closet, and then went down to the kitchen for a quick lunch of yesterday's leftover potatoes fried with onion and butter.

Then it was time to go. He left the house by the back door, grabbing a thick leather motorcycle jacket on the way out. It was spring now, a gorgeous

213

perfect sunny day. The mountains were crisp in the distance beyond North Van, the snow on their peaks diminishing more and more each day, like ice cubes left in the sink, melting more and more each second.

Straddling the big Harley and urging it to life was a thrill Josh never tired of. He remembered one day when he and Jessie first got together, that blessed painful three weeks before Charlie came home and messed everything up. It was cold then, but cold is relative in Vancouver. People sail in January, they golf year round. So he and Jessie had taken a ride on the bike, her wearing this very same jacket as a guard against the cold, and he in an old one he'd worn when he was twenty. They'd cruised up into the mountains and found a quiet rest stop where he'd pulled her against him and kissed her with the urgency only a lack of time can bestow, querying the universe as to why such perfect moments always had to come at a price.

Thinking about that particular ride, Josh paused and thanked God for getting the two of them through that initial coming together and through everything that followed. There was an old wooden fence erected on the northwest side of that particular rest stop, a split rail type like the one at the *Drifters* camp. Even now, a few years later, Josh's gut ached to hold Jessie the way he held her that day, him leaning back against the fence, this amazing new love in his arms, each desperately wanting to trust the other, learning to trust, the bike parked a few feet away, a surreal vista of English Bay and dotty channel islands laid bare at their feet.

He couldn't remember what they'd talked about, only that they didn't discuss her impending marriage at the time, or Charlie's painful affairs that left Jessie lonely and hurting. Instead, Josh recalled the feelings, the physical sensations that rocked him to the core—his hand under the black jacket, under her sweater, the newness of her, his fingers against her skin, protecting, hoping, wanting. Even now, he tingled at the way their skin felt when it connected, even the slightest brush of a fingertip—his or hers, it didn't matter—on the other's cheek was enough to elicit soft moans of longing.

That particular motorcycle trip into the mountains had ended with both black leather jackets on the ground, Josh on his back, Jessie on top, and neither feeling the cold seeping a warning in and around them. *Magic*, he thought, remembering. *Simply magic.* He'd taken her home on the bike, to his place, not hers, in case they were spotted, and he'd never felt so in love, so free. In those early days he knew Charlie was an issue, a barrier, but he believed from the first moment Jessie's soft gaze met his—in the garbage, no less—that their connection was infinite, everlasting. Solid.

The ride home that day? Divine. The cool wind raced over his face along-side the euphoria in his heart, and an unexpected lover rode behind him, their thighs touching as she wrapped her arms around his waist. It was one of those rare moments gifted from the universe he'd banked away for days like this, when he was about to get the Harley out and cruise downtown to terminate a connection that terrified him for its unknown power over his body and mind, and over his and Jessie's lives.

He revved the Harley and kicked away the stand. The bike was upright and raring to go, like a good horse, trembling between his legs with a lust for the road and the freedom it wrought.

～～～

In Miami, Jessie was over the moon. She hugged Kelly deeply and sincerely, and silently thanked Michael for what she thought must have been one scin-tillating night for the new couple, because Kelly was in a rare, gracious mood today. She likely hadn't slept—much, at least—based on her regular yawns and sleepy eyes, but she was glowing, and she'd showed up for an early call, focused and determined. It likely didn't hurt that Michael was red as a beet on the perimeter of the set all morning, Jessie thought, but she could care less. Thanks to Kelly's good graces, Jessie was going to be able to fly home early.

"Kelly, I'm actually going to miss working with you," Jessie was saying enthusiastically, standing back after their hug to linger in Kelly's presence for a moment longer.

"You'd better be back next season, girl," Kelly responded sincerely. She gestured to Michael, who was chatting with Jacob behind them. "In case he gets out of hand and I need some girl talk to straighten us out."

"Ah ha," Jessie smiled knowingly. She leaned in closer and whispered in her co-star's ear. "So how was it? Worth the wait?"

A wide blush bloomed across Kelly's cheeks, which Jessie didn't think was possible, as far as this hoity-toity star was concerned. Raising her eye-brows, Kelly answered, "Put it this way. He knows where all the buttons are."

Laughing, Jessie peeked over at Michael, who noticed both girls looking mischievously at him, like two little waifs eyeing wrapped Christmas presents, and he licked his lips uncomfortably and looked away, but not before grinning boyishly at Kelly and turning a deeper shade of red than her.

"Damn, he's cute," Jessie stuck the tip of her thumb in her mouth and sucked on it.

"Who?" Kelly's eyes narrowed playfully. "You talkin' 'bout my new man, or Jacob?"

"Ha! Jacob's appeal has long been established. No, I mean your man. He looks like Matt if you look at him in a certain light." She angled her head and grinned at Michael, who couldn't resist turning to see if he was still the object of the girls' seductive stares.

Kelly regarded Jessie with a naughty smile. "You ever want to go there? With Matt? I mean, maybe not now, but back in the lonely Charlie days."

"Ummm," Jessie nibbled on her thumb thoughtfully, studying Michael, the way he moved so easily around the craft table, the way he placed a hand casually on his hip as he scanned the semi-dark set, the way he swiped at his hair as if he still had long layers to play with. "I always thought Matt was cute but he was all business in those years. I was a little afraid of him." She grinned, then added, "But there was always something sweet and gentle about his eyes. Despite the ornery security guy bullshit."

"Answer my question, girl!" Kelly rocked back on one heel and crossed her arms, eyes twinkling.

"Kelly! Really!" Jessie was laughing but she, too, was suddenly an interesting shade of red. "Noooo! I mean, not really! Not in the 'Biblical' sense!"

"Um-humn…" Her lips puckering thoughtfully, Kelly nodded behind Jessie as Matt unknowingly walked into a conversation he would have thought was very strange, had he known what was on Jessie's mind at the moment.

He touched her shoulder lightly and she jumped, eyes darting to him to see who had come up behind and touched her, and then she gave Kelly a half-hearted death-ray stare before grinning and turning her head away to purportedly study a handful of grapes on the nearby craft table.

"What?" Matt asked curiously as Kelly broke into robust laughter.

Jessie air-palmed Kelly. "Don't you dare," she demanded, a little afraid of what might emerge from between those usually unfiltered pink lips.

With a sidelong wink at Matt, who stood looking confused a few feet away from her, Kelly positively appraised his choice of conservative pale blue dress shirt unbuttoned at the neck, smartly rolled up jeans anchored with a wide leather belt, and designer calfskin cap-toe Balmorals, before she sauntered over to Michael and wrapped both arms tightly around his waist.

"What the hell was that about?" Placing both hands on his hips, Matt sucked on his bottom lip and watched his brother whisper into Kelly's ear while brushing tendrils of blonde hair back from her face.

"Um…" Jessie started, still blushing and unable to look at him. "You don't want to know."

But Matt was a smart guy. He clued in pretty quickly and took a moment himself to rub a thumb and forefinger over his mouth before trusting himself to speak. He, too, blushed at Jessie and a hint of a smile curved up one corner of his lip.

He reached an arm out to her. "C'mon girl," he said, chuckling. "The jet's fueled and ready to hit the skies. We've got people waiting for us back home."

"Yes, we do," Jessie replied, happily wrapping an arm around his waist as they started towards the door in the far corner. She stopped by Jacob and took his hand.

"Bye, you big baby. I'll miss your stupid butt." She leaned back and frowned, then reached out and ran a finger over the red bandana he had once again tied around his head. "What the hell's this? Two days in a row? We really need to find you a woman. Preferably one with some fashion sense." She slipped both arms around his back and squeezed tightly before rocking him back and forth a little.

He couldn't help himself—Jacob stuck his nose in her hair and breathed in the scent of lavender that followed Jessie everywhere, and which seemed to visit him in his dreams, the ones he never wanted to wake from. He snuggled her closely.

"Be safe, Annie-Jessie. I'll see you soon."

"'Kay," she said a little too brightly, regarding him closely, affectionately. "Next week, for the concert."

"Yep," he answered with a sigh. The concert. No doubt Jessie's hubby would be present. But he brightened at the prospect of playing music on stage with her in front of the expected few thousand fans.

Jessie turned and wrapped an arm around Matt's waist again, letting her fingers slip out of Jacob's hold as she left him standing alone to watch her exit his life yet again.

"Damn," Jessie murmured disconsolately to Matt. "This leaving thing just never ends, does it?"

"Not in this crazy business it doesn't," Matt replied honestly, a ripple of sorrow in his voice. Sorrow for the boy they were leaving behind, sorrow for Jessie's seemingly never-ending sad moments, and sorrow for his wife and Katy, who were on their own so much while he was away.

"Let's rock, Matt," Jessie said suddenly, as the door opened and light poured in. She could see the sky, blue and beckoning. She picked up her pace.

Matt followed, holding her hand now as Jessie moved ahead of him through the door. At the last moment he turned to salute his brother, and then he disappeared outside.

Chapter Twenty-four

Her breathing changed to rapid short intakes when Caryn spotted Josh on the Harley. The star of the biggest film on the circuit right now, *Freedom Ride,* which, incidentally, featured Josh Sawyer at his freakin' sexiest on a Harley, cruising to a halt outside Revolver to meet her, ON A HARLEY? She exhaled slowly, admiring the bike and its rider before she stepped lightly forward to greet her coffee date.

"Nice bike," she cooed sincerely, letting a finger graze the classic red bumper and white trim. "Old, or just old style?"

Unbuckling his half-helmet, Josh placed it on his seat before answering. He unzipped his motorcycle jacket. "Remake of a classic style. A smooth ride." He lifted his right hand and cut it forward through the air, fingers together, palm down, to accentuate the word smooth. His eyes were still shining from the exhilaration the *smooth ride* bestowed.

"Hmmm, your second love?"

He broke into a full grin. "Something like that."

Grasping Caryn's elbow with one hand, the helmet with the other, he gently steered her down the little hill and then up the few steps into Revolver. He glanced around—a few people had picked up on his presence. At least no one was asking for autographs, and he didn't see any visible cell phones; still, Josh sucked in a breath. Being seen with the exotic Caryn in public was maybe not the wisest idea. He chided himself for getting caught up in the woman's mystique, and made a point of telling himself he would talk to Jessie when she got home tonight. The guilt of sneaking around behind her back was consuming him whole. *And anyway,* he thought, *I need her side of this weird story.*

In the small narrow Revolver, with its rustic aged wood booths and iron filigree trim, Josh set down the helmet while he shrugged off the heavy black jacket, which he laid over a metal chair by the coffee shop's large window. He gestured to Caryn to take a seat, noting as he did the short, tight white leather jacket she was at this moment unzipping to reveal an elegant sequined tank top. He averted his eyes from the exposed half moons of her perfectly round breasts. She folded her arms on the bar-style tabletop that ran the length of the window, and smiled up at him, doe eyes sweet and beckoning.

"Drip coffee?" he asked, still standing. "Or something laced with sugar?"

"Plain old drip would be great, Josh, thanks."

"Treats?"

"Ahhhh," she breathed inwardly, her gaze drifting over his thick black motorcycle boots, denims, and the wrinkled grey hoodie. She met his eyes and bit her top lip, exhaling slowly. "Yesssss…"

His smile faded and he shook his head just the slightest bit, then looked away, embarrassed. "Not the kind of treat I had in mind," he admonished her in a low voice, quickly swiping the back of a hand across his cheeks and nose as if the hand could hide a thinly disguised desire. *Damn this woman,* he thought.

She shrugged as if to say *your loss,* and then threw in a curve ball. "Eric and I have an open relationship, Josh. We sleep with other people. It's perfectly natural, and in fact helps a lot of relationships." The statement was delivered in a matter-of-fact manner, but it shook the ground underneath Josh's feet. Memories of the on-set hair gal on *Freedom Ride* came back to haunt him.

Caryn wasn't finished. She lifted a delicate hand and placed it over his, which he was resting on the counter. "Nobody has to get hurt."

He stared hard at her, one lip's corner inching downwards. His words were rock hard, and they chilled him even as he spoke them. "You asking me… or Jessie?" Angry glints flicked in his eyes, and his knuckles whitened under hers—but Josh didn't move his hand. Despite his honorable intentions in meeting her, he was powerless under Caryn's touch. Yet his next few words were husky, low and insistent. "Or both?"

Josh couldn't deny it. The thought of having sex outside of his and Jessie's bedroom, lighting a deeper fire, as they say, adding some interest and fun and spice…was erotic in itself. Actually doing the deed? Could he? Was that why he kept meeting Caryn? Because she represented something he was curious about? He was now a very famous actor, an A-lister on the major film circuit. He could have whomever he wanted, when he wanted. He could grab this woman by the arm and take her somewhere, now. He could live a life filled with danger and excitement, and thrills likely beyond the reach of most couples.

But—he wasn't that kind of guy and, despite the increasing blood pressure pounding in his ears, he was glad of it. He got what he needed at home, when Jessie was, in fact, home. He regarded Caryn thoughtfully, waiting for her response. But it was slow in coming. She'd seen the waves of emotion cross his face like a movie trailer—first lust, then intrigue, naked desire, reflection (of Jessie, likely—Caryn could read him like a book when thoughts of his wife crossed his mind), and…a certain peace. Contentment, even.

"So that's it, is it?" was her response, finally, delivered in a small voice with a lingering wistfulness. "Not even going to try?"

Slowly, Josh looked down at their hands. He gently pulled his away from underneath her delicate, tapered fingers. He grinned boyishly, that ornery cascade of hair falling over the stubble on his cheek. "Maybe if you beg," he said jokingly, quietly, since he knew they were still being watched.

"Oh, I can beg," was Caryn's response as her heart rate picked up dramatically. She straightened hopefully, but then caught the glint in his eyes. She swatted him on the arm. "Damn you," she said irascibly. "I'd like to take you and that bike of yours," she nodded in the general direction of the Harley just up the hill outside, almost out of view, "for a test run."

"I'll bet you would," he answered, the slow teasing grin readily apparent now.

"Go!" She waved him off. "Get me coffee, will you? Before I lose my mind!" She watched him weave his way over to the counter, shaking his head in amusement.

Then Caryn straightened and tensed. Her eyes had flickered back to the window and scanned down Cambie Street, people watching; she recognized a few folks from the neighborhood, and wondered about the others—who was aimless, lost, scared? And then, just as she was remembering the day she found Jessie hunched on a step, shivering with fever in the freezing rain, she had looked up the street, and something caught the corner of her eye. *Someone.*

"Noooo," she breathed, elbows on the counter, both palms squeezing her cheeks before covering her eyes. "No." She was afraid to open her eyes, and desperately afraid to turn around to warn Josh. But she had to move.

Slowly, the hands came away from her cheeks. She had glanced back up Cambie to take a peek at Josh's bike, to admire it and dream about the hopelessly sexy man who swung a leg over it to greet her just a short time ago. And there, a moment ago and still, now—frozen, staring—was Jessie.

The girl was staring wide-eyed up at Revolver's large open window, where Josh and Caryn—and their entwined fingers—were, a moment ago, clearly visible. She moved now, just a hair's breadth, enough to look sideways at Josh's Harley, the classic red, the only one of its kind in Vancouver. The one she'd ridden on many times, holding her man close, the heady smell of leather filling her nostrils, the feel of Josh's windblown hair tickling her cheek.

Caryn saw her chest rise, but she didn't see it fall. Jessie was barely breathing and now, as the shock was sinking in, she was fisting her hands into tight little balls. She mouthed something slowly, eyes now on fire, and Caryn didn't have to guess what she said. Three simple words. *You little bitch.* Not emphasized by a fist in anger, but spoken simply, accented with angry tears.

"Oh, shit," Caryn whistled through clenched teeth. "This can't be good." Thoughts were whirling through her mind as she waited to see which direction this was going to go—would Jessie back off, or would this internationally renowned star come barreling through Revolver's door with guns blazing? And what the hell was she even doing here? Josh said she wasn't expected home until six.

She didn't have to wait long. Josh picked that moment to come back and ask Caryn if she wanted cream or sugar. She didn't answer him.

He followed her gaze…and met Jessie's confused, hurt, angry stare.

"Jesus!" he cursed, both feet stuck to Revolver's bare narrow-planked floor. Inadvertently, he dropped a hand on Caryn's shoulder, for balance, but he quickly realized Jessie didn't take it that way. He was locked in the terror now apparent in those captivating ice-blue eyes, and it immobilized him.

Jessie moved first. She wheeled around, suddenly, while in Revolver Josh and Caryn both gasped, at once, for breath. Josh didn't take the time to grab his helmet and jacket. He vaulted through the door and down the steps, two at a time, almost knocking over a very pregnant woman, who had to clutch the iron banister at the last second to keep from toppling over.

"Jessie!" he cried, streaking up the sidewalk, as many sets of eyes followed him, alerted by the panic in his voice. "Wait! Hold on!"

She was running now, too, swiping angry tears away as she barreled around an older couple with a small husky dog, and then a woman with a baby in a stroller. She had to stop at the corner on Hastings Street, though; it was either that or get run over by one of Vancouver's big speedy buses. Josh caught her there, and he grabbed her arm.

She threw him off, screaming, "Get the hell away from me!" She was shifting her feet hurriedly, her breath coming in short, quick rasps, her mind too confused with weird images and messed-up memories to know what to do, how to react, where to go.

Around them, someone clued in as to who they were, and whipped out a cell phone, which was immediately pointed towards the celebrity couple screaming at each other on the sidewalk.

"You don't understand," Josh was crying, "just hold up and listen for a goddamned second!"

"What's there to understand, Josh? Jesus, first it's that woman in Virginia, and now…and now…" But Jessie was sobbing openly now, and so the words couldn't quite form on her lips. Her eyes shifted down the hill and hardened, though, and Josh knew without looking that Caryn was somewhere behind them.

Jessie heaved her arm out of her husband's grasp and backed away. All kinds of visions crossed her mind. Josh, sickeningly adorable in his old grey hoodie and loose-fitting frayed denims, rolled up once at the bottom over black motorcycle boots so they wouldn't drag on the sidewalk (they did anyway, as evidenced by many loose threads dragging low); Josh, liquid chocolate eyes now wet, tortured, aching; Josh with…Caryn?! Jessie shook the cobwebs away. *Seriously? Really?!*

A soft liquid sugar voice floated through the air to Josh and Jessie.

"Jessie, honey, please…can we go back to Revolver and have a coffee? To talk about this?"

Incensed, Jessie's wrath aimed itself at her old employer and…lover. "You," she growled in a voice Josh recognized as Jessie's about-to-implode tone. "You fucking little bitch. You couldn't have me so you went after my husband? Is that it?!" She threw out the word husband with such spite and distaste that Josh, sickened, bent over, a bile rising in his belly that he was fairly certain was going to erupt—soon.

Caryn raised both arms, which were full of Josh's discarded jacket and helmet, and held both palms outward, facing the girl she'd once rescued. "That's not what this is, Jessie. Calm down."

"If that's not what it is, then what the hell is it?!" Tears were now freely pouring down Jessie's cheeks, which was heartbreaking for Josh and Caryn to witness, and even painful for the not-so-discreet fans with phones raised to film the confrontation.

"Wait a second," Jessie was adding, too calmly, as if the world was suddenly rotating properly on its access again, "I don't FUCKING want to know!"

Josh tried to breathe and speak in a normal tone. He was suddenly aware of the people filming around them. The thoughts of where those videos would go, and the power they held, scared the freakin' bejeesus out of him. "Jessie," he begged. "Not here, okay? Let's not do this here." He tried to grab her arm again, but she screamed and yanked it away.

"Let go of me! Let me go!" Then, as her mind tried to make sense of the situation, a moment of clarity hit her between the eyes. She forced herself to meet Josh's terrified expression. "Why, Josh?" she begged to understand. "Why?"

Heartsick, his shoulders sank. He whispered to her and, despite the cacophony of the city street, she understood every word. "I needed to know," he said. "I needed to know."

Which was when the full impact of what the man she loved now knew about her hit Jessie with a gale force wind big enough to almost take her down.

He saw it register in her eyes first. They caved in, like an earthquake from the inside of her soul, cracking, splintering, and blistering her in two.

She bent over and wrapped her arms around herself, choking back her next words, which came from some disembodied voice she didn't recognize, even though it was her own. "Oh sweet Jesus," she moaned over and over. "Oh sweet Jesus, sweet Jesus." Josh knew some of her most deeply guarded secrets now. *Who else knew? Who else knows?!*

She managed to get a grip long enough to straighten and then, since Josh knew about her past now anyway, she voiced something she'd wanted to say to Caryn for years.

She pointed a trembling finger at the beautiful woman who once cared so lovingly for her in a way Jessie desperately needed at a time when her whole world had completely disintegrated. "Caryn," she whispered, the woman's name a painful blister on her tongue, "You...threw me away." She started to back away but didn't lose the woman's steady, albeit distraught, gaze. Josh stood by, too shocked and terrified to move, lest Jessie shrink from him and back into traffic.

Jessie jabbed her finger at Caryn and said it again, a bottomless unfathomable pain coloring her features, sinking her even deeper into a sinister dark abyss. This time the words were fraught with an emotion too big to contain, and they came out in choking sobs. "You! Threw! Me! Awayyy! You fucking bitch!!!" And she ran for Caryn and shoved her the same way she shoved Josh that night when she first came back to Vancouver. But at least that night she and Josh were hidden away from the world, and so her pain was delicately guarded amongst people who loved her. Today it was laid bare for the world to see, and neither Josh nor Caryn was even remotely prepared to stop it from happening.

She turned then and ran for her car, the red Mustang she lovingly brought out on this beautiful spring day to test its motor and set it free from a dank winter's dark imprisonment.

Josh wanted to run to her, but he had to let her go. He knew her; she needed space, she needed time to drive and drive and drive and hopefully to think more rationally as her emotions settled. He stooped over and laid both palms on his thighs, adjusting his breath so he could speak sensibly to Caryn. But first, he looked painfully up at the throng gathered nearby, not close enough to touch, but certainly close enough to film the day's hapless climax.

"Please," he begged, putting his hands with palms facing out in front of his chest, "please respect our privacy. This is an old wound that needs some time to heal."

And he followed Caryn down the sidewalk to his bike, took first his jacket from her and then his helmet, and then he swung a leg back over the bike, started it, and regarded Caryn critically. "It's my fault," he admitted mournfully into her searching eyes. "I did this. I promised Jessie I wouldn't keep secrets, that I'd be honest with her."

"All hell's going to break loose, isn't it, Josh?" Caryn's face was pinched and pale.

He scrutinized her thoughtfully before answering. "I think it already has," he said as a dark gloominess sank deep into his body. Josh sighed, kicked the kickstand away, gave Caryn one final hard look, and motored off, solemnly and justly defeated.

Chapter Twenty-five

"Hey, Charlie?"

Josh had the phone against his ear in one hand, and with the other he was rubbing his head forcefully, elbow high in the air and hair starting to look as if he'd stuck his hand in a light socket. For sure, that was how he felt, his whole body juddery and unbalanced, his breath uneven, his eyes blinking hard against unshed tears. He had ridden to the spot on the mountain where he'd taken Jessie so long ago. Somehow he thought—he hoped— he could feel her here, in spirit, at least. If not, well then at least he was closer to God so he could sink to his knees in prayer after calling Charlie, who he knew was his best chance in breaking this latest crap to Charles and Dee.

"Yeah! Josh? What's up?" On the other end, Charlie was bouncing baby Stella gently on one hip but, at the agony in his friend's voice, he laid the baby down in her crib and gave his full attention to the drama now unfolding over the phone.

"Hey Charlie, you remember the day Jessie and I got back from P.E.I. and you sensed something was up? Well, the proverbial shit has hit the fan." He made a *plopping* sound, which in his crazed state Josh thought sounded like shit actually hitting a fan. He tried to laugh at his own funny, but couldn't muster any saliva in his dry mouth.

Charlie inhaled slowly through his nose. Anything to do with Jessie was usually…well, dramatic and difficult.

"Is she okay?" he asked, his voice small and suddenly very, very afraid. "Jessie?" He didn't need to ask. Josh's voice was trembling enough for Charlie to discern two things—one, this call was of course going to involve Jessie

227

in one way or another, and two, of course she wasn't okay. Nor was Josh, apparently.

"Not really, no," Josh managed, balking at the truth. "Well, physically, I suppose, at least I hope so, but mentally and emotionally—"

Charlie cut him off. "Josh! Talk to me. What the hell's going on?"

Sighing, Josh collapsed onto a picnic table at the look-off and related, as best he could, the events of the last while. He told Charlie about the pictures, about Jessie's retrieval from the streets by Caryn and Eric, and he didn't hold back when he told him how disgusted he was that these people kept Jessie in their grasp for as long as they did. What he did not tell Charlie was why he kept going back to see Caryn, that he'd talked alone to Arnie at the studio, and that he was...well...somewhat intrigued and captivated by Caryn and her...relationship...with his wife.

Silence reigned on Charlie's end of the line when Josh mentioned the number of cellphones he knew had filmed the altercation on the Downtown Eastside.

Josh was quiet, too, and hung his head in shame. He watched a gutsy dandelion frolic in the breeze off the water, and wished he had the energy the weed had to beat the elements, to continue to survive in a harsh environment.

Finally, Charlie rallied. "Josh, first of all, this is not a real surprise to me."

Catching his breath, Josh hesitated. Charlie heard him gulping for air, for stability, for a leg to stand on.

Charlie's next words were succinct. "I knew she lived with someone for a while. Jack, my dad, heard it from someone in the acting workshop. We didn't know who. And not like Jessie ever talked, as I guess you're also figuring out." Those words were almost spiteful, but Charlie looked back over at his gurgling, happy baby girl and he relaxed a little. "What I didn't know was what kind of relationship they had, but really, at this point, does that even matter?"

"Charlie, I don't know what the hell matters anymore." The weariness in Josh's voice caught Charlie off guard.

"Tell me you didn't sleep with this Caryn chick."

"Hell, no!"

"Josh?"

"No! Jesus, Charlie!" Josh stood suddenly and kicked the dandelion, which, despite his heavy boot, still fluttered hopefully.

"Okay then," Charlie said. "You know where Jessie will go in the short term. She'll go for a long drive, and then she'll either go to your place or to her downtown condo." He added reflectively, while rubbing his chin between two fingers, "I don't think she'll go to see Charles and Dee. This is too much to drop on their doorstep by herself, likely, at this point."

"I don't even know if they're home."

"They're home," Charlie replied. "They were here today to see Stella."

Josh's gut wrenched for the thousandth time that day. "Of course they were," he muttered, picturing the couples' glee at visiting with the 'son' they likely wished they had. Jacob, too, entered Josh's mind unbidden, and he winced and buried his head in his hands again.

Sighing, Charlie ignored the wince. "All right. So there's not likely a damned thing we can do about those videos hitting YouTube, so let's not stress about that just yet. What we need to do is get Dee to work her PR magic with whoever's doing their publicity these days. I think they've got someone new? Someone well versed in Social Media?"

"Yeah, they do. Someone Michelle recommended, actually. From her firm. A guy."

"Right. Yes. Josh?"

"Yeah."

"Don't go there, okay? Thinking about Michelle and old relationships. It'll just sink you."

Something in his voice hit Josh hard. He bit his lip. "You do that, Charlie?"

"Course I do. All the time. I'll always regret fucking things up with Jessie. But I know I've got it pretty good now, so I'm not complaining." His words took on a gentle timbre. "I knew I didn't have a chance after you came along with those big brown eyes." He added, "I'll call Charles and Dee. To prepare them and to get some counter-media happening. And Josh—don't worry about Jessie. You guys have a lot to learn about managing relationships. All new couples do. Secrets suck, and they have a way of sucking the blood out of marriages. They don't work in a marriage. They don't belong there. So the way I see it, this is just one more thing Jessie's responsible for. She should have told me, or you, or at the very least, Charles and Dee."

"I think she's so scared of being called on her past...that...that..."

229

Charlie cut him off. "I know. She's scared, period. Of her own shadow, some days. But that's beside the point right now. Look, I gotta go give Dee a call before this tiny little female in my care decides to start a whole new drama. We try to time Jane's trips to the store to in between feedings, but sometimes that backfires on us. Stella is only a few months old and already she has a mind of her own and is running the household."

At that, Josh managed a tiny lopsided smile. "Okay," he said, picturing the conversation Charlie was going to have on his behalf with Jessie's manager and producer.

Charlie broke in with one last question. "You going to be okay, buddy?"

"Not at the moment," Josh said, fearing the explosions he knew were going to come his way before this thing settled. Hopefully Jessie wouldn't divorce him…but Charles and Dee might.

"Go home," Charlie insisted as Stella entertained Josh with gurgles in the background. "She'll show up somewhere."

"All right," Josh agreed, somewhat placated with Charlie now on the case.

After they signed off, he considered placing a call to Stephen, but he wasn't up to explaining things again. Steve would have to wait.

He stayed on the picnic table for a while, his butt on the table part and his booted feet on the bench, contemplating life and marriage and black box studios and Caryn and Eric and Jacob and Jessie. Then, climbing back onto the big bike, he pointed it, anxiously, towards home.

Chapter Twenty-six

*F*ootsteps finally echoed on the flagstone walk at about ten thirty that night. Throwing open the door, Josh was less than pleased to see Deirdre Keating standing there, arms crossed and fatigue lining her face in little streaks that emanated from her eyes and lips.

"Can we talk?" she asked in a voice Josh considered neither menacing nor friendly.

He moved aside to let her pass, but looked behind her first to see if…

"Charles isn't here. He'd put you through that wall if it was up to him."

Josh swallowed. The wall she was referring to, lining part of the back deck, was solid stone.

He didn't speak.

Dee crossed the floor and sank into a comfy leather couch. "The thing about being married to Jessie, Josh," she started, pressing a tired hand to her forehead, "is that when unexpected surprises like this appear, we have to deal with them. Immediately. In fact," she eyed him carefully, "your stature in the entertainment biz these days also requires, shall we say, increased management. I hope you've called Hilary."

Still, he was silent. He sat across from her and waited.

"Have you heard from her? Jessie?" This was Dee asking Josh. His shoulders sank further as he blinked away a new threat of tears.

He shook his head and managed a somber, "No."

"Nor have we. Matt has eyes on her place downtown. She hasn't shown up there, either." She counted to three and sucked in a breath before continuing. "Josh, I understand from Charlie there are…photos…and films."

Josh saw through Dee's formidable exterior then. She, too, was crumbling. He ran both hands through his unruly hair and made a small *pffftt* sound.

"There are," he finally got hold of his voice box. "Caryn—uh—this couple—tells me they will never be released. Some kind of Downtown Eastside code or something."

"The thing about the existence of this kind of material, Josh, is that—well, especially in this day and age—it can be pretty easy to get your hands on it, and," she put both feet up on an ottoman, one at a time as if it hurt to move them, "put it online. Too easy," she added unnecessarily.

"That's why I went there, Dee. I wanted to ebb that flow, y'know?" He looked at her, a wistful hopelessness lending a somber plea to his face. Josh spoke as he now felt, in the knowing there wasn't a sweet damn thing he, or anyone else, could do, should Jessie's photos and / or films get released.

"I know that, honey," Dee softened, but she still spoke frankly. "But somehow that doesn't ease my mind when I picture this woman's hand on yours at a downtown coffee shop."

"Wh-what?" Josh asked, incredulous. Someone posted *that* on YouTube? *Jesus.*

"Why was she even there, Dee? Downtown? At four o'clock? She wasn't supposed to be home til six."

"Matt said she finished up early and they flew home. It was seven o'clock Miami time. As for downtown, I'm guessing she found you gone and decided to drop in on Mary Helen at the shelter. Why she apparently didn't call or text you about her early arrival is beyond me. Unless I suppose she wanted to surprise you."

He cringed. *Yeah, she surprised me all right.* He'd asked himself the same question until he found a hastily scrawled note on the kitchen island—*home early, back by six. Cell toast, will charge in car.*

A startling buzz jarred Josh's analysis of that, which made perfect sense in 'Jessie world', and Dee pulled her cell out of the pocket of her light soft tweed jacket. She glanced at the screen and squinted to read it, then pulled her reading glasses out of another pocket, placed them on her nose, and swiped the text message so as to get the full effect in larger print.

"It's Matt," she said to Josh. She looked up and exhaled heavily. "She's driven up to Whistler. She contacted Matt to try to find access to our condo. He notified someone on the condo committee and they let her in with the spare key."

Sitting back on the chair, Josh rubbed his stubble with one hand, and looked away. *Okay,* he said to himself. *Okay. She's okay.*

Dee removed her legs from the ottoman and used both arms to propel herself off the couch. "I'm leaving now. I'm old and I need sleep. Tomorrow I will be at Jessie's door before she gets her lazy butt out of bed, and Charles will be with me. You," she pointed a finger accusingly at Josh, "will not."

He stood too, and faced her, shoulders drawn back with determination. "I've got news for you, Dee," he said, feeling a new tremble overtake him, "she's my wife. I need to see her."

"You will not see Jessie because Charles will skin you alive, Josh, if you're near his esteemed company any time in the near future. This was too big of a secret to keep, for both you and Jessie, and the image of that woman's hand on yours is just a little too fresh at this point."

She didn't add *for Jessie, too* but Josh felt the unsaid words echo through his bones, regardless.

"What am I supposed to do, Dee?" he asked, posing the question as a heartbroken child, arms flailing at his sides, eyes glistening.

"You wait," she said, moving towards the door. She gestured downwards with her hand and glanced at the chair he'd just vacated. "You wait, and you see her when she's ready to see you. And maybe, if you're lucky, and keep trying to get in touch, she'll take your call."

The slamming of Dee's car door was the final bit of icing on the cake. He couldn't hold it in any longer and, when Steve tried to call Josh later after seeing the video of Josh and Jessie's very public fight, Josh didn't even look up. By then he was sitting on the floor, leaning against the wall, a mess of tears and snot.

He was alone, wallowing in a pool of misery essentially very much his own doing, despite it being grounded in Jessie's need to hide, and he was inconsolable. He considered driving to Whistler anyway, but then, when he finally settled enough to check his phone, Josh saw a note from Matt.

233

I'm with Jessie she will be okay hang tight will be in touch

"Good ole Matt," muttered Josh miserably.

He hung his head and took a deep breath.

"Good ole Matt."

~ ~

"Oh honey," Jessie said to Matt when she opened the door of the condo at twelve-thirty in the morning. "You need to be home with Julie. Not here fixing another one of my glorious messes."

Judging by Jessie's piqued face and red-rimmed eyes, Matt didn't agree. He held up a bottle of Baileys. "For our coffee," he said definitively. In the other hand he held a recyclable tray containing two large coffees from the twenty-four hour Tim Horton's down the road. "ROAM Whistler was closed," he told her.

Matt had been in Whistler for the last half hour, but he'd sat in the Audi and watched Jessie through the window of the condo before he drove off to gather the coffee and Baileys. He knew he was, technically, a little out of line doing that, but he was trying to put his finger on the aura surrounding this often troubled girl. Why was her music so special? Why did she mean so much to people, to the world? Regardless, he knew she'd survive this latest blow, because her fans were deeply faithful. They needed her; they needed her music. They wouldn't care if they discovered her association with the mysterious blonde in the YouTube videos. If photos got released? Or films? Matt didn't dare speculate. But now, she was family, pretty much, and she was hurting. So he was here.

Watching through the window of the two-story townhouse condo as he sat in his car, Matt saw, against a backdrop of shimmering yellow light, a woman who always turned to music when she was upset. It helped her breathe, he knew, the same way a salty ocean tang welcomed home people who lived by oceans.

The condo's living room window was open a notch to let fresh air in. Poking a button on the car door, Matt had watched his window slide down. He left it about halfway open to the biting breeze, and he didn't really care if he got a bit chilled, because music was wafting through. Jessie was sitting on the edge of the wide sofa in the open concept space, strumming on her dad's old Gibson, which she'd hastily retrieved from home before leaving Vancouver. The song she was playing? Matt strained to hear, and then the chords were suddenly illuminated. It wasn't one of her songs—this was a Gordon Lightfoot tune, 'Sundown.' Melancholy and rare for its lyrics and music, the song was easily a hands down Canadian favorite from the 70's. It was about drugs, Matt thought, and there were some words about a 'room where you do what you don't confess.' He listened to Jessie play and sing the tune, giving her unknown audience of one all she had, and he contemplated the truths of its minor key and lyrics while chewing on a fingernail.

She was surreal, even when she thought she had no audience. In fact, Matt liked her this way, alone in a living room playing music she wanted to play, with no sound guy, no lights, no screaming fans. Her voice cracked on some of the notes as emotion caught up and tried to take over, but she kept it under control, although she focused on a spot on the floor and sang to it, seemingly lost in some ethereal dream brought on by the music.

Now, at the door, which Jessie finally let Matt enter, he had a closer look at the girl with whom he'd only that afternoon flown home from Miami in the Keating jet. She was clearly exhausted, her eyes bloodshot and bleary, and heavily shadowed underneath. She leaned her head against the doorframe and studied him right back.

"You're off duty," she yawned, blinking at him. They'd agreed to let Jessie move around Vancouver without security unless a special occasion demanded it. This didn't always sit well with Matt, though, and he generally stayed closely in touch. Today, and maybe for the next bit, well…he might ask her if he and his team could just stick around until the dust settled. For her…and for Josh who, given his own difficult past, was likely to become a bad-boy target once again.

"Julie sent me up to see you," was the answer Matt gave Jessie as he moved past her and went to the kitchen to pour some Baileys in their coffees. Jessie hesitated, and put her hand out to signal she didn't want alcohol in her coffee. She avoided Matt's eye when he handed her the steaming cup.

Matt went on, "Julie's your biggest fan, Jessie. She…saw the video. One of them."

Jessie groaned.

"She swept me out the door like an old rug. Said 'get up there and make sure that girl's okay.'" He lingered at the kitchen island and watched Jessie for signs of severe anxiety or trauma. Apart from bruised hands from, likely, fingernails, she seemed surprisingly okay.

"Josh didn't come up with you? Is he hiding out there somewhere, scared to come in?" Taking a sip of the hot drink, Jessie plunked her butt onto one of the high stools at the island across from Matt.

"No," Matt said quietly. "He knows you're here, though. Safe. I texted him."

"K," she said. "Fine."

"Have you called Trudy?"

"Trudy?" Jessie looked surprised he'd brought up her therapist. Did he think she was going to break, or shatter like the candy glass they used on *Drifters* when cowboys came flying through supposedly plate glass windows? She shifted uncomfortably. "No. I didn't call Trudy. I'm fine, Matt, really."

He considered yesterday's fight with Jacob in the Miami studio. Shook his head slowly from side to side. "I disagree, Jessie. It's been a tough couple of days for you."

The honest comment from a man she loved and trusted brought the heady emotions—that indeed did come from the last few days—gushing to the surface. Jessie moaned and leaned her head on her hands, which were supported by her elbows on the counter. She rubbed her hands hard over her face as the tears started to slowly drop, one by one.

"I just can't believe he was with her, Matt. Caryn. And it obviously wasn't the first time." She rolled her eyes, remembering Caryn's hand covering Josh's, and the odd expression on his face, something between desire and mischief.

"Do you think he slept with her?"

Sighing, Jessie drooped further as Matt reached behind him, found a Kleenex, and pushed it across the counter to her. "No. I don't. I really don't, Matt. I mean, if he didn't, he has a helluva lotta willpower because, believe me, that woman has bewitched many an unsuspecting victim. And not many turn her down, I've…I've seen that. Including…including me, once upon a time."

"I see." Matt delivered the simple acknowledgement tenderly, without accusation.

She glanced across at him. "Yeah," she breathed and said it again.

"Including me. But Matt—I only just started remembering all this. The whole Downtown Eastside thing. I knew I lived with someone but it was all hazy and murky in my brain. Until…well, until Trudy started poking around in there and bringing up all this old shit, and then…well, the day we got back Josh and I saw Caryn and her husband Eric at Revolver. And then it was like the proverbial light went on. All these memories came rushing back."

"So call Trudy, get some help dealing with this."

"I can't, Matt. Not yet, at least." At his concerned look, she acquiesced. "Look, I will, I swear. Just not in the next day or so. She's already called me, anyway, and left a message, along with the rest of my pseudo-counsellors, those being Charlie, Steve, Maggie, and Jacob, at last count."

"Why not Trudy, Jessie?" Matt was leaning on the counter, trying to act nonchalant, when in fact his heart was racing. He was glad she seemed to be doing okay, but she was likely still in shock after the day's events.

"I just know where she will try to take me, that's all. What she'll try to convince me of. But I know the truth, I know who I am, where I stand."

"You don't like yourself very much."

"Know anybody who does? Like his or herself?" She twisted her coffee cup between her fingers and stared at it, her eyes losing focus. "The thing is, Matt, I'm trying to like myself, and some days I do, but on the bad days I quite clearly know who I am. In fact, I know *what* I am. Where I came from, what I've had to do to survive." She looked coolly up at him. "It's just everybody else that seems to have trouble accepting it."

"You're something else, Jessie, I'll give you that." His heart was in his throat, and the words came out sounding like they'd been stuffed with cotton.

"I am who I am, Matt. I've long ago accepted that, and yes, coming back to Van and running into Caryn, and then having all those memories rush back, really sucked. But I learned a lot with Trudy, how to handle those things and how to like myself better—most days—so I was dealing with it, you know? And now…" her face fell.

"And now Josh knows, too."

"And apparently the whole fucking world."

"Not necessarily, kid. The world only got garbled bits and pieces out of those cellphone videos."

SUSAN RODGERS

"But they know who Caryn is. Her business."

Matt straightened, stretched and cracked his back. "Ouch." He regarded her carefully. "You've been on the internet today."

"Hell, yeah. I watched some of those videos and I read some of the crap that's been posted."

"Does it matter, anyway? What the rest of the world thinks?"

Fresh tears started rolling down Jessie's pale cheeks, big wide drops, and her eyes gazed at Matt with a mixture of pity and fear. "Yeah," she said. "Because they'll make him a target again, Matt. Won't they?"

"You're worried about *him*." Jessie's capacity to care about Josh more than herself constantly amazed Matt. He scrunched up his shoulders for another big stretch and answered her. "Nah. You guys are going out to the ranch anyway, aren't you? And back to P.E.I. for some of the summer? Stay off the net. This, too, shall pass."

"I hope you're right."

"You need to talk to Josh. He's in agony."

"Humph. Let him suffer. He's got a lot of explaining to do."

Despite himself, Matt chuckled. Jessie looked up, surprised. Her eyes narrowed. "You find that funny, Spike?" She reached out to touch his hair and he grabbed her arm. In a menacing voice he growled, "You've been warned. DON'T touch the hair, missy." Then he added, "And yeah, it's funny. I can't tell you how many times Julie and I had the same kind of fights. She'd give me the silent treatment for a day or two, until she'd get lonely, and we'd make up. That's always the best part."

Frowning, Jessie remarked, "Yeah, and your fights were about porn. Uh, you being IN IT, by the way. Or her. Oh, and then there's the possibility of cheating...can't see you going there, Matt."

"Look, most of the fights you and Josh are going to have are going to be about stupid little things, like the way he leaves pots and pans on the stove for a whole day before washing them. Stuff like that. But, Jessie, there will be other rough patches along the way that will escalate into bigger issues because of your careers. Because of who you have become over the last number of years."

"I'm not sure I like the sound of that. Although," she smiled, "I like the
238

idea of lots of fights if it means we'll still be together." The smile turned upside down, and the childlike part of Jessie Wheeler was back. "Although right now I'm still so pissed at him for seeing Caryn behind my back that he might have to do a lot of sucking up before I forgive him."

Matt took Jessie's hand in his, and the wisdom Jessie was starting to count on more and more from this man was reflected in his gentle eyes. She paused, and tilted her head to listen.

"You need to forgive, Jessie. In a marriage. You forgive quickly, and don't hold grudges. Ever."

"Hmmmm." She lifted a finger and ran it slowly over her top and then bottom lip, then slipped the finger up to twist a ringlet. "That's the Matt I know and love. Giving me all his secrets to sweet success in life."

He withdrew his hand. "I just know what I've learned, Jessie. What Julie and I have learned," he corrected himself. "Life's too short to be mad at the person you love the most in the world. Here you are, up here alone, miserable as hell, and Josh is down there in Vancouver, suffering alone. The two of you need to shut out the world and talk this over. You know Josh, you *know* him, Jessie. If he went to see that Caryn woman, he did it for a good reason. And I'm guessing it wasn't to get laid. He would do anything for you. You know that. Anything to protect you."

As would you. The thought slipped its way into her mind, and Jessie let a smile accompany it.

"Do you know why he went to see her, Matt?"

"I think I do, yes. Although to be honest, I haven't talked to him today. I left him alone. As did Charles and Dee, until later in the evening, I think."

"You left him alone." Jessie digested that, and then, realizing there were a lot of heady emotions involved on everyone's part, she set the thought away til later. Instead, she pursued the other issue. "So why do you think he was with her?"

"I am guessing he wanted something from her. Files, likely. Maybe photographs."

"Of me."

"Yes."

"Yes, well I expect that's what he wanted, too. But the thing I don't understand is why they looked like they were friends. Or—more than friends, even. Who just haven't slept together yet. Maybe. Hopefully not."

"I guess you'll have to ask Josh that."

"I lived with them for a long time, Matt. She was kind to me."

"I gathered that. What about…him?"

"Eric? I can't get used to that name since it's also the name of Carlotta's baby grandson. Big Eric is not quite as innocent as Little Eric." She frowned, dug a nail into the back of her thumb, and watched a new crescent form. "He was okay most of the time. Didn't say much. He was nice to Caryn, though, and a good cook." She looked up and added, as an afterthought, "He did most of the cooking. Taught me a few things." She drifted off, thinking, and Matt let her take her time sorting out the muzziness in her brain, although he did pull her right hand away from the left, where more new crescents were forming.

Jessie's eyes darkened and she stared at the countertop between them. "He was okay except for a few times near the end, before they kicked me out. Usually when," she swallowed, "when there was sex, it was, well, not me and him alone. But then I guess he decided he wanted me alone, so there were a few times that…well, that that happened." She blinked nervously, and chanced a quick glance up to Matt's kind eyes.

"Go on," he said quietly, afraid of what she was going to tell him.

"He wasn't mean, ever," she said remorsefully. "He was just…quiet. And so he did things without telling me what he was doing, and it freaked me out. I wasn't talking then either, so it was like being stuck in a cave. But then one day Caryn caught him at it, and she lost it. So they got rid of me. Their toy." Bitterness edged her voice.

Matt pushed her gently. "What kind of things, Jessie? He didn't hurt you, you said." *Thank God,* he was thinking.

"No. Things with…toys." She looked up and was pained at the sadness in Matt's eyes. She laid a hand over his. "It wasn't a big deal, Matt, really. Lots of couples add a little spice to their lovemaking." She winked. "You oughtta try it."

Groaning, Matt straightened and averted his eyes.

"You shy thing," Jessie teased.

"Julie and I do just fine, thank you, Jessie. I guess I just see Josh's point of view in all this a little more clearly now." A haunted twenty year old who doesn't speak, a couple who bring her to their home and use her, who put her in erotic films and photos? He was disgusted.

A little tug came at his sleeve. He glanced down and then over at Jessie, who was pulling at his cuff, pleading with him.

"Do you hate me now, Matt? After finding out what I did back then?"

He turned his wrist over so he could take her fingers in his. A slight sad smile accompanied his remark. "Nobody on this planet could ever hate you, Jessie. Ever."

"I'm hoping that includes Charles and Dee."

"Well, kiddo, I guess we'll find out. On that note, we should likely try to grab some shuteye before dawn, as I expect the illustrious Deirdre Keating will be on the road before the songbirds sing."

A wail slipped from between Jessie's lips. "She's coming here?"

"Not alone, kid." He waited for that to sink in.

"Oh geez."

He reached across the kitchen island and rustled her hair. "It'll be fine, Jess. Now go and get some sleep."

"I probably shouldna had that coffee, Matt. You know that wonder drug they call caffeine?"

But she slipped off the stool and started towards the stairs. Then she paused and slowly turned to face him, shoving fingers in her jeans pockets as she did so. Knitting her brows together, Jessie hesitated before meeting his eyes and speaking. "Matt, there's one other thing."

"What's that, kid?" He paused in his cleanup duty, and stood, both hands wrapped around cups of half-drunk coffee.

"Well," she swallowed before speaking. "It's like this, um, I'm...well, I think I might actually be pregnant."

Her admission was rewarded with a slowly widening grin. "Well. That's the best news I've heard all day." Matt didn't sound overly surprised, but he seemed genuinely happy.

"You knew."

"I suspected." He knuckled the Baileys and screeched it across the countertop towards her. "I've never known you to turn down Baileys in your coffee. Plus you've had kind of an avocado green aura over this last little while. C'mere, Jessie."

She smiled shyly as he rounded the kitchen island and met her halfway, taking her in his arms and giving Jessie a big old bear hug.

"I mean it, Jessie. That's really great news."

"I haven't been to a doctor yet, Matt. So it's not official, but it...well, it seems likely."

"Get on back to the city, then. Get the final word so you can start taking care of yourself and that beautiful new baby. And by the way, you might want to cut out caffeine. It's not necessarily on the good list of food and drink for pregnant women."

"I am! Taking care of myself. Us. Caffeine?" Inadvertently, she placed a hand on her belly and bashfully glanced at the floor before meeting his eyes again, a happy upturn to her pink lips and a rosy blush highlighting her cheeks. "Seriously? I turned down the Baileys."

Matt laughed heartily. He placed both hands on Jessie's shoulders and deeply searched her tired eyes. "Get on the internet. Do some research. Are you feeling okay? With nausea and that kind of thing?"

"Yeah, I'm okay. Nauseous but not overly. I'm on the hunt for crackers. I've tried a bunch that help dry up the acid but I'm more of a Fudgee-o fan." She shrugged.

"How about I ask Julie for a brand that worked for her?" He frowned. "Actually...I suppose you could check with Jane as well?"

"About that, Matt—the thing is, you're actually the first person I've told. You're the only one who knows."

A wave of genuine surprise flitted across Matt's kind features. It completely humbled him, a man who found it unbelievable that Jessie cared enough about him—and trusted him enough—to share this wonderful news first with him, someone who was technically her employee. "Not even Josh yet?" he asked quietly.

"No. I want to tell him in person. It didn't seem appropriate to scream it at him on Cambie." The old sadness flitted across her eyes. "Now I think I'll wait until the doctor confirms it. There's not much point in getting his hopes up, and anyways I'd rather tell him when things settle down and there's not this aura of crap hanging over our heads."

Matt pulled his charge close and held her for a moment before gently taking her shoulders again and swinging her around. "Up those stairs, young lady. Sleep. I'll take the downstairs bedroom so when Charles and Dee land here in a few hours I can halt them at the pass so they don't disturb you."

"All right," she reluctantly agreed, eyeing her iPhone, where texts and missed call notifications lit up her screen. There were a number from Josh but Jessie still felt sickened and not yet ready to hear his story. Nor did she want to discuss hers, although opening up to Matt somehow felt safe.

She turned off the phone, ignoring the calls and messages from all of her friends.

Matt watched her do it, and so was glad he'd made the trip to Whistler. Arriving at Jessie's doorstep was the only way anyone would have reached her, and he was glad it was him.

You'll be okay, he said to her back, as the realization hit that if she was indeed pregnant, a lot of things would soon be changing in the Wheeler-Sawyer-Keating camp. Hopefully the changes would all be good. He caught his breath and said a little prayer before heading to the back bedroom for some zzzzz's.

His last thoughts before drifting off started with astonishment that Josh was not yet aware he was about to become a father. He smiled at the elation sure to pepper the young man's face when Jessie told him. Quickly, a new thought replaced the happy vibe. Matt grimaced and prayed Josh hadn't crossed too many weird lines where Jessie's old Downtown Eastside hosts were concerned. He wondered how Charles and Dee would react to the news of the pregnancy. He hadn't thought to ask Jessie's opinion on the subject. *The powerful Keatings.* Dee would likely be over the moon, once this latest blowout settled. Charles? Yeah. The big guy too. Although Matt thought it might be a while before Charles relaxed around Josh again, which wouldn't necessarily be a good thing.

He yawned. *Well, I'll see in the morning how that's going to go,* he thought.

Quiet tiptoes stole down the stairs, and Matt tensed, hoping he wouldn't hear the front door opening. He didn't—instead, the toes made their way quietly back upstairs. Momentarily, gentle strumming started on Jessie's Gibson. But the tune she was playing was one of hers this time, that old well-known ballad Matt knew she had written for Josh.

A broad smile creased Matt's face, was stifled with a yawn, and then the chief of all things Keating-Wheeler-Sawyer security drifted peacefully off to sleep.

Chapter Twenty-seven

$\mathcal{A}$s expected, Charles and Dee arrived in a flurry of angst mixed with generous helpings of still fresh anger. Matt met them at the kitchen island, where he was spooning some yogurt from ROAM into a cup. Thankfully the trendy cafe opened before Jessie awakened. He figured rightly there were no groceries in the condo, and his girl was now likely eating for two.

Matt reminded himself not to slip up in front of Charles and Dee. That bit of news was Jessie's to tell and, well, it wouldn't likely be first in line today.

He tried to hush his bosses, so Jessie could get a few extra winks, but they weren't having it. As far as Dee was concerned, she'd waited long enough. Just when she was about to fly up the stairs to wake Jessie, the singer herself sauntered casually to the landing, and down to the first floor. She was wearing the same outfit as yesterday, jeans and a cute floral sweater, and she hadn't showered. At the bottom of the stairs she stopped and faced two of the people she dreaded hurting the most, ever. A few curse words directed at her husband were muttered under Jessie's breath, and then she looked wide-eyed around the room, thinking he might in fact benefit from hearing them in person. She cocked her head and narrowed her eyes at Dee.

The older woman read her thoughts and responded. "No Jessie, he's not here." She sounded exasperated.

"You didn't bring him?" Diminished, Jessie let out a slow breath. "Why am I not surprised?"

She followed Dee's quick sideways glance to Charles. Jessie's producer was as intimidating as ever, although generally not so much to Jessie herself. Today he was rumpled and tired, and apparently severely annoyed and frustrated, judging by the way he directed his drawn lips and dark eyes towards her.

"Oh," Jessie said staunchly, "I see."

"Your husband is not on my list of favorite people today, Jessie." Charles stood his ground, while Deirdre came forward and drew Jessie into her arms for a big hug. Jessie was somewhat relieved of that, but as Dee hugged her she didn't take her eyes off Charles. She could see Matt behind him, silently eating a dish of yogurt, watching with interest and a glimmer of amusement. If she wasn't so damn frustrated and hurt, Jessie might have rewarded him with a wink and a knowing smile at their shared secret.

Instead, she planted her feet as she let go of Dee. "This is not really his fault."

"Jessie," Dee tried to halt the conversation, which was clearly off to a bad start, but Charles cut her off.

"Not entirely, no. But flirting publicly with other women who he may or may not have—"

"Charles!" Dee flashed angry eyes at her own husband, whose behavior she knew she would have to guard today. She looked worriedly at Jessie, who appeared more pale and downcast than ever, and even a little green around the gills, with limpid eyes subdued but still locked on Charles.

"Fine. I'm sorry, Jessie. But despite any good intentions Josh may have had, it's apparent he dived in a little deeper than he should have, regardless of how things ended up. So I, for one, am happy to give him some space." Charles avoided acknowledging the tears forming in the corners of Jessie's eyes. Matt cringed then, and shot Jessie a *sorry* look he hoped she would see from across the room.

"You've never liked him." The low growl surprised all of them, especially Charles, who stole a quick look at Dee, knowing before he looked that she would be tense and poised to call him off Jessie, should things heat up too much.

"What?" He faced Jessie again, cautious but still too angry and exasperated to completely back off.

"Josh. You've never approved of him. You wanted me to marry Charlie, but now he's off the market, so let me guess who Charles Keating's number two is. Oh—I know—Jacob. Fucking Jacob."

"Jessie." Dee again, who was the first to notice the red bloom across Jessie's face. "Easy."

"No, Dee. I won't go easy. Charles—and maybe you, too—are probably hoping Josh did cheat on me. So I can divorce him and hook up with Jacob. Is that right, Charles?"

"No! No, Jessie, of course not!" Charles wheeled half around and appealed to Matt for help, but before Matt could enter the fray Jessie lost it.

"Don't lie to me!" she cried, swiping a fist across her eyes. "Josh is everything to me, and what he did or didn't do hurts like hell! And you both come waltzing in here with guns blazing, ready to call him down and scheme and plan ways to get around this whole terrible mess that I in fact made, and I bet you ordered him to stay home and stay out of it. As much as I appreciate Matt driving up last night, I can honestly say it's Josh who I wish was here, Josh! Not you, Charles, and not you, Deirdre Keating! I want Josh. I want—my—husband! I haven't seen him in ages, or touched him or talked to him, hardly, and I miss the hell out of him."

She whipped around and grabbed her coat from where she'd tossed it on the couch the night before. Keys were in the side pocket; she fished them out and turned back to the Keatings and Matt. "I'm sorry," she said, "I'm truly sorry about all this. I know we need to talk about it but right now what I need more is to go do my hollering at home. Which is where I belong. With my careless husband who, I assure you, is not getting out of this unscathed. I will call you later, Dee."

She made a point of saying Dee's name with lots of emphasis in order to exclude Charles, which crushed him. At the door, Jessie turned to Matt. She hesitated before striding over to him for a hug. "Please bring my Gibson, Matt. And thank you for the coffee last night. I'll see you. Please don't follow me."

At that, with his generous hug for energy, accompanied by a bowl of yogurt he spooned out for Jessie and thrust into her arms, spoon sticking out, she swung around on one brown boot and left the condo.

They let her go, and stood their ground for a good few minutes before any of them spoke. It was Charles who broke the ice.

"Damn that girl."

Deirdre sighed loudly and sank down onto the sofa. "It's true, Charles. What she said. Josh was never our first choice for Jessie."

"He was doing fine until that stunt he pulled last summer, running off to Virginia to film *Freedom Ride*. And then yesterday—"

"Yesterday he was trying to protect Jessie." Matt sidled over and offered his calm wisdom to the tired couple.

"He did a helluva job," Charles replied. "I'd like to hang the boy's balls from the rafters. With crazy glue."

"He'll be fine," Dee interjected, patting her husband's knee as he sat beside her. "Regardless, the part we have to worry about is the reckless media. Jessie will have to learn to deal with her husband. And I have to admit, I'm glad she's going home and not trying to hide out here any longer."

"What about this couple, Dee? And the films?"

"We'll talk to Jessie after she's had a chance to see what Josh discovered. If he was amicable with that woman, then maybe the films are safe." She was heartsick at the thought of films, or photos. But somehow it wasn't really a surprise to have discovered the truth about how their girl survived on East Hastings not all that long ago.

"Films like those are never safe," Charles was muttering. "Not celebrity films, at least."

"We'll deal with them if and when we have to," countered Dee softly, taking her husband's hand.

Behind them, Matt stole up the stairs and packed up Jessie's guitar. He sent a quick text to Josh warning him Jessie had hit the road, supposedly for home. Matt himself was anxious to get on the road, too, to spend some time with his family and also to stay just a few miles behind Jessie, should the Mustang prove too cold on a windy day like today. He knew he wasn't really needed. But he liked to watch over her, anyway.

She was family.

Chapter Twenty-eight

The Mustang's souped-up engine was what alerted Josh to Jessie's approach, rather than any phone call or text from her. Thanks to the notification from Matt, he was listening for it; its bass thump-thump-thump timbre was usually pleasing to him, a man who appreciated vintage vehicles (and the driver of this particular car), but as it rounded the far corner Josh's body tensed from the tips of his toes on up. Granted, it quivered over him in harmony with a serious sense of relief that Jessie was indeed coming home, but he knew there would be no winning this particular battle.

Josh was outside sweeping bits of old leaves and crud off the deck when the gate clicked open and then clanged shut, and he felt a vibration tremble across his gut in nervous anticipation. His knuckles whitened around the broom, which he futilely held in front of him in some odd hope for protection.

The first thing Jessie laid her eyes on, coolly, were his bare toes. Despite her lingering anger, her heart raced.

She raised her head and met her husband's aching eyes, her lips opening in fear. Jessie's voice was unsteady, a tiny tremor discernible underneath the accusatory tone. "What the hell are you thinking, Josh? It's April."

He whistled through his teeth, a slow exhalation that helped muster courage and bought a tiny speck of time. He didn't want to set her off. He had to choose his words carefully. "It's fine. The sun's been on me the whole time I've been out here."

"Getting sick is not an option, Josh."

"I know what my options are, Jessie." *So much for staying calm and cool*

249

crossed his mind, but the way she stubbornly raised her chin and stared spitefully at him pushed his defensive buttons even more.

"Do you." It was not a question.

"Can we get this over with?"

"Which. Part."

"I didn't sleep with Caryn."

Her throat twitched and the lips parted again. Relief? Josh wiped his knuckles nervously across his mouth and tossed the broom aside, but he didn't move towards her. Jessie stayed put as well, ten feet away.

"Then I guess you have balls of steel. Or else you just didn't get there… yet."

He swallowed past the sticks in his throat.

Jessie shifted her balance from one foot to the other and continued. "She's not known for being turned down. Pretty much ever. Male or female."

"Apparently."

"Don't you dare turn this around on me."

"Ahhh," Josh growled in frustration, grabbing a fistful of his own hair, then dropping his hand and turning his hips to face her more straight on. "Look Jessie, I went to see her with one goal in mind, and that was to get the files. I need those fucking files in my hand, where I can bury them!"

Her voice rising, Jessie responded angrily, "What good is that gonna do, Josh? Files these days are all digital, they'll keep coming back, multiplying like, I don't know, fucking rabbits!"

He wanted to laugh at that but in the heat of the moment Josh ignored the urge and dove deeper into the fray instead. Glaring right back at his wife, he declared, "I realize that, your good friend Arnie drove the point home, but—"

Arnie? Jessie blinked, and placed both hands on her hips.

"Somehow I still feel like if I had something in my possession—"

"There's not a damn thing you can do. It's done. It was done a long fucking time ago. It's over. Let it go."

"It's not over, Jessie. It's not going to be over—ever! These people took advantage of you, a sick girl who was suffering from post-traumatic stress. They've got incriminating photos and films of you that could ruin your career, that have the power to change the way people look at you, the way they feel about you. If something gets leaked, you know what'll happen—first an internet feeding frenzy, and then you get pulled from projects, your music gets taken off iTunes, people won't let their kids go to your concerts. Entertainment is a vicious business. It takes no prisoners."

The chin came up again as a wetness slicked across Jessie's eyes. She clenched her fists at her sides. "So whose career are you most worried about, Josh? Mine or yours?"

"Don't give me that bullshit." His tone was low and menacing, and his glare was pointed sideways at her.

"Admit it. You're on a roll. If something gets leaked, you'll suffer as much as I will. By association."

"No. That's not what this is about. That's never been what it's about."

"Yeah, hanging out with Caryn was never about *your* career. Uh huh. That helps." She paused only for a quick second, to rock back on one foot and cross her arms, before she continued her attack. "So what were they about, then? All those visits? Plural. Because the nauseating way you undressed her with your eyes at Revolver yesterday sure as hell made it look like the two of you are friends. And it should have only taken one visit to ask for files. So how many trips, Josh, and when did the seedy Downtown Eastside become your favorite neighborhood in the city to hang out in, anyway?" She used the back of her hand to wipe away a tear.

"Awww, Jessie." Standing ten feet away from her, watching her hurt this way because of him, was crushing Josh. He tried to extend an arm, but she wasn't budging. "C'mon. Don't do this."

"Don't do what? Don't try to find out what intrigued my husband so much about a woman whose bed I shared years ago?" She switched gears then, and shifted her weight to the other foot again. "By the way, I should warn you it may be a few years before you're likely welcome again in the Keating home. Thanks for that. Dee—I dunno, she might cave over time, but Charles?" She shook her head and sucked on her top lip. "Not so much. Not for a while, anyway. We'll have to ask Carlotta to come here if we ever want her chicken crepes again."

"I didn't sleep with Caryn, Jessie! Tell Charles to shove it up his fucking ass!" The old fire was back, but the pain in Josh's gut was not easing. He felt like he was being eaten alive from the inside out.

251

Finally, Jessie marched forward, but only to point a trembling finger in her husband's chest and accost him directly. "I saw the way you looked at her. She had her hand over yours, and yeah, you were trying so hard to pull away that the goddamned counter-thingy was shaking."

She glared righteously into the flickering eyes of the man she loved. "What do you think, I don't know you, Josh? I know every expression on that pretty boy face of yours, and most of your thoughts as well, and yesterday you were all about lust. You want to know something? Charlie didn't always cheat on me. In the beginning, it was great. I actually felt like a princess for a little while, a couple of years, maybe. But then it started, first a gorgeous blonde, and then some playboy model he met at a party." She nodded, emphatic, remembering. "You remember the first few, you do, but then after a while they all fade into one messed up mash-up of beautiful women with clit rings and Brazilians and perfectly round breasts." She stuck her hands under her own breasts and pushed them upwards for emphasis. "And then after a while you stop caring. Cuz like…what's the goddamned point?"

Angry tears were coming more regularly now, and Josh tried again to reach for his wife but she backed off.

"Jessie, I'm not Charlie, okay? I'm not. I will never be."

"First there was the woman in Virginia, and now Caryn. Admit it, Josh. They intrigued you. Sex with a woman other than me intrigues you. At least enough for you to go to some woman's hotel room and then get drunk with remorse; at least enough to stand there above Caryn at Revolver with her hand over yours, and smile stupidly at her like you've been friends for years. Even if you didn't sleep with her, and I guess I believe you, at least I'm trying to, I bet it wouldn't have been long in coming. Like I said, you'd have to have balls of steel to turn that woman down. She's something else." She gulped for breath before adding, "I know she is, Josh." Pointing at herself, Jessie added, "Because I went there myself, remember? I don't have balls of steel, apparently."

"You don't have balls at all, girl." He tried unsuccessfully to lighten the mood but was met with a broken-hearted frown. Sighing, he said, "Yes, I admit it, Jess, I'm a man. There are times I do find certain women attractive, I won't lie. And there was something mystical about Caryn. There is, I mean. She has some weird powerful aura."

"And she's sexy as hell."

"That's not fair. You're around Jacob all the time, and I know what women say about him. I've Googled the guy, I admit it. And just for the record I don't understand why any woman in her right mind would be attracted to a slob who wears his jeans two sizes too big and slouches around under oversized shirts with his hands shoved in his pockets."

"Let's leave Jacob out of this, okay? I'm not going down that rabbit hole with you—or him, either, by the way—anymore. I'm tired of it."

"Back to Caryn then. Yes, there's something about her, but I didn't go there with her. We sat, we talked (he left out the *we cried* part), and it was all about you. Okay? About you. About what you were like when she found you—sick, apparently—and how and when you seemed to be feeling better. That's all. You were away, I was lonely, I went there looking for files, I stayed in touch with her because she was a link to you."

He took a few steps towards Jessie, holding his breath, which he didn't set free until he saw that she was holding her ground. Slipping his right hand around her left, he was relieved when she didn't pull away. He reached up with his other hand and gently wiped away her tears with his thumb. "I'm not like Charlie, little one."

He would have missed her response if he hadn't been watching her closely, watching that sensuous little mouth form its challenge and fire it at him.

Eyes blazing, without missing a beat Jessie whispered, "Fucking prove it."

Slowly, he blinked at her. "I will," he said, eyes begging her to give him a chance. "If you'll let me."

She nodded. The knot in her chest was heavy. For the time being, it was blocking her voice. Eventually the words came, hoarse and demanding. "I better not hear anything goddamned different in the meantime. That you slept with her, or anyone, for that matter. Charles will crucify you."

Josh squared his shoulders and stubbornly raised his chin. "I'm not going to ask why Charlie never even got a reprimand."

"He did, from Dee a few times. I think Charles just thought I didn't really give a damn."

"Ahhh. I see."

She punched him lightly in the belly. "Exactly. He knows if you cheat on

253

me you'll break my heart." Wrenching sobs she'd held back during their conversation finally won the battle, and Jessie leaned into Josh's steady embrace and wrapped her arms around his back.

"I'm sorry," Josh murmured into her hair, "for ever going to see Caryn and Eric in the first place. I thought I could…I dunno…I guess maybe part of me was just curious, Jessie." He wrapped both strong forearms around his wife's head and shoulders and pulled her as tightly against him as he could manage. "It was stupid," he breathed into her ear, his own tears mingling deeply with the loose curls. "I'm so, so sorry."

The sun ducked behind a cloud just then, and Josh shivered in his T-shirt.

Jessie pulled away. "Please Josh, come in. You can't get sick. I…I need you." She gulped as a wave of nausea floated over and then through her.

"All right," he said. "You win. The messy deck loses." He looped an arm loosely around Jessie's shoulders and kissed the side of her head as they wandered towards the sliding door.

Childishly, she murmured up at him on the way in, "Matt says making up after a fight is almost worth fighting for."

Josh sighed. "I don't deserve you," he said. "I really don't."

"You're, like, the sexiest man on the planet right now, Josh. At least according to the female editors at People magazine, the ones who've never had to sit on a cold porcelain toilet in the middle of the night. Or wash your dirty boxers."

"They *wish* they were washing my dirty boxers."

"I'll send them some. Snail mail. I love you, you dork. Don't be stupid again. And no more secrets."

"I love you back, little one." He turned her shoulders to face him. "Look, Jess. You need to go see Caryn, okay? Just once. I'll go with you. We'll say our goodbyes."

Her sorrow was so sudden and complete he instantly regretted bringing that up just when things seemed to be lightening up between them.

"Why?" she pleaded, heartsick and childlike.

"Because, for some crazy reason, that woman loved you once upon a time. And we need to keep her on our good side. So the images she has don't find their way to a computer, anywhere. Ever."

Swallowing hard, Jessie stared at Josh's bare toes before she looked up and answered him. She leaned in for a soft kiss before speaking. "So cute," she whispered. "Okay. Once. That's all. One time."

"Okay." He let his lips brush hers for a moment longer, and then Josh slid open the glass door.

She stopped him. "Josh," she started. "There is one thing…about Caryn. That might help you understand."

"Go on," he waited.

"Well, I don't always know how to explain her. Even to myself. Or…or why…why I let what happen between us happen."

His voice was quiet, yet earnest, his eyes searching and attentive. "I'm listening." "Well, it's like," she hesitated, and then found the words, the impossible words, that might somehow make her sketchy past go down easier. She looked up at him, this man who loved her beyond all others, and told him what she believed to be the God's honest truth. "She loved the 'broken' me. Before I was Jessie Wheeler, the singer and actor."

Josh shook his head slowly from side to side. "Hell, Jessie, we all love the broken you. We're all broken, Jessie, everybody's broken in some fucked up way or other."

"I know, I know, it's just that…don't you see? There was something really pure in the way she loved me, back then. When I was nothing. For a time… it was so…*real*."

"Babe," Josh placed both hands on Jessie's cheeks and pressed her to listen, to understand. He leaned his forehead against hers and sighed heavily against her. "You…were never nothing." He closed his eyes and pressed his lips softly against her forehead, so she would believe him and never again question her simple worth in the world.

She trembled, grasped his arms just above the elbows, and thanked God for the chance to love this incredible man another day.

Behind and above them, perfect clouds floated over the horizon, cottony soft and dreamlike, their simple presence over the vast ocean timeless and surreal; whispers of home craved by lovers in a dimming light.

Chapter Twenty-nine

*D*ee didn't wait for Jessie's call. Instead, she speed-dialed her girl's number during Josh and Jessie's ride downtown the next day. She'd tried numerous times in the previous 24 hours but Jessie wasn't interested in connecting just yet. She was still incensed over Charles' sideways inference about giving Josh space and, besides, she'd been in Miami much too often and for too long, in her opinion. She wanted to be with Josh; she needed to connect with him again while, around them, the social media world was imploding with unanswered questions and unfounded deductions both Josh and Jessie wisely decided to ignore.

When the phone vibrated it was in Jessie's chest pocket, that is, in the pocket of the thick black leather biker jacket Josh gave her for Christmas four months prior. She was sitting behind him on the classic Sportster, hands comfortably on his hips as he nosed the Harley into the busy traffic downtown. After he eased the bike into a parking spot in front of Caryn and Eric's building, Jessie pulled off her helmet, sorted her hair in a detached kind of way, and retrieved the phone from the inside chest pocket. After staring at Dee's name on the display for the umpteenth time, she simply dropped the phone back into the pocket, unzipped the coat all the way, and ignored her manager altogether.

Sucking on the corner of her bottom lip, Jessie looked anxiously into Josh's nervous eyes before taking his outstretched hand and walking alongside him towards the building's entrance. Caryn was expecting them. Hopefully this would be a quick—and absolutely final—visit.

There were changes inside the home Jessie found comforting, in a way,

256

as if time was telling her she was different now, that this weird world was no longer hers. The infrastructure was the same but she was relieved to see new furniture and even shiny new countertops in the open concept space. These alterations gave the mixed bag of recollections a good doughy squishing in Jessie's already roiling belly. As a visual person, the last thing she wanted was to be stimulated by too much of the 'same old'.

One thing that did stir up odd feelings was the staging where the bed sat, which was raised higher than the rest of the room. That hadn't changed, it was the same, although the bedding was different than she remembered, and some of the Inuit soapstone carvings were obviously new.

It was early afternoon, and the vista of the mountains and, below it, Burrard Inlet, was shockingly vibrant, a saturated deep blue sky punctuated by snowy mountain peaks; below them, container ships and bridges dotted their way to some place or other. The overall image was that of high art, as if the window wall in the place was but framed artwork. The only thing giving the truth away was the railing around the outside deck, around which Caryn had placed window boxes of petunias and pansies—floral offerings of peace parallel to those at the building's entrance. It struck Jessie funny, the analogous brightly colored flowers. Either Caryn had a lot of say in the building's green scheme, or else she volunteered her time as a gardener. The idea didn't seem to fit, somehow, and Jessie shook her head to clear the image of Caryn's elegant fingers softly dredging up dirt.

Josh's fingers were still wrapped around Jessie's, as if he was afraid she'd bolt if he let go. Next to him, she raised her chin high and fixed narrowed eyes at the woman who once saved her life.

"Caryn," she said simply in greeting. She glanced behind the woman in white to see Eric, and she shivered involuntarily despite the tall man's kind but questioning eyes. She nodded at him, and swallowed nervously before slipping her second hand into Josh's as she moved a little behind him.

"Come in, you two. Sit. Have a drink." Caryn waved them in the general direction of the large chaise in the living area. Josh peeked over his shoulder at Jessie half behind him. He hadn't told her about the large photograph, but he tightened his hold on her hand and, with soft moist eyes, silently pleaded with her to understand.

They didn't sit. Once they arrived at the chaise, the couple remained standing. And Jessie didn't speak for a very long time. Instead, she studied the shocking photograph at length, teeth set and jaw clenched. She left both hands locked in Josh's, and then her body sighed as she leaned her head on his shoulder.

Regarding the diminutive tender movement, Caryn flinched, and crossed her arms across her chest.

A knock at the door jarred them all into action. While Eric moved forward to heave open the big door, Jessie threw Caryn a hard look that wasn't wholly successful in masking a whole lot of pain, and an entire library of emotions, which were mostly a lingering ennui derived from confused feelings and an old but tough love affair.

"Jessie?" The voice from the entrance was calm and tender.

"Arnie?" Jessie paused before finally letting go of Josh's hand and padding over a thick white bearskin rug to fold herself into the arms of a trusted friend she would always consider a kind of savior. Her voice sounded loud and echoey in the acoustically reflective space. Her words tumbled over each other. "God, it's good to see you again. Did you have fun in P.E.I. at the wedding? We hardly chatted, you were so busy running around to all the beaches."

He ignored the rambling, anxious comment, and instead held her aloft to study the tired eyes. "Will you take a break? You're exhausted," he reprimanded.

"I just had a break. Last summer. And a ways before that, remember?" She slumped dejectedly in front of him, her hands in his.

Arnie glanced over at Josh, and nodded a wordless hello. Josh responded in kind, the nerve on his cheek twitching slightly.

"Drinks, anyone?" Caryn threw in, clapping her hands together once. She turned and glanced at her husband over her left shoulder. "Eric?"

The tall man acknowledged the request with an amiable grunt, and marched off to do his wife's bidding. The others sat, Jessie with Arnie on her right and Josh on her left, and Caryn kitty corner across from them. Jessie gazed up to the photograph once more and then eyed Arnie conspicuously to see what he thought.

He shrugged nonchalantly. "That's about what you were like, when you came to me."

She didn't hesitate. "When they threw me away, you mean."

In the kitchen over and behind them, past the entryway between the two spaces, Eric paused in his pouring of cranberry juice and ginger ale. He looked over their heads and met Caryn's eye.

She tossed her blonde and pink mane and fought back. "Jessie," she urged, "You need to understand—we didn't throw you out. We had to let you go to…uh…" She halted when she met Josh's eye, and Jessie tensed, noticing.

Arms folded diminutively and gracefully on her lap, Caryn's exotic jade eyes darted back to Jessie. Caryn was sitting on one butt cheek, long legs crossed, one elbow barely gracing the arm of the Scandinavian chair Josh usually sat in during his visits. She continued, but cleared her throat first. "To save our marriage, actually."

Tenderly, Arnie patted Jessie's hand. "You were getting in the way. I think it had something to do with that lost orphan look you wear so well."

"I think it had to do with Caryn walking in on Eric and me," Jessie spat, thinly disguised daggers in her eyes.

On the inside, Josh moaned. Jessie felt him stiffen beside her.

Caryn was non-plussed. "Eric had access to any woman he wanted. But he knew you were special to me. So yes, I was less than impressed."

"Less than impressed," Jessie intoned drily. "I suppose that's one way of putting it." She was remembering the day, and a rare fight that had her cowering in a corner. In her memory the words were muzzy, the air fusty from the heat of a hot summer day. Behind the couple, who were tossing anger around like knives, was the bed, and that's what impaled itself upon Jessie's retinas now. It was mussed-up and wrinkled, and in the corners were cuffs Eric had hastily undone—from Jessie's wrists and ankles, no less—when Caryn arrived unexpectedly home from the office.

"That was a long time ago, Jessie. Let it go." Arnie gently interrupted her thoughts, which left Jessie's eyes wide and frightened.

A drink in a tall frosted glass came into Jessie's peripheral vision and floated before her. A hand balanced it—Eric's, large and obtrusive. Hesitating, Jessie wrapped her fingers around the glass, trying not to touch Eric's as she did so.

Her voice broke the ensuing silence as everyone else sipped the fizzy red drinks. She spoke directly to Eric, leaning away from Josh and towards Arnie for support.

Momentarily panicked, Josh grabbed his wife's left hand and eased her back towards him, but only the arm came. She spoke with less anger now as she groped for some even footing beneath the painful memories of feeling used and abandoned. "I wasn't afraid of you, Eric. You were always nice to me. I just...the Deuce McCall thing...Charleston...it wasn't that long after, that I was here, you know." Barely a whisper delivered the next remark. "But you couldn't know that. You guys couldn't know."

Her drink sat balanced on one thigh, untouched. It left a wet ring that soaked through her black jeans, but Jessie was beyond noticing anything but the horrid, confusing memories.

"Bullshit." Josh was cringing. He took the drink from her and set it on the coffee table beside his before she leaked red juice all over the carpet. His eyes flashed. "Remember the part about not speaking, Jessie?" He shook a fist at the photograph. "That damned picture! How could anyone see that kind of hopelessness in a young woman's eyes and not recognize the suffering?"

"Josh, it's okay." Jessie squeezed his hand then, and begged him with those same sad eyes to understand. Quietly she added, "I need to say this. There needs to be some forgiveness here. So we can all move on." Matt's wise words from a few nights before were suddenly bouncing around her brain. His gentle eyes were encouraging; as chief of all things Jessie Wheeler-Sawyer security, Matt's almost constant company over the years had evolved into a steady and trusting friendship. She decided his words were worth listening to.

"Caryn, Eric," she focused on Caryn first, and then scanned the room abstractly before landing on Eric as she searched for the right words. "Guys, the first thing I want to say is thank you. Thank you for taking me on when you had no idea what I'd been through. I expect you now, like the rest of the world, know my story."

A solemn reverence accompanied their nods.

"Well," Jessie continued, sliding her right hand into Arnie's and clutching Josh's thigh tightly now with the other, "the thing is, Eric—I wasn't ready. That particular night. For you. Like that. You know?"

"I scared you." The man who rarely spoke sat down across from Jessie. "I'm sorry."

"No it's okay, like I said, you couldn't know." The restraints he'd used on her that night flashed again across her mind. "But now," she looked earnestly back at Caryn, "I need to apologize to both of you. Caryn—Eric may have been out of line, as far as you're concerned, but I didn't resist him when he approached me that night. In fact, I understand so much more now, about sex, about women, about men and their needs," her hand tightened around Josh's thigh and she felt him freeze, "that I figure I likely led Eric on, on some level. You know, short skirts, tank tops, lacey bras."

"The way a woman dresses does not give a man permission to have sex with her, Jessie." Arnie spoke quietly, but it was clear he was determined to be heard.

"He didn't—oh, you guys!" Exasperation edged Jessie's words. "God, this sucks, talking about ages-old sex with you bunch of goofballs!" Her cheeks bloomed red. "No, it was just one of those things where we couldn't quite communicate. Heck, he talks now about as much as I did then! And so things got all SNAFU, you know? Situation Normal All Fucked Up. He used the cuffs, Caryn wasn't there," her voice softened and she gazed at Caryn sympathetically, "she was…softer, somehow. I trusted her in a different way after…after Deuce. Anyways, the thing is, by the time Caryn came home I was pretty messed up."

She hung her head, shamed. "I think I was screaming by then. Maybe."

"Jesus," Josh said, wrapping strong fingers around hers on his leg. He leaned his left elbow on the arm of the chaise and balanced his forehead in it.

Apologetic, Caryn ignored him and spoke directly to Jessie. She leaned forward and laid a hand on Jessie's knee so she could see more deeply into her eyes. "You were screaming all right. Bloody murder. The neighbors were ready to call the police."

"So naturally you thought Eric hurt me."

Caryn shot Eric a sideways glance. "I honestly didn't know what to think, honey."

"So you and Eric had this big fight and decided to ship me off to Arnie, here."

"We did," Eric admitted. "Thank you for clearing me on that count, Jessie. I don't think Caryn ever quite believed I didn't hurt you that day."

"Hurt is subjectable," Josh broke in, a little more harshly than was likely required for the moment.

"Let it go, Josh," Arnie warned.

Eric shrugged his shoulders and stood. "He has a right to feel the way he does." To Josh he said, "But you weren't here. You didn't see her then."

Josh eased himself off the chaise and strode over to the large framed photograph. "I do now, Eric. Every day. Every day I see this image in my head, and it breaks my heart."

Cuddling into Arnie, both hands grasping his left and right hands now, Jessie folded her legs up underneath her on the chaise and emitted a great sigh. Caryn took advantage of Josh's absence, and she rose and then dropped into Josh's vacated seat, her right leg curled up underneath her. She laid the same arm over the back of the chaise, slowly so as to gauge Jessie's reaction as she did it. Leisurely, she arced her left hand across to run elegant fingertips down Jessie's cheek, ostensibly to push a strand of rogue auburn curls behind her guest's ear.

Watching, stunned and increasingly uncomfortable, Josh poked his thumbs into his jeans' pockets and stood poised, feet apart, ready to rescue Jessie from the woman who so often crossed his mind over the winter; the woman who had often taken Jessie to her bed to comfort and love her during a dark time.

At the remembered touch, Jessie sucked in a breath and let go of one of Arnie's hands. Her eyes flitted shut and she turned her body slightly towards her old lover. Caryn leaned closer and touched the strand of hair again, this time with the backs of her fingers, slowly, while she murmured softly in Jessie's ear. Unable to help herself, Jessie, still with a light hold on one of Arnie's hands, turned her cheek just slightly towards Caryn, so their faces were close together. Caryn let a willowy thumb brush Jessie's lips. Quietly she leaned in and brushed her own moist lips across her visitor's cheek.

This all happened in an instant, no more than a few seconds, but it was enough to heat up the tension in the room to a point of no return. Eric was silent and still as a dull rage started to beat in his heart, a rage he had pulled inwards for many years, where it festered and boiled. Arnie was slightly amused but also well aware of Caryn's powers. He maneuvered his right arm across his body and touched Jessie's knee. He gave her a little shake to encourage her to come back to them, to their space, for he could see she was remembering a long ago touch that comforted and caressed when it was needed.

Captivated, outside their bubble, Josh felt his body respond in a way his mind now knew he solidly wanted no part of. Sure, the tingling in his groin felt good. He and Caryn had built a wary friendship based on a shared love of the same woman. But now, standing underneath the portrait of his stricken wife in younger days, all of the mixed emotions he'd struggled with since he first understood the tall couple's business and Jessie's possible part in it came rushing to a head. It was erotic as heck watching Caryn's warm breath bring a flush to Jessie's cheeks, and even in those brief moments Josh could see his wife's breathing change. It quickened, and her lips parted. It confused him more, or his body at least, but still—this wasn't going to be a part of he and Jessie's life together. The touching, the subdued whispers, the elegant tapered fingers on his wife's neck...no.

Caryn was still whispering, still gently grazing Jessie with her touch. But even at Arnie's provocation, Jessie didn't stir. Instead she let Caryn kiss her, and then brush the backs of her fingers over a breast. A tiny *ahhhh* escaped Jessie's throat, and she reached for Caryn and held her close, allowing her own lips to open against the woman's neck, allowing her tongue to dart out and leave a moist trail in the delicate crevices. Caryn pulled her close, and wrapped an arm around Jessie's back.

"Please," Josh, in his stunned stupor, finally heard Caryn moan. "Please please please..."

But Josh shifted then, and the floor creaked under his thick-soled motorcycle boots. Jessie's eyes flashed open, and met his. Caryn's left hand was under Jessie's top now, underneath the biker jacket Jessie had not bothered to remove. It was warm and soft, and it rubbed and kneaded and pushed Jessie's body against hers. But when it slipped around to her belly, and then up and under her bra, Jessie moaned once and then slowly grasped Caryn's arms at the wrists, and pushed them away.

She held her old lover aloft. "No," she said, hurting at this, leaving someone

263

else wanting. Not Jacob this time, and never Josh, but someone who she honestly knew in her heart once truly loved and cared for her. Breaking Caryn's heart was not her first choice in coming here today—she only wanted to talk, to explain, to listen…to forgive and to offer forgiveness. But now—now there was only a new trail of pain.

"Caryn, sweetheart," she said, touching her old lover's cheek as Arnie slowly rose to give them some privacy, "this is not happening. Not between you and me, or you and Josh, or any combination thereof. It's not. I'm sorry."

"Why?" Caryn begged, pleading, trying to free her arms so she could touch Jessie, bring her closer again. "We made a mistake that night. I—we…" She looked hopelessly at her husband, who was watching the way he always did, with sympathy and concern, mixed with fear and a simmering rage, "We made a mistake. We should never have let you go."

Jessie shook her head. "No, honey. You did the right thing. You helped me heal, didn't you? And then it was time to let me go. I didn't understand it at the time, but I think I am starting to now." She leaned her forehead against Caryn's and brushed her hair with her hand, again and again, from above Caryn's ear and down. "I can't go there again. Things have changed."

Caryn swung around and glanced wildly at Josh over her shoulder, then back to Jessie. "We can do this, Jessie. No one has to know, if it makes you uncomfortable. Couples do it all the time!"

"Not this couple." It was Josh who spoke this time, from behind Caryn. He moved forward and took his wife's hand away from Caryn's hair, and then gently tugged her up off the couch towards him. His eyes were bright, and they searched Jessie's for the pain he knew he'd find there. He wiped a thumb slowly across her mouth as if it could erase—or absorb?—Caryn's touch, and then he wrapped both arms around Jessie and held her close.

Arnie took Caryn's arm and pulled her up off the couch. She turned to face Jessie and Josh, while Eric watched discordantly from a new post against the back wall.

"Please, Jessie. Just lie down with me, okay? Let me just hold you. Okay? For old time's sake. Just for a little while. I need to hold you." She was almost whimpering now, her pride gone, lost and forgotten, her strength and refinement diminished.

"I love you," Jessie was whispering softly to Josh, her back still to Caryn. "I love you so much."

Still confused, Josh was scared at the power this woman in white seemed to have over both he and his wife. Arnie intimidated him, and Eric's imposing presence both scared the heck out of him and sickened him, for his part in crossing the line of comfort, in Josh's opinion, so many years ago. He grasped Jessie's hand tightly. Over her shoulder, he met Caryn's injured jade eyes.

The weighty connection between them had changed now, somehow, with the erotic touches and Jessie's seeming willingness to revisit those touches, even just for a few moments. Now the power fused in a secret friendship was alive with a different kind of electricity, with an unshakeable faith in something greater than themselves. It was now about a love so simple and complete and necessary and pure that it went beyond touch and it existed beyond time. It was deeply set now, in Josh's eyes, in Caryn's, and on the invisible thread that traversed between them; that joined them irreversibly, to each other and to the woman that stood between them.

Caryn let that power consume her then, and she offered Josh one last peach on that difficult day. She told him, shining emerald eyes moist and sorrowful, in a low husky voice thick with emotion that ached for him to understand, and which drew him into a bubble that precluded all other souls in the room, "She is so responsive. To love." She finished the proclamation with a slight dip of her chin, and a direct stare that elicited new tremors in Josh's soul. "Isn't she?" Her hands floated towards him, towards Jessie, on whispers of air unable to grasp anything tangible to hang on to. In the end she let her arms drop to her sides, clenching and unclenching nothing but a hollow emptiness.

Jessie felt a shiver pass through Josh's body at Caryn's words, and she stilled, knowing his expression would be the same as the one that crushed and shocked her a few days ago outside Revolver. His cheeks would be flushed, his eyes a little lost but still radiant with a barely concealed lust, and his lips would be parted, wanting.

Jessie stared at the floor before turning. She didn't want to see him like this, at such a loss, at such odds with himself. Connected with Caryn like this, on the inside. Ever.

"Goodbye, Caryn," she whispered, her heart racing. Her eyes drifted over to the silent Arnie, and then to an all-knowing Eric. "Bye."

Josh didn't say his goodbyes, but he forced his gaze away from Caryn's to see both Eric and Arnie watching him closely. He knew they were not surprised at Caryn's power over him, and he understood the clear warning they were shooting wordlessly at him—*stay away*. He looked back at Caryn once before he let the door close behind him. She was staring at Jessie's photograph, her mouth working as if she had more to say, but her perfect lips were devoid of sound.

"Jesus," he moaned to the elevator's back wall, when the door slid with a *swooshmph* behind them. He leaned his forehead and sweaty palms against its rough carpeted surface and tried to swallow, but his mouth was dry. He couldn't summon up any saliva to help the process along, and so he had no more to say.

Jessie tucked an ankle up behind her, leaned her body against the side wall, and dropped moist, shaking hands into the leather jacket's pockets. She stared straight ahead.

When the elevator found the first floor, Jessie exited first. Josh was close behind, and she handed him his half helmet for the Harley ride home without looking at him. He swung himself onto the bike first, shoved up the kickstand, and leveled the bike so Jessie could climb on behind. Abruptly, he turned the key and their ride home sprang into life. Only then did he turn his head slightly so he could speak to Jessie over his shoulder.

"You ready?" he asked hoarsely.

She wrapped her arms around his still trembling body and spoke in a small voice. "Yes."

The phone in her chest pocket vibrated again. "Not now, Dee," she demanded in a crushed murmur as Josh eased the Harley out onto the street.

Through the side mirror, behind them, she saw Arnie step out of the building. He stood and lit up a smoke, and then raised a silent watchful hand in goodbye. Jessie whipped her head around in time to see him fade into the distance, but she didn't let go of Josh's waist in order to wave back.

She held on for dear life, closed her eyes, and let the cool wind caress her hot, tender cheeks.

Chapter Thirty

"It's just a check-up," Jessie was saying to Josh early the next morning as she dropped her cellphone into her purse. "I'm going to see Dee later, to clear the air if I can. If the dragon man is there, believe me, you don't want to be. Not yet."

"I can handle the dragon man," Josh pouted, with more confidence than he felt. "And you look a little green today. I'm not sure *you* can handle the dragon man. Or the dragon lady. Are you feeling okay?"

Jessie turned her back to Josh so he couldn't see the flush rise across her cheeks. Over her shoulder she tossed, "I'm never having sushi again. Like pretty much ever. Stop bringing me sushi. You're supposed to be cutting down on takeout, anyway."

"You usually like those spicy rolls."

Not last night I didn't, thought Jessie, wincing in hard remembrance as her belly threatened to erupt. Josh watched her pause by the door, a hand on her stomach. Her back to him, he couldn't see the closed eyes and tightened lips, but her slightly bent-over countenance puzzled him.

Huh, he wondered. "Seriously, Jessie, I can drive you."

She grabbed her keys from a bowl on the table by the sliding door at the back, turned around to face him, and blew Josh a kiss. He looked so dejected that she sighed and, with a tiny smile, stepped forward and wrapped her arms around his waist. She looked up, rubbed her cheek against his stubble, and kissed him tenderly. "I love you muchly, Sawyer," she said, before wheeling around again. "I'll be fine. But thanks."

At the door, she stopped and did that thing she often did before leaving him, gazing at him and memorizing him, before she crossed the threshold in her black flats and clopped off down the pool deck towards the flagstone steps.

"Um hum," Josh muttered to himself, cocking his head to listen for the Mustang's telltale roar. "Well, then." He looked idly around before absently snapping his fingers by his side a few times as he digested his wife's seemingly ailing countenance as well as the warning about Charles. Would the distinguished older man ever truly accept him?

He trudged up the stairs to his and Jessie's shared office, lowered himself into a chair, and propped his feet up on the desk. He was going back to Toronto soon, to work with Steve on Jonathon's show. They'd finally gotten the green light to produce a full pilot, and Josh was raring to go. He yanked the script off the top of a pile and settled in to learn his lines.

His cell chimed—Facebook Messenger. It was Caryn.

You around?

He hesitated, and answered *no*.

It chimed again.

Jessie close by?

He typed *not right now.*

Caryn wrote *Eric moved out last nite*

Josh rubbed his forehead. He typed back *I'm sorry.*

Can I call you?

Not a good idea

Please and then *just for a minute*

After a moment Josh typed slowly, with one finger, *quick call*

"Hey," Caryn's lilting voice said when he answered, a touch of urgency evident therein. "Thanks. I just needed someone to talk to."

Josh tapped three fingers on the desk and stared at a handwritten yellow post-it note Jessie left for him by his keyboard a few months earlier, which he chose to never stick in the recycling, ever. It featured a silly happy face and a sweetly scrawled *Jessie loves Josh xoxo*.

"I don't think I should be that someone, Caryn."

"What are you so afraid of, Josh?"

He guffawed loudly. "Around you? Everything."

He could hear the smile in her voice when she responded, "Maybe that's a good thing."

"It's bad. It's very, very bad. Trust me."

"Josh, honey, come see me. Please. When will Jessie be back?"

"Not happening, Caryn. Look, I just took your call because I am sorry about how yesterday went. And I'm sorry about Eric, I really am, but—"

She cut him off. "He left because of Jessie. And you, I guess. I haven't really been into him lately, Josh. Not since—"

"Leave me—us—out of this, Caryn." Josh was tense now, and diplomacy was going to have to fly out the window with this woman. "Please," he said, echoing her agony yesterday, "leave us alone. We—I—can't have you in our lives."

"Why not?" she was whispering. "Even if it's just you and me. You know it would be unreal, between us. You know that. Accept it."

Jessie's poolside chat came to mind, the part where she talked about Charlie and how his escapades started. Josh blanched at the thought of ever disappointing that beautiful face, at seeing those tears start up again because of him. "Not in this lifetime, Caryn. Because I'm planning to be faithful to my wife until the day I die, and then some," he answered honestly, using a thumb and forefinger to squeeze his temple. He shifted his position to lean his elbows on the desk, and inadvertently knocked another small post-it note off. He bent over to pick it up. It was just a reminder of Jessie's doctor's appointment, with a Doctor Wyatt. Absently, he put it back on her desk. "I really am sorry about Eric. That sucks."

She sighed heavily. "It's been coming for a while. It's not really a surprise."

"Still sucks, though, eh?"

"Yes, Josh. It sucks."

"I'm going to say goodbye now, Caryn. I'll tell Jessie about Eric. I know she'll be sorry. She cares, okay? But…please. Don't call again." He considered changing his number. It may have to be an option. He'd see whether she kept calling in the next few days and then decide.

She read his mind. A big slow exhalation accompanied her plea. "Don't."

"Don't what?"

"Change your number. I'll leave you alone. I won't…stalk you."

269

SUSAN RODGERS

A chill ran up Josh's spine. He was shocked she would even consider saying that, given his and Jessie's recent history. He couldn't speak.

"Goodbye, Josh." The phone went silent.

"What the hell kind of Pandora's box did you open, Sawyer?" he berated himself harshly. "Geez Louise."

He sat for a while, and then got up and blended himself a banana-chocolate-peanut butter smoothie. Only then, after time to prepare, blend, pour and wash, did his nerves settle. When he sat back down at his desk, script in one hand and smoothie in the other, he laid the cold glass against his side, where his spleen had been removed and his body marked with a large obnoxious scar.

It was a long time before he could read any lines without having to repeat them many times over.

～⌒～

"It's so kind of you to grace us with your presence, Your Highness."

Dee had swung open the front door of La Casa and was standing with her arms crossed, leaning against the doorframe, as Jessie hoisted her tired body out of the Mustang and slammed the door.

"Look, we don't have to do this today, Dee. In fact, we don't have to do this at all." In leggings and a long floral top, and a short jean jacket over top, Jessie was cold and not in the mood for a stripping down. She didn't expect a north wind, and she'd left the top down on the Mustang. Warm weather seemed to have come and gone in Vancouver and, to make matters worse, today was grey and rain was now threatening. She was overly nauseous and not interested in standing outside freezing while Deirdre threw a temper tantrum. "And don't call me Your Highness."

Dee scooched over to let Jessie storm by.

"Is Charles here?" was the first thing Jessie asked when she landed on one of Dee's new high leather chairs at the kitchen island. She set her purse on the counter with a soft *ploompphh*.

"These are nice." She ran a finger over the expensive buttery leather on the chair next to her. "What country of cow died to make these? Fancy."

Flat heels descending the stairs at a quick pace decisively answered her earlier question. She groaned. *I am really not feeling up to this today.* She hung her head in her hands.

"Moo-A," announced Charles as he swept into the room.

"Ah," responded Jessie warily, eyeing him as he made his way over to his wife and brushed his lips lightly against her forehead. "Italian. Italian cows died so you two lovebirds could have fancy chairs."

"The Irish ones were green." He shook his head at Jessie. "Not for us."

"Ha ha. Charles Keating made a funny." She grimaced.

"Speaking of green," he looked at her curiously.

"I'm fine. Last night's sushi didn't agree with me, that's all."

Scowling, Charles cut in rather unnecessarily, "Don't you two ever cook?"

"Don't you?" Jessie spat, and gestured towards the sound of Carlotta's vacuum in the back media room.

"Touche," responded Charles hotly.

"Tea?" Dee interjected quickly, reaching up into the cupboard for cups. "Something pepperminty might help your indigestion, Jessie."

"Sure. Okay. You really should get one of those Keurig things like Trudy has. They're pretty slick."

"Oh, pshaw." Dee waved an arm in the air. "Charles doesn't like those newfangled things. He's too old fashioned."

"Who's old fashioned?" Charles urged his wife into the curve of one arm and spun her around on one heel, in some old jive move they learned years ago. Then he leaned closer and dropped a lingering kiss on her forehead that, for some reason, touched Jessie immensely. She couldn't resist a small smile, finally, which Charles caught when he let Dee go. He flipped around to lean back against the counter while his wife filled the kettle.

"You are, honey," Dee finally answered him, laughing. "Terribly. Old fashioned, that is."

"He's a music producer!" Jessie grinned, mellowing. "Can't be too behind the times. He's got two songs in the top ten right now."

"He has minions. They're the real brilliance behind Charles Keating." Dee ducked out of the way of her husband's flailing arm.

"And I have you and Jacob. Hence the two songs in the top ten right now." Charles winked at Jessie, but frowned when her smile faded.

"What?" he asked.

"Be prepared. My song might get pulled. Or sink rapidly."

271

Charles moved forward and leaned both elbows on the island across from Jessie. "Things have settled down, Jessie. The social media consensus is this—Josh likely had an affair, or was considering an affair, despite Hilary's announcement to the media that he was just having coffee with a friend."

"Geez Charles, you don't have to sound so glib."

Her producer raised a hand and palmed the air, closing his eyes and counting to three as he did so. When he opened his eyes, Charles took a deep breath before speaking, looking at Jessie directly as he did so. "Jessie, no one, especially me, is overly thrilled with Josh right now."

"He is my husband, Charles."

"Yes, I'm well aware of that. Thank you for the charming reminder."

"Charles," Dee chided, as she placed peppermint tea bags into mugs.

Jessie straightened and glared at Charles. "Why do you hate him so much? You know, I'm not the only one who thinks you'd rather I stayed with Jacob. Or Charlie. You guys are always bouncing over to Charlie's place."

"We enjoy the baby, honey," Dee responded. She eyed the kettle and willed it to boil. In her world, a hot cuppa tea or coffee solved a lot of problems. Silently she thanked Carlotta for her ever present influence with such graces.

"Fine, but it's still a kick in the ass to Josh. You hardly ever have dinner at our place."

"That's because you're rarely there."

"Oh, and whose fault is that? Who got me the job in Miami?"

"Don't blame this on Miami, Jessie." Charles was regarding her frankly, flashes of light dangerously close to the surface of his eyes. "After Friday's concert, I hear you're taking off to the new ranch for a month."

"Then to P.E.I. again," Dee declared, the hurt in her voice palpable. "For the summer."

"I don't know," Jessie shook her head, unsure. "Maybe. Josh has the pilot to shoot for Jonathon in Toronto. He's just waiting for word on when. And he's thinking about another film this summer, in New York, I think. Same director as *Freedom Ride*. It'd be tough to pass that one up. So we'll see, although I admit New York is not where I want to spend my summer."

"So don't go to New York. Go to your island and I'll come stay with" you for a bit," Dee announced, a little too brightly. "I'll keep you company. Besides, you have a few guest appearances on the calendar so that will spice things up."

"Hmmm," Jessie said, eyes narrowing as she accepted a steaming teacup from Dee.

"What?" asked Charles.

"I wouldn't be surprised if you're exec producing the New York film just to separate me and Josh."

"Jessie, you have to stop this. Charles has nothing against Josh. He never has, except maybe in the very beginning and then…" She didn't need to finish that sentence. The summer of loneliness and fear and Jessie's eighteen-month absence would always be a part of the collective Keating-Wheeler-Sawyer memory. And although that wasn't Josh's doing, he was definitely the reason Jessie isolated herself from everyone in her circle.

"Got a Bible in the house, Dee?" Jessie asked drily. "So Charles can swear on it?"

"No, Dee," Charles stood taller and glanced at his wife before fixing his gaze on Jessie. "Jessie's right. I wouldn't pass the Bible test."

"Charles—"

"No. Let's be honest here. I know you're happy with him, Jessie. And I'm glad of that. Sincerely. What I want most in this world is to see my girls happy. Carlotta included. Or I get liver for dinner."

Jessie folded her arms across her chest, angled her chin sideways at him, and frowned.

Charles continued. "But I am not liking what I am seeing from Josh lately. He doesn't always travel with you, and I hear he got involved with a woman from the crew on the shoot in Virginia."

"Nothing happened. He walked away."

"He told you? Well, I guess that's a start. But no, Jessie. That's not what I heard. I've been told he didn't walk away."

"Wh-what?" Disbelief etched her voice.

"I'm not saying he slept with her, exactly. But he was seen engaged in some heavy activity at the woman's door." Charles' voice was subdued and sincere. He watched Jessie to see how she was taking this before he continued.

She pursed her lips and stared hard at him.

He continued, while Dee watched Jessie anxiously. "You wouldn't listen in Whistler. But listen now," he demanded. "This thing with the woman downtown has been going on all winter. When you were in Miami, Josh was seen with her. A few times."

"I know. We've talked about that." And then, incredulous, as she realized what he was getting at, "You were *spying* on him?"

She jumped off the stool and faced both of the Keatings. Her eyes darted from one to the other. "Seriously, Charles?"

Dee closed her eyes and groaned.

Shrugging, Charles nodded. "Yes Jessie, I had him followed now and again. Look, I just don't want to see you hurt."

"By who? Who followed him? Matt's team? Was Matt in on this?!"

"Matt had nothing to do with it. I engaged Big Dan and Ulysses a few times. Unbeknownst to Matt."

"Duh, he's their boss, Charles!"

"I'm their boss. Matt's, shall we say, partial to Josh. I chose not to put him in an awkward position. Plain and simple."

"Oh, aren't you the bloody martyr!" Angry tears shot to the surface of Jessie's sea-pearl stare.

"Enough, Jessie. I had my reasons for following Josh, and it turns out I was right on the money."

"And how many times did you have Charlie followed? Huh?"

"Deirdre was Charlie's conscience, Jessie. You know that."

"Yes, because you were too busy sucking up to him. Because he was so damned perfect in everyone's eyes."

"I learned my lesson with Charlie. Josh is starting down the same damn road, Jessie. And I don't want to see you get hurt again. Ever!"

"Oh, so what are you planning to do? Have him shot? You know, you could just send for your Golden Boy to accomplish that dirty deed. In fact, he made a very recent threat against Josh."

Dee gasped. "What? What kind of threat?"

"The killing kind, Dee! The fucking killing kind!" Jessie was losing it again. "You know something? The last little while I've been getting kind of tired of all this innuendo and underhandedness around you two. In fact, I haven't heard shit-all from the Peterborough relations, and I wouldn't put that past the two of you, either, to have some hand in keeping them away from me! And then there's Caryn...you got her on your payroll, Charles? The one marked 'decrepit old whores?' Jesus, you two!"

She wheeled around on her ballet flats and headed for the door.

"Jessie, stop this," Dee demanded. "We have things we need to discuss today. You're overreacting!"

Slowly, Jessie turned and faced her, and was sorry to see the angst in her manager/pseudo-mom's eyes. But Charles was behind Dee, reeling still at the Golden Boy comment, and not at all impressed with Jessie's quick-trigger responses these days.

To Dee, Jessie stated flatly, "You had Josh followed? You do realize what that makes you both, eh?"

They were still, and listened. Charles wrapped an arm tenderly around his shaking wife's waist.

"Stalkers," Jessie winced, hugging her woozy belly. "It makes you stalkers."

And, with a final *hrummpphhh,* she left the pretty house, slamming the door loudly behind her.

~ ~

A few nights later, as Jessie was sound asleep on the Keating jet, heading back to Miami for the live *Mystic Nights* end of season promo concert and subsequent wrap party, Doctor Wyatt was leaving a message on her phone. At the same time, Eric was alone in his and Caryn's place, taking one last look around before leaving with the remainder of his things.

For the most part Jessie was content, although she was desperately uneasy about her now floundering relationship with Charles and Dee. At this juncture, somewhere over the Midwestern U.S., serenaded by the roaring hum of the trusted jet, she was snuggled in a big chair with Josh, half on top of him and arms wrapped around him. He was asleep, too, feet up on a large ottoman, Jessie's head cradled protectively against his chest.

Behind them, Matt was reading the Globe and Mail. Every once in a while he looked up at his two charges across and just up the aisle, and he swore there were tiny smiles lighting up each of the two faces he'd grown to love.

Home, he thought, realizing just how completely the two loved each other. *That's home.*

Doctor Wyatt's message was short and sweet and, in fact, quite jubilant. It was an adrenaline rush being one of the only people in the world who knew Jessie Wheeler and Josh Sawyer were about to have their first child. One person was of course Jessie, one was Matt, and one was the good doctor. Doc Wyatt didn't know about the trusted *Mystic Nights* crew member who'd delivered the home pregnancy test to Jessie a week or so earlier, but Jessie had confided to the doctor she hadn't yet told anybody else. "Until it's confirmed," she'd said. "I don't want to disappoint anybody. Especially my husband."

As for Eric, while Jessie and Josh slept in each other's arms, he spent a considerable amount of time just standing in the middle of the lush white palace he was vacating, and looked absently around. The moon popped out from behind a cloud and bathed Jessie's large photograph with a swath of opalescent blue light. To Eric, it was a sign. He tugged at his iPhone, which was snugly in a back pocket of his tight black denims, and he snapped a photo of the framed work. Rather mournfully, he turned off the iPhone and shoved it back in his pocket. He left, quietly closing the door behind him, a last small box of incidentals tucked underneath the crook of his arm.

Chapter Thirty-one

Skidding to a halt outside Jessie's dressing room, Jacob grabbed the door-frame for extra help in braking.

"Damn, these floors are slippery," he announced to Josh, who was leaning against the far counter munching on a Granny Smith apple. Jacob stepped inside, hesitant, eyeing Josh out of his peripheral vision while he snuck what he thought were subtle peeks in his quest to find Jessie.

"She's not here," Josh answered matter-of-factly. "She went down the hall to say hi to Kelly." He took another big bite of the apple, then reached behind him and grabbed a second one out of a basket, which he tossed to Jacob. "Here. If you're anything like she is before you hit the stage, you've eaten crap all."

"Thanks," Jacob said. He studied the apple. "You poison it?"

"Nah," Josh replied, a slow grin spreading across his face. "I'm leaving that shit up to you."

"Yeah. Thanks for that. Considerate as always, Sawyer." Jacob hopped up on the counter kitty corner to Josh and sank his teeth into the apple. "I don't think I will ever get used to the nerves," he admitted reluctantly.

"Jessie still gets nervous." Josh crossed his ankles and leaned back as he relaxed into the conversation. Time alone with Jacob was rare, and he wanted to stay on the guy's good side as much as possible, since Jacob was likely always going to be a conduit to Jessie, however unwelcome. "Until she gets behind the microphone. Then she disappears. She goes someplace else when she sings."

Gazing over his apple at Josh, Jacob agreed. "Since we met I've been trying

277

to figure out what it is about her music that makes her so special. That gives her a deeper edge over other performers, and I think I've got it figured out."

Josh answered for him, casually munching on the apple as he remarked, "She doesn't leave anything behind. That's what it is. She's raw. It gives her an intimacy people crave."

"Huh," Jacob said, surprised that Josh, a non-musician, thought enough about Jessie's music to lay his finger on this realization. "Wouldn't have figured you for the kind of guy to care enough about the music part of her to bother trying to go there."

"Why not? It's a pretty big part of who she is. It's worth my while to try to understand the woman I love on every level." Josh's belly creased with anxiety over the memory of the angst-ridden days before they'd boarded the jet for the Miami trip.

Jacob paused before answering, his apple held aloft, forgotten. He met Josh's steady gaze. "I guess I was hoping you'd leave a part of her for me."

Shifting his eyes to study the toes of his boots, hair falling forward over one cheek, Josh replied, "You've got enough of her, Jacob. You're always two steps behind me." He looked up, and Jacob acknowledged this statement with a dejected shrug.

"I don't have nearly enough." While Josh digested that, he added, "And from what I heard about last week in Vancouver, I think maybe I'm now only one step behind."

He waited for Josh's stunned response.

It was a few moments in coming.

Outside the dressing room, hurried footsteps echoed down the shiny hallway, mingling with layers of shouts and excited laughter in anticipation of the long-awaited *Mystic Nights* promo concert, which had been sold out for weeks. The show was in a cozy old theater not unlike Vancouver's Orpheum, with faded purple velvet seats, gorgeous old Art Nouveau carvings and moldings, and rich high-polished mahogany woodwork. The theater sat a good 2500 souls, and the stage was intimate enough for everyone to climb as deeply into the music as they wanted.

"She's mine, Jacob." Josh's voice was quiet and determined, but he couldn't disguise the constant fear Jacob's presence decreed.

Jacob didn't miss a beat. "I'm never giving up," he said into the fearful chocolate eyes of his one-time lover's husband. He jumped off the counter and tossed his apple core into a nearby garbage bin. "Even if she doesn't give me everything. Even if she always loves you more."

Josh swallowed. "Jacob," he started. "Just leave us alone. Give us a chance." He had seen Charles place an arm around Jacob's shoulders earlier that day at the rehearsal. The spiteful image jumped into his mind, and he cursed under his breath at the way his stomach had lurched at the sight.

"Every man for himself," Jacob proclaimed, flinging his arms wide as he backed out of the room. He paused when he reached the open doorway, and cocked his head at his nemesis. He eased up when he realized that, for some reason, Josh was actually silently telegraphing a fear of losing Jessie.

Jacob grinned. "Hell, Sawyer. Don't look so scared. She's so deeply messed up in you she practically can't breathe when you're not around." He added, "In all honesty, I don't have a fucking chance with you around. And I know it."

He slapped the doorframe for emphasis and then, leaving Josh immobilized and speechless, went sliding off to find the girls.

Kelly had been applying a final layer of lip-gloss when Jessie dropped in. She peeked at Jessie through her reflection in the mirror as Jessie bounced onto a comfy couch on the opposite wall behind her.

"Hey," Jessie enquired. "Excited?" She frowned when she noticed Kelly studying her clothing choices with an air of barely concealed disapproval. "What?" she asked, throwing out her arms and gesturing to herself. "Not liking the slightly western feel of the old denims and boots?" She lifted her boots onto the ottoman, exaggerating the movement. Kelly frowned down at the barely discernible old black smiley faces Jessie had re-emphasized on the boots with a Sharpie during the afternoon's rehearsal and sound check. Jessie did it while perched in the theater watching a segment she wasn't performing in, boots propped up on the seat back in front of her, Sharpie borrowed from one of the production assistants helping out with the show.

"Classy," was the blonde's response to Jessie's comment.

Kelly, as usual, was dressed to the nines in an expensive mini-dress with an empire top. She wore long chandelier earrings that twinkled from the lights around her make-up mirror. On her feet was a new pair of high-heeled sequined Manolo Blahniks. She re-crossed her legs over the knees, non-chalantly shrugging, eyebrows raised. "You could at least pretend you care about your appearance."

"What, afraid I'll make you look bad? This *is* my appearance. This is who I am."

Kelly peeked back at her through the mirror, the lip-gloss poised above her top lip. "I like the top, at least. Is it backless?"

"Yep." Jessie was long past letting Kelly's comments grate on her nerves. It was as if the girl didn't have a social filter. Or maybe it was a defense mecha-nism, she wasn't sure. She twisted around so Kelly could see the back of her top, which was entirely backless with the exception of a strap that buttoned in back just below her breasts, and a button at the halter-style fastener at the neck. The sides were open and flowing, the halter itself the only part of the floral cotton fabric tight against her body.

"It's cute," Kelly agreed, softening. She finished applying the lip-gloss and then turned in her chair just as Jessie was asking how things were going with Michael.

"Good," Kelly answered, brightening, as Jessie smiled and filed away that topic for future openers with her co-star as an obvious pick-me-up in the world of Kelly Reilly. "He told me about what happened to his wife and little girl, Jessie." She glanced surreptitiously towards the door in case the object of the conversation should happen to wander in.

"Matt told me a little," Jessie said, reclining gracefully against the cor-ner cushion, adjusting it behind her back, putting a hand above her head and leaning back against it. "Nasty." Her heart ached at the thought of kindly, funny Michael witnessing an accident that brutally tore his family away from him. She sucked in a breath and laid a palm against her belly. *No more sad-ness*, she said. *You, little baby, will have only joy.*

Kelly didn't notice the involuntary movement. "He was having an affair, Jessie. His wife caught him basically necking with a woman he was about to go on tour with. A dancer. His little girl was in the car."

Sighing deeply, Jessie hesitated. What could she possibly say to dignify the agony of Michael's past, that would give Kelly hope they, as a couple, could live in a fulfilling and joyous way forever? She knew that was what

Kelly was grasping at—how can you guarantee your relationship will survive, when there is so much pain in the world? How could Kelly, in the man she loved, ease an ache he carried with him since the day of his tragic loss? An ache that was his shadow; no, that was a part of him, now and forevermore?

Kelly was staring at her now, twisting her lovely fingers in her lap, imploring Jessie to respond, to say the right words, to voice thoughts with the power to promote healing.

Jessie leaned forward and sank her elbows onto her knees. "Honey," she started, recognizing there was oh so much more to the abrasive Kelly Reilly than the world, or those in her inner circle, would ever see, "there is only one way to help him. Or to make your relationship work, if that's what you're asking me."

"What's that?" Kelly blinked, tossed her newly curled blonde mane, and raised her chin aristocratically while the rest of her body remained still and quiet. She eyed Jessie carefully from just above her on the stool, the guard over her heart well in place.

"You just love him," Jessie said simply. "Through all the fights, through all the nights when he feels distant and remote, when he leaves the toilet seat up, or…" she reached for the words, "or when he's lost so deeply in sorrow you're wondering if he'll ever again see the light of day."

Kelly smiled softly down at her, her shoulders visibly relaxing. "That's how you guys do it, huh? Get past all the crap?"

Reaching across the space between them, taking Kelly's hand in hers, Jessie applied a little pressure. "There's no other choice, honey. Sometimes it'll be lonely as hell. But there's no other choice. That's what love is."

When Jacob rounded the corner a few moments later, he found the girls holding each other tight in a big ole hug, wiping tears from the corners of their eyes. They turned to him, laughing at themselves and their capacity for emotion at the slightest provocation, and then Kelly became Kelly again.

Giving Jessie's fingers a squeeze, she winked sideways at her and said to Jacob, "Ryan, it's a good thing there's wardrobe crew on this show."

Jessie forced a smile at their interloper and gulped. "Geez, Jacob, you do clean up mighty fine." Silently she breathed *thank you, wardrobe!*

Their eyes met across the room and Jacob grinned. "You like?" he asked, gesturing to his tight fitting blue western shirt that fell pleasingly over body hugging over-dyed denims.

Jessie's eyes fell to his feet. "New boots again?" She eyed him appraisingly, and didn't hide her satisfaction and a little jealousy as her eyes roved upwards. She shifted uncomfortably when their eyes met. Jacob held his ground and sent Josh a telepathic addendum to their recent conversation. *I'm never giving up.*

Hooking a thumb over his jean pocket, he held Jessie's gaze as long as he dared. Kelly noticed.

"Stop it, you two. Stop undressing each other with your eyes. Her man's just down the hall." She let go of Jessie's hand and moved forward to give Jacob a small hug and a kiss on the cheek. "You are positively adorable. It's about time you ditched that old plaid shirt and, by the way, did you ever wash those jeans? Hope you burned 'em."

She turned to Jessie and whispered behind her hand, "Isn't that cross on his back sexy as hell? I'm going to ask Michael to get one for me."

At that, the old lingering sexual tension was broken, and Jessie moaned before laughing heartily. She put a hand over her eyes. "T—M—I. Too much information, Kelly."

Her eyes twinkled at Jacob and he grinned back. He was picturing Jessie asking Josh to get a similar tattoo. Somehow, he just couldn't see that going over very well.

"You girls ready for tonight?" he asked instead, trying to recover from the blush that bloomed across his cheeks at Jessie's undisguised stare of approval when he walked in.

"Yeah," Jessie jumped in. "I changed that note in our ballad. The C that just never felt quite right. Here, try it with me."

Kelly slipped back onto her high chair and nodded her approval after Jessie took Jacob's hand and ran a few musical phrases with him. "That's better," she agreed, as the two waited on her opinion. "As good as it's going to get, anyway," she teased, "with you two on stage."

Jessie leaned into Jacob and brushed her lips across the stubble on his cheek. Inadvertently, he raised a hand to her back, as he always did, and lingered there, breathing her in.

"You gotta stop wearing those backless tops around me," he murmured, inhaling quietly, his eyes locked in hers, his hand moving up her back, a finger slipping under the strap.

She took his arms, as she'd done with Caryn, and lowered them. "I'll see you on stage," she said quietly. Waving at Kelly, she slipped out of the room.

Kelly eyed Jacob curiously. "I thought you two came to some sort of peace after we recorded those songs in the studio."

"So did I," Jacob breathed. "But I guess Vancouver wasn't the dreamy fantasy she expected."

"Do you think he cheated on her?"

He shrugged. "I don't know. But maybe that's besides the point."

"What do you mean?"

"I mean…does it matter? Shit like that's gotta rock your foundation, regardless of the truth."

"Ahhh," Kelly said, nodding. "And you'll be around to pick up the pieces when the whole thing goes up in a flash of dynamite."

"That's the plan." He didn't bother smiling at the satisfaction the thought brought him, of holding Jessie in his arms and comforting her. He just let himself feel it, his whole body suddenly alight and tingling. He gazed at Kelly, and waited for her reaction.

It didn't come. She just watched him, a blank unreadable expression on her face.

"I just want her to be happy, Kelly."

"Happiness, huh?" She smiled wistfully at him. "And you think that's the answer? Loving someone who doesn't love you back?"

He paused, taking that in. "She does," he said. "She loves me back."

"But she loves Josh more."

"For now." His voice was a whisper.

"Oh, honey," Kelly said softly, suddenly loving Jacob for the hurts she knew he had endured, for the intolerable hurts he was enduring, and for the hurts bound to come down the road.

Just then, a greasy-haired assistant stage manager ducked his nose into the room. "There you are, Jacob. I've been looking for you. Outside," he signaled. "In the hall. Your grandparents are out here."

"Oh. Okay. Cool!" With a last look at Kelly, Jacob turned, waving *so long* behind him as he sauntered out of the dressing room. He whistled as he turned the corner, but stopped suddenly, frozen, when he saw his grandparents.

They weren't alone. He ducked his head shyly and watched for a bit before wandering over, both thumbs hooked over his pockets now, his heart racing.

"Hey," he said.

"There's my handsome grandson!" His grandmother hugged him tightly. Over her shoulder, he nodded and said *hi* to his grandfather, and then eyed the third person in the group.

Tom Ryan extended a hand. "Jacob," he said gruffly.

Guarded, Jacob took it. "What are you doing here?"

The handshake was tight, strong, and his father held it for a few moments before he answered. "I got tired of listening to Charles Keating's over-produced shit on iTunes," he said in that recognizable Tom Ryan voice that was low and hoarse from years of smoking and hundreds—no, thousands—of performances. "I wanted to see if you could hold up live on stage."

Jacob had nothing to say—there was no saliva in his mouth, but it didn't matter because the words wouldn't come anyway. His stomach growled loudly.

Tom grinned. "Did you puke yet?"

At that, Jacob nervously lightened up. "Once or twice."

"What?" his grandmother interjected, concerned.

"It's okay," Tom said, resting a hand lightly on her shoulder. "It's a performance thing. Nerves." Then he motioned lightly towards Jacob. "Or should I say it's a Ryan thing. Not everybody gets that nervous before shows."

A wide grin spread across Jacob's face. "A Ryan thing, eh?"

"Yeah. So listen son, tell me how you play that bit in *Smokescreen*. I like the song, but I can't get my head around the bridge."

Despite a gnawing resentment and uncertainty at his estranged father's unexpected reappearance in his life, Jacob was on a *Mystic Nights* fueled adrenaline high, so he pushed the past behind for the moment. He and his father ducked their heads and started talking shop, which helped immensely in getting Jacob's mind off his pre-show nerves, and off the sizzling feel of Jessie's skin under his touch.

Fifty feet away, Jessie was wandering the hallway looking for Charles and

Dee. She had to look twice when she spotted Jacob's back hunched over in conversation with his folk rock legend dad. *Ohhhhh,* she said to herself, stopping in her tracks when it hit her that Jacob's famous dad had come to see his son play live. A glow touched her cheeks and imbedded itself in her soul at the sight of them, accented by the comforting presence of his grandmother's hand on Jacob's back. *Damn,* Jessie whistled under her breath. *Good ole Jacob.*

She sighed wistfully. *Grandmother. Family...sister.*

Charles' clipped business voice interrupted her mellow glow. "Jessie, Dee's looking for you."

"I know," she answered quickly, forcing her thoughts to abruptly change tack. "I've been trying to find her too. Where is she?"

The assistant stage manager marched up the hall hollering, "Fifteen minutes, everybody! Those with tickets for the show are asked to take your seats. Theater doors are closing promptly at seven thirty."

"In your dressing room."

"Crap. I was just there. I must have just missed her." She started to walk away, but Charles grabbed her elbow, and she turned around to see his eyes searching hers. "Jessie," he said. "Look, I know things have been a little strained between all of us lately, and I'm sorry about that." New wrinkles lined his eyes, which were gray underneath as, sometime over the last while, new harsh shadows had settled in.

"Me too," she answered in a subdued tone, regarding him carefully. "You have to leave Josh up to me, though, Charles."

"I am tired of seeing you get hurt, Jessie," he said, letting his moist eyes speak more than the simple sentence proclaimed. He let go of her arm.

She studied him for a moment, and then stepped forward and wrapped her arms around Charles. The simple relief of hugging this man, her producer and second father, eased the ache in her heart substantially. *Home,* she thought, inhaling his musky Charles Keating spicy aftershave scent. *He feels like home.*

Letting a small smile linger on her face, she breathed, "Come find Dee. You guys need to take your seats."

But he pulled back. "Not yet, Jessie," he said, wavering in an uncharacteristic Charles kind of way.

She frowned, and as the realization of why he wouldn't go into her dressing room marched across Jessie's eyes, they transmitted the pain instantly. "Seriously," she groaned. "You won't come in because Josh is there?"

His shoulders slumped. "I'll talk to him after the show. We'll try to come to some sort of peace."

Eyes watering, Jessie implored him to stop this persecution of the man she loved. She had to work hard to muster up what she felt she had to say to him, to make him understand. Her voice was thick with emotion, her eyes pleading desperately. This time she articulated it with an extra emphasis that left no room for doubt as to the importance of Josh in her life. "He's my *husband,* Charles. My *husband.*"

"I know," he responded, frustration swelling his response into something bigger than it should have been. "You don't ever forget to remind me."

"Yeah," she replied, swiping at a tear before it could make her mascara run, begging him to understand. "Because you don't seem to get it." She whipped around on one booted foot and left him there wanting.

Martinique LaVois was in town. In fact, she was a few feet away. Her singsong voice cut into Charles' bitter reverie. "If you love her, sexy man, you have no choice but to love her choice of husband." She sipped on a martini and watched Jessie disappear into her dressing room.

"I do, Martinique. I like Josh. But I'm having a hard time with some of his choices, that's all."

"Has his cake but wants to eat it, too?" she mouthed, her lips forming a perfect glistening red O around the straw as she faced him.

"Something like that." Charles realized then that he was still staring at the door through which Jessie had just disappeared. He exhaled slowly and wheeled around to spy Jacob down the hall, bent over in a serious discussion with Tom Ryan.

Martinique followed his eyeline until she, too, saw Charles' protégé lost in his dad's eyes. "Oh," she said. "The boy's father is here."

"Something like that," Charles muttered again, disconcerted. Suddenly he didn't feel much like anyone needed him anymore. He was being shut out, and it hurt.

He rallied, though. He had to. "I'll see you at the half, Martinique. It's almost show time." He started to walk away, and then flipped around and walked backwards a few paces. He narrowed his eyes at her. "You're going to fall off your seat if you keep poisoning yourself with all that booze."

"Hope so. I think I'm sitting next to you, big man. I'd like to fall right into your lap!" She winked and waved gracefully, leaving him with her musical voice ringing in his beet red ears. "Bye, my dah-ling! I'm off to pee!"

His eyes darted once again to Jacob as Charles waited outside Jessie's dressing room to collect his wife, who was inside now wishing Jessie a good show. Jacob was just leaving his family, waving to them as they went off together to find their seats. He looked happier than Charles had ever seen him, cheeks glowing and flushed with excitement. Charles caught the boy's eye and raised a hand in greeting. Jacob waved back enthusiastically.

"Give 'em hell," Charles called in encouragement, forcing a smile.

"Thanks, Charles," was the cheerful response as Jacob literally skated down the shiny floor to his own dressing room. "See you at intermission?"

"You got it."

And then Jacob was gone for a last hair and make-up check, and for a tweak of the shiny new wardrobe.

Dee appeared, and marched across to her husband. She slipped her arm around his. "There's no bigger rush," she exclaimed, "than watching Jessie sing live. Come on Charles, let's get out there so we don't miss anything. I said good luck from you."

Grrrr, was his silent response. Thankfully, Deirdre was too wound up to feel the tension in her husband's body. She tucked a lock of her bobbed hair behind an ear and held on tight to him so her fancy heels wouldn't slip on the over-waxed tiles.

In her dressing room, Jessie was smiling gently at Josh as she ran a hand up the buttons on his denim jacket and leaned in for a kiss.

"Go find your seat," she murmured, "before I have to forgo the show and do naughty things to you."

"One minute," he said, pressing a hand into the bare skin on her back and running his tongue over her high-glossed lips.

"They're gone," Jessie said, pouting and pulling away a little. "Charles and Dee. You don't need to worry about running into him."

"I'm not," he answered. "I just want a few quiet moments with my sexy wife."

A high-pitched voice from the hallway broke into their thoughts. "Five minutes. Five minutes, everyone."

"Go." She turned Josh and pushed him lightly. "Or they won't let you in until after the first song. And I don't want you to miss anything." She put up a finger to stop him from speaking when he turned. "Don't say it. The songs reflect our characters on *Mystic Nights*. Go. Sit."

Josh leaned against the doorframe for a moment and soaked up Jessie's essence. "I was just going to say I love you, Wheeler."

"Wheeler-Sawyer," she retorted softly. "Love you back. See you at the half."

He blew her a kiss, and was gone.

Chapter Thirty-Two

Josh did okay during the show. He let himself believe the magic floating between Jessie and Jacob when they sang together wasn't them, that it was their characters on *Mystic Nights*. He had to. Otherwise he would have lost his mind.

At the half, he avoided Charles and Dee as they headed backstage in front of him. He ducked into a washroom and, when he exited, he landed in Jessie's arms.

Exuberant, she hugged him tight. "It was good, wasn't it, Josh? The first half. With all the cast. Isn't Kelly amazing? Her voice is a dream, all wispy and full of longing. And the standing ovation when Michael came on stage to sing with us! I just about burst into tears with the thrill of it all. I wasn't sure I'd be able to find my voice at all."

She leaned back and stared at him. "Hey. Do you think everybody's streaming this? Charlie? Steve and Sophie?"

He laughed. "You're vibrating. Yes, of course they're watching this. Millions of people are watching this show, Jessie."

"Ahhh." She sank back on her boot heels. "Crazy."

"Yeah. Crazy." He thumbed a wet glob of sweaty hair back from her forehead. "Because of you. You know that, right?"

"I don't really get it." She was subdued now, running a hand down the front of his jean jacket and letting her gaze fall there instead of meeting his adoring eyes.

"Stop it," he whispered. "You are a beautiful captivating light people are drawn to."

289

Instead of answering, Jessie regained her earlier vibrancy and enthusiasm. "Come on!" She grabbed his hand. "Everybody's in the dressing room. Let's go see what they think of the show."

By everybody, he knew she meant Charles and Dee, which made his intestines clench, and likely Matt, who was never far away from his girl in public arenas like this. He murmured a prayer Jacob wasn't there as well. There were limits, after all.

They breezed hand in hand towards the dressing room, Jessie waving happily at other cast as they wove their way through a buzz of excitement. A few looked at her oddly, but she didn't catch it, so lost was she in the adrenalin rush that always accompanied live shows. Josh caught the looks, though, and by the time they got to the dressing room a strange confusion was infiltrating his thoughts, crisscrossing his face like a lengthening shadow, grey and insistent.

A stark silence greeted them when they made their entrance.

Jessie paused at the door, her hand in Josh's. "What?" she asked, feeling the earth shatter beneath her feet before she even knew what precipitated the tears on Dee's cheeks and the deepening anger flashing towards Josh in Charles' eyes. As for Matt—well, at first she was afraid to look at him, for fear of what his gentle eyes would tell her, but then she did, and a sickening thud hit her in the chest at the same time the old caverns in her soul started to fill in with a thick sludge and mud.

From across the room, her sharply dressed security chief was begging her, with nothing more than an earnest plea flickering deeply beneath his eyes, to stay calm, and not to lose it.

Inhaling sharply, Jessie let go of Josh's hand and started into the room, afraid to lose Matt's gaze because, lately, he was the only person she really felt connected to, besides her perhaps misguided husband. Matt was always a steady rock, and right now she had the sick feeling she was going to need him.

He moved, his right hand slipping down to the top left edge of a slim silver MacBook Pro that sat unconcerned on the counter, as if it didn't have the power to rock her world, to destroy everything that had finally begun to matter to Jessie once again.

Matt pointed the screen outwards. Twitter was open. The image from

Caryn and Eric's wall—Jessie, larger than life, a tear on her cheek and her breasts exposed—stared out at her.

Matt spoke, but it wasn't until a few moments later that what he said registered with her. "It's a photo, Jessie. A picture of a picture." Of course that meant someone took the picture. Someone with access to Caryn and Eric's private quarters. So…either Caryn or Eric.

The rejection in Caryn's eyes, the desperate pleading from the other day, launched itself into her brain, and shattered Jessie's soul. The fact Eric might have done this wasn't even a consideration.

"How could she?" She clenched her fists, and the people in the dressing room, those closest to Jessie, recalled another night just more than a year earlier, when they saw the same rage and hopelessness build to an explosive potential in the girl's icy eyes.

Those same eyes flitted to the screen's left. "I'm trending," she said abstractedly, and she laughed, a high-pitched choke that was also, in itself, a warning. "Look," she said weirdly to Matt, pointing. "I'm number one on Twitter."

He reached over and closed the lid on the laptop, but he held Jessie's gaze and it was he who first saw the strength crack then, and the girl they all loved crumple.

"Jessie," he started, reaching for her. "We knew this could happen. We'll deal with it."

Despite the love and trust in the man's expression, the words were futile, then—at the moment of impact. For to Jessie, the release of this lonely girl she once was, on the Internet, was no less devastating than a missile through her heart.

The ice-pale eyes ruptured and melted in front of Matt, and his lips parted at the futile agony of not being able to help her.

"Steve and Sophie," she was whispering. "Charlie. My aunt Evelyn. My… my relatives in Ontario. No one'll want me now. Nobody."

He took her arm and tried to pull her towards him while, behind her, Josh stood immobile, unable even to breathe.

Josh couldn't meet Dee's tortured face; she stood with both hands over her mouth as she silently sobbed. He didn't dare look at Charles, but Josh could feel the imposing man's presence in the room larger than anyone else, larger even than the simple silver computer on the counter that destroyed them all in the first place.

But then the energy changed, and it came from Jessie just as Jacob was skidding to a stop outside the door, oblivious.

Jessie turned, slowly, her shame and rage now complete. And it was focused on Josh. She strode towards him in slow motion and then sped up at the last minute and clutched the jacket she'd only moments before been touching tenderly. She started shoving him the same way she'd done just over a year before, the night she first came home from Scotland.

"You," she growled on the first push. "You. You couldn't stay out of it. Could you. You had to go and raise the dead. You had to go and make her want me again! You had to make her want *YOU!* And now," she whipped an arm behind her in the general direction of the computer. "LOOK WHAT YOU'VE GONE AND DONE!"

By then she was pounding on him uncontrollably as everyone in the room stood by in shock, helpless. "YOU'VE RUINED EVERYTHING! EVERYTHING!!!"

She was choking on her sobs now as they racked her body, and when Matt finally hollered at Jacob to get Michael, and moved towards her, she was in that place where blind white rage takes people, beyond agony and beyond hope.

Matt couldn't subdue her because Josh was no help, lost in his own sweet pain in the stark knowledge of the demons he'd unleashed by going to see Caryn in the first place; and in the knowledge it was for love of Jessie that took him there. Jessie, who was now swinging at Josh, leaving bruises on his body that would turn yellow and remain for days afterwards, painful and unwanted souvenirs. The pure hate in his wife's eyes broke him in two.

Somewhere in her grief Jessie felt Matt trying to get a grip on her. But before she swung around to scream at him to leave her alone, she had more to say to Josh.

"I AM SO ANGRY AT YOU RIGHT NOW!!! I AM SO FUCCKK-IIINNNNGGG GODDAMNED ANGRY!!!" Then she backed off, her body shaking uncontrollably, and watched him struggle.

292

"I'm sorry, Jessie," he was crying, trying not to lose himself entirely. "I am so fucking sorry."

Her eyes flicked behind Josh to Jacob, who was standing in the doorway, his body on high alert and his eyes boring into hers, wide and shocked. Someone else had gone to get Michael. Jacob was frozen.

Matt grabbed at her again, now that she was still, and managed to grasp an arm, but his touch set Jessie off again. She whipped around and stared hard at him, directly into the trusted eyes, the eyes that carried yet another secret.

She pointed a finger at him. "Don't you fucking say anything. Matt, don't you fucking say anything!" And at that, Michael, who had just been alerted to the Twitter photo, vaulted into the room, pushing Jacob aside as he did so. He was breathing heavy, accustomed to hauling Kelly out of bars not all that long ago, but not sure what he would find in this dressing room. What he found was Jessie firing death rays at his brother, white-knuckled and shaking violently, eyes wide with terror.

Matt shook his head at Jessie. He turned to Charles and Dee. "Leave us," he demanded. Josh was next. "Go."

Nobody moved. Matt looked at Michael and at Kelly, behind him. "We need your dressing room. Take them."

Josh stood his ground, shoulders shaking. "I'm not going anywhere." He felt the fusty air move when Charles and Dee moved past him like ghosts in the night.

"Oh yes you are," Jessie breathed, her gaze not leaving Matt's. "Get the hell out of here."

It was Jacob who grabbed his elbow, which Josh shook off immediately. But Jacob understood Jessie as well as Josh did, and he knew she needed space. He spoke quietly. "Josh. Let's go."

They moved off just as the assistant stage manager came striding down the hall. "Five minutes. Jessie and Jacob, please be ready at the curtain."

The door clicked shut. Matt and Jessie stood apart, telegraphing their thoughts across an unseen wire. Then he spoke.

"What do you want to do?"

"Disappear," she said, eyes leaking a new waterfall.

"Not an option. Not again."

"For a little while?" she sobbed. "Just for a little while, Matt? Go and… be normal somewhere?"

"Don't you do that again, Jessie." His eyes were flooding now. "You promised. You promised me, you promised Charles and Dee, you promised everybody."

"Josh." Her shoulders sank, and she sobbed at the floor. "I could just kill him. I swear to God, Matt." A thought popped unbidden into her head. "Whose account posted the photo? Was it Caryn's?"

He shook his head. "No. Someone with the handle Oscar99. We'll find out."

A sardonic laugh appeared suddenly through her tears. "Oscar was a cat they had once. They're old Gretzky fans. They use that password for everything."

"Okay," he nodded. "So we know, then."

"Yes," she whispered in defeat. "We know."

A knock came at the door. "I'm sorry." It was the ASM. "We've gotta move, Jessie."

"Jessie?" Matt needed to know.

"I never seem to get to wrap parties," she said softly. "Fuel the jet, Matt."

"Vancouver?"

She turned slowly and gazed at her reflection in the mirror. She was a little older now, but the tears and sadness etching her eyes made her appear just as lost as the Jessie in Caryn's photograph. She grabbed a Kleenex and swiped at the mascara running on her cheeks. "No," she said. "Alberta. The ranch. We were going there in a few days anyway."

"Josh?" The question was posed quietly. Matt still hadn't moved.

"I don't know. I don't know yet, Matt."

He turned to her then, and urged her to face him. He put a finger solidly under Jessie's chin and pointed it upwards so she had no choice but to look at him. "Hey. Didn't I teach you anything?"

Another knock came at the door, and this time it opened. It was Jacob, pale and afraid. "Jessie?"

"Yeah," she said, studying Matt's solemn expression. "God," she murmured. "Julie's got herself one helluva good man."

At Matt's small smile, Jacob visibly relaxed. "It doesn't matter, Jessie. No one cares. It's just more celebrity gossip. And my dad's here. We gotta do this duet."

Behind him, the ASM was losing it. "They need you, Jessie. Now. They need you."

"They need me," she murmured to Matt. "One last time maybe, eh?"

He released her chin but she stood without moving. He turned her shoulders towards the door. "Go," he said. "Show them you're strong, Jessie. That you can handle whatever shit the world throws at you."

She sighed, and faced Jacob, who moved forward and pulled her into his arms. "Come on, girl," he said, hugging tightly. "Let's rock their world." He released her, wrapped one set of fingers around hers, and led her out into the bright hallway, where many pairs of eyes, including Josh's, watched them go.

Josh waited a few seconds before catching a movement at the door to Jessie's dressing room. It was Matt.

Eyeing Josh as he walked by him, Matt followed Jessie and Jacob, still hand in hand, on their way to the stage.

Josh was lost, alone now. He was still trying to get his breathing under control, and it wasn't going well. He was struggling for breath when he noticed Matt stop and turn to face him, from about fifteen feet away. Matt raised his fingers and signaled to Josh to follow. "Come," he said. "You haven't made it this far to give up on her now, Sawyer."

Shoulders hanging in shame, Josh made his way towards him.

Matt swung an arm loosely around his neck.

"I don't know, Matt. I don't see how we're supposed to crawl back from this one. I think she's finally had it." He watched his wife with Jacob, now bent in a tete-a-tete at the side of the stage, hands clasped and foreheads touching. Jessie was nodding as Jacob spoke fervently to her. Josh got his breathing under control; his breaths started to come in more regularly as he used his thumb and forefinger to wipe away the excess moisture around his eyes, and on his cheeks. "Do they always do that?" he asked Matt, his tone subdued and afraid.

"Yeah," Matt replied, hands on his hips, blazer flaring. "Always. Suck it up, Sawyer. Deal with it."

"Damn," Josh breathed quietly, watching them. He flinched and moved towards them when Jacob kissed Jessie full on the lips after the emcee introduced them, but Matt grabbed his elbow.

"And that?" Josh whispered.

"No," Matt said definitively as, before them, Jessie walked onto the stage ahead of Jacob, taking her Gibson from the hand of a tech as she breathed in deeply, afraid of what she would face. Jacob was right behind her, waving to the crowd and shooting them a big wide grin, his way of telling the ones who knew about the damaging Tweet to let it go, that this girl was hurting and that they, as a musical couple, had magic to share.

The cheers were overwhelming, some of the crowd on their feet in solidarity before Jessie even had her guitar over her shoulder.

"We love you, Jessie!" someone in the balcony shouted heartily.

Jessie didn't look up. She was still trembling as she grasped her guitar pick between sweaty fingers. She glanced over at Jacob, wondering if he was thinking the same thing, which was *I wonder if that person knows. I wonder if he has seen the photo.*

Jacob wasn't. He was thinking *this is it. This is my time with her, with Jessie. This is all I get, for now.* He was living in the moment. For at least the next few minutes she was his and, as far as he was concerned, his alone. A broad smile creased his face and he licked his lips, tasting the salty energy transferred from Jessie's soft lips when he'd kissed her.

She was on the opposite side of the stage facing Jacob and, by default, in the wings, Josh.

The audience quieted as the opening chords of the haunting ballad begged them to listen. In simple 4/4 time, the song was a tender thank you between friends, an easy tune for Jessie and Jacob to play, with the exception of the raw emotion that underscored it here tonight.

Jacob nodded encouragement to Jessie when he saw her waver, when he saw the bottom lip tremble and the pale eyes reaching, the lungs gasping. He mouthed *you are not alone,* and so her fingers played despite the agony settling deeper, second by second, into her heart.

With Jacob's presence and Trudy's healing thoughts in her head, Jessie found strength somewhere, in the mystical stage lights maybe, or in the accompanying drums or banjo, or perhaps in the fairy-tale enchantment, mystery and thrill of live music. She locked her eyes into Jacob's, where she found strength and an intimate hope, and then she lifted her chin and moved a knee just slightly, involuntarily keeping time. During the musical bridge, Jacob leaned towards her and brushed his lips against her ear; he whispered, *love you,* because they were in a bubble where the music was theirs, and because he knew she needed to hear and believe those simple words, and feel his warm breath on her cheek.

And so it was Jacob who lovingly nurtured Jessie through those first anguished moments; through knowing the image she presented to the world was once again being rocked off its already tenuous foundation.

From the sidelines Josh watched, desperately wanting to catch her eye, to let her know he'd done it for her, approached Caryn *for her.* That he loved her, and that he would always love her, despite how she might be feeling about him right now.

But he had to acquiesce for the moment, and stand back. He had to let Jacob have her right now. Because it was Jacob's hold over Jessie that got her through the ballad, not Josh's here, today; it was Jacob's unwavering gaze holding her aloft, that helped her go where she needed to go in order not to feel the pain, in order not to sink into the numbness that saved her so many times before, but which now she understood was simply an escape, a temporary respite from the bitter cold.

When the song ended, and their voices and souls were quieted, Jessie's lips turned up in a little smile meant for Jacob, and Jacob alone. Josh watched her mouth *thank you, babe,* to Jacob, her eyes lost somewhere in his where Josh could never go. He ached to run between them, to sever whatever it was that connected them, and Matt sensed his anguish, because once again he wrapped his fingers solidly around Josh's bicep.

Josh felt a presence behind him—Dee. He knew it was her by the smell of her perfume, something floral and, tonight, bloody overpowering.

In the theater, the cheering was dying down, and Jacob started to pull off his guitar. But Jessie's eyes flickered, her body stiffened and, offstage, Josh tensed. He knew that look only too well. He sucked in a breath, and waited.

"What's she doing?" he heard Dee exclaim, astonished, as Jessie started to play the first few chords of a song NOT on the playlist, NOT part of the *Mystic Nights* soundtrack, and NOT rehearsed with the band. But it was a song everybody knew, a Gordon Lightfoot classic, and so it wasn't long before the band picked it up.

Josh breathed in and out, slowly, savoring every lungful of air as the shock of what Jessie was doing reverberated through him.

He answered Dee the best way he knew how.

"She's sending someone a message," he bit off.

He tilted his head towards the stage and lost himself in Jessie's voice while at the same time longing to place both of his big hands on her bare back, and draw her to him so he could love the ache away.

This time she was facing the audience—the cameras actually, Josh figured rightly. She sang directly into one and, as their friends and the playback video would loudly proclaim later, she never wavered. The anger in her eyes flashed wildly as she snapped off the lyrics with a disdain and contempt that righteously told *someone* exactly what she thought of her.

At home in Vancouver, alone in a big apartment devoid of any lovers, in the darkness lit only by the glow of her iMac's big screen, Caryn hugged her knees to herself and shook as she cried. In one hand she was clutching her iPhone, open still to Twitter. On the floor at her feet was the beloved photo of Jessie, torn to shreds, a large butcher knife embedded in one breast.

The famous lyrics of the song soaked and chilled her as Jessie delivered her coup de grace, eyes on fire and one foot tapping to the beat.

I can see her lying back in her satin dress,
in a room where you do what you don't confess.
Sundown, you better take care,
if I find you've been creeping round my back stairs.
Sundown, you better take care,
if I find you've been creeping round my back stairs.

She's been looking like a Queen in a sailor's dream
and she don't always say what she really means.

Sometimes I think it's a shame
when I get feeling better when I'm feeling no pain.
Sometimes I think it's a shame
when I get feeling better when I'm feeling no pain.

I can picture every move that a woman can make
getting lost in her loving is your first mistake.
Sundown, you better take care
if I find you been creeping round my back stairs.
Sometimes I think it's a sin
when I feel like I'm winning
when I'm losing again.

I can see her looking fast in her faded jeans,
she's a hard lovin' woman got me feeling mean.
Sometimes I think it's a shame
when I get feeling better when I'm feeling no pain.
Sundown, you better take care
if I find you've been creeping round my back stairs.
Sundown, you better take care
if I find you've been creeping round my back stairs.

Sometimes I think it's a sin
when I feel like I'm winning
when I'm losing again.

She changed one word—*man* became *woman*. The rest was true to Gordon Lightfoot's haunting lyrics.

When she was finished, Jessie didn't hesitate. She swept the guitar off over her head and, with one final hard look at the camera, she bypassed Jacob, squeezing his hand as she stomped off the stage.

"Matt." He took the guitar from her without hesitation.

She strode past Josh and Deirdre without acknowledging either. Matt nodded at Josh before following Jessie. They didn't stop at her dressing room, although during the performances Matt had texted Michael to get Kelly to pack up some of Jessie's things. He grabbed them on the way by.

Charles stepped out in front of Jessie as they passed her dressing room.

"The jet is fueled and ready. Susanne is in Calgary with her man, she'll meet you at the airport and get you into a car. Dee and I are flying with you."

"No," was Jessie's icy response.

"No to the ranch? Do you want to go somewhere else? To P.E.I., maybe?"

She slid him a nasty look. "No, you're not coming tonight. Or tomorrow. Or the next day, or the next, or the one after that."

He grimaced. "Don't do this, Jessie. Don't…cut us off."

"Look Charles," she snapped, fists clenched. "We all know how this started. How this photo got leaked. Don't we?"

His silent angry glare was enough of a response.

"Well," she continued, "things need to cool down. I don't know what I want right now, or," she touched her belly, ever so lightly, "whom, in the immediate future. But I know one thing. I don't want you and Dee in our faces, staring at Josh the way you looked at him when we went into that room tonight. Like he just committed murder!"

"Jessie, we—"

"No," she said, putting a palm up between them. "Just no. Not right now. Okay?"

"All right," he agreed, stepping back. His throat caught on his next words. "We're here if you need us, okay, Jessie?" A quick look at Matt eased his mind. He knew they were close. Matt had her back, he'd stay in touch should she not calm down anytime soon. Should she choose to eliminate them from her life…again.

Charles glanced behind Jessie to see his wife walking towards him. Josh was farther back, leaning up against a wall, watching, his stubbled face sunken in misery.

When Jessie started to walk down the hall away from him again, Josh didn't know what to do, whether to go forward or just to leave, to give her space. But he couldn't take Charles' withering glare. It was humiliating to stand in the hallway amongst Jessie's co-stars and be the sole object of their derision and scorn. So he turned away and headed for another set of stairs—not the ones Jessie was heading down, towards the limo, but a set of stairs that would spit him out into the warm Miami evening, under not-yet-lit artificial lights and neon splendor. Maybe he could find a place nearby where he could have a beer, where he could hide from light and lick his wounds.

But then something came crashing into him, and grabbed fistfuls of his denim jacket. It was Jacob, who had been watching the whole thing go down.

"Where you going?! Where you going, Sawyer?"

Recoiling, Josh swiped the back of his hand across his eyes and faced Jacob. He didn't have to speak. His lost eyes said it all.

Jacob grabbed him again and shoved him backwards, hard against the wall so that Josh hit his head. "Coward! Fucking coward!"

"Geez Ryan, back off!" Josh rubbed his head and shoved Jacob away from him.

"YOU don't get to walk away from her. YOU started this mess, now you fucking clean it up!" Jacob was incensed, his entire body an overheated mass of shakes and tremors, his voice rising and falling with the effort to make this man *see*.

"I can't..." was all Josh managed.

"Don't be stupid, Josh! Don't let her walk away from you! Don't be a goddamned idiot! God, do you know what I...what I would give...?" Jacob started to back away, and turned in circles a few times as if he was lost, as if he had forgotten where he was.

Josh's voice stopped him cold. "You should be with her, Jacob. You should be with her."

Slowly, Jacob turned back and stared at Josh, incredulous.

Josh continued, stepping away from the wall as he pointed a finger at Jacob. "The way the two of you are when you're together...the music...you're in your own fucking universe, the two of you!"

"The music, remember? That's our thing, that's always gonna be *our* thing." Jacob's eyes flashed and said *stay the hell out of it!*

Josh waved his arms out to the sides and looked helplessly around him at all the little groups of hushed folks watching, including Charles and Dee. The older man had a viselike grip on his wife's arm so she wouldn't jump into the fray with two potentially violent wound-up men.

301

Josh heaved in a great breath and refocused. "You should be with her, Jacob. The way you two sing together. The way you look at each other." He swayed a little from side to side as he spoke. The whole hallway seemed over-lit, bright, slippery as grease. Out of control.

"You handing her to me, Sawyer? You giving up?"

"Look what I've done to her. How am I in any way good for that girl? All we do is hurt each other. Over and over."

Jacob studied him as the thoughts whirling around in his own head careened out of control. "If you let her go now, Sawyer, you're not ever going to get her back. Is that what you want?"

"I want her to be happy," is what Josh said, pinching his forehead hard to try to keep the pain away. His arms dropped. "That's all I want, Jacob. It's that simple."

Reeling, Jacob had to fight for breath. His lungs hurt, and the breaths he did manage to take were ragged and uneven. He stood still, and raked his mind over what Josh was telling him. Could it be true? Could it be possible? *Can I have Jessie, finally?* The sight of the distraught man in front of him, the one who was now rubbing his palms against his jean jacket as if he had to be moving or he would explode, was pitiful. *Maybe I am the better man,* Jacob caught himself thinking.

He straightened. He shook the cobwebs away and said to Josh, "You said you would never let her go. You just said that, in her dressing room, before the show!"

Locking his eyes into Jacob's, an even calm to his voice, Josh answered quietly. "No I didn't," he replied disconsolately. "I said she was mine. That's what I said. But I wasn't considering..." He left the sentence hanging, as if by speaking the words *she might not want to be, anymore* they might actually come true.

Swallowing, a surfeit of ragged feelings traipsing across his face, Jacob actually considered leaving Josh standing there alone while he, Jacob, took off down the hall after Jessie. But a sound off to his left caught his attention. It was Deirdre Keating, whose husband wouldn't let her go to Josh or Jacob, but she had a voice, and she used it. It wasn't a word, it was just a sound, a low clearing of her throat that jarred Jacob into looking over at her. When

302

he did, he saw only the slightest movement of her head—a shake? Not even, just a slight sideways motion that meant, clearly, *no*.

Crushed, Jacob knew he could do whatever the hell he wanted. And in the days to come he would kick himself again and again because he might have wedged his way in between Jessie and Josh on this night, or at least he thought perhaps he could have. He wasn't afraid to defy Dee, but there was a timeworn honor in battle, and so how could he take Jessie tonight, as Josh's war weary gift to him, when the night's new crushing defeats had yet to even settle?

He stepped forward, shoulders back, a defeated pride flooding his eyes. "Well, the thing is, Josh," Jacob started, inhaling deeply, "I can't do that. I can't take her like she's your goddamned concubine, free to give away to the highest bidder when you're too weak to hang on."

He let that register with Josh before continuing. "You see, the music is a temporary thing. It's only a small chunk out of our lives, out of who we are. Yeah, it's awesome, but," he gave Josh another push as his voice cracked again, "I had her for a while, remember? Without you? And you know something?"

Josh turned his face towards him and listened, his downcast eyes struggling to understand.

Jacob finished with a flourish of his arms, waving Josh towards the exit through which Jessie and Matt just disappeared. "I don't ever want to see that sadness in her eyes again. Go. Go, before I change my mind and talk myself into following her myself anyway. Please," he begged. "Just go."

Searching his eyes, Josh faltered. He wanted to run, to hide, to bury himself in booze and pass out on some barroom floor. He wanted to pound Jacob into a bloody pulp so the guy would leave his wife alone. But in the guy's eyes was a pain that decreed he was already battle-hard, and that he knew, at least for now, he had already lost the war.

"If you don't go," Jacob was now saying, cutting into Josh's thoughts as he shoved him again, his voice breaking, "I will. But the thing is, Josh, she's not gonna want me. She might be angry right now, but you know when she comes out of it, it's you she's gonna want."

Josh didn't move. He just stared at Jacob, unsure, and not quite understanding.

Jacob touched his shoulder, and gave him a gentle push this time. "Don't fuck this up," he said evenly. "She needs you. Don't walk away from her."

At that, incredulous because it hit him like a sucker punch that he'd almost let Jessie go, to Jacob who, in the end, proved to be a bigger man than Josh felt he himself could ever be, Josh finally lifted his shoulders and walked down the hall, trying to avoid the stares of everyone around him. He had to pass Charles, who now held Dee in his arms, and he stopped and looked at them, his desperate eyes searching theirs in a vain attempt to tell them he was not the enemy, and he would do his best to help get Jessie through this.

"I don't even know if she will have me," was all he managed before he started walking again.

Michael was at the end of the hall, holding open the door, and Josh saw him nod through the open door. The nod, Josh realized, was likely his acknowledgement to his brother Matt that Josh was coming with them.

"Thanks, man," Josh gulped as he slid by Michael and jogged down the stairs to the bigger door that opened into a back alley where their limo was waiting.

He looked up at Matt as he passed him, too, and as Matt closed the car door behind Josh and got into the front passenger seat, he half expected Jessie to start pounding on him again, to push him away. They sat in stoic silence as the car ghosted its way through the city's still light streets, and Josh marveled that this was possible, because he felt the streets should be as dark as he felt right now, with that sinister photo now out in the world for everyone to see, because of him.

He stole a look at Jessie once, and was surprised to see her sitting up straight, both hands folded in her lap, staring out of the window. He thought she would be slumped over.

He whispered to her, "Would you rather I was Jacob?" He touched her, and she recoiled. "I need to know, Jessie. Would you rather it was Jacob here in the car with you? It's not too late."

She hung her head then, and turned a little away from him. He didn't see the single tear slide down her cheek, but he knew it was there, because he felt it in the still air between them, a lonely marker for a lonely girl. He watched her wipe it away, and then he went back to staring at nothing on his own side of the big car.

At the airport, Matt jumped out and opened the door for them to exit. Josh got out quietly, and paced in a circle behind the car as Jessie slid over the seat and accepted Matt's hand to help her rise. She paused for a second as Matt stepped aside, ducking behind the steps that led up to the small jet.

Jessie started towards the plane without looking at Josh, the loose sides of her top flapping in the warm breeze, her bare back glistening in the new sundown, the magic hour photographers covet that was now making the sides of the white jet pop out in a radiant orange haze. But she stopped when she got to the bottom step, and Josh saw Matt signal to her. The man's eyes sought and then found Josh's. Slowly, Jessie turned.

She raised both hands to her mouth and covered it, as her shoulders finally slumped and she gave in to the exquisite pain that came with loving someone who had just so badly hurt her.

"I need you," she sobbed, to Josh's overwhelming and excruciating relief. "Not Jacob. I need *you*!"

And then she was in his arms, hanging on tight, and Josh's knees almost gave way at the thought he almost, a short while before, walked away and let Jacob have her.

The pretty pale eyes searched his as, behind Jessie, Matt bowed into the jet to confer with the pilot.

"Home," she whispered. "This is home. Anywhere with you."

Then Jessie took Josh's big hand and placed it against her belly. She laid her own hand over his and told him, "There's a little tiny heartbeat here, Josh. A little *tiny* heartbeat. And it's there because we love each other. And because we made it."

He stared at her, not hearing at first. Unbelieving. But then Josh swore he felt it, the heartbeat, pulsating just below his fingers, deep in the belly of the woman he loved, and he almost crumbled. But he couldn't, he couldn't crumble because he had to be strong. For her. For them. And because Jessie just told him she needed him. *Him.*

"Really?" He sought the truth in her eyes, and he found it when a certain peace passed over the diaphanous gaze watching him now for his reaction, after the type of news that could only do one thing—change his life.

Forever.

SUSAN RODGERS

"Yeah," she said, wiping away the last tear she had left to give the harsh world this day. Dipping her head in that Jessie way of hers, she smiled. He started to sob quietly, and held her close.

"It's okay now," she said, backing away after a moment and laying a warm palm flat against his cheek. "We'll go to the ranch for as long as we can, before you have to go to New York, and then we'll face the world again. Together."

"No P.E.I.?" He asked her.

"Not this year," she answered. "This year it's your turn. The ranch and then New York. You're sexy as hell on a horse."

Laughter floating on the warm breeze was what brought Matt to the open doorway. His heart melted at the sight of a couple he knew was so in love with each other that nothing could keep them apart for long. Not even a semi-nude photo that the world, by now, was tweeting and re-tweeting and probably publicly condemning.

He stepped lightly down to the asphalt and touched Jessie's shoulder. "It's time to go," he said.

Josh's moist eyes blinked in the orange glow-light, which accented his newfound amazement and wonder. "We're having a baby, Matt. Can you believe that?"

"Congratulations." Matt stuck out a hand, smiling with genuine happiness for both of them.

"You're not surprised," Josh's voice rose curiously.

Attempting to put out another small fire, Jessie rather hastily interjected, "He tried to give me Baileys the other night."

Josh's laugh was sincere, and he gripped Matt's shoulder with one hand as he and Jessie passed by. He draped his other arm around his wife's shoulders and led her to the jet.

As they mounted the few steps, Matt called out to Jessie. "Would you please tell Charles and Dee, Jessie? I'm having a helluva time keeping this secret. It's too big!"

She turned, and smiled down at him. "You tell them, Matt. I don't plan on seeing them for a while. But you come see us. Bring your family."

As the outdoor crew closed the jet's door, Matt backed away. He sighed. *I'm not telling them,* he told himself. Then he resolved to make it his business to reunite Jessie with her Vancouver parents. He would do whatever it took to restore their faith in Josh, and crush the divide that had grown between them. He just hoped Josh would do his part.

He sat by the driver in the limo as the Keating jet taxied down the runway and flew off into the setting sun, its passengers' destination a small unknown ranch in Alberta's Kananaskis country.

He told the driver, "Back to the concert, Gustavo. I'd say it's just about over now."

Matt had to collect Charles and Dee and look into their pained eyes and not tell them the waif they'd raised into a star was going to give birth in... when, November? He had high hopes for this baby. It alone would likely have the power to bring the families back together.

Forgiveness, was the thought he sent on silent wings to the big jet. *You hear me, Jessie?*

He was sure the plane dipped its sun-kissed wings just before getting lost in the willowy fluff of a feathery white cloud.

But then the car turned a corner, left the airport, and the plane was out of sight.

Chapter Thirty-three

Josh had to leave for a week to shoot the pilot for Jon's show in Toronto, but Jessie chose to stay behind at the ranch and hang out with her Aunt Evelyn. She was in hiding mode, and the chipmunks and squirrels she met on the steep woodsy hiking trails around Canmore or on the banks of the sparkling Bow River seemed less judgmental than a curious public. After Josh's return, they settled in to their ranch at the base of the Canadian Rockies, but eventually had to go back to Vancouver so Josh could pack for the film shoot in New York. Jessie planned to meet him there after the press junket for *Mystic Nights*, which was premiering in September. It was with heavy hearts that they left the gorgeous mountain vista where they'd stayed sequestered from the world for two short months riding horses, reading in the sun porch with their heads in each other's laps, and arguing playfully over whose turn it was to do the dishes.

Before they left, during their sequestered time in the historic Bow Valley, Jessie communicated with Deirdre over email, business stuff only, but she refused to correspond with Charles. She canceled previously scheduled engagements, including visits to her North American shelters, and when Dee asked to come visit, Jessie's answer was a staunch *no*.

One day, at the end of their Alberta stay, one of Dee's emails was worded differently, in a different style and using language not normally used by Dee. Jessie read it before noticing that, at the end, the email was signed *Charles*.

Figures, she said under her breath so she wouldn't wake Josh, who was napping next to her in the sun porch as she checked emails as well as the Internet buzz about herself and Josh, which had faded as expected in the last few weeks. Surprisingly, what she discovered was most people saw the image the way Josh did, which was not as porn, per se, or even as erotica, which she knew Caryn claimed it was—either that or 'art.' Instead they perceived, in the image of Jessie, a sad, lonely and very lost young woman.

Now, she re-read Charles' email, which saddened her. After the initial fury of that heated night, and the ones before it, she wasn't surprised to find she truly missed the power couple. *But making up is always harder than fighting, isn't it*, she told herself.

Jessie, we had a frank discussion with Matt today. Imagine our surprise when he told us you and Josh are expecting a baby. He said he was waiting for you to tell us, but now that you're coming back to Vancouver he's afraid the beans will inadvertently be spilled when someone recognizes you. So he felt inclined to tell us himself. I won't pretend we're not hurt. But at the same time we want you to know we're very happy for both of you and that we pray every day for you to allow us back into your lives. We understand the due date to be sometime in late November or early December, around the time Mystic Nights starts shooting season two. They'll be excited to have a new baby on the set, I'm sure. We hear Jonathon's new series has finally been greenlit. Josh must be happy about that since he'll be working with his good buddy Steve again. Not sure when it is starting up, but I gather it's sometime after the New York film, perhaps around the time Mystic Nights starts up again. Do you plan to be in Toronto for the birth of the baby? On that note, I pray again you will come see us when you get back to Vancouver. Safe travels, Charles.

It was the first time he'd used Dee's email address to try to get through to Jessie. Her heart softened at this, and she wistfully chewed on a fingernail as she considered writing back. In the end she punched in a short note that finally included Charles' name in the salutation.

Hi Charles and Dee,
I'm glad Matt finally told you. I asked him to before I left Miami but he's a stubborn old goat, isn't he? As am I, I know you're thinking. I will come and see you when I get back. I'm sorry things got so messed up. Josh is well, and happy.

*He's napping here beside me, or practically on top of me I guess you could say,
with his head on my lap and a hand on my belly, which makes it hard to type
since he's kind of in the way. I love him desperately and I know he will be a wonderful father. I just wish the two of you could believe this as well.*

Hugs, Jessie

She backspaced over the 'Hugs' part, deleting it, before hesitantly frowning and retyping the word. She closed the laptop after hitting 'send.' Ruefully,
Jessie woke her husband by bending down and blowing on the hair covering his forehead.

He stirred underneath the gentle loving feel of Jessie's breath and then the
touch of her fingers on his cheek, and he opened sleepy eyes at her, blinking
as a dreamlike fog dissipated and floated him back to reality.

"Hey, you," she said, beaming down at him. "Good dreams?"

"The best," he replied with a grin as he laid his head back down on one
folded arm, wrapping his fingers around hers with the free hand. "I dreamed
about you."

"What was I doing?" She bent over and brushed her lips along his forehead.

"Walking," he answered. "In some kind of field, or meadow. And you had
our little girl by your side. You were both so happy…covered in, like, this
golden light. I was watching from the side."

"Little girl, huh?"

"Yeah," he said, yawning. "She was beautiful, really beautiful. Like a little mini you. Her name was Grace."

He looked up at her again, and she melted at the simple hope and peace
in his eyes.

"Grace," she echoed. "I was thinking, if it's a girl…"

"What," he asked, pulling himself up to a sitting position and looping an
arm around her shoulders so Jessie could rest her head against his side, "is this
a name question?"

"Yeah," she laughed, poking him in the ribs. "Just listen. I was kind of
wondering how you feel about maybe calling her Emily. Like my mom."

"My mom's middle name was Grace," Josh offered quietly. "I suppose
that's why in the dream our daughter was Grace."

310

"Grace-Emily," Jessie said simply, entwining her fingers through his.

"Hmm. Or Emily-Grace. Wow. Okay." Josh said it again, trying it out, his voice humbled at the way the name passed between his lips. "Emily-Grace. Sounds better that way."

"And if it's a boy?"

"David, I think." Josh's eyes softened as he smiled down at his wife, who was playing with the sleeve of his T-shirt, absently wrapping it around and around one finger as they talked.

"David Wes," she wondered idly, "or David Jonathon?"

They shook their heads simultaneously. "Nah!"

"Just David," Josh said. "That works for me. We can't have Wes and Jon fighting over our baby."

"David it is." She twisted around and stretched so she could kiss him. "Thank you, Josh."

"I guess we have to have at least two rug-rats, then," he said. "Thanks for letting me sleep today. I may need to stock up on my zzzzzz's."

"Sorry I had to wake you at all but Evelyn and Gary will be here soon. And I'm aiming for five, by the way. Kids."

He stretched adorably, catlike, and Jessie watched, her eyebrows raised in approval. "Damn," she said. "Do you think we have time for a snuggle before they get here?" She slipped a hand up under her husband's T-shirt and pressed it against his stomach. His abs tightened in reflex and she bent down and brushed her lips over his warm skin.

Her question was answered with the sound of tire treads on the loose gravel outside. "Damn," she said again, groaning. "Later, maybe. Okay, husband?"

"Anytime, little one," Josh agreed. He kissed her tenderly before wandering over to the screen door and yanking it open to greet their visitors. It screeched as it always did on its old hinges, and then again as Jessie followed him.

"Hey, Evelyn," she waved. "Glad you two old lovebirds could make it!"

As the men went off to inspect the horses and talk about the care of the ranch during Jessie and Josh's upcoming lengthy absences, the ladies settled into wicker chairs on the verandah. They sipped on lemonade Evelyn had made and poured into a thermos. It was a hot early summer day, and they were melting.

"I have news," Evelyn told Jessie after they were comfy.

"News?" Jessie's heart picked up its pace. "About what?" She wrapped both hands tightly around her cool glass.

"Your grandmother decided she wants to meet you after all." Evelyn delivered this whopper the way she'd delivered the lemonade, matter-of-factly and pragmatically.

"Oh," was Jessie's response. "Is that all." She looked over at her aunt. "I just thought…you know, after the photo…she would never want to meet me. Ever. I figured that horse left the stable ages ago."

Evelyn threw back her head and chortled. "We need to get you back to the city, Jessie. You're turning into a country girl."

"It's scary, isn't it?" Jessie replied, twisting a sweaty muck of hair into a ringlet. "How quickly a person adapts to their environment? Can you believe the first radio station I turn on in the morning now is country?"

"As long as you don't start playing it," was Evelyn's cautious response. She paused at the innocent wide-eyed expression on Jessie's face. "Oh no," she hollered to the breathless air. "You're not writing it, though, are you? Just playing old Garth Brooks tunes for your husband?"

Jessie nodded slowly, eyes still wide. Then she crumbled and joined Evelyn in her raucous laughter. "I can't help myself," she moaned. "Maybe it's the being pregnant thing. It sure as hell changes other stuff, like my sense of smell!"

"The world of pop music will never be the same," said Evelyn wisely. "Nor country, I expect."

With a final giggle, Jessie steered the conversation back to her Ontario relatives. "So she wants to meet me, huh? What about my sister?"

"Not so much. But she'll come around. Martha's old, Jessie. My mother has come to realize her time on earth is short. I think she was just afraid, before."

"Afraid of what?"

"Of the river of emotion seeing you is going to stir up. Do me a favor?"

"Of course. Anything, Evelyn."

"Don't stir up any more than you have to? Just go easy on her, okay?"

"Okay. I promise."

They sat back and relaxed, sipping on their lemonades and admiring the majestic mountain panorama before them, while Jessie wrestled with a new knowing, that she could now make plans to meet her grandmother and, hopefully, her half-sister.

Josh had crawled underneath the split rail fence to the corral, Gary right behind him, and both men were slapping the chestnut horse, Misty, here and there, as they discussed her care. Josh grabbed the horse's hoof and pried it upwards, and pointed deep inside it as Gary stooped over to look.

"Gawd, I love the way his hair falls over his face like that when he bends over," Jessie remarked dreamily, tucking her feet up underneath her on the wide cushioned chair. "He's something, isn't he, Evelyn?" She let her eyes wander over Josh's body as he showed off his horse—the western boots, the loose jeans, the white T-shirt that clung to his chest, moist and grungy in the heat. As if he knew she was watching him, Josh stood and wiped the rogue hair off his cheek. He smiled broadly at his wife, and even Evelyn felt the air suddenly stir.

"He is a good man, Jessie," she said, patting her niece's knee. "You have my permission to keep him. Should you decide to keep him, that is." She winked and Jessie slapped her arm playfully.

"Always and forever," she whispered. "He's my guy." She laid a hand protectively over her growing belly.

She turned to Evelyn, her face curious, her mind drifting back and forth between the images, known and unknown, who were now peopling her consciousness. "So the old broad wants to meet me after all."

Evelyn chuckled, and tipped back her lemonade. "Old broad, huh?"

"What's she like? My grandmother? Is she an old broad?"

"Nah. She's sweet."

"But you and my mom cut her off." Jessie's voice was quiet, contemplative.

"Life got in the way, honey. You'll see."

"I can't believe she finally wants to meet me. Maybe it's because of the baby."

"Maybe she just got used to the idea, Jessie." Evelyn smiled deeply. But then she sighed. "No, honey," she said then, retracting her statement and changing course. "That's actually not it. The truth is, she saw that photo—"

"As did everyone else in the world, apparently," growled Jessie.

"Well, be glad it got out there, hon."

"Why would I ever be glad of that?" The thought sickened her.

"Because after your grandmother saw it, she called me. You want to know what she said?"

Tentatively, Jessie answered. "What?" A curious frown replaced the earlier happy smiles.

Evelyn leaned close to Jessie and whispered conspiratorially. "She said 'call that girl and bring her to me. That child needs a hug.'"

When she sat back, Evelyn sipped on her lemonade quietly. Jessie needed to compose herself. Then the older woman touched her niece's knee again. "You will love her, Jessie. I swear. You've got her smile, you know. It lights up your whole face, when you're happy and willing to let others in."

Jessie ducked her head and fought the wetness that suddenly appeared in her blue eyes. "Okay," she said. She looked up. "Soon, okay? Before I chicken out." Dee flashed before her mind and she paused. Evelyn caught the hesitation.

"What is it?"

"It's just…Deirdre, that's all. Suddenly I'm missing her."

Evelyn took her hand and held it tight. "You know, Jessie," she said, tapping two fingers on her knee as she held the hand, "there's this thing about a woman's heart."

"Oh? You're not going to break into lyrics from a country song, are you, Evelyn?"

Evelyn's smile was as broad and wide as her freckled face beneath the ubiquitous grey ponytail. "No, honey," she said. "I just wanted to tell you there's room for lots in there. Lots of people. In a woman's heart. Many, in fact. But you have to let them in. That's something only you can do."

"Evelyn?"

"Yes, Jessie?"

"Thank you."

Evelyn sat back and finished off her cool drink. "You're very, very welcome, my dear."

Together they watched their men wander around the corral, chatting as men do, legs apart and arms crossed.

"Jessie?"

A contented sigh stretched between them. "Yeah?"

"There really is a mighty fine view from this verandah."

Their laughter made its way to the corral, and Misty whinnied in response. Josh looked up from the dirt he was toeing during his deep discussion with Gary, and he leaned one arm on the split rail fence. He lost Gary's voice for a second as he watched his pregnant wife laugh and swap secrets with her aunt, and he stifled the urge to go over and tell her he wanted to keep her there in the protective sphere the Alberta ranch offered in the shadow of the Rocky Mountains. That taking her back out into a very public life could not be good for her—for them—ever again.

But he choked the thought back, and then he looked up at Gary again. "What was that? Sorry, I—I was watching the ladies for a second. Not sure what's in that thermos your lady brought." He was grasping at straws, because he knew Evelyn would not have brought alcohol to his expectant wife. But it was such sweet joy to see Jessie happy. There was no doubt in Josh's mind that taking her home would break the magical spell.

He looked over one more time, and caught Jessie's eye, but he shrugged off the niggling worry and waved. There would be time for worry another day, for tonight there was good company, a beautiful landscape, a happy woman by his side and, in a few months, there would also be a new child to light their lives.

He clapped Gary on the shoulder. "Come on," he said. "It's sweltering out here. Let's take our gals inside where it's cool, and you can show me how to make those barbecued ribs you're always bragging about."

When he got to Jessie he took her hand and helped lever her off the chair.

She parted her lips and studied him, a hint of a smile on her flushed cheeks. "You missing me?" she asked him.

"Always," he said, placing both arms around her waist and leaning over her newly swelling belly for a sweet salty kiss.

"But you were just over there," she teased. "Like, maybe fifty feet away? You could see me the whole time." She kissed him back, running her tongue over first his top lip, then the bottom. He shivered involuntarily.

315

"Sometimes that isn't enough," he said, recalling the night of the *Mystic Nights* concert when he'd watched her on stage with Jacob, so close, yet so untouchable.

"Yeah," was her simple answer, and they shared an intimate kiss that contained its own sweet promise of the night to come, after their bellies were full and their guests on their way home.

"Charles and Dee know about the baby," she whispered before she let him go. "And my grandmother finally wants to meet me."

Silently, Josh wished he could climb inside Jessie and protect her forever. Not just the physical her, but the soul part too. He swallowed down the fear but not before she saw it rise to the surface.

"Sweet Josh," she said tenderly, letting the tips of her fingers trace his cheek, from the corner of his eye to his lip. "Stop worrying. We've weathered some pretty rough storms, you and me. And yet here we are, together, in this incredible place. We'll be fine. I'll be fine."

"Promise?"

"I do. I promise."

The eerie *scriitttcch* of the screen door pulled them apart, finally. Gary stood there with a cook's apron over his shirt, and a jar of Miss Diana's sauce in his hand.

"This is it," he called to Josh. "This is my secret. I admit it. My sauce is bottled."

Josh's laugh warmed Jessie's heart as they walked towards the door arm in arm.

"I should have known," he said, still chuckling as he held the door for Jessie. "Things are usually simpler than they seem."

"You got that right," she said in response, touching his stomach and then hooking her fingers over his belt and pulling on it as she walked by. "Come on, cowboy. Me and Emily-Grace are starving."

Emily-Grace. Josh rolled the name around on his tongue, and pictured the beautiful little golden girl from his dream. He thought about the mother he'd long ago lost to cancer, and the texture and musky scent of the velvet seat as he sank down into it as a child to watch her perform with the symphony.

As he followed Jessie into their ranch home, the thought crossed his mind that good times come, and then they go. The world never stands still. It rolls around and things change.

Some days are dust.

But some days are diamonds.

From the corral over yonder, Misty neighed her agreement. Josh sidled his way into the kitchen and dug out a knife. He had ribs to cut, to sauce, and to barbecue. He laughed his way through dinner prep and eating, and then that night, in bed, he made love to his wife.

Early the next morning, he gathered their things and packed them into the back of their rented SUV. He guided his sleepy wife to the passenger side, propped a pillow behind her neck and head, and closed the door gently behind her.

And then Josh pointed the vehicle down the long driveway, and started them on the journey towards their Vancouver home.

Chapter Thirty-four

"We're making them Pad Thai," Jessie was saying to Dee as, from the side window in the kitchen she eyed Steve and Sophie, who'd just arrived and were out in the driveway conversing with Josh as they swapped stories and reveled in the sheer thrill of being together again.

God, I've missed Steve, she said to herself as an afterthought. *And Jacob,* she added. *I miss Jacob, too.*

Charles stepped into the home from the back door by the pool deck. He slid the glass door shut behind him and strode nervously into the center of the living area. Fidgeting with her fingers in front of the swollen belly she knew he'd notice right off the bat, as Dee had, Jessie turned to greet him.

He didn't hesitate. Charles marched forward and took Jessie into his arms. He held her tight, his throat constricted. When he found his voice, he held her at arms length and chided her gently. "We love you," he affirmed. "I love you. And I'm sorry. We missed you terribly, Jessie."

She accepted the hug and ducked her head, ashamed for shutting this couple out of her married life. She held onto Charles' sleeves and looked up at him. "I love you too," she said while, behind her, Dee bit her knuckles to keep herself from becoming too emotional at this sensitive reunion. Charles pulled Jessie close again, speech not forthcoming. There were no words adequate for the sorrow all of them felt during Jessie and Josh's last week in Vancouver, and then in Miami. The ache hung heavy over them today.

"You can stay," Jessie tossed in hopefully, trying to lighten the mood. "For the Pad Thai. Charlie and Jane are coming, too. With Stella."

"No, that's fine, Jessie," Dee said, coming to her side while her husband composed himself. "You enjoy your friends. Us old fogies are meeting Jack and Lydia for dinner, anyway, at that new French place in Kits."

Jessie couldn't stem the wave of caution passing over her. Was this relationship fully salvageable as long as Josh was her husband?

"Because of Josh?" she asked, raising her chin as alarm bells went off in Charles and Dee's brains. "Is that why you won't stay?"

"No, honey," Dee replied honestly. "Not because of Josh." She took her husband's hand.

Jessie sighed and wandered back over to the window. She stood on her toes and strained her neck to see Charlie and Jane pulling into the driveway in an SUV. "Charlie looks weird driving a Mommy car. Don't you think?" She added dejectedly, "I kinda miss the old days, like the *Drifters* season two days. Before Deuce." *Before Jacob.*

There was no response for that comment that anyone could find in their stores of careful and appropriate remarks, and besides, the Keatings knew a rhetorical comment when one was placed before them.

Dee turned the tide. "How are you feeling, honey?"

"Oh, I'm good," Jessie responded, smiling carefully. She took Dee's hand and placed it at her side. "She's kicking now. Can you feel that? Busy little thing."

"She?" Charles asked hopefully. "Do you know for sure?"

"No, Charles, we actually don't know," Jessie answered. "We want it to be a surprise. But we feel like it's a girl. Josh had this dream, actually..." She shrugged and let her thoughts drift off.

"She can play with Stella, " Dee offered brightly. "She won't be all that much younger, really."

"Or marry Stella if it's a boy," Charles threw in.

"Starting already? Really, Charles," Jessie chuckled. But at the quick tension that creased his face, she added gently, "Don't worry Grampie, boy or girl, we'll let you choose the partner. Okay? Might as well not try to hide the elephant in the room, eh?"

He shot her an anxious look before realizing she was joking. Then what she'd called him sank in. "Grampie?" he asked as a thin film of moisture once again assailed his buoyant eyes.

"Well, it's either that or Poppie, and I think you look more like the Grampie type. What do you think, Grammie?" She posed the question to a quickly blushing Deirdre.

"I think I like it. Very much," Dee said, wrapping an arm around Jessie's blooming waist. "We'll go now, dear, and leave you to your dinner and your friends. But come see us tomorrow, okay? For brunch? Matt will be there with Julie. Carlotta's making a cream cheese quiche and some variation of an arugula salad."

"I don't know, Dee." Jessie grabbed a dish towel, and started wringing it around her hands. "I don't know if we're ready for that."

The back door slid open then and the gang marched in. Hugs and greetings were shared, before Josh cautiously made his way back to the kitchen where the Keatings were still talking quietly with Jessie.

He nodded at Charles, but had a hard time holding the man's gaze. Dee was a little kinder, but not overtly friendly.

"I think we won't do that brunch," Jessie said, the tension in the air thickening as nobody seemed to know what to say.

Josh tried to find words that would help heal the wounds he'd caused, but it was a losing battle. His mouth was dry, his eyes searching, hurting. He looked over at Jessie and she smiled in sympathy. She reached out a hand. He took it, brushed his lips against the back of it, and then he wheeled around and wandered back into the living area.

Charlie and Steve were there, swapping stories of their TV and film set lives, when he approached, glum, hands in his pockets. Their women had wandered to an upstairs bedroom to try to settle Stella for a nap.

Steve slapped Josh on the back. "It's been a while, soldier. You doing okay?"

"Working on it," was Josh's downcast response. He glanced over his shoulder at Charles and Dee.

Charlie was never one to hold back his thoughts. He dove in headfirst, his voice low so as to avoid alerting Charles to what he wanted to know. "Did you cheat on her?"

At Josh's shocked expression he added nonchalantly, "We see Charles and Dee all the time, Josh. I know that's what's driven a wedge between you."

"That and the other thing we won't bother mentioning," Steve said, raising his eyebrows.

"Can you two clowns maybe not stick your heads up my butt right now? And I already told you, Charlie. The answer's no." Josh was adamant and, in all seriousness, really quite afraid of what Charles might overhear. He gestured towards the back pool deck, and the guys went out there instead.

"Look, Josh," Charlie started. "This may be the only chance I get to talk to you without the girls around. Whether or not you cheated on Jessie is your business. The two of you. As a couple. But that doesn't mean I'm not going to offer you a word or two of advice."

"I didn't," Josh exclaimed again. "Okay? I didn't. As I already told you. I—well, I'm not going to say I wasn't tempted, but I knew what I had waiting for me. So I didn't." He swallowed bitterly before adding, "I worked too hard to get her, you know? We lost so much…so much time. There was no way I was going to take a chance on messing that up. Okay, Charlie? Is that what you want to hear? So you can take it back to Charles?"

"This is the thing, Josh." Charlie was sitting on a chaise lounger across from Josh. He stared hard at him, demanding he listen, while Steve, standing nearby, quietly looked on. "Whether or not you caved that time, or the one before that—"

"Oh, Jesus," Josh gasped, making a move to get up and go. "I don't need this."

Charlie stood and faced him. "Yeah, you do, actually. You need to hear this, Sawyer."

The earnest, sympathetic cast to Charlie's flecked eyes stopped Josh in his tracks. He paused, and looked back through the glass door to see Jessie watching them, curious.

Josh ran a hand through his hair and sat back down. Charlie followed.

"It's like this. Once you cross that road—and believe me, after a few solid years of the same old car the shiny new ones start to look pretty good—well, it gets damn harder to come back. And then, each time it just gets worse. The guilt, the avoidance, the lies. It's a cold dark road, Josh. You could lose everything." He paused. "I did."

"He put you up to this, Charlie? Is this a threat?" Josh looked back inside. Charles had wandered to the door and was watching them, stoically.

"No," Charlie insisted, as Steve's eyes narrowed. Steve stepped over behind Josh in solidarity. "Let's call it 'making up for past wrongs.' I screwed her over big time. And I won't stand by and let you do the same. She deserves someone she can depend on."

"Our relationship is none of your business."

"The hell it isn't."

The two men glared at each other, one rather emphatically eyeing the other, who was firing daggers at his friend.

The glass door slid open and Charles stepped out. Inside, Jessie tensed and locked her eyes into Steve's, who shrugged nonchalantly as if to say *what the hell?*

Charles wandered over to the boys, who stood to greet him without losing the sizzling eye contact between them.

"Charles," Charlie acknowledged.

"Charlie," Charles replied.

"We're having a heart to heart," Charlie told him. "Got anything you want to add?"

At that, Josh finally broke eye contact with Charlie, and looked over at Jessie's producer. Sticks were suddenly in his throat, piling in and choking him. He felt so cornered he thought he might actually be sick. It had been a while since Charles Keating and he were in the same space, and it hadn't been pleasant. Like Jacob, Josh felt intimidated in the man's presence at the best of times. And this day was not one of the best.

Charles tilted his head and regarded Josh. Something in his heart broke when he saw the anguish in the younger man's eyes, and he tried to smile, but it came out lopsided.

"I'd just like to add that I'm sorry," he said, to Josh's surprise. "I am sorry I doubted you, Josh. But I'm also sorry you got messed up with that Caryn woman."

Josh moved his mouth to speak but Charles stopped him with a raised hand. "Let me finish," he said. "You were never my first choice for Jessie."

Someone in the open doorway gasped. It was Jessie. In the silence, the muffled sounds of little baby Stella gurgling and the quiet laughter of Sophie and Jane, who it seemed were playing with the baby instead of trying to encourage her to sleep, floated through an open window.

Jessie stepped into the fray and accosted Charles. "I think you should leave," she said, shoulders rising and her heart sinking.

"Please, Jessie. I need Josh to hear me out." Charles was the closest to tears he'd been since…well, since the night he and Dee were told by Matt that Jessie was pregnant. Not by her. By *Matt*. Months after she knew herself. Instead of a joyous announcement, it was a pained proclamation.

Josh squared his shoulders and faced the man. But Jessie could see the fear in his eyes. They all could. But she backed up and stayed by the door. This was between two men she loved dearly. She would have to wait to touch Josh, to let him know she was there for him.

Charles knew the stakes, but he had talked this conversation over with his wife, who stood by Jessie now. They rehearsed it like they rehearsed Jessie's lines with her, sometimes. But the plan was almost thwarted when they arrived at the Sawyer home and found it about to be full of good friends and dinner plans.

"Josh, let me try this again. I accepted you because you made my girl happy. But I have always been nervous that you'd regress back into addictions or lose your temper with her or," he hesitated, "or accept the many offers that come the way of a good looking actor whose star has skyrocketed rather quickly."

Blinking back at him, Josh waited. He still didn't trust himself to speak, despite the comfort of his good friend Steve nearby.

"You left her alone in P.E.I. You messed around with a woman on the set in Virginia where, I have been told, you laid down your bike and almost got killed."

From the door, Jessie groaned at the reminder.

They both ignored her, although Josh knew he'd likely get a few extra hugs and admonishments from Jessie later.

"You got involved with this Caryn woman insofar as even going to her rather seedy place of business. More than once."

Jessie leaned her head against the doorframe and closed her eyes. She pictured Misty in the corral, romping and playing, Josh happy and carefree on the horse's back, the wind in his hair and the muscles in his arms bulging.

"You stirred up a hornet's nest that has changed the perception of Jessie in the public eye. Although, granted, I know it wasn't your intention. Your actions backfired on you."

Josh stood his ground, but his shoulders were sinking under all the weight Charles was dumping on him. It wasn't rage he was feeling at the man's statements, it was more of a broken down feeling, like he'd let everyone down with his bad decisions. But most of all...well, he'd let Jessie down.

"What I have to say to you now, Josh, is I understand some things better now. I've had some time to think, and between my wife and Matt I think I've come to some conclusions. The main one is Jessie loves you so, by affiliation, I have to accept you." His eyes softened. "I want to accept you. You're going to be the father of my first grandbaby." Charles' eyes were moist again now, and he knew the impact he was having on Josh, who was still standing before him, trembling slightly, fists clenching and unclenching.

"I won't lie to you and tell you I'm thrilled you were Jessie's choice, Josh. It means you have a lot of proving yourself to do. For me and for my girls. All my girls. But I've accepted that you were, and nothing makes me happier than," he was choking on his emotion now, as Josh stood before him and sucked up his own discomfort in order to let the man have his say, "nothing makes me happier than seeing Jessie wrap her arms around the man she loves. Nothing."

Dee snuck out from behind Jessie and crawled under her husband's arm. He looked down at her. "Well, maybe one thing," Charles said, and kissed the top of her head.

Jessie stayed where she was, but her small voice drifted over to them. "Nothing makes you happier than the money you make from the music I write about being in love, Charles."

That broke the ice, and they all laughed, with the exception of Josh, who understood the nature of Charles' honesty, but who still felt it was in fact some sort of veiled threat. As the others regrouped, and Jane and Sophie joined them with a very non-sleepy baby wriggling around in Sophie's arms, Josh fixed his gaze on Charlie.

"I'm not you, Charlie," he said simply. "I will never go down that road."

"Never say never," was Charlie's response. And then he walked away.

"Wow," Steve remarked to Josh when the gang had gone back inside, oohhhing and ahhhing over the baby, "that wasn't intense or anything." For the second time that afternoon, he asked his friend, "Are you seriously okay?"

"Not really," Josh answered. "But I will be." He looked over at Steve. "Have you ever considered stepping out on Sophie?"

Steve threw up his arms. "Not this dude," he exclaimed. "Just that one time, with..."

"Yeah. With Jessie." Josh frowned. Then he inhaled deeply and changed tack. "Did you actually really say dude just then? Man, it's good you finally left California."

"Now I'll start saying eh again. Eh?" Steve slapped Josh on the back and wandered over to Jessie, who was still leaning on the doorframe, watching them. He placed a hand flat against her belly and smiled at her, his dimples lighting his face in a way that made her smile broadly at him.

"Hey, little girl," he said before gathering her into his arms for a hug. "Momma to be, huh? Looks good on you."

"You're next," she said, moving his hand to a place near the side where the baby usually kicked. "Sophie's not putting Jane's baby down."

"That's cool," he remarked, grinning, when he felt a butterfly motion beneath his fingers. "Weird, but definitely cool."

"I guess we'll finally be seeing more of you? And hopefully Sophie?"

"In Toronto, yeah. I hope you'll be around some."

"Lots," she answered, smiling over at Josh, who was hanging around like a lost puppy, waiting for his turn to hold his wife after Charles' confession, which was still weighing heavily on him.

Steve glanced behind him and saw the electricity pass between his two good friends. "Okay, okay," he grinned. "I'll make my own Pad Thai. That's what we're having, right? Pad Thai? Why don't we just order from the Noodle Box?" He moved off into the house, pecking Jessie's cheek on the way in.

Josh finally made his way over to Jessie, and leaned against her so their foreheads touched. He placed his hands on her hips and closed his eyes.

"You're trembling," Jessie said, worry lines suddenly manifesting by her eyes. "Are you feeling okay?"

"No," he answered dismally. "Not really."

She leaned back and laid a palm across his forehead. "Babe, you're warm."

Instinctively she slipped a hand under his shirt and ran fingers over his scar. "This feels warm to me."

"It's a hot day, Jessie." Josh couldn't muster the energy to open his eyes.

"Charles was hard on you."

His heavy sigh was founded in his toes. "He's a tough nut to crack."

"He's all bark and no bite, Josh. He'll settle down."

"Yeah. If you say so." But his tone said he didn't believe her.

"Come. We have to feed the masses. Then it's early to bed for my adorable husband."

Finally, Josh opened his eyes and looked at her. He smiled once, just a little, to reassure Jessie. They went inside, to family, to friends, and to a hard earned but somewhat reserved joy.

Chapter Thirty-five

"You didn't dedicate a song to me, Jacob. What was that about?" Tom Ryan wrapped an arm around his son as they ascended the steps to the legendary singer's private jet. In his low rumbly nicotine-nurtured voice he joked, "Why did you send one out to Jessie Wheeler and not to me?"

"You're doing just fine. Jessie needs all the help she can get."

"That's a lie. She's one of the biggest stars on the planet."

"Hence the need to send her a song. With a few prayers tossed in." Jacob bounded up the rest of the steps and disappeared inside the plane as his dad watched in wonder.

"Ah. I see. Women trump dads." Tom Ryan trudged upwards, a small smile on his lips. He lifted a hand to secure his battered fedora a little more tightly. Inside, he dropped down next to Jacob and immediately started rolling a joint.

"You can smoke in here?" Jacob asked, somewhat incredulous.

Tom shot him a look. "It's me fecking plane, son. I can set it on fire if I want to."

He handed the smoke to Jacob, fished out a lighter, and together they settled back as the plane's crew prepared for takeoff.

"Press junket was okay, son?"

"Tolerable," Jacob grunted, an edgy verve coloring his quick response.

"Hence the shout out for Jessie? She's on your mind?"

Jacob thought about that for a moment. "Yeah. But the shout out wasn't anything special. She's always on my mind." He shrugged further into his seat, stretched out his legs, and crossed one ankle over the other. "The extra

327

prayers part…those were actually for me." He closed his eyes as the pot worked its way through his system.

His father watched him start to smile slowly.

Tom Ryan settled deeper into his own seat, and then took the smoke from between his son's calloused fingers. He inhaled deeply, relying on his years of practice as an old musical legend.

"Ah," he said again. "I see."

~~ ~~

Michael and Kelly trundled down the road in Michael's old red pick-up. He pulled into his lane, in the home they were now sharing and, whistling, he swung around the front of the pick-up and opened the passenger side door. He lifted Kelly out, and adjusted the long white veil she'd tucked into her hair earlier.

He kicked the door shut behind them, and carried her up the walk and then up the steps to his 1940's two story home. He almost tripped once, but her laughter stopped him, and so Michael tried harder to stay upright the rest of the way.

At the door he fumbled for the keys. When his fingers found them, he inserted a key in the lock. It didn't work, so he tried another key, with more success this time.

He kicked the door open and carried his new bride inside.

Outside, the old red truck stood guard. On its downward drift, the sun melted into a glorious pink and orange ribbon, and its fingers touched the older home, nestling the newly married couple in its warm embrace.

~~ ~~

Matt stood at the Keatings' kitchen counter and thumbed through the Globe and Mail. Casually, he scanned a few articles while, around him, Julie and Carlotta fussed over a cake they were icing for Charles and Dee's wedding anniversary. He turned his head slightly to watch them at the far counter, where they were arguing over which tips to use for the decorating tube.

Shaking his head with a smile, he went back to the paper.

A caption caught his eye, and the smile disappeared.

More nude photos of Jessie Wheeler-Sawyer released

He read the article, stunned at what it told him. A leather photo album containing more than a hundred photos was found in a garbage bin on East Hastings. They all featured Jessie at a much younger age, they'd been scanned into digital images, and they were now, as Matt read, making their way around the Internet. Matt was floored, but he speed read the last bit of the article as the sharp staccato of Charles and Dee's footsteps descended the stairs. He looked up to greet them, shifting his weight and putting a false smile in place, and wiping a stray tear away as he did so.

He closed the newspaper and, as soon as he got a chance, he ran it out to his car.

This news could wait another day.

Today was a day to celebrate.

A deep rumble started up the driveway. It was Josh's Harley Sportster, making its presence known.

Matt stood at the doorway and greeted the couple, who were finally visiting *La Casa* while on a break from Josh's shoot in New York.

His heart was sinking. But this was the life Matt signed up for. This was a life where people were targets. This was a life where people got hurt on a global scale. This was a life where people suffered at the tempestuous unpredictable mercy of the masses.

This was a life that, frankly, sometimes just hurt.

～～～

Caryn sat on the floor of her condo, in the center of the rug below the Scandinavian chair, and forced herself to look up at the hole where the large portrait of Jessie was displayed for so long. She was ensconced in a white T-shirt, a big one that hung down over her arm, leaving a shoulder bare. She was twisting the stem of a wine glass around and around on the rug by her bare feet.

Soft footsteps padded towards her. Caryn looked up. The smudged mascara underneath her emerald eyes lent her an eerie appearance in the diminishing light as the day's end hastened. The girl in front of her bent down and wiped a dark smudge away. Then she leaned forward and placed her lips against Caryn's, finding them soft and welcoming.

"You're so responsive," she murmured when Caryn's body responded

329

to her touch. Caryn looked over the girl's shoulder towards the drawer where her photo albums had been kept for so many years. It remained slightly open, testament to recent usage. Testament to a missing album.

She hung her head, and let the tears come.

Chapter Thirty-six

A pale moonlight washed a luminescent blue aura on invisible waves into the room as Josh slid in bed beside his wife. He wriggled deeper under the light summer coverlet and then rested his head on one elbow on the pillow. He peeked over at Jessie, who smiled before reaching out to move that favorite rogue bit of hair off Josh's cheek and back behind his ear.

She moved towards him and let her lips touch his. Running her pink tongue over his top lip, she murmured, "So cute."

"Tired?" he whispered softly. "Or do you want to play tonight?"

"Play," she answered instantly, her tongue probing his lips, his teeth. "But you'll have to go round my growing belly."

"Your belly," Josh managed between low gasps of pleasure as she reached between his legs and gently started massaging him. "Our daughter, you mean. Emily-Grace."

"Emily-Grace." Jessie smiled, testing the name on her lips as she opened her sleepy eyes. She was pleased to find her husband's liquid chocolate eyes on her, and even more pleased to watch his body move and sigh in response to her touch.

Ahhh, Josh moaned, wrapping his hand around hers as she massaged him. Then he let his hand slip around to her back, and he pressed her to him, as close as he could get, anyway, with their unborn child in between them, and he ran his hand slowly up and then down her back.

There was a soft breeze that night, and Josh had left the balcony door open so it could waft inside and cool them as they slept. With it came the moon, on beams of bluish-white light, it seemed. There was a whisper in the room that somehow took their senses and focused them securely on themselves and on their small place in the infinite universe. It had the power to eliminate the rest, the extraneous stuff that hurt and wrestled and tried to pull them apart.

This whisper was airy, lighthearted; it had the power to soothe, and it had the power to heal.

Josh moved over Jessie and cautiously slipped himself inside. She parted her legs wider and sighed, glad that even in the middle stages of pregnancy sex was still so damned pleasurable. This night he filled her perfectly and, as he throbbed inside her, she cried out Josh's name to let the moon and the whispery breeze know just how much she loved her man and his tender ministrations.

After, Josh lay on one side as his breathing eased, and he touched soft lips to Jessie's breast.

Some days are dust, he reminded himself as he held his wife and rocked her gently in the cradle of both arms. *And some days are diamonds. And,* he added to himself as he lifted himself on one elbow, brushed stray locks of hair out of his wife's eyes and kissed each beautiful closed eyelid, *some days are just—plain—surreal.*

They slept in peace as, around them, the glittering dust of diamonds turned an ethereal blue-gold in the scattered moonlight, and the wind whispered to them a promise of home.

The End.

Hello!

Thank you for reading *Whispers of Home*—I truly hope you are enjoying the Drifters series! I wonder if I can ask you a small favor—writers like
myself rely on ratings and reviews to help other readers discover our books.
If you could take a moment to go to Amazon (Kindle), Goodreads and/or
Smashwords and rate and/or review any of my books, I will remain humbly
grateful forevermore. Thank you so much! Happy reading!

www.susanrodgersauthor.com

Facebook: search **Susan Rodgers, Writer**

Twitter: **@srbluemountain**

www.bublish.com

email: **fatcat@pei.sympatico.ca**

Susan Rodgers' first novel *A Certain Kind of Freedom* was a Finalist in the Writers' Federation of Nova Scotia Atlantic Writing Awards for unpublished manuscripts. Her short story from the novel of the same name, published in two anthologies, has received rave reviews, as have the Drifters novels, Susan's all-time favourite books to write.

Owner/Operator of Bluemountain Entertainment, Susan is a 'Diploma With Honours' graduate of Vancouver Film School. She produces mostly documentary style client films and short dramas with plans to one day shoot a Feature Drama based on the novel Atlantic Blue.

Formerly a Museum Curator, in winter Susan lives with her partner Steve and her striped cat Oliver (Lucy Maud Montgomery once said the only good cat is a striped cat) in Summerside, Prince Edward Island, Canada. In summer, she hides in a small trailer in Darnley, P.E.I., where she writes novels, paddles kayaks, and crafts sandcastles on the beach. She makes frequent trips to Vancouver to visit her son Christopher, where she enjoys life in the hippie city while listening to great music and sipping on good espresso.

Books by Susan Rodgers

Drifters series:
A Song For Josh
Promises
No Greater Love
Riptide
Whispers of Home
And Then There Was Silence (2015)
Let the Music Cry (2015)
If I Could Sing You Home (2015)

Other:
A Certain Kind of Freedom (2015)
Seasmoke (2015)
Atlantic Blue (2015)

Feature Screenplays:
The Story of Jack & Emma
Atlantic Blue
Beautiful Jane
They Were Dreamers (adapted)

Short Stories:
S12
A Certain Kind of Freedom
A Gentle Peace